Thirteen Stops Earlier

SANDRA HARRIS

POOLBEG

This book is a work of fiction. The names, characters, places, businesses,
organisations and incidents portrayed in it are either the product of the author's
imagination or are used fictitiously. Any resemblance to actual persons,
living or dead, events or locales is entirely coincidental.

Published 2022
by Poolbeg Press Ltd.
123 Grange Hill, Baldoyle,
Dublin 13, Ireland
Email: poolbeg@poolbeg.com

© Sandra Harris 2022

The moral right of the author has been asserted.

© Poolbeg Press Ltd. 2022, copyright for editing, typesetting, layout, design, ebook

A catalogue record for this book is available from the British Library.

ISBN 978178199-451-1

All rights reserved. No part of this publication may be reproduced or transmitted in any form or by any means, electronic or mechanical, including photography, recording, or any information storage or retrieval system, without permission in writing from the publisher. The book is sold subject to the condition that it shall not, by way of trade or otherwise, be lent, resold or otherwise circulated without the publisher's prior consent in any form of binding or cover other than that in which it is published and without a similar condition, including this condition, being imposed on the subsequent purchaser.

www.poolbeg.com

About the author

Sandra Harris is a Dublin writer, poet, film-blogger, autism mom, animal lover, serial eavesdropper, horror fan, history buff and self-confessed bookworm.

In response to the many people who have asked the question of her in casual conversation over the years, she would like the words '*Yes, Sandra Harris is Still Plugging Away at the Auld Writing*' to appear on her headstone.

Even then, she still expects to be asked the question in the afterlife …

Acknowledgements

Thanks again to Lisa and Reuben — you brighten my days.

Thanks to my agent Jonathan Williams, my editor Gaye Shortland, my publisher Paula Campbell and everyone at Poolbeg.

To Lisa and Reuben, always
and ever my greatest achievements

Chapter 1

LAURA

Christmas 2014

Laura Brennan, babes, you look *abso-fucking-lutely fabulous,* she told herself confidently as she turned away from the mirror in the Ladies' room and made for the door. Who cared if those snotty bitches still clustered round the mirror were giggling and sniggering at her and quite obviously bitching about her behind her back, the very second she turned it on them? The girls from the typing pool at Phelan's were proper little bitches anyway. Laura had only been working there since Halloween but she already knew that much. They had disliked her on sight, most of them, and hardly gave her the time of day, even now, two months later – unless she had to ask them a direct question about the work, and even then they smirked and shrugged and made faces at each other like witches round a cauldron when they thought she wasn't looking. It was because they were jealous, that much was obvious. Jealous of her slim figure, pretty face and gorgeous fall of long blonde hair, straightened arduously earlier on that day for the Christmas party. It was the straightest it had ever been and she was thrilled with it. She tossed her head and sent the shimmering golden locks flying as a little parting 'screw you' to the watching women as she left the Ladies' room, letting the door slam shut by itself behind her.

Outside, in the darkened room upstairs in the just-off-Grafton-Street bar where the Phelan's 2014 staff Christmas party was being held, the noise had risen to almost unbearable levels and the crush at the bar was beginning to resemble a rugby scrum. Laura grimaced and stood, undecided, teetering on her high heels at the edge of the crowd. She could wriggle her way through to the front of the queue, maybe, being small enough, but some oaf was bound to spill beer on her new little silver top with the spaghetti straps and the new butt-hugging black-leather skirt in the crush. She looked at her watch. It was a quarter to eleven. She could slip off home now if she really wanted to, she supposed. She'd temporarily lost sight of Paul since nipping to the loo, and he was one of the main reasons she'd come to this stupid party on her own tonight, hoping to catch a glimpse of him and maybe chat to him in person, away from the workplace. She'd attended the formal, sit-down dinner earlier — for which she'd bought a pretty pricey ticket — and she'd mingled with the crowd at the drinks party afterwards, so that was her professional duty done for tonight. She hadn't really enjoyed the dinner. She'd been seated with some of those bitchy women from the job who'd ignored her, which had been pretty uncomfortable, but afterwards during the drinks party she knew she'd caught the eye of several of the men (including Paul, who'd been flirting with her pretty much since she'd joined the company) as she floated around the venue with her long blonde hair swishing, her wine glass in one hand and her little silver clutch purse in the other. At the end of the day, the men were the ones who mattered. Laura didn't give a tinker's curse for the women. What had women ever done for her, except to be constantly competing with her for the men she liked?

"You look a little lost, just standing there – can I help at all?" said a voice suddenly in her ear.

Laura looked up, startled out of her embittered musings. "Oh, hi," she said, *faux*-casually, her heart skipping a beat when she saw who it was.

Paul Sheridan, the best-looking of all the junior managers at Phelan's, was grinning down at her with that kind of lopsided smile he had that made all *'the gals in the typing pool'*, as they were jokingly known by everyone who worked at Phelan's Freight & Warehousing Ltd., go weak at the knees. From the snippets of gossip Laura had managed to garner about the junior managers, Paul was not only the handsomest but the most openly flirtatious as well. Married, too, unfortunately, but that had never stopped her in the past. In fact, in some ways she kind of preferred it. She liked the challenge.

"I was just deciding whether it was worth fighting my way to the bar for another drink, or whether I should just call it a night and head home," she went on, looking up at him coyly from underneath her fake eyelashes, which she was fluttering like mad, to good effect. He was looking down at her as if he'd like to *eat* her. She felt like Little Red Riding Hood in the presence of the Big Bad Wolf, and it excited her. She felt a familiar fluttering in the pit of her stomach that made her want to stand even closer to him and press herself against him.

"It's always worth getting another drink," he said, accompanying his words with a dazzling smile, "but why don't you let me go get it for you? What're you drinking? Wine, is it? A white wine? No problem."

"*Um*, thanks," she simpered. "Shall I wait here for you then?"

Paul shook his head, making a lock of his thick dark hair fall forward over one eye, Hugh Grant-style, in a way that caused the fluttering in Laura's stomach to intensify. God, but he was a big ride! "There's a little room across the corridor; d'you see it there?" He took her arm proprietorially and turned her bodily, gently, so that she was pointing in the direction he indicated. "Some of the run-off from in here is drifting across to over there," he continued. "It's a little less crowded, anyway. Why don't you go across and wait for me a minute? Get us a nice little quiet table or something? I'll be back with your drink in two ticks." He grinned lopsidedly again and disappeared into the crowd.

Her arm tingling from where he'd touched her, Laura did as he'd suggested and crossed the corridor to the room where a few little knots of people were seated, chatting, or milling about holding drinks. No one paid any attention to her as she picked the most private little table for two she could find, a slightly rickety one towards the back of the room where hardly any of the dim night-time light penetrated. Not that Laura was afraid of the light. Oh no. She wasn't some old biddy who shrank from natural light and only looked presentable in semi-darkness. She had perfect peachy skin and no lines or wrinkles yet (well, she was still only twenty-six), and, although she wore tons of make-up every day, she didn't really need it. It was just for the glamour. Glamour was so important in these days of social media. It was no longer about what kind of a person you were; it was about what you looked like, on and off camera. People judged you on your appearance these days, and usually harshly too. Laura wasn't afraid of being judged on her appearance. In that department, she knew she was the equal of most other women. She may not have been the most beautiful woman who ever lived, but she made the most of what she had, and that was what counted.

He was back in about five minutes with her glass of white wine and a pint of something for himself. "See?" he said, as he placed the two drinks on the table. "Didn't I tell you I'd only be a minute?" He swore loudly then as the table wobbled and some of his beer slopped onto his trousers.

Laura laughed, carefully picking up her own glass. "Table's rickety," she said. "You'd better watch out."

"A toast?" he said, raising his pint glass to clink against her wine one.

"To what? Christmas, I suppose?" The madly fluttering eyelashes were working overtime.

"Nah, that's boring. Every single person here is drinking to bloody Christmas. Who cares about bloody Christmas? It costs me a fortune and I never get what I really want. I'd like to propose a toast to . . . let's see now . . . how about to the most beautiful girl in Phelan's?"

"What? Where? Who is she? Is she here?" Laura pantomimed looking round her.

Now it was Paul's turn to laugh. "Oh, very good, very good. I see what you did there. No, come on, seriously. You must know how hot you are. Don't they have mirrors where you come from?"

Laura smirked. "You're very sweet to say so. You know, you're not so bad yourself," she added, pretending to study him critically now with her head on one side. As if she'd only just thought about it. As if she hadn't spent hours covertly studying him from her desk in Phelan's! The junior managers all worked in little glass boxes, barely bigger than toilet cubicles, that you could easily see into from outside, and Laura had watched his comings and goings with keen interest from her vantage point out in the typing pool, more or less since she'd come to work there a few weeks ago.

"How are you enjoying working with us?"

"Oh, it definitely has its . . . interesting points." She was flirting for all she was worth now, the long curled eyelashes going like the clappers and her voice soft and breathy, like a Hollywood starlet's. She drew her bare arms close to her body, knowing it had the effect of pushing her boobs together and up, even though the lacy bra she wore was already doing a more than good enough job of that. The whole performance was certainly having an effect on him. His dark eyes were locked on her face and he liked what he saw, she could tell.

"Are you by any chance, *uh*, single, Laura?" His eyes now lightly grazed her bare ring finger.

She shrugged carelessly. "Just for the moment," she said, hoping to imply that she was merely between boyfriends and could be deliciously embroiled in a hot and heavy relationship again at literally any minute.

"I see," he said with a slow grin, his eyes travelling from her breasts in the little silver top to her red parted lips. While she knew she had his undivided attention, she bit down hard on her full lower lip, aware that guys in the past had always found the gesture sexy. He reached over and gently touched her full, quivering bottom lip.

"Don't," he said softly. "You'll make it bleed."

The hairs stood up on the back of Laura's neck. "What about you, anyway?" she said breezily, in an effort to seem casual. "Is that a wedding ring I see before me?"

"Well, yes, technically," said Paul, a kind of reluctance in his voice now. "*Technically* it's a wedding ring, yes."

"What does that mean?" Laura breathed. "What does *'technically'* mean?"

"It means, my dear Laura, you vision of loveliness, you, that Barbara's and my marriage is a marriage in name only. We don't love each other any more. After ten years of marital bliss, the spark has well and truly gone. The magic's gone too. We don't even sleep together any more, not since our second child was born."

"How long ago was that?"

"Just recently."

He sounded like he was being evasive, but she had no way of telling. How recent was *just recently,* anyway? Yesterday? Last week? Six months ago, what? Best not to press it, though, this early in the game.

Now it was Laura's turn to say slowly: "I see."

"And what do you see, my lovely Laura?" He reached across the rickety table and took one of her hands in both of his. "I sure as fuck hope you see an unhappy guy who's waiting for a beautiful girl with long blonde hair wearing a little silver top to come into his life and make him feel whole again."

"I see an unhappy guy," Laura said with a smile, "who's

waiting for a beautiful girl with long blonde hair wearing a little silver top to . . . what was the end of that again?" She laughed out loud. All the wine she'd had tonight had gone straight to her head. She felt wonderfully uninhibited, sophisticated and sexy, like Rita Hayworth as Gilda in that old movie her mum loved. It was a fantastic feeling.

". . . to come into his life and make him feel whole again," Paul prompted with a grin.

". . . to come into his life and make him feel whole again," parroted Laura obediently.

Paul nodded in approval. "Where do you live, lovely Laura?"

"I have a flat near the Stephen's Green Shopping Centre. It's only about five minutes' walk from here." Her heart leaped. Guys only ever asked that question for one reason. This was going exactly the way she'd hoped, ever since she'd looked up to see Paul standing over her at the fringes of the crush for the bar. Ever since she'd first seen Paul around the office, if she was to be perfectly honest with herself. He was good-looking, sexy, well-built, well-dressed, charming, and she wanted him for herself. He was wasted on his wife, as most men were.

"That close? Sounds perfect. For, *erm*, commuting, I mean. The Luas and everything. Can I walk you home, lovely Laura? I'd consider it an honour and a privilege."

"Don't you have to go home to — what's her name? Brenda? Belinda? Bernadette, is it?" Laura knew perfectly well it was Barbara. There was nothing wrong with her memory, thank you very much. She was simply being the bitch she knew so well how to be.

"It's Barbara. And not for a few hours, lovely Laura. The night is still young. But this party's getting old. I say we split now, while we're still relatively sober. What do you think?" He drained his pint and looked over at her questioningly.

For answer, she drank down the last of her wine and nodded assent to an early(ish) departure from the Christmas party.

"Well, then, I'm ready when you are," she said, giggling when her first attempt to stand up went awry and she ended up flat on her butt again on the seat. "*Ooops*, what am I like?"

He leaped up manfully and helped her to her feet. Her legs felt a bit wobbly in the high-heeled shoes after all the wine she'd drunk, but Paul's big strong hand on her arm felt so right. He steered her through the room and down the corridor to the cloakroom. Laura was a bit annoyed that he'd deliberately, or so it seemed, chosen the fast track to the cloakroom rather than their having to go out through the party room again. She would have given anything to have those bitches from the typing pool watch her as she swanned out of the party on Paul's arm, Paul Sheridan, the hottest and, apparently, most up for fun of all the junior managers. *But never mind*, she consoled herself as he tenderly enfolded her in the little pink fur jacket that went so well with the tight black-leather skirt and the high-heeled silver strappy shoes that matched her top. *Paul Sheridan is coming home with me. Me, Laura Brennan. And if I play my cards right, this won't be the last time it happens, either* . . .

The sex was fantastic, as Laura had predicted it would be. Guys like Paul were always good in bed. After confirming with her that she was on the Pill, he managed sex a good two times before they both fell asleep, his arms wrapped lightly around her naked body. As they'd made love each time, her legs locked round his waist and her fingers pushing his hair back from his face or caressing his handsome features, she'd repeated to herself like a mantra: *I have you now, Paul. I have you now. I have you now. I have you now* . . .

Even in the morning, when they'd woken up gritty-eyed and hungover, he seemed fine with her, and with being there with her, in her flat and in her bed. Sometimes, as Laura knew all too well, in the morning, men often regretted their actions and choices of the night before and couldn't wait to get away. Laura personally thought that this was the most unflattering thing a man could do to a woman: let her know the morning after the night before that he regretted sleeping with her and that she was a mistake in his eyes. With Paul, however, there was none of that, which was how Laura knew for sure that he and she were meant to be.

"Morning, lovely Laura," he said when he opened his eyes. Then, "Shit, what time is it?" as he sat up, leaned over the edge of the bed and scrambled about on the floor for his scattered possessions, his wallet, phone and keys.

"Half-ten," she obliged.

"Ah, that's all right then. That's okay. So long as I'm home by lunchtime or thereabouts."

"Where does your wife think you are right now? I mean, what will you tell her?" She couldn't help being curious, even a little jealous.

"I have a couple of mates I watch the footy with. Sometimes it genuinely runs into the next morning. This will just have to be one of those times, won't it? I told her I might be staying over with one of the lads after the party, so as not to disturb her and to watch a match or two."

"You're so clever," she flattered, not caring that she was laying it on a bit thick. "You think of everything, don't you?"

"I try," he said modestly, before grabbing her and kissing her hard on the mouth. "You taste gorgeous first thing in the morning, has anyone ever told you that?"

Her reply was muffled by his lips and probing tongue.

Laura packed a small bag a couple of days later, locked up her flat and went home to spend Christmas with her mother Eleanor in Phibsborough. She would have preferred to stay home in her own new little modern flat, just in case Paul happened to text or phone (he'd assiduously keyed her number into his phone in front of her before he'd left her flat, the morning after the Christmas party), but it wasn't worth the hassle she'd get from her mother.

"Oh, just leave me here to rot on my own at Christmas /Easter/Halloween/Mother's Day/my birthday/Yom Kippur/Labor Day, why don't you?" was a favourite refrain of Eleanor's.

To which there usually seemed no answer but: "Oh Mum, it's not like that, honestly it's not!"

"How is it then?" her mother would invariably say, to which there seemed no answer that wouldn't give offence or cause further argument. Eleanor was notoriously touchy. And weepy and waily as well. She lived her life constantly in a state of high emotion that frequently gave way to crying fits and outbursts of shrieking.

Now Laura put her key in the door of her mother's council house with the same sense of foreboding she always got when she unlocked this door. What kind of mood would her mother be in today? The house smelled of nicotine, like it always did, and cheap perfume with maybe a squirt of air freshener to disguise the fag smell. The house had smelled the same for as long as she could remember. Eleanor Brennan made occasional half-hearted attempts to give up the smokes, but the habit was as ingrained in her as self-pity and blaming others, mostly men, for her own ill-fortune. Laura didn't suppose she'd ever give it up for real.

"Mum, I'm home! Are you in?" she called out to the house in general.

She listened carefully then and heard the muffled noises and bumping sounds coming from upstairs. Taking a step or two up the stairs, she recoiled when she realised that she was hearing the sounds of two people having noisy sex in the main bedroom at the top of the stairs. Her mother's room. Laura looked at her watch. Jesus Christ. It was two in the afternoon, on the day before Christmas Eve, and her mother was in bed, having sex with God-knows-who. She'd mentioned a new man-friend when Laura had talked on the phone to her last, but Laura hadn't got the impression that it was anything serious. Feeling utterly grossed out and not daring to take her bag upstairs to her old bedroom in case she heard or saw something she'd regret, that might scar her for life (who, after all, wants to see a parent having sex?), she went into the sitting-room instead and took off her coat, draping it over an armchair.

The artificial Christmas tree was standing in its usual

corner of the room, but the decorations and lights were still in the two sad little battered cardboard boxes sitting beside it. So Eleanor was leaving that job to Laura, then. The rest of the house was undecorated too. With a sigh, Laura got down on her knees and began to untangle the long string of Christmas lights. Christ! How old were these relics? They were probably a fire hazard by this stage. And why was it that, no matter how meticulously she unwound them before she put them back in their box every New Year, they always managed to tangle themselves up horribly once more for when she took them out again the following Christmas? It was one of the great mysteries of the Universe, like the way a supposedly sick child or pet will happily bounce off the walls in the doctor's surgery or vet's clinic and make a liar out of an anxious and embarrassed parent. Or the way a guy will always somehow lose your phone number, even if you saw him with your own eyes input the correct details into his actual phone.

Laura wondered miserably as she worked if that was what had happened with Paul. He hadn't texted or phoned since their wonderful night together, and Laura was afraid to contact him in case it made her look too eager. Although how eagerly had she gone to bed with him, she fretted now, and how much of a giant slut did he probably already think she was for doing so? It was so unfair, and the double standard was so frustrating! Paul, even though he was a married man with a family, would be hailed as a big stud for bedding the new hot little blonde in the typing pool, whereas she, as a woman, would be branded a slut for taking her knickers off for one of her bosses. They wouldn't be back in work together until the day after New Year's Day (it would be a Friday), and Laura was starting to feel like she genuinely couldn't wait that long. She missed him so much it almost resembled a physical ache. Sure, they'd only slept together the once, but Laura had known it was going to happen, was practically *fated* to happen, ever since she'd seen him for the first time a few weeks ago. And she could not, *would* not, believe that it was over between them before it had even started. The noise of people coming down the stairs jerked her rudely out of her Paul-daydream.

"Laura, I didn't know you were here! I never heard you come in!" exclaimed Eleanor, coming into the sitting-room in the wake of a scruffy young man with longish hair and a beard who immediately parked himself on the couch and began rolling a smoke with a mumbled *"Howyeh"*.

"You were . . . busy," Laura said curtly, unable to bring herself to allude to the sex noises she'd heard. "Mum, who the hell is this?" Indicating with a jerk of her head the man on the couch, rolling himself a smoke with the general air of someone who feels very much at home where he is, and an expression of annoying complacency on his unshaven face that Laura wanted to slap off him.

"There's no need for that snotty tone, Laura." Eleanor was instantly on the defensive. "This is Thomas. He's staying here for a while."

"What d'you mean, *'staying here'*, Mum? Why is he staying here? Hasn't he got anywhere of his own to go to?"

The man called Thomas grinned and lit his own cigarette before handing one to Eleanor. "Smoke, love?" he offered to Laura then, who ignored him as if he hadn't spoken. His was a very strong native Dublin accent that grated on Laura's ears.

"Well?" she demanded.

"He's . . . between residences at the moment," Eleanor said coolly, seeming none too happy at being quizzed. "I've said he can stay here for a while, just until he can get on his feet again."

The feet in question, clad in socks with a hole in the left big toe, were parked now on the coffee table with the dog-eared magazines, the ashtrays and the plant that Eleanor never remembered to water. If Laura didn't pour a drop in every now and then when she visited, it would have died long ago, the poor thing. Laura longed to kick those arrogant, presumptuous feet off her mother's coffee table. During her childhood, when she wasn't being packed off to relatives because *"poor Eleanor"* couldn't cope with being a mother, she'd eaten all her takeaway dinners on this coffee table in front of the television. When the damn thing was working, that was. Eleanor had a decent telly now, but the one from Laura's childhood was an old wreck, a temperamental dinosaur of a machine that belonged in a museum.

"Have you given him any money?" she asked her mother now, while the man called Thomas just kept smirking and smoking.

Eleanor flushed a dull brick-red. "That's none of your business, Laura. You've no right to ask me questions like that."

"Right? Right?" Laura snorted. "I'm your daughter, aren't I? That's my *'right',* as you put it. Anyway, I'll be the one who has to pick up the pieces when *Thomas* here —" she couldn't keep the sneer from her voice, "buggers off with every cent of your Disability money and anything else you might have squirrelled away as well. If that doesn't give me a *'right'*, I don't know what does."

"How *dare* you? How dare you talk to me like that, Laura?"

"Ladies, ladies, please!" intervened Thomas in his North Dublin whine. "Don't be bleedin' fighting over me. Not unless yiz are going to wrestle in a bath full of mud wearing bikinis." He laughed, an unpleasant grating sound.

"Oh, fuck off, you!" said Laura, before stalking off to the kitchen. She returned instantly for her handbag, which she'd left sitting on top of her bigger bag with her clothes in it. Giving the amused Thomas a filthy — and pointed — look, she stalked off again with her nose in the air. "Either he goes or I do," she told Eleanor, who'd entered the kitchen behind her and was now putting on the kettle. "I'm not staying under the same roof as *that*."

"Laura, lovey, don't be like that." Her righteous anger dissipated, Eleanor's tone was wheedling now, cajoling. "I haven't given him a penny, I swear. And he's not as bad as you think. He's great company, and he makes me laugh. You don't begrudge me a bit of happiness, do you, love?"

"Happiness?" expostulated Laura. "Mum, how old is he?"

"He's — I don't know. Nearly thirty," Eleanor fudged.

"Nearly thirty, my arse! He's twenty-six if he's a day, which makes him my age, Mum, and seventeen years younger than you."

"Why are you always going on about age?" Eleanor was sulking now. "Age is only a number. And besides, he's over eighteen, isn't he? I'm not some cradle-snatcher. You're making me feel like a bloody paedophile or something."

"No one's saying that, Mum." Laura sighed, exasperated. "And, yes, I suppose you're entitled to a little bit of . . . light relief every now and then like the rest of us. But this one! Come on, Mum. He looks like a thug. If he doesn't knock you about and rob you, I'll . . . I'll eat my hat. Where did you even meet a person like that?"

"At an AA meeting, if you must know," said Eleanor in her snippiest tones.

"Have you been going to AA again?" Laura asked, her hopes sky-high.

"I was, but I've stopped again, so don't go getting all excited. It doesn't work for me. It doesn't work for Thomas either, so we both decided to quit going on the same night, the night we met there. He asked me for a euro for a cup of coffee after the meeting. I felt sorry for him. I offered to take him for a coffee *and* a hot meal as well. He accepted, we got talking and it sort of went on from there. That's all there is to it. Oh, please, Laura," she cried, changing her tone — and her tune — in an instant, "don't make me send him away! I've promised him he can stay till after Christmas. Don't make me put him out on the streets before then, please! And don't make me choose between you, please, because I'd have to go with my heart, you know that!"

Yeah, and put some scumbag you only know five minutes ahead of your daughter, just because he has a couple of body parts you value more than the whole of your own flesh-and-blood put together, Laura thought in dismay. Out loud she said: "Let him stay, then, if it means that much to you. But you're responsible for keeping him out of trouble, okay, and don't expect me to make merry with him. My Christmas cheer only stretches so far."

"Don't worry, Laura," trilled Eleanor, delighted now that she'd got her own way as usual. "I promise you, you won't even know he's here. He's such a free spirit and a creative thinker, though. Some of the things he says would really make you think. Go on in the sitting-room now and keep him company, will you, while I make us all a nice cup of tea and bring it in."

Laura sighed, feeling the beginnings of a dull headache behind her eyes. It was going to be a long and tedious Christmas.

"Aunty Vee, it's me, Laura. Have you got a minute?"

"Oh, hi, Laura. What's up?" Vera Donohue sounded harassed as usual. Not surprising, really, as she'd had eight children in an era when families were traditionally becoming much smaller, and now had God knows how many grandchildren for her trouble as well.

"It's Mum." When was it not? "She's behaving oddly again." When was she not?

There was the unmistakeable sound of a long sigh on the other end of the phone. It made Laura's heart sink. Everyone in the family had had their fill of Eleanor Brennan's dramatics. It was getting increasingly harder to get any of the relations to pitch in and help when Eleanor was going through a wobbly patch. And the problem was that she had so *many* wobbly patches! Laura felt like she was for ever putting out little Eleanor-related fires.

"What is it now? Is she taking her meds?"

"As far as I know. Her depression and anxiety ones anyway, and her sleeping pills. No, it's not that. It's . . . something else."

Now she could hear the sound of Vera lighting a cigarette and taking a long, grateful puff of it before saying tiredly: "What is it, then? Laura, I'll be honest with you. I haven't got a lot of time on my hands at the moment. I still have so much to get ready for Christmas, and our Marge is going in to be induced first thing after Christmas, if the baby doesn't come before then. And it won't. All the Donohues who ever lived were never on time for anything."

"I'm sorry, Aunty Vee. I know you're up to your tonsils in it. It's just that I don't really have anyone else to turn to."

Vera Donohue's voice softened. "Just tell me what's the matter, love."

"She's brought home another lame duck! A man-friend, I mean, but you know he's *more than that, don't you?*" The last few words came out on a note of hysteria.

Vera sighed again. "Where'd she pick this one up, then?"

"At an AA meeting, of all places. If she'd only kept going to them, it might have been all right. As it was, though, the night she met him there was coincidentally the night she decided the meetings 'weren't working for her any more'. Apparently she just stopped going. *Again.*"

"How old is this one?"

"Mid-twenties."

"Employed?"

"Between 'residences' so presumably between jobs."

"Criminal record?"

"Not that I know of, but I wouldn't be at all surprised, going by the look of him."

There was a silence, then: "Look, Laura, I know it's difficult for you, love, but there's not much I can realistically do from over here in Inchicore. If I were you, I'd just wait this one out. He'll wander off in his own time, like they all do. Then you'll have to be there to help pick up the pieces for your mam so, if I were you, I wouldn't be in that much of a hurry to get rid of him. At least while he's there with her, she'll be happy and quiet."

"But, Aunty Vee! He could be anyone. He could be a murderer, a robber, a rapist. He could be Jack the bloody Ripper or Larry bloody Murphy for all I know! I can't just leave him here with her and do nothing. It's Christmas, for God's sake."

"Laura, my advice to you is just to wait this one out. It'll peter out like all the rest. Hang on a second, would you? Someone's trying to ring me on the other line . . ."

After a two or three-minute absence, during which Laura fidgeted with her hair and tried to be patient, Vera came back on the line, out of breath and panicky. "Laura, love, I have to go. That was Brandon on the other line there. Marge's waters are after breaking by themselves, so it's really happening this time. Give my love to your mam, and happy Christmas to the both of you."

"But, Aunty Vee! I need to know what to do about . . ."

But Vera was gone, off to assist at the birth of her oldest child Marge's fourth baby. It was all right for Marge, sulked Laura as she was left hanging up the phone in frustration. She *had* a husband, Brandon, who would be there for the birth of this child as he'd been there for all the others, as far as Laura knew, so what did she need her mother dancing attendance on her for as well? Brandon was one of those so-called "*New Men*", as Eleanor dubbed them scornfully, but Eleanor was only jealous, because the father of her only child had deserted her as soon as he'd found out that she was pregnant with Laura.

Laura sat for a while on the couch with her head in her hands and her phone on the coffee-table in front of her, on the off-chance (the *very* off-chance) that Vera would get an opportunity to call back, but that was probably it for the time being. Eleanor would get a text in due course informing them of the baby's eventual sex, weight and potential christening date, and that'd be it. There was never time for much more. Laura sighed. She could have really done with her Aunty Vee's comforting, practical presence in the house at the moment, but the problem with her Aunty Vee was that she just had too many damn children and grandchildren taking up all her time and attention. That had always been the way of it, for as long as Laura could remember.

She'd had to stay in her Aunty Vee's house a lot when she was growing up, every time Eleanor was having a really bad bout of depression and had to "go away for a little rest", for a couple of weeks or even longer. Laura, though she missed her mother, had always loved staying in Aunty Vee's house, with its perpetual warmth, cheer and noise, so different to her own home which always seemed to have an atmosphere about it of cold hush and a recent bereavement. Aunty Vee's husband Derek was a genial giant of a man who always had two or three kids hanging out of him and one up on his shoulders, and Aunty Vee was a great cook who was always trying to feed people up whom she thought needed it. She'd done her best for her pale-faced, skinny little niece, Laura, but there was just so little time to devote to her individually. Every time Laura climbed up onto her aunty's lap for a cuddle, or a chat about how worried she was about Eleanor or when Eleanor would be able to come back home from her "rest", a load of other kids would come bursting in, with cut fingers and skinned knees or other ailments, and the moment was lost. How many times had Laura wished, during her childhood, to be a legitimate part of Aunty Vee and Uncle Derek's brood, and not to have to go home to that cheerless, joyless council house in Phibsborough!

The word *legitimate*, of course, conjured up its much uglier converse, *illegitimate*, a word that, in fairness, none of her peers or schoolmates had ever thrown in her face or accused her of being (maybe because they'd never even heard it, old-fashioned and obsolete as it was), but Laura knew it, and it had always bothered her. She was illegitimate, a bastard, as they used to call it (a cruel, ugly word), because her father hadn't wanted to marry her teenage mother when he'd made her pregnant. It was an old, old story, and they were by no means the first or only mother and child to which it had happened, but why, oh *why*, Laura still wondered several times a month, had it had to happen to *her*, to *them*? Other people had things so much easier. Life was so bloody unfair sometimes.

She got up from the couch and stood indecisively for a minute. What to do with the rest of her day? It was early afternoon on the day before Christmas Eve. Her mother and the awful Thomas person had taken the bus into town, supposedly to buy each other Christmas presents, but Laura could totally imagine how one-sided the present-buying process would be. If Thomas had a single solitary euro to his name, she'd be gobsmacked. Maybe she'd go for a wander around Phibsborough by herself, do some Christmas shopping of her own. If the gruesome twosome were in town, there'd be no danger of bumping into them locally. That's what she'd do, then. It was her Christmas break, too, after all.

She ran upstairs to the bathroom and redid her make-up, then she gathered up her coat, hat, scarf, handbag, phone and keys and left the house. It only took her a few minutes to walk to the shopping district. It was jam-packed with people. She went to the chemists' first and bought a lovely little lily-of-the-valley bath-set for Eleanor and a jasmine one for herself. She spent ages looking at the after-shave products for men, wishing that she could buy a box of his favourite brand for Paul, but, for one thing, she didn't know the name of that dreamy smell he sprayed on himself that had her nearly weak at the knees the night they'd slept together and, secondly, how could she buy a present for a man she'd slept with only once but who mightn't want anything to do with her ever again, for all she knew? Certainly it didn't look like he wanted anything to do with her so far. It wouldn't be appropriate at all. Would it? Still, though, some of these boxed sets were really classy-looking. She sprayed several of the testers on her wrist and concentrated really hard on trying to identify the scent of after-shave Paul used. When she was nearly sure she had it, she marched right up to the counter with a big boxed set of it before she could change her mind. She paid the exorbitant price with only the merest of twinges, then she stuffed the box down into the very bottom of her shopping bag where no one would see it. If anyone asked (although no one was likely to), she'd say she was buying it for a cousin, or for a friend or a work colleague or something.

She mooched around a bookshop wondering what kind of books Paul read, or if he read at all. The customers in the bookshop were all queuing up to buy the latest expensive hardback biographies of the sports star or sports critic *du jour* to give as presents to unsuspecting people who presumably deserved better. It bored Laura endlessly, the Irish public's obsession with sport, both watching it and reading about it too, and she guessed that, if she was pressed, she'd have to say that Paul probably didn't read a whole lot, whether about sports or otherwise, but that didn't matter. She wouldn't hold it against him. She didn't love him for his razor-sharp intellect. Laura really only read magazines herself, the celebrity gossip and fashion kind. With a start, she realised that she'd used the word *love* in connection with Paul. Was she in love with him, then, properly in love? Head-over-fucking-heels, instantly replied the little voice in her head that told her how she was feeling about things or people. Her heart beating a mile a minute with the shock of her discovery, she took her favourite magazine to the counter and paid for it. How can you love someone after only five minutes? said her inner critic then. Laura could explain that, though. She'd always formed close attachments to men very quickly. She knew almost on sight, on first meeting, in fact, if she wanted to take things further with them. And, with Paul Sheridan, she was absolutely convinced now she wanted to go all the way.

Here was a man she could love really hard, did already love with every fibre of her being.

Unable to concentrate further on her shopping, she gave it up as a bad job (at least she had something small, a token, to give to Eleanor; she doubted if her mother would try much harder in the purchasing of a present for her daughter) and found a vacant table for herself in a coffee-shop that wasn't as jam-packed as some of the others. Reading her magazine while sipping her latte and crumbling a gooseberry muffin in her fingers, she became depressed pretty quickly at the sight of all the loved-up, happy couples between the pages of the glossy weekly rag. Even though she knew that a lot of that lovey-dovey-ness was just for show, she was still jealous of the beautiful women with their handsome, rich and successful husbands, their perfect, beautifully dressed babies and children and the show-houses they were lucky enough to call home. (Unless they rented these palaces for the photo-shoots and, in reality, they lived in a kippy trailer-park?) Laura sighed. She was done with shopping. She was done with Christmas, for that matter, and Christmas presents and shiny, happy Christmassy people and the whole festive kit and caboodle. If only, if only, if *only* Paul would call or text. She tossed her crumpled napkin on top of the magazine and left them both behind her on the table, as she exited the coffee-shop and made dejectedly for home through the throngs of excited shoppers.

Christmas was every bit as tedious as she'd predicted. All the preparations had been left to Laura, as Eleanor was "in love", and, when she was "in love", things like housework, cooking, cleaning, shopping for food and presents and getting ready for Christmas were off her radar completely. Laura didn't like the way it was just assumed that she would take on all her mother's jobs just because her mother had yet another boyfriend who, after all, would probably turn out to be just as short-lived as all the others had. Eleanor had always seemed to abdicate her responsibilities at the drop of a hat, and it was always just assumed that Laura would always be fine about taking them up in her turn. Growing more irritable by the hour, she braved the crowds of pushy, shovey shoppers for the second time and cobbled together the makings of a Christmas dinner for — oh, please, just let the awful Thomas leave! — three people and bunged it all in the oven on Christmas morning. She had a bottle of wine beside her as she worked away at the sink, peeling potatoes and chopping vegetables, wearing rubber gloves to protect her lovely nails that there was no one for miles around to admire.

Eleanor and the awful Thomas were ensconced together on the sitting-room couch, with enough cans on the coffee-table in front of each to stock a small off-licence. They were both looking utterly ridiculous, in Laura's opinion, in the matching Christmas jumpers Eleanor had bought them. Eleanor also had on a pair of reindeer antlers and Thomas was wearing a Santa hat. Both of them were pissed long before noon and squabbling loudly over whether to watch perennial favourite *The Snowman* on one channel or perennial favourite *A Muppet Christmas Carol* on another. In the end, they ruined both by flicking back and forth wildly between the two programmes before eventually losing the remote down the side of the couch, where it was never seen again.

Thomas kept getting calls and texts on the new fancy phone Eleanor had bought him for Christmas (how much did she pay for a phone like that, while she was only on a Disability allowance herself, Laura wondered resentfully), and Eleanor was furious at the way he kept nipping out into the hall to take the calls and respond to the texts in private.

"*Who is she?*" she demanded, after he'd been out in the hall for a fourth time.

"I told you, it's only a bit of business, will ya chill yer tits, woman!" he defended himself hotly.

Mother and daughter hadn't exactly pushed the boat out when it came to buying each other presents to mark the festive season. Eleanor had barely glanced at her lily-of-the-valley bath-set and Laura hadn't been at all pleased to receive an exactly similar set from her mother, only with lavender in place of lily-of-the-valley. Lavender, an old lady smell! Her mother had clearly put no thought whatsoever into choosing a present for her only child, but then, when had she ever? Laura still remembered the Christmas when her mother had given her nothing but a book of coupons, for money off various fast-food meals and services like shoe shine and repair and car-valeting in the local area, that had been shoved through the letter-box sometime the week before. Tossing her lavender bath-set onto the couch with a muttered "Thanks," she retreated to the kitchen to angrily down a glass of white wine in record time while checking on the stupid turkey, which, she was beginning to realise, was way too big for only three people, even though she'd deliberately tried to pick a smallish one. But what had seemed "smallish" in the supermarket was now crowding their little oven and Laura realised with dismay that they'd be eating turkey well into March at this rate. The sound of raised voices from the sitting-room made her open the oven and jab furiously at the turkey's ample hindquarters with a fork. *Owwwwww!* she almost heard him spit and sizzle.

"Cook, will you, for Christ's sake?" she muttered, praying inwardly that the argument in the sitting-room wouldn't escalate into a fist-fight, on this day of all days. Frustrated, she turned the knob on the oven from four and a half up to nine to speed things up.

"Thomas has a girlfriend AND a child!" declared Eleanor dramatically, marching into the kitchen with her glass in her hand, her face red with booze and indignation.

"No kidding," Laura said under her breath, as she closed the oven door on the turkey and straightened up. It would be at least an hour, though, before the stupid thing would be safe to eat. Eleanor would be well pissed by then, and she'd probably have fallen asleep on the couch and missed dinner completely, like she'd done on so many Christmases in the past. "What do you expect, Mum?" she said out loud, sitting down at the kitchen table for a minute and taking a good big drink of her own wine. "You've only known him five minutes. Surely you must have realised that he had a life before you? He could have a wife and six children, for all you know. Maybe they're all at home somewhere right now, crying and waiting for Daddy to come home." Laura knew she was laying it on a bit thick, but so what? Eleanor never gave the remotest thought to the consequences of her actions.

"You never show me any sympathy, Laura," her mother said petulantly. "Why are you always so hard and unfeeling towards me? You're a hard, cold person, do you know that?"

"I show you nothing *but* sympathy! I show you too much sympathy. You'd probably be better off if I showed you some tough love instead. Look, does this Thomas fella want a leg or a breast, when this monstrosity in the oven is finally cooked, or what?"

Eleanor stared at her daughter blankly. "Thomas is a vegetarian. I thought I told you?"

Now it was Laura's turn to stare blankly. "No, you bloody *didn't*! Mum, if Thomas is a vegetarian, then why am I stuck in this poky bloody kitchen trying to cook a turkey that's big enough to feed a small army?"

"No one asked you to. Stop playing the martyr," huffed Eleanor, turning away to go back to the sitting-room, from where angry voices began immediately to be heard once more.

Laura couldn't help it. She started to cry. Stuck here cooking dinner for the two most ungracious, ungrateful people in Ireland, while Paul, the new love of her life, was probably at home right now enjoying an elegant, love-and-present-filled Christmas straight out of bloody *Hello!* magazine. She could see it now. Paul and his beautiful wife Barbara and his two charming little daughters, one of them a new-born (they were called Jessie and Lucy; she knew this from office gossip), would be dressed in matching Christmas jumpers, and they would all look like something out of a TV ad for the perfect family Christmas. They'd be opening expensive, thoughtfully chosen gifts while gathered round a fairy-tale Christmas tree lit with a thousand twinkling candles, and the air would be deliciously redolent of the real pine Christmas tree (which they'd have had specially picked out and felled for them in a nearby forest by a friendly smiling woodcutter) and the hot, spicy mulled wine Paul and his wife would be sipping from crystal tumblers that had been in the family for generations. The thought of it made Laura cry even harder. Life was so unfair sometimes. How come some people got the Dickensian picture-postcard Christmas, and other less fortunate people got to share their festive season with a couple of argumentative drunks and an oversized turkey that just wouldn't hurry up and *cook*, goddammit? She blew her nose loudly on a segment of kitchen paper and got up to see to the vegetables.

A loud crash and a scream issuing from the sitting-room had her rushing from the kitchen suddenly.

"What the hell, Mum . . .?" she began. Thomas was flat-out on the couch with his eyes closed and a bump on his forehead the size of an egg. The lamp from the sideboard was on the couch beside him. Eleanor was standing over him, her hand over her mouth. "Mum, did you hit him . . .?" Laura stared in amazement at the still, unmoving figure of Thomas and a cold feeling of dread began to creep towards and over her.

"I didn't mean to," Eleanor whispered, pale-faced and aghast. "I only meant to throw the lamp. I never meant to hit him. You know what a bad thrower I am. I can't throw to save my life. You know that. Is he . . . dead?"

"I don't know," her daughter replied, leaning over the prone figure and tentatively lifting one of his wrists to check his pulse, like she'd seen people do in medical dramas on television.

She screamed when a hand grabbed her own wrist and an angry male voice mumbled: "I'll kill you for that, you crazy bitch!"

"I didn't touch you, you fool. That wasn't me, so will you pipe down?" Irritably she shook his hand off her. "Get a wet cloth for his head, will you?" she directed her mother, who stood transfixed. "Mum, *please!* Wake up and stop standing there like you're in a trance or something and go get him a wet cloth for his head, I said!"

Eleanor scuttled away, galvanised into action.

"I'm outta here," growled Thomas, heaving himself to his feet with a pained groan. "I'm not staying here to be murdered by you two mad bitches."

"Sit down, can't you?" urged Laura. "We need to put something on your head. You might have a concussion or something."

"*Gerrout me way!*" Thomas pushed past her and out the door.

She heard him pounding up the stairs and, just as Eleanor was returning to the sitting-room with the wet cloth, he was back with a kit-bag into which he began throwing bits and pieces of his belongings that he'd left scattered around the room, including a pair of stiff, dirty socks that his poor girlfriend would now presumably have to wash. Good luck to her, Laura thought with a grimace.

Eleanor stared at him, appalled.

"You're not leaving?" she squeaked. "Tommy, you can't! I never meant to hurt you. I never meant to hit you, you must believe me! I'd never hurt you. I love you! And it's Christmas Day. Tommy, you can't leave me, not now, not on Christmas Day!"

But the Awful Thomas was not to be dissuaded. With a few muttered curses and dire threats, he zipped up his bag, pulled on his jacket and was out the front door and down the garden path before either woman could really do anything.

Eleanor collapsed onto the couch, most recently vacated by her lover, and gave vent loudly and messily to her grief.

Laura, sighing, sat down beside her and attempted to comfort her. Her heart sank at the thought of all the comforting she would have to do now over the festive period. A thought suddenly occurred to her.

"Would he have stolen anything?" she asked her mother.

"Like what?" Eleanor sniffled. "There's nothing here worth taking."

"I'll run up and have a quick look round anyway," Laura decided. "Just in case."

Upstairs in her mother's bedroom, she averted her eyes in distaste from the sight of the rumpled unmade bed. It didn't look like anything in the room had been disturbed. Her mother's jewellery box still stood open on the dressing-table with all her little bits and pieces of costume jewellery in it. Eleanor's purse was in her handbag and the handbag was on the floor beside the bed. Laura sat down on the bed and opened the purse. It contained two twenty-euro notes and several coins, so it was unlikely that Thomas had been in there. Well, at least he hadn't robbed them. That was something to be thankful for, she supposed. She replaced the purse in the handbag and was standing up to go back downstairs when she heard the sound of the smoke alarm coming from the kitchen and smelled the unmistakeable smell of burning meat. Oh, bollocks.

"*The turkey!*" she shrieked. She'd completely forgotten about it and the fact that she'd turned the oven all the way up to maximum a while ago to speed things along a bit.

She bolted downstairs to attempt to save their Christmas dinner. The kitchen was filled with smoke and the smoke alarm wouldn't stop wailing until she hit it several times with the handle of the sweeping-brush. The cover came off and hit the floor, but at least the damn thing shut the hell up. She opened the oven and was nearly choked with the clouds of black smoke that came billowing out. Grabbing up a tea-towel so as not to burn the hands off herself, she lifted out the big stainless steel oven tray with the turkey on it, only to drop it on the floor with fright and a loud clatter when Eleanor came charging into the room suddenly.

"He *did* steal something after all!" she exclaimed. "He nicked our two bath-sets. Probably going to give them to his girlfriend as a Christmas present, the bastard! Laura, what have you done to our turkey?" she added, only then noticing the outsized, almost black bird sitting on the kitchen floor in a bed of burnt stuffing and charred roast potatoes.

Laura stared at her mother. No words would come. There *were* no words. She heard her mobile phone ringing then from the back pocket of her jeans, the way a person in a nightmare might hear something — hearing it, while not exactly registering what it was or where it might be coming from. As if in a daze, she took the phone out of her pocket and stared at it. *Private number,* it said. She answered it and, rather robotically, said hello.

"Hey, babes," said the voice with the melty chocolatey undertones she'd been longing to hear all Christmas long. "Happy Christmas! How's your day going?"

Chapter 2

SUZANNE

"I've . . . I've broken up with Mark," Suzanne Carragher said nervously. She'd been working up to it for several minutes and so it came out of her in a kind of rush, like it was all one sentence. *I'vebrokenupwithMark.*

Barbara stared at her sister in dismay. "Suze, no!" she exclaimed. "When? What happened? How are you? How's *Mark?* Who did the breaking-up?"

The sisters were seated on the high stools at the breakfast island in Barbara's kitchen, drinking coffee and chatting while Jessie, aged two-and-a-half, and Lucy, eight weeks old, napped in front of kiddies' television in the sitting-room across the hall. All the doors were open so the two women could hear the kids if anything happened.

"If you'll allow me, Your Honour," Suzanne teased with a faint grin, "I'll field those questions one at a time. Firstly, I did the breaking-up. I broke up with Mark. His ego's a bit bruised, but otherwise not too much damage, I'd say. He'll get over it, if he hasn't already."

"You broke up with Mark?" exclaimed Barbara, her eyes wide. "But I thought he was such a good catch! Good-looking, well-mannered, cultured, solvent, never raised his voice or lost his temper . . .?"

"Wow, Barb, it's a wonder you didn't ditch Paul and marry him yourself, you've such a high opinion of him!"

"Don't tempt me," replied her sister grimly. "I still bloody might, let me tell you. But seriously, Suze, if he's such a great catch, then why'd you dump him? What's he done?"

"Well, nothing as such. It's a bit more complicated than that." Suzanne dipped her chocolate digestive in her coffee and took a bite out of it, chewing thoughtfully.

"Why? What'd you mean? How is it complicated? I mean, what did he *do?*"

"I told you, sis. Nothing. He's done nothing. It's more a case of what he *has* than what he's done."

"Ah, stop being so cryptic and mysterious, Suze! What are you talking about, it's more a case of what he *has?* What exactly does he have, apart from a nice car and a decent bank balance and a good haircut?"

"Well, not to put too fine a point on it, sis — and if I may interrupt the Mark-love, which, by the way, is becoming very hard to stomach — for a moment, a *penis.*"

Barbara started, her mouth agape. "A penis? You mean . . .?"

Suzanne nodded. She chewed on her bottom lip the way she did when she was nervous and waiting for an answer to something.

"You mean, you don't fancy men any more, you fancy women? You're gay? Oh, Suze!" Barbara burst into noisy sobs there and then at the breakfast counter.

Alarmed, Suzanne took her sister's hands across the counter and said: "Barb, honey, what's the matter? There's no need for you to be upset! I'm not upset, there's nothing in the least to be upset about, so what's wrong, Barb, love?"

"I'm not crying because I'm sad, you muppet! I'm crying because I'm happy, happy that you've finally figured out what you are and that you're happy about it. You *are* happy about it? Please tell me you're happy about it!"

"Well, I'm not so much happy about it as resigned, as in I can finally accept it instead of trying to fight it all the time, which I was. But what do you mean, you're happy that I've finally figured it out? Are you saying that you knew all along or something?"

"Well," said Barbara, after blowing her nose ferociously on a tissue from the open box on the counter, "do you not remember when we were kids and I'd be there playing with my dolls and my Barbies and you'd be tying the boy next door to a tree, wearing his red Indian costume and threatening to scalp him with his own tomahawk?"

"Vaguely," grinned Suzanne.

"And when we were in secondary school, and me and everyone else had a huge crush on Mr. Lomax, the science teacher, but you spent your days mooning over Miss Lambert, the home economics substitute for Old Ma Henderson?"

"Oh yeah," Suzanne said, remembering with a vague sense of wonder at memories unveiled.

"And when you were making your Confirmation, and you cried so hard and so long when Mum was trying to get you to wear the green dress with the puffy sleeves and the little bows round the hemline, and in the end she had to let you wear trousers or you wouldn't go to the ceremony?"

"How could I forget?" Suzanne said wryly. She'd never

seen her mother so upset. The notion of her eldest daughter making her Confirmation in trousers, actually appearing in front of the bishop in a pair of tan corduroy dungarees and a checked shirt and going up for Communion in them as bold as brass, had very nearly been too much for Eileen Carragher. Suzanne wouldn't be surprised at all to hear that their mum still carried the mental scars of such a dreadful trauma.

"Well, let's just say that I *suspected*. I didn't say anything because I wasn't sure how much you knew yourself. I always thought you'd figure it out for yourself when the time was right, and now it looks like you have. This calls for a celebration. Pass me down those Jaffa cakes from the secret cupboard behind you. No, not that one, the other one. They're behind that pile of plates there. I have to hide them from Paul or he'd scoff the lot, *and* try to pin the blame on the kids. As if a new-born baby can climb a chair and hand down the Jaffa cakes to her sister! Here, now, have a few of these to mark — *oops*, sorry, I said *Mark!* — this auspicious occasion."

"Thanks, Barb," said Suzanne gratefully, a glint of a tear in her eye as she dipped a Jaffa cake into her coffee and munched on it. "Not just for the Jaffa cakes, although I *do* appreciate your breaking out your hidden stash. No, I mean, for understanding and being there for me and stuff, even though I'm . . . I'm maybe not the sister you thought I was."

"Don't you dare say that!" Barbara took Suzanne's hand across the breakfast island and squeezed it to emphasise her point. "You're exactly the sister I thought you were and you always will be, so don't you dare ever change, okay? Anyway, listen, do you mind me asking, why now? I mean, you and Mark splitting up? Has something happened to push you into making the decision to come out? I mean, that's if you *are* coming out? Is this it?"

Suzanne took a deep breath and nodded slowly. "I think so, now. I've been fighting it for years, but I genuinely don't think I can fight it any more. I'm gay, Barb. I'm gay. I can't believe I'm sitting here saying it out loud to another living human being but I am. It's true. I'm gay. I'm a gay person. A gay woman."

"I'm so proud of you," said Barbara tearfully. "I'm so proud of my wonderful big sister."

"Steady on, Barb. I'm only coming out. I haven't actually found a cure for cancer."

"I know, I know. But it's still a big deal. We should have a nice big dinner to celebrate."

"Don't you want an answer to your question first?" Suzanne said shyly.

"What question was that?" demanded her curious sister.

"You know, whether anything's happened to . . . *erm*, to spark all this off? Me and Mark splitting up and everything, and me coming out as . . . well, as gay?"

"Well, has it?"

God bless her, thought Suzanne, she sounded so excited!

"*Erm*, yes, in a way."

"What d'you mean, *in a way?* Has something happened or not?"

"Well, kind of. I've met someone, Barb."

"You've met someone? A woman? Well, of course a woman, what am I saying? Who is it? Oh my God, Suzanne, I'm so happy for you!"

"Well," Suzanne said self-consciously, "her name is Rachel and she works at the college. She teaches yoga and mindfulness on the same nights my art classes are on, so we kept on bumping into each other in the staffroom on the breaks, and before and after the classes and stuff. That's how we got to know each other. It kind of happened organically."

"And what's she like? Is she nice? Well, of course she must be nice, if you've chosen her!"

"I love that you have so much implicit faith in my judgement, Barb. She's a lovely calm person, actually. All that yoga and mindfulness, probably," Suzanne said with a laugh.

"And does Mark know about her?"

"Yes. I thought it was best to be honest with him, even though Rachel and I were careful not to do anything about furthering our own relationship until I'd broken up with him properly. It was the right thing to do. You know I couldn't ever cheat on anyone or be deceptive if I could help it. I'd just feel too uncomfortable about it. My conscience would never let me relax."

"And was he okay about it?"

"He was civilised about it, put it like that, but I wouldn't exactly say that he was okay about it. He won't be throwing any parties to announce it to the world, put it like that again. It's been a big blow to his ego, more than anything. Ours was a relationship based on companionship more than actual love; just someone to go to art galleries and symphony concerts with was all we were each looking for. We were never madly in love, like kids."

"And are you madly in love with this Rachel person?"

"I think so, yes. Yes, yes, I am. And so is she. I hope!"

"And what about Rachel? I mean, is she openly gay? Or is she only just coming out now, like you are?"

"No, she's been out for a while, I think. A few years, anyway. Her parents and siblings were a bit iffy about it at first, but now they're fine about it and she sees them all the time. She's thirty-two, by the way, so she's a couple of years younger than me but, in terms of living her life openly the way she wants to and on her own terms, she's had a bit of a head-start, as you can see."

"Oh my God, Suze!" Barbara's hands had flown to her mouth and her dark eyes were wide.

"What?" Suzanne said, alarmed.

"What you just said there about parents; about Rachel's parents being fine about her being gay. Oh, Suze, Mum and Dad! I've only literally just thought about them."

"I wish I could say the same," said her sister wryly. "I've hardly thought about anything else over the last few days. Telling them is going to be hard."

"Are you *going* to tell them?"

"Well, I'm going to have to, aren't I? I can't go around telling my only sibling that I'm coming out as gay and not tell our parents the same while I'm at it. I'm tired of living a lie, anyway. I just want there to be no secrets between family. The only problem is *when* to do it. I thought maybe this coming weekend? Are you and Paul and the kids going over there for Sunday dinner?"

"Well, we're invited, but I can cry off if you'd prefer to have them to yourself while you tell them. I could say I'm just too knackered from Lucy and the night-feeds and everything, which is still true enough, anyway."

"Would you mind? It'd only be this once. It's probably best if I go over on my own."

"Suze, are you sure about this? You know Mum and Dad. They're old-school. No to divorce, no to abortion, no to everything else as well. If that referendum they're talking about for gay marriage ever actually happens, you can bet your bottom dollar that Mum and Dad will be the first to the polls with a big fat 'no'. No to everything, that's them."

"They might change their minds if they think it'll affect someone in their own family who's close to them. That's what I'm banking on, anyway."

"Suze, I'd love to think so, but Mum and Dad are dinosaurs. Face it. Shure, they still turn over if a sex scene comes on the bloomin' telly, even if it's hetero. Even if it's only kissing."

"They'll be fine about it when I talk to them, I'm sure. If I can just get them in the right frame of mind . . ."

"Suze, you're an idealist," said Barbara with a sigh, as she slid off her high stool. "Look, here's Paul's car in the driveway now and me with not so much as a spud peeled or a child in the house washed. And they've been napping for so long now, they'll never sleep tonight. You'll stay for dinner, won't you?"

"Of course I will, if I'm invited."

"Of course you're invited, you muppet! Now get peeling," Barbara added, with a mischievous grin and a jerk of her head towards the sink and the not-so-little basin of potatoes and vegetables requiring attention.

"*A-ha*, I knew there was a reason you invited me," Suzanne countered with a grin. "By the way," she went on, rolling up the sleeves of her shirt and getting to work, "will you tell Paul my news for me? About my splitting up with Mark, I mean? And, I suppose, my getting together with Rachel as well? I mean, it's not fair to ask you to keep things like that from him. He's your husband, after all. But wait till I'm not here to tell him, will you? If he's got any pervy remarks to make about girl-on-girl action and that kind of thing, I think I'd rather not be here to hear them. No offence," she added hurriedly. "I'm sure he wouldn't say any such thing."

"Don't worry," Barbara said grimly. "If he does, I'll stuff him with sage and onion and serve him for Sunday dinner. He's not sullying my wonderful big sister's first proper gay relationship with his filthy mind."

There was just time for Suzanne to flash her younger sister a grateful grin before Paul Sheridan breezed into the kitchen looking extraordinarily pleased with himself. More so than usual, even, and that was saying something. "Ladies, ladies," he said, mooching in the biscuit barrel for a digestive to take the edge off his ravenous just-in-from-work hunger. "Don't all crowd me at once. There's plenty of Paul Sheridan to go around."

Suzanne glanced across the kitchen at Barbara, then stepped aside from the sink and handed him the potato peeler.

"*Get peeling*," chorused the sisters.

Paul's face fell.

The following night, when Suzanne was back in her own flat in Rathmines, Rachel came over and they discussed what had happened with Barbara. Rachel was thrilled that it had gone so well with Suzanne's beloved younger sister, about whom she was always talking.

"One down, two more to go," Suzanne said with a wry grin.

She was sitting up in bed with a book open in front of her, her glasses on and her long straight dark hair piled up on top of her head, held in place by two pens and a tortoiseshell comb.

Rachel was seated at the one dressing-table chair, brushing her longish blonde hair in front of the mirror. "Do you really think it's such a good idea to tell your parents about us so soon?" she asked, putting down the brush and starting on her night cream. "I mean, from what you've told me, they're not exactly Mr. and Mrs. Open-Minded and Tolerant, are they? No offence meant, by the way."

"None taken. I just feel like, well, if I don't tell them now, when *will* I tell them? If I'm going to be living an openly gay lifestyle from now on, which is what I'd like, wouldn't it be wrong to leave them in the dark?"

"There's no shame in protecting yourself, either, though, from people who might give you grief about it." Rachel, dressed in just her pyjama top, finally finished up her night-time preparations and climbed into bed beside Suzanne. "I know plenty of gay women who are still keeping their sexuality and lifestyles a secret from certain family members, because they know for sure that those particular folks won't understand."

"I don't think I could live like that, though. It was different when I was denying it to myself, because there was literally nothing to tell anyone then, but now that I've finally figured this whole thing out for myself, with your help, of course," she added with a shy smile, "it would just feel wrong to me not to tell them. I mean, they're my parents, aren't they? Don't they have a right to know that their eldest child is happy at last with the person of her choice? I'd want to know if it was my son or daughter."

But you're a million times more enlightened than a couple of hardcore old-schoolers, were the words that hung unspoken in the air between them.

Rachel shrugged. "If that's what you want, Suze, love. I just don't want you to get hurt, that's all. As I know myself, all too well, people don't always react to things the way you want them to. A friend of mine from college got completely cut off from nearly everyone in her family when she came out to them a few years ago. Mind you, the climate for it was a lot frostier back then. It wasn't nearly as tolerant as it seems to be these days. She's always saying she wishes she'd waited a bit to make her big announcement, until there was a more favourable climate, maybe, or even that she wishes she'd never told them at all. It just wasn't worth all the hassle it caused her, in the end."

"It won't be like that for me!" Suzanne sounded confident. She took off her glasses, closed her book and put them both on the night-stand. She smiled when Rachel began to gently pull the pens and tortoiseshell comb from her hair, the long dark hair that was so like Barbara's. "My parents love me," she went on, still in the confident tone. "They'll want me to be happy. And, if the only way I can be happy is by being with a woman, then I'm sure that they'll be happy *for* me. They've always loved us and wanted what was best for us, even if they were a bit stuffy and uptight in the way they went about things. That's why I intend to be straight, if you'll excuse the pun, straight, open and honest with them. I owe it to them."

"What do you think they'd say if they could see you now?" purred Rachel, running her fingers through Suzanne's well-cut and conditioned locks (Suzanne and Barbara both were justifiably proud of their shampoo-commercial hair) and sliding one hand up under Suzanne's Snoopy nightshirt to find her breast, soft and warm and the absolute right size for cupping. "Do you think they'd approve?"

Suzanne laughed. "I think they'd have a bloody blue fit, that's what I think."

Rachel laughed too, then leaned across Suzanne to put out her reading light. She left Lyric FM, which they both liked, on the radio for soothing background noise, and she pulled Suzanne down with her to the pillows. "Should we just forget them for a bit, so?" Her hand snaked its way to between Suzanne's bare thighs, to where her pussy was damp and already twitching with excitement.

"There's nothing I'd like more," murmured Suzanne.

Suzanne pulled into the driveway of her parents' house and turned off the engine, staying sitting in the car for a minute or two to gather her thoughts before going in. She'd had a lovely morning, which she'd thought had helped to relax her, but here she was again now, as nervous as a kitten. *There's nothing to be afraid of*, she repeated to herself over and over, as per Rachel's instructions. *They're only your mum and dad.*

She and Rachel had slept late this morning as it was Sunday; then Rachel had gone out to get the newspapers and she'd come back to the house with a big bag of warm croissants to go with their coffee. She'd made the coffee and brought up everything to Suzanne, who'd been enchanted, especially by the bag of warm croissants. They'd drunk the coffee, eaten a few of the croissants, ignored the papers completely and then snuggled back down under the covers to make love, and it had once more been magical. When the pair spent the night together, it was usually at Suzanne's flat in Rathmines, as she shared with no one and Rachel had two flatmates sharing with her out in Chapelizod.

The last thing Rachel had said to her lover this morning before Suzanne had set out on the momentous trip to her parents' house was a reiteration of the mantra she'd taught her: "They're only your mum and dad. There's nothing to be afraid of." To which she'd added: "And never forget that I love you very much and I'll be here when you get back, and you can tell me all about it."

Suzanne had kissed her gratefully then before starting up the engine of her car and driving away, a little glow inside her from Rachel's words of encouragement. It was particularly decent of Rachel to give her such encouragement, especially when Rachel seemed to be secretly convinced that Suzanne coming out to her ageing, narrow-minded parents wasn't a good idea in the first place.

Now Suzanne got out of the car and was greeted by a ferocious volley of barks from the family dog, a Jack Russell called Scooby-Doo, who barked the longest and hardest at family members trying to gain access to the house but who pretty much ignored everyone else. If you were a burglar or any kind of dangerous criminal or escaped lunatic, Scooby-Doo would lick your hand and fall asleep devotedly at your feet. If you were a Carragher family member, however, or the postman, or perhaps a visiting doctor come to see a sick patient, Scoob wouldn't let you go until he'd practically denuded your ankle-bones of all flesh. He was a proper little piranha when it came down to it.

"Ah, go on out of it, Scoob, you mad thing, you!" Suzanne said affectionately, as she danced round the little yapping terrier and nipped rather niftily in through the back door of the house, which was always left open when Eileen and Dermot Carragher were at home.

Eileen was in the kitchen as usual, seeing to the dinner, and Dermot was in and out between the sitting-room and the shed in the back garden, bringing in logs for the fire, which was always lit on Sundays after the dinner, except on the hottest of summer Sundays. The little table by the window in the sitting-room was already set up for the chess game Suzanne always had with her dad after Sunday dinner, and Eileen's knitting sat on her favourite armchair by the fire, ready for when every last trace of the dinner had been cleared away and Eileen eventually allowed herself to sit down and relax a bit. Even then, she still had to keep busy with her knitting because the devil made work for idle hands.

"Any news?" Suzanne asked her mother as she joined her at the sink and began to dry up a few plates that Eileen had been washing. "How was Mass?"

"Father O'Donnell broke his wrist," said Eileen, with the air of someone imparting really important news.

"Jesus! How'd he do that?" Knowing how much of a big deal Sunday Mass and the Catholic Church and Father O'Donnell were to Eileen and Dermot both, but especially to Eileen, Suzanne tried her hardest to infuse an air of shocked surprise into her voice.

"He tripped on the hem of his surplice coming down off the pulpit after morning Mass one of the days since last Sunday. He put out his hands to save himself, and got a broken wrist for his trouble. You could tell he was in terrible pain during the Mass this morning, lifting the chalice and everything."

"God, that's terrible!" Suzanne hoped she'd infused the right amount of shocked solemnity into her words. "Could no one else take over from him for a bit?"

"He's very devoted to his parishioners. He'd have to be in a really bad way, he's always saying, before he'd abandon his flock."

"Good old Father O'Donnell. What a trooper he is. *Erm*, how's Dad?"

"He's grand. Go on in there now and say hello to him while I finish up in here."

Suzanne went into the sitting-room. "Hi, Dad, how are things?"

Dermot Carragher, a big, tall bearded man, was on his knees in front of the fire, coaxing it to light with firelighters and a lighted newspaper. He was obviously taking no chances with his precious fire. *Me, man. Man make fire. Make fire for food and wo-man.* The same words came to Suzanne every time she saw her father wrestling with the fire. It was obviously a sort of primeval desire within all men, she'd often thought, the way they seemed to feel the need to create fire every so often. It explained why they always hogged the barbecue in the summer-time, and why they burned rubbish on bonfires they built in their back gardens and marched round them in satisfaction, often clutching a big dirty stick. *Me, man. Me have stick, make big fire for cook food. For wo-man.*

"Did your mother tell you that next door's dog dug up my cabbages?"

"Are you sure it was next door's, Dad, and not Scooby?"

Her father snorted. "That useless fecker? Ah shure, he couldn't dig up a bone." He put out a hand and gently rubbed Scooby's soft head. Everyone loved little Scooby-Doo, despite the ferocious yapping. He'd padded into the sitting-room a little while ago, worn out from barking at Suzanne and dancing round her, and had lain down for a snooze on the hearthrug, regardless of whose way he was in. That was Scooby-Doo for you.

Dinner went off well, with Eileen's chit-chat about Father O'Donnell taking up most of the conversation. Eileen was a deeply religious woman. It was the kind of family she'd come from herself. She'd gone more or less straight from school into marriage with Dermot, having seen little of life and even less of the world. She'd never worked, outside of the home. Inside the home, she'd cooked and cleaned and scrubbed and polished her fingers to the bone, to keep a clean, comfortable home for her husband and two daughters to come home to every day. If marriage hadn't been what she'd expected or if it had disappointed her, she'd certainly never mentioned it. Dermot had worked in a biscuit factory for most of his life; then, when the factory closed down, he'd done security work for the libraries and museums. He'd liked walking up and down in the National Gallery, wearing a lanyard and a uniform and answering the public's questions about where the toilets were, if they could take photos of the paintings and how long was the Jack B. Yeats exhibition going to last. But he was retired now.

"Mum, Dad, I've got something to tell you both."

Dinner had been pronounced more than satisfactory and then cleared away, and Eileen had brought in the tea, which they always had in the sitting-room after Sunday dinner. Suzanne was sitting on the couch and Dermot was seated at the table by the window, ready for their chess game. Eileen immediately looked worried. Her hand flew to her mouth. To Eileen, a bit of news could only mean bad news. Someone had died, had cancer or had been run over on the way to the corner shop. No news was ever *good* news, that was for sure. She was a proper worry-wart, a big panicker. She was one of those women who, if they ever found themselves at a loose end with nothing in particular to worry about, would promptly invent something. Clearly, Suzanne had often thought, her mother felt that worrying was just part and parcel of the female condition and that was that.

"Will you relax, Eileen," Dermot said. "Let the girl tell us herself, in her own time. I'm sure it's nothing bad. She didn't say she'd anything *bad* to tell us, did she, only that she had some news."

Suzanne smiled gratefully at her dad. Maybe this was all going to be fine after all. She cleared her throat and self-consciously began with the words: "Dad's right, Mum, it's nothing at all bad, it's just something new. News, that's all. A bit of a surprise."

"Will you hurry up and tell us, Suzanne love, for the love of God?" pleaded her mother. "I don't think my heart can stand the suspense. You can't imagine what I'm going through with all this dreadful worrying."

"Will you give the girl a chance, Eileen?" Dermot said, but she merely clicked her tongue at him in annoyance and continued staring intensely at Suzanne as if to say: *'Well?'*

"Well, in the first place, I've broken up with Mark."

Eileen's hand flew straight back to her mouth. "I knew it! Oh, Mother of God, I knew it!"

"Don't dramatise, Mum," said Suzanne, getting annoyed herself now. "It was mutual. Well, pretty much mutual. It was me who did the breaking-up, but I promise you Mark wasn't that bothered. He'll be fine, Mum. You've no need to worry about him."

"But he was such a good catch! And so very good-looking and romantic and everything!" wailed Eileen.

Whoa, get in line after Barbara, Mum! You're not the only one who loves Mark and thinks he's the greatest catch since Moby Dick.

"And secondly?" said Dermot, looking keenly at his eldest daughter.

"Sorry, what?" Suzanne had been totally side-tracked by her mother's apparent grief over Mark.

"You said, in the first place, and that was about Mark. What was the second thing?"

"Well, that's the real thing I wanted to tell you." Suzanne's hands and voice were shaking.

This was it, then. This was the moment she'd pretty much been waiting for, albeit subconsciously, her whole adult life: the moment she told her parents that she was gay. After all, she'd told her sister Barbara about it, and Barbara had been fine, more than fine, with the news. Having a sister like Barbara was like having your very own cheering section or mammy lioness, someone in your corner who'd tear other folks limb from limb if they so much as looked crooked at you. Barbara was a great support, a really decent person and a smashing sister to have.

"You see, I've met someone else . . ." Her voice came out

in a pathetic squeak. She cleared her throat and tried again. "I've . . . broken up with Mark, you see, because I've . . . I've . . . I've met someone else."

"Who is it?" Eileen's eyes were as round as saucers and her face still wore the expression of impending catastrophe. "Whoever he is, he can't possibly be a better catch than Mark. Mark had his own home, his own car and all his own teeth and hair. That's very important to someone like you, someone who's getting on in years a bit, or at least it should be. But young people nowadays, they've no concept of what's good for them or what really matters."

"Mum, will you please stop going on about how great Mark is?" Suzanne was growing really annoyed by now. "You're really not helping. Yes, I know Mark is a great catch and all that, and I'm sure he'll make someone a terrific husband one day, but will you please get it through your head, Mum, that it won't be me? Mark's actually the most boring person I've ever known in my life and, even though he's done nothing wrong, I'll be glad to be shot of him. Even if I hadn't met someone else and fallen in love, me and Mark would never have lasted. We'd have split up sooner or later. So now will you please stop going on about him and fan-girl him in your own time, Mum, *please?*"

Muttering dire warnings about people who hadn't the remotest idea what side their bread was buttered, Eileen subsided into a huffy silence.

Strangely shy now after her outburst, unable to look either of her parents in the eye as she spoke, Suzanne fixed her eyes on the slumbering Scooby-Doo, blissfully unconscious and as warm as toast on the hearthrug.

"Her name is Rachel. She works in the college as a yoga and mindfulness teacher. That's where we met. She's really a . . . a very fun person. I just know you'd like her."

Eileen was as white as a sheet. "A woman? Oh, Mary Mother of Jesus! What on earth are you saying to us, girl?"

"I think you know perfectly well what I'm saying, Mum," Suzanne replied, as calmly as she could manage it. "I'm saying that I'm . . . that I'm gay, and that I'd like to live as . . . as an openly gay person from now on. That means I won't be dating . . . be dating any more men . . ." She trailed off, conscious of a distinct, dramatic dip in the social temperature.

Her mother sat stock-still, looking like she was in shock. At last, Suzanne chanced a glance at her father. He was looking out the window, away from her.

Then he turned his head, the expression on his face giving nothing away.

"D-Dad . . .?"

"Get out of my house."

"Wh-what . . .?"

"Get out of my house."

"But, Dad, this is me, Suzanne, your daughter! You can't mean that, surely?"

"Get out of my house! I don't want to see you here again!" It was a roar now.

Eileen nearly jumped out of her skin at the unexpectedness of it. Dermot half-rose from his seat at the table by the window and overturned the chessboard. A queen somehow made its way across the floor to land at Suzanne's feet. She leaned down, picked it up as if in a trance and looked at it in wonder. Then, the tears starting to spill down her pale face, she closed her trembling fingers around the little wooden figure and fled from the house.

"He wouldn't even look at me," she told Barbara afterwards. They were back at their favourite posts on the high stools at Barbara's kitchen island, sharing a bottle of medicinal wine and a family-sized bar of chocolate. "I obviously disgust him so much that he couldn't even bring himself to clap eyes on me." Suzanne's voice was hoarse from crying. She was finished with crying for now — she'd done plenty of that on Rachel's shoulder when she'd arrived home from her parents' house last night.

Rachel had been wonderful, she'd been more than understanding and she'd never once said 'I told you so' — and now Suzanne just felt bone-weary and filled with self-loathing.

"Come on now, Suze," Rachel had said, her voice warm with sympathy. "On the couch now, come on, sit down. I'll bring you a large brandy for shock."

And she probably had been in shock, too, Suzanne reckoned when she thought about it afterwards. She'd been shaking like a leaf, her teeth actually chattering as if she'd been suddenly plunged into icy cold waters. Rachel had sat her down on the sitting-room couch, wrapped a blanket around her trembling shoulders and helped her to hold the brandy glass to her lips, as her own hands were shaking so much. Then Rachel had slipped Suzanne's shoes off and rubbed the circulation back into her frozen feet. It really was astonishing, how cold she'd been after the encounter with her parents, and how much the shock had resembled an unexpected dip in freezing cold waters. Suzanne would remember for the rest of her life how cold she'd been that day. No subsequent winters, no matter how chilly, would be able to touch it. Neither would she forget how kind and supportive Rachel had been that day. Not once did she say 'Oh, if only you'd taken my advice and kept schtum!' for which Suzanne would be eternally grateful. There was nothing more annoying than someone who said, 'I told you so!' Rachel hadn't said anything at all, except that she was so sorry Suzanne had had to go through something so awful, and was there anything at all she could do to help? She'd been an absolute sweetheart about the whole thing.

"I'll murder him," Barbara said grimly now. She was very angry indeed at their father. Yes, she too had been aware of the ultra-conservative nature of both their parents (no to divorce, no to abortion, no to any kind of family barring the traditional two-parent one, and, of course, even then, one had to be male and the other female), but she'd never dreamed that their father would react so violently as to order his beloved eldest daughter out of his house.

"Look, talking like that won't help, Barb. Thanks, I know you're only trying to stand up for me but, honestly, I don't think that tearing round there to give Dad a bollocking will help the situation any. It'll just make things worse. You do understand that, don't you, Barb? You know what he's like. He'll only dig his heels in and there'll be no shifting him then, ever."

"He needs a good boot up the jacksy with the new millenium." Barbara's face and tone were so militant that Suzanne had to laugh. "He's living in the bloody past, he is."

"Well, maybe he is and maybe he isn't, but I don't think

it'll make him warm to the new me somehow, you telling him all that, do you, sis?"

"Maybe not," Barbara concurred, but reluctantly. "I still think he was well out of order, though, ordering you out of the house like that. Paul agrees with me."

"Did you tell Paul about . . . about my coming out?"

"Yeah. He whistled through his teeth, said, 'Imagine, good old Suzanne a lezzer? Deadly buzz, fair play to her,' and then he wandered off to watch *Match of the Day* with a slice of pizza in his mouth. Trust me, he's fine about it."

"Maybe I should have stayed in," Suzanne joked feebly.

"Stayed in? What do you mean?"

"You know, I was supposed to be coming out and it didn't go too well? I'm just thinking that maybe I should have stayed in? It's a joke, Barb." She trailed off miserably.

"Don't you dare let that prejudiced old fogey ruin your precious coming-out!" Barbara said fiercely. "You did a very brave and courageous thing, telling your loved ones that you were gay. It's Dad's own fault if he chooses to take offence at it for some mad reason. Don't let it detract from the brave and beautiful thing you did."

"Barbara, I love you, you know that?" Suzanne reached across the counter and squeezed her sister's hand. "Did I really do a brave and beautiful thing? You still think that?"

Barbara nodded staunchly. Good old Barbara. She was golden. She was a rock. She was a star. She was *all* of those things!

"Me thirsty, Mummy," said two-and-a-half-year-old Jessie suddenly, coming into the kitchen from the sitting-room, trailing her favourite teddy along behind her by one leg.

"Daddy's supposed to be minding you, sweetheart, while Mummy talks to Auntie Suzanne!" Barbara hopped down from her high stool and picked up her daughter. Together they went to the fridge to look for juice. "Where's Daddy, Jessie honey? Where's Daddy?"

"Daddy phone again," Jessie said, before taking the small bottle of orange juice from her mother's hand and drinking it down. Her mother put her down again and the little girl trotted back the way she'd come, still trailing poor Teddy by the leg.

"Is everything okay, Barb?" asked Suzanne, noticing the dark cloud that had come over her sister's face when she'd heard that her husband was on the phone again.

"It's nothing. He's just always on the bloody phone lately, that's all."

"Busy at work?"

"Yeah. That must be it." Barbara seemed to give herself an infinitesimal shake and then she changed the subject. "I've been thinking, though, about Dad and the way he overreacted to your news. Do you remember our Uncle Ray?"

"Jesus. There's a name I haven't heard mentioned in years. What about him?"

"Well, do you not remember there was always a big mystery around him and around why he was more or less kicked out of the family?"

Suzanne stared at her sister. "Oh my God, yes. Uncle Ray, yes, I remember now."

When they were teenagers, Suzanne and Barbara had once asked their mother why their father's younger brother Ray was never allowed to visit their house or the houses of anyone else in the family. In hushed tones, their mother Eileen, as frightened of controversy as she'd always been, told her two daughters that Daddy couldn't stomach Uncle Ray (and neither could anyone else in the family) because, sadly, their Uncle Ray was *"a practising homosexual"*. She'd said the words the way someone else might have said *"a practising Satanist"*, or *"a practising cannibal"*. Then she'd mouthed, too fearful obviously even to whisper it: *'Don't let on to Daddy that I said anything, shure you won't?'* So, the subject of Uncle Ray was *verboten* then, was it? And that had been the end of that, except that Suzanne had some notion that their Uncle Ray had gone abroad somewhere to live, presumably because Ireland had become too hot to hold the likes of him, a *"practising homosexual"*.

Poor Uncle Ray, thought Suzanne now. Kicked out of the family for being gay. Jesus Christ. She'd always thought of her parents as being fuddy-duddies in general, or the type who routinely objected to everything that wasn't their own norm, but never active homophobes. Did they hate 'foreigners' too, she wondered? They were always complaining about the way that Dublin was now nearly as cosmopolitan and diverse as New York, but using less politically correct terminology. The thought nearly took her breath away. She wondered as Barbara topped up their drinks if anyone in the family had ever bothered to check up on Uncle Ray and his whereabouts. Was he well, was he happy, had he enough money to see to his daily needs? Was he even alive, or had he died in a foreign country somewhere, surrounded by no one but strangers? Even if her own father never spoke to her again, Suzanne decided there and then that she was going to somehow find her Uncle Ray — find him and let him know that there was at least one member of the Carragher family who cared that he existed and who knew how he felt.

"Sorry, what?" She'd been so lost in thought, she hadn't heard what her sister had said.

"I said, at least you've still got Rachel, and of course you've always got me and Paul and the kids, and you've got your art classes and your own painting too. When are you meeting with that agent lady, by the way? What's her name again? Granny O'Toole?"

"Grania O'Toole, you nutter. It's actually next week. I nearly forgot about it in all this bloody 'coming out' disaster."

"It wasn't a disaster," Barbara said firmly. "It was something you felt strongly about and you had every right to want to share it with your friends and family. If Dad wants to take it as a personal insult, well then, that's on him and not you, okay? It shouldn't take away one iota from what you did. Anyway, good luck with Granny O'Toole, although why she can't just call herself 'Gráinne' like a normal bloody person, I'm sure I don't know. What kind of posh name is Grania, anyway? Artsy people are so bloody pretentious. Present company excepted, of course. Anyway, I'm sure she'll be so impressed and bedazzled by your artistic genius that she'll buy every painting you've ever done and set you up in a snooty gallery in the very poshest part of town. You'll be the talk of Dublin! Suzanne Carragher, up-and-coming artist, admired by all and sundry."

"That's the dream, anyway," grinned Suzanne, touched by Barbara's constant, everlasting faith in her. "But I'm not counting my chickens just yet, okay, sis? I just need to keep a cool head for now."

"A cool head? Hell, I think we should throw a bloody

party to celebrate your coming out. We don't need any negativity or haters right now. We need positivity and bottles of pink sparkling champagne and some of those little cocktail sausage roll things from Marks & Spencer, that's what we need." Barbara nodded her head, the very picture of grim party-planning determination, and Suzanne wanted to cry again with love for her.

"Barb, Lucy's crying," announced Paul suddenly, strolling into the kitchen with his hands in his pockets.

"Can't you see to her?" snapped his wife.

"I don't think I can physically provide her with what she needs right now, sweetness." He grinned as he pointed to his nipples.

Barbara sighed and climbed down from her high stool again. "I'll be back in a minute," she promised her sister as she left the kitchen, unbuttoning her blouse as she went to give her daughter the evening booby-feed.

Paul mooched about, taking a square of chocolate from the big bar of Fruit & Nut the sisters had been sharing and popping it in his mouth. "Chocolate and wine, eh?" he said approvingly at the sight of their little pick-me-up. "You gals sure know how to live it up all right."

"It's only a bottle of supermarket plonk," Suzanne told him. "It's not exactly Moet & Chandon. You don't begrudge Barbara that, surely? Anyway, she only has one glass at the most, now that she's breastfeeding again. It's me who's drinking it really."

"I'm not criticising, Aunty Suze. Not a bit of it. In fact," here he lowered his voice confidentially "I just wanted to say to you how brilliant I think you are for coming out the way you did. I mean, it's not easy deciding to be a lezzer in a society where male-female relationships are still, well, you know, the norm. Not that I'm suggesting you're not the norm, Aunty Suze. Not at all. Not for one second. You're the coolest aunty the girls could ever have, and we'll make sure they know all about it when they're older. But, *erm*," his voice grew lower still, "there was one thing I've been wanting to ask you about it all, if that's okay with you?"

"Fire away," Suzanne said, resigned. Might as well let him get his asinine, juvenile schoolboy-ish questions out of his system straight away. She couldn't wait to hear this. What did lezzers do in bed? Was Suzanne the man or the woman? Did she do sixty-nine? Could a mere tongue really achieve what it normally took a penis to do? Is it really even riding if there's no penetration involved? Come on, Paul baby. Hit me with it. Do your worst.

"Won't you . . . *erm*, no offence meant now, Aunty Suze . . . but, I mean, won't you . . . well, won't you miss *dick* at all . . .?"

Suzanne stared at him, noting the blob of chocolate on the side of his mouth and the toast crumbs on his shirt front, and thought about it. For about a nanosecond.

"Not as much as you might think," she said.

Chapter 3

FAUVE

Fauve Delahunty was the first to arrive in work that day, or so she'd thought. Humming tunelessly to herself, she entered the little office kitchenette with her yogurt and banana lunch, intending to put the yogurt on her shelf in the fridge and the banana in the cupboard over the sink marked '*Fauve*', only to find Dr. Cross seated at the little kitchen table in tears. This was a highly unusual occurrence. It had literally never, in fact, happened before in living history.

"Marcia, what is it? What's wrong?" cried out Fauve in dismay. In front of the patients, Fauve and Molly, the two receptionists, called their boss 'Dr. Cross', but she'd told them they could call her 'Marcia', in private. Dumping the yogurt and banana on the sink, she sat down beside the sobbing doctor and put an arm gingerly around the woman's shaking shoulders. She was not in the habit of willy-nilly touching her boss in the normal course of events, but this was obviously a special circumstance.

"It's okay, I'm okay," hiccupped the doctor, but it was clear that such was far from the truth. "If you'll just please grab me some tissue from over there, Fauve, I'll be fine."

Fauve leaped up and pulled a great big wad of paper off the kitchen roll on the sink. She wadded it up and handed it to the doctor, who blew her nose on it loudly.

"How about a nice strong cup of your coffee?" Fauve suggested, and was glad when Dr. Cross nodded gratefully. It made Fauve feel better to be doing something useful, something practical. Though the doctor didn't normally take sugar in her coffee, Fauve slipped in two heaped spoonfuls for shock. She didn't know exactly if the doctor had had a shock as such, but the sugar couldn't hurt. When the drink was made, she placed it in front of her boss and sat back down beside her tentatively. She was more than willing to listen if the doctor wanted to talk, but she wasn't sure if her boss would want to confide in the staff something which was obviously of a personal nature. Why else would she be sitting crying in the office kitchen at this hour of the day, a good hour before the first patient of the day was due to darken the doors of their cancer surgery? A dreadful thought occurred to Fauve.

"Oh God, Marcia, you haven't found a lump anywhere, have you?"

The doctor immediately shook her head. "No, no, no," she hastened to reassure her worried receptionist. Here, in the offices of one of Ireland's most respected cancer specialists, Dr. Marcia Cross, Fauve and Molly saw people every day of the working week who had lumps, cysts, boils, moles, lesions, odd-looking freckles, you name it, some of which would turn out to be cancerous and some of which, thankfully, would not.

"Thank God for that!" Fauve said. "*Erm*, is there anything I can do to help at all?"

Dr. Cross took a big drink of her coffee, then involuntarily grimaced when she tasted the two heaped teaspoonfuls of sugar. "*Mmmm*, this is lovely," she murmured politely. "Just the job. No, you've been a great help, Fauve, thank you, just by being here. But I suppose I owe you some kind of an explanation for all this." She extended her hands to indicate the table, the unexpected crying, the works.

"You don't owe me anything, Marcia, honestly," Fauve responded fiercely, while inwardly her mind was saying: *Tell. Me. Everything.* Well, she couldn't help being insatiably curious about her fellow man (or woman), could she? It was what made her such a hit with the patients, who all loved the lovely warm, empathetic Fauve with the bright dyed-red hair and ready, white-toothed smile. (Well, her dad *was* a dentist, after all. You'd hardly expect her to be sporting manky gnashers.)

"No, it's all right, Fauve. It'd probably do me some good to get it out of me, anyway. The fact is, Fauve, that . . . well, Gregg and I are splitting up. Well, no, that sounds like it's mutual, doesn't it, and civilised, when in fact it's not at all. Gregg is leaving me."

Fauve was aghast. She and Molly had had many a juicy gossip about Dr. Cross's handsome younger husband, Gregg Korda, a half-Greek plastic surgeon who mostly specialised in celebrities who wanted nose jobs and lip plumpening, titty-lifts and ass-sculpting and stuff like that. He was in his late thirties, early forties, maybe, a good bit younger than Dr. Cross, his second wife, and he was always being pictured in celebrity magazines with the movers and shakers whose noses he fixed and whose tits he lifted for money. Big bucks too, everyone knew that. He really was tall, dark and handsome with deeply tanned skin, thanks to his Greek heritage (his father was Greek and his mother Irish), and his thick dark floppy hair, elegantly tinged with grey, a little too long for convention, fell down over the silver-rimmed spectacles he wore that made him look like an intellectual. Fauve always privately thought he looked a little sleazy, however, like a millionaire playboy sex addict or something, who should be cavorting in nightclubs or on a yacht in the Mediterranean with a bevy of bikini-clad supermodels while snorting cocaine and doing big-bucks drug deals with the Cubans or the Colombians on the yacht's golden phone.

"Is . . . is there another woman?" she asked nervously now. How could there be though, she told herself sternly, when Dr. Cross was the kindest person you could ever meet in a day's walk, and not half bad-looking and well-preserved for a woman in her fifties? To her horror, Dr. Cross nodded slowly while a tear tracked a solitary path down her make-up-less face. Well, she didn't *need* make-up really, did she? Fauve would have challenged anyone who said 'boo' to the doctor about it. Her skin was well-hydrated and unlined and practically perfect for someone of her age!

"Is it someone you know?" she whispered, trying to walk the desperately fine line between being agog with a natural curiosity and not wanting to upset her employer any more than she obviously had been, by quizzing her about things she might not want to discuss.

The doctor shrugged. "Yes and no. I've never met her personally, but I've seen plenty of photos in magazines and on social media. She's called Rosaria Kelly."

Fauve's jaw dropped. "Rosaria Kelly? *The* Rosaria Kelly?

The model? She's bloody everywhere at the moment."

"Gregg did her breasts. That's how they met."

"*Oooooooh!*" Fauve murmured approvingly. "They're lovely, her new tits. Doireann, that's my housemate, and I, well, we were wondering who'd done them so nicely for her."

"Well, now you know," said Dr. Cross dryly. "I'll pass your compliments on to Gregg."

"Oh, well, just because she has nice tits doesn't mean that she's not still a husband-stealing skank," Fauve back-tracked furiously. "And they'll probably implode on her, anyway, shure, the first time she takes a flight anywhere."

"Thanks for your loyalty, my dear, dear Fauve. I really do appreciate it, but it doesn't change the fact that I'm being thrown over for a twenty-eight-year-old fashion model with the face of an angel and the body of a, well, a twenty-eight-year-old fashion model. And I'm sure she's a lovely girl as well, behind all the make-up, but it still hurts like hell, you know?"

Fauve nodded. A lovely girl behind all the make-up, my hole, she scoffed inwardly. You didn't get to be where Rosaria Kelly was today, on all the television shows and on the covers of all the magazines, by being a Lovely Girl. She'd have to be a walking bitch at the very least and, anyway, from the photos Fauve had seen of the young woman's face, in which she always seemed to be looking down her perfect little button nose (Gregg Korda again? She made a mental note to ask Doireann) at everyone around her, she looked like one and so therefore probably was. It was so like the generous and fair-minded Dr. Cross to give the evil cow the benefit of the doubt, but Fauve had the skank's number all right. Fauve was not one to have the wool pulled over her eyes in matters of the heart. It wasn't that long since she'd been dumped herself by a guy for another woman, and the hurt was still very much alive and kicking. And how could Gregg Korda, or any other plastic surgeon for that matter, fancy someone whose breasts they'd sliced open in order to squash in a couple of chicken fillets, then sewed up again afterwards like Frankenstein's Monster? How could he ever bear to touch them, kiss them, suck on them, after what he'd seen? *Eeuw*. Fauve was quite sure she could never fancy someone whose inner workings she'd seen laid out in front of her like that, fashion model or no bloody fashion model. It was grotesque and yucky.

"Wasn't she going out with someone, though? That bratty bad-boy actor, Johnny Somebody?" Fauve remembered suddenly. Their 'stormy' relationship, as the newspapers had delighted in calling it, had been plastered all over the press and social media for months.

"They broke up, supposedly before she met Gregg, but I rather suspect some overlap."

"*Hmmm*. Very bloody likely, knowing these so-called 'celebrities'. Has he moved in with her yet?" Fauve winced herself at the expression of pain that crossed the doctor's sensible, kindly face. Fauve had read the recent celebrity magazine with the glossy pictures in it of husband-stealer Rosaria Kelly lounging glamorously around her gorgeous new Docklands flat. Fauve knew all about that slut's state-of-the-art new coffee machine, the football-pitch-sized den for 'unwinding' in and the little room that actually jutted out *onto* the water from where the slut planned to write her extremely popular health, fitness and beauty blog, as if she wasn't enough of a walking bloody cliché as it was! She'd be bringing out a bloody cookbook next. *Stupid Recipes for Stupid old Health and Happiness, for Stupid People who need to be told what to eat by a famous person because they've no minds of their own,* by Rosaria bloody Kelly.

"Not yet, but it's happening. He's at home today, packing. It'll probably be the weekend."

"The hussy! She doesn't waste any time, does she?"

"Gregg has a choice in this too, Fauve, remember," the doctor reproved her mildly. "I can't get into the business of blaming Rosaria for everything, or I'll just be eaten up with hate and envy inside. Do you see what I mean?"

"Oh yes, absolutely, of course," trilled Fauve, while inwardly thinking: *That skank! If it were my hubby she'd set her sights on, she'd be on a slab in the morgue by now.* "*Erm*, will you be okay to work today, Marcia? Maybe you'd prefer to just be at home by yourself? Because Molly and I can certainly call everyone and put them off till another day?"

Dr. Cross shook her head emphatically. "That wouldn't be fair on the patients, Fauve. They wait long enough for their results as it is. Some of them are driving up from Cork and Kerry to get them. They'd be on the road already, shure. And anyway, I don't want to be at home while Gregg's there, packing to leave me to go to *her*. I couldn't stand that. I'd be better off here, doing something."

"Yes, yes, I guess you're right. I forgot he's there. Better off keeping busy here, so."

"Exactly. Oh, and Fauve? Thank you so much for listening, and for being here for me today, but . . . well, you *will* keep all this stuff to yourself, won't you? I don't want it getting around any sooner than it has to. I mean, when Gregg moves out and into her flat and the two of them start being photographed around the place together, at events and parties . . ." Her voice broke off and she blew her nose loudly again on Fauve's big serviceable wad of kitchen roll.

"You can trust me," promised Fauve.

She spent the rest of the day — in between clients, of course — trawling through all their waiting-room celebrity magazines, even the old ones in the recycling bin, for articles about the omnipresent Rosaria Kelly. Never let it be said that Fauve didn't do her homework. The model was going through her period of peak exposure now, so the magazines were naturally full of her. She wasn't half bad-looking, either, Fauve grudgingly admitted, with her superb figure, her long fall of wavy, warm-honey-brown-coloured hair and those glorious greeny-grey almond-shaped eyes that gave her an exotic look, even though she was no more foreign than Fauve was, and her family was from Ballyfermot. She had learned to repress her native Dublin accent, though, and replace it gradually with as close to a Dublin 4 one as she could muster. Look at her in that photo there, pretending to be 'relaxing' on her designer couch in her designer tracksuit with a book! As if that sort ever read a book that didn't have colouring-in pictures in it, Fauve scoffed. They simply didn't have the cerebral wherewithal, these modelling types. She could not *wait* to tell Doireann her news.

"I just can't believe what a bitch she is, doing that to poor old Dr. Cross!"

Doireann's reaction to Fauve's news had been infinitely

gratifying. She had *oooh*ed and *aaah*ed in all the right places, her eyes as wide as saucers, as Fauve had unwrapped and unfolded her tale before her as carefully and painstakingly as a merchant of old showing off a skein of valuable silk to a customer. Fauve was careful not to leave out a nuance, an action, an inflection, an expression, a single variation in tone that would have damaged her retelling by its omission. Orla and Sasha, their two other housemates, came late to the performance and were thrilled to have Fauve obligingly start over again at the beginning for their especial benefit. When the show was over, all three of them had to actively stop their hands from coming together and making admiring clapping sounds.

"*Wow, what a skank!*" Orla said feelingly. Like Fauve, she had just broken up with a guy and her wounds were still raw enough for her to regard any man-stealer as a traitor to the sisterhood.

"Yeah, I mean, a real skanky tramp," Sasha put in. "And poor Dr. Cross! I mean, have they got any kids together?" Naturally she addressed her question to Fauve, the expert on the subject.

"Not together, no, but they both *do* have kids. Marcia has two grown-up sons from her first marriage and Dr. Gregg has a teenage daughter from *his* first. God knows how she's going to react to her father hooking up with a girl who's barely a decade older than her."

"What's the betting that Little Miss Skanky will be knocked up by the end of the year, and they'll all have to get used to a baby in their new so-called 'blended family'?" This was Doireann's contribution, and now it was her turn to be gratified, as Fauve, Orla and Sasha all gaped at her with their mouths hanging open. "Can't you just see it? The two of them on the cover of *VIP* magazine, his hands all over her bump, and her wearing barely anything, just enough for modesty! *'Oh, I've literally never been so happy!'*" simpered Doireann in a fake, gushing 'celebrity' voice. "*Dr. Gregg really does it for me sexually; he gives me so many orgasms I don't know whether I'm coming or going (that's obviously the Greek lover in him), and I simply couldn't be happier to be having his baby, because it's a baby made of pure love and . . . and the best sex ever!*" Doireann finished triumphantly and everyone in the house in Kilmacud (which was everyone currently occupying the sitting-room) stuck two fingers down their throat and made some pretty damn realistic vomiting noises.

"Poor, *poor* Dr. Cross!" chorused Orla and Sasha together, shaking their heads sadly.

"*Hmmm*," murmured Doireann, scrolling down through Facebook on her phone. "There's an event here that might interest you, Fauve."

"What is it?" Fauve immediately moved from the arm of the couch where she was perched to the vacant seat beside Doireann.

"Well," replied Doireann slowly, as she read down through the event on her phone, "it looks like Little Miss Skanky Husband-Stealer is launching some kind of stupid new exercise ball in the Stephen's Green Park on Saturday morning. Weather's meant to be great, and a big whack of the proceeds from the exercise ball goes to some charity or other."

"Which charity?" scoffed Orla. "Free Lettuce Leaves for Anorexic Supermodels?"

"Or, what about this one — *a free go of someone else's*

husband for every skank who applies?" said Sasha, not to be outdone.

Fauve's turn. "What about this one — *a charity that provides free special goggles with no peripheral vision, to teach skanks and ho's to keep their eyes away from other women's blokes?"*

The three girls stared blankly. That one might have been a bit too sophisticated, Fauve conceded mentally. A bit too intellectual.

"Ah shure, it's one of those anyway," Doireann said, when the tumbleweed moment had passed. "Who cares? The main point is that this husband-stealing wagon will be in the Stephen's Green Park this Saturday morning. With a camera crew, I might add." She paused and looked directly at Fauve. "Are you thinking what I'm thinking?"

Fauve leapt up instantly and said: "Great idea, I'll get the spoons!"

"What for?" Doireann looked bemused. "What do we want spoons for?"

"Your idea wasn't to go get the ice cream?" Now Fauve looked bemused.

"Well, yes, obviously, ice cream at some point, always ice cream, Fauve, you know that! But for now, just look at this, will you?"

In front of Fauve's eyes, she clicked *'going'* to the charity event, then looked at her friend meaningfully, her beautifully shaped eyebrows raised. (Doireann always had fabulous eyebrows. If she went to the trouble of raising them at you, you knew there was something up.)

Eventually, Fauve copped on to what her friend was trying to communicate to her and nodded grimly.

"So, we're on for Saturday, are we then, girls?" Doireann grinned.

"*Oh yes*," Fauve said, and Orla and Sasha nodded their agreement also.

"Good," Doireann said approvingly. "*Now* you can go get the ice cream, Fauve."

"What's happening Saturday?" said Sasha, looking up from a text on her phone. "What was I just agreeing to there?"

Fauve had always known that Liam wasn't The One, but breaking up with him had still hurt. He was only twenty to her twenty-four (her friends had all laughingly called her a cradle-snatcher), a Trinity College science student from America, and he was drop-dead gorgeous. They'd met when he'd been delivering Indian takeaway leaflets (his part-time job) to all the businesses in the building where Fauve worked, and they'd hit it off instantly.

"How'd you get past Security?" she'd asked him wonderingly, that first day.

"He's fighting with someone on the phone. Wife or ex-wife, by the sound of it." Liam's mischievous grin had sent shivers of lust up and down Fauve's spine. They'd gone out for drinks together that first night (Liam had apparently binned the remainder of his Indian takeaway leaflets outside their building) after Fauve had finished work and, despite her promises to herself to be good this time, she hadn't been able to resist bringing him home to the house in Kilmacud and falling into bed with him, he was that good-looking, with a kind of naïve, devil-may-care youthful transatlantic charm to boot.

Three blissful months had followed, during which time the pair of them met up nearly every day and Fauve's housemates became used to the sound of the two of them riding each other ragged most nights. (Used to it; not necessarily happy about it. The noise of the headboard banging against the wall on top of Fauve's sex-moans was something else.) Then, without any warning, Liam had come over to the house one night and said he wouldn't be around for the next three weeks because . . . Here, he'd shuffled his feet a lot and looked down at the carpet and tried to avoid Fauve's eye. Well, because his girlfriend from the States, Amy, to whom he'd been engaged practically since they'd both been nippers because their two families were staunch lifelong friends, was coming over for a visit and she'd be expecting his undivided attention while she was there.

"You've had a girlfriend in the States this whole time?" Fauve had squeaked, shocked. "One you're engaged to? Why didn't you tell me?"

He'd shrugged then and said: "You never asked."

This was like a red rag to a bull to Fauve, who'd always considered it a low blow in the battle between the sexes. "Well, excuse *me* for assuming that a guy who asked me out and then slept with me was free to do so!"

They'd had a huge row then, even though Liam had insisted that they could go back to seeing each other like before just as soon as Prissy Little Miss Amy (Fauve's words, not Liam's) had returned to the States.

"*I'm not your bit on the side!*" she'd screeched at him in huffy outrage as she ushered him down the stairs and out the door into the Kilmacud night. As soon as the door was locked and bolted to find him, she'd flopped down on the hall carpet with her back to the front door and bawled her eyes out. Her housemates, who'd all heard the row, had come rushing out to offer support and sympathy in the form of ice cream and bitchy remarks about this Amy person. They'd offered some surprisingly racist and stereotyped insights into her possible appearance and character.

"Of course she's a total skanky cheerleader type." This was Doireann.

"With perfect teeth because the Americans are made to wear braces when they're still in the womb." Sasha, nodding her head emphatically to lend weight to her words.

"Probably knows how to make an American Quilt," put in Orla. "American women are always quilting things."

"And putting things in stupid boring scrapbooks that no one will ever look at again, but does that stop them? My hole, it does!" Doireann again.

Doireann had such a posh voice, it always made Fauve smile to hear her say 'my hole' like that.

"And losing their virginity in the back seats of cars to their captain-of-the-football-club boyfriends, who give them their class rings and their stupid college jackets in exchange for a blowjob and, you know, *swallowing*." Orla, excitedly, really getting into the groove.

"Total skanks." Doireann was nodding emphatically now too.

"Probably has the clap from all that shagging in the backseat of cars at the drive-in movies. You don't want to get the clap too, do you, Fauvey-Wauvey?" Orla, kindly, stroking Fauve's tear-soaked hair back from her face.

Fauve shook her head and bawled all the louder.

"Was Liam the captain of his football team?" Doireann asked suddenly, as if it had only just occurred to her and it was a matter of the highest urgency. "And did he have a class ring?"

Fauve shrugged. "I don't know. Maybe." More tears and more tissues.

"Does he have one of those stupid college jackets, d'you know?" Doireann again.

Fauve shook her head in alarm. "I've never seen him wearing one."

The other girls exchanged wise, knowing looks, then Orla shook her head and said sadly, patting Fauve on the arm the whole time in a way that was obviously meant to be comforting: "That's because *she's* got them. The ring and the jacket. That Amy one. What a slut."

After a bit more stereotyping in the draughty hall, the party moved to the kitchen for easier access to the fridge and the Ben and Jerry's. When Fauve eventually went to bed that night, it was with a strong dislike for the Other Woman (not Amy in particular; she'd never met the woman, after all. Just Other Women in general) imprinted on her heart. Now, her beloved employer and friend Dr. Cross had fallen foul of such a personage. Well, Rosaria Kelly had reckoned without the fierce love and loyalty Fauve had for her boss (for whom Fauve had worked almost since she'd left school), and the strong antipathy Fauve had to the kinds of women who broke up relationships, even if they were the legitimate girlfriends who'd met the guys first, as in the case of this Amy one. Rosaria Kelly, lovely new tits or no lovely new tits, had one hell of a Day of Reckoning coming. Fauve was glad about it. The Other Woman had it coming to her, big-time. Fauve couldn't wait to see to it that she got it.

Saturday, or Double-D-Day as they'd nicknamed it, dawned bright and clear, if a little breezy. It was the perfect early autumn day, and there was no earthly reason to suppose that the event in the park would be called off. Fauve, Doireann, Sasha and Orla all made their way from Kilmacud into the Stephen's Green by Luas, and it was only Doireann's practised flirting with the ticket checker that got him to agree to all four of them carrying their cumbersome home-made placards on board with them to their destination. Doireann's sister Gabby and Gabby's friends Celestine, Colette and Marla met the four of them outside the main entrance to the Stephen's Green Park, the entrance opposite the lobby of the shopping centre. They all carried home-made placards too, much to Fauve's delight, consisting of the backs of cereal boxes sellotaped to mop-and-broom handles like those of their friends, and seemed well up for the project in hand, having been thoroughly briefed on the 'sitch' by Doireann.

"Hustle your bustles, lads," said Fauve busily. "This thing starts at eleven and it's nearly bloody well five past already."

"Don't worry — shure, these things never start on time," Doireann.

"Which part of the park is she in?" This, from Gabby, looking down at her lovely shoes. "I won't have to wade through any muck, will I?"

"The event just said Stephen's Green Park," Doireann said, looking at her phone. "It doesn't specify what part, precisely. We'll just do a circuit of the whole thing. It'll only take a minute, shure."

Five minutes later: "*She's in the summerhouse!*" screeched Fauve. "That's her in the bright yellow tracksuit, you can see her from space!"

And the eight placard-waving women tip-tapped their way precariously across first the tarmac and then the mucky grass to the summerhouse, where Rosaria Kelly was bouncing around the big wooden structure on something that greatly resembled the giant space-hoppers that Fauve and Doireann remembered from their childhoods. Three or four delighted-looking male photographers were snapping excitedly away as if they were at an American presidential press conference, while a couple of (also male, also delighted-looking) executives in suits, presumably from the company launching the so-called 'exercise ball', looked on and clapped admiringly.

Rosaria Kelly was looking fabulous, the octet of female protestors had to admit, and flashing her dazzlingly white smile non-stop. She was indeed wearing a bright-yellow tracksuit, unzipped all down the front to reveal the new breasts in an outrageously low-cut white vest top with the slenderest of spaghetti straps. They bounced and boinged magnificently with every bounce of the giant ball she took, holding on for dear life the whole time to the 'ears' of the thing. Her long warm-honey-coloured hair bounced in its ponytail along with the breasts. The whole performance was a beautiful and moving symphony of bounce, and the air seemed chock-full of gigantic round bouncing things. The watching men were lapping it up, and now some passers-by were starting to slow down and watch the proceedings as well.

"Look this way, Rosaria!"

"Smile for the camera, Rosaria!"

"Over here, Rosaria baby! To me, love, eyes to me!"

"How's your love life going, Rosaria babes? Any sign of a new boyfriend on the horizon yet, love?"

"She's not even wearing a bra," spluttered Fauve indignantly.

"Would you, if you had tits like those?" said Orla, goggling in awe at the magnificent new breasts. Each fresh leap of the exercise ball took the splendiferous pair of bosoms closer to the heavens from where they surely *had* to have materialised. Everyone in the crowd was mesmerised by them and their fluid bouncy-bouncy movements. They were in danger of bouncing free of the white vest top altogether if she went at it any more enthusiastically.

"Are you protesting about something, dear?" This, to Fauve, from a tiny little old lady in a red hat with plastic cherries on it who'd suddenly appeared at her elbow, with a white uppity-looking poodle on a lead in tow.

"Darn right we are! *Girls, placards up, now!*"

All eight placards went up simultaneously. The small crowd turned to look at them with mild interest. *GET YOUR OWN MAN,* read one or two of them. *SKANKS OUT,* read another, without specifying a possible destination for the women concerned. *MAKE HUSBAND-AND-BOYFRIEND-STEALING ILLEGAL,* read yet another. Fauve was particularly pleased with Doireann's sister Gabby's effort, which was extremely specific in content: *ROSARIA KELLY IS A DIRTY CHEATING MAN-EATER* in black marker on one side of the cornflakes box, and *GIVE FAUVE'S BOSS HER HUSBAND BACK,*

YOU SKANKY FECKER in blood-red marker on the flipside.

"What's all this about, ladies?" inquired one of the photographers.

"Are you collecting for a charity, dear?" asked the little old lady in the red hat with the plastic cherries on it. She had her purse out and was proffering a one-euro coin to Fauve.

"Well, more protesting than actually collecting, as such," said Fauve, waving away the coin and yelling "*Boooooo!*" and "*For shame!*" and "*Down with this sort of thing!*" in the direction of the summerhouse.

Rosaria Kelly was starting to notice the hubbub. She and the breasts were staring over at Fauve resentfully now (well, her nipples looked like eyes, they really did!) and were gradually coming back down to earth with each succeeding bounce of the exercise ball.

"We're like Father Ted and Dougal, protesting about the dirty fillum!" giggled Sasha.

"My shoes are destroyed," mourned Gabby.

"Who the hell are you lot?" demanded a now-earthbound Rosaria Kelly, dismounting from the ball and marching across to Fauve and her cronies, her spotless, obviously new white trainers sinking into the damp muddy grass as she went. "What's all this about? You're interrupting our photo-shoot." She was wearing so much make-up she didn't even look like a real person, a human being.

"Oh, is *this* the *dirty cheating man-eater*, dear?" said the lady in the red hat.

"Got it in one, ma'am," said Fauve belligerently.

"*How fucking dare you, you cheeky bitch?*" exploded Rosaria

Kelly, shoving Fauve in the chest so that she lost her footing and fell on her backside on the damp grass.

"How fucking dare *you* push my friend around?" said Doireann, pushing Rosaria Kelly in the chest in retaliation, just above the magnificent breasts, while around them the photographers snapped like mad and the grinning passers-by took pictures on their phones.

"Whomever did you cheat on, dear?" the lady in the red hat asked Rosaria with interest.

"That's none of your fucking business, Grandma," snapped Rosaria, her *faux* posh accent slipping about a dozen notches in one go. She was struggling to get at Doireann but unable to move, as one of the execs-in-pinstriped-suits was holding her back, entreating her to: "*Stay calm now, Rosie love, just stay calm, the lads will sort all this lot out!*" while Rosaria screeched: "*Get off me, you fucking thug! Let me go! I'm going to rub her face in the fucking dirt for pushing me, who the actual fuck does she think she is?*"

Fauve was back on her feet, ready for the fray once more whilst vigorously rubbing the muck off the backside of her jeans, all set to wade in and defend Doireann, just as the sound of bugles and drums and people cheering began to make itself heard in the park. After entering through the side-gate nearest the summerhouse, a little procession of children in wheelchairs and on crutches was making its way slowly to the summerhouse while Fauve, her friends, the old lady in the red hat with the poodle, Rosaria Kelly, the photographers, the execs-in-pinstriped-suits and the passers-by all stood and watched. Two boys in wheelchairs at the front of the procession were banging little hand-held drums and two boys in wheelchairs beside them were tooting, discordantly but joyfully, on bugles. A little girl in a wheelchair was stroking a puppy with a bandage round one soft paw and a patch over one eye. Two slightly more able-bodied teenagers to the front were holding up a banner between them that read: *'ST. HILDA'S REHAB SUPPORTS ROSARIA KELLY AND THE NEW SUPER-BALL!'* All the children, without exception, wore beaming smiles and their eyes were aglow with hope and anticipation. Some of them were waving little flags with Rosaria's face on them.

"What the fuck . . .?" said Fauve.

"Half the proceeds of the sales of the Super-Ball are going to these poor kiddies," supplied a nearby photographer helpfully.

Fauve's hand flew to her mouth. "But if I'd known that . . ." she began, aghast.

"Oh, and that's Rosaria's little sister," the helpful photographer added, as the fashion model of the hour got down on her knees in the dirt before the little girl in the wheelchair with the injured puppy and hugged the child, who was crying with delight on recognising her big sister.

Fauve, horrified, immediately lowered her placard, which read *SKANKS OUT,* and faced it away from the child.

"Oh, don't worry about that," said the photographer. "Poor kiddie's blind since birth. Can't see a dickybird."

Fauve gasped, tears coming to her own eyes at the joyful sight of able-bodied sister embracing younger, differently-abled sister. She was enveloped in a sense of shame and humility so strong she doubted if she would ever shake it off.

"Shame about the puppy, though," the photographer commented then, shaking his head.

"What about the puppy?" demanded Fauve.

"He's being put down this afternoon, poor little sod. Kid's had him since birth as well. This launch is his last ever outing. He's been hanging on just to make it to today, the poor mutt. Going straight to the vet for the old euthanasia after this."

"I have to go," mumbled Fauve, indicating to her friends to down tools and follow her.

"Puppy's blind too," said the photographer to her retreating back. "Lost his sight in a terrible car accident. Or it might have been a fire."

Fauve stopped and whirled round. "You're doing this on purpose," she accused.

"Doing what?" replied the photographer, all innocence. As Fauve walked away, her head hanging low, he called after her: *"Two people died in that fire!"*

"It was just so nice to feel a part of something for a change," said the old lady in the red hat with the poodle to no one in particular. "I'm quite sad now it's all over. Maybe you young ladies could let me join in your next protest? My Bert was always saying I was probably a suffragette in a past life. He even called me Emmeline in bed sometimes. You know, after that lovely suffragette lady? Even though my name's actually Dot. Every time I sucked him off, he used to say it, God rest his gentle soul. *'Fuck me, Emmy!'* he'd roar. So sweet. I used to laugh so much about it with my dear departed sister Emma. Anyway, may I join you ladies?"

"We'll call you," Doireann said, trailing her placard dispiritedly along the ground as she followed along behind Fauve and the others.

"How exciting!" trilled the old lady.

"My shoes are fucked," complained Gabby.

"Oh, shut up about your shoes, will you?" retorted Doireann.

"But I haven't given you my number . . .?" said the old lady sadly. The poodle yapped and lifted its leg against a tree.

The debacle in the park made the news. For a day or two, it *was* the news. Fauve cringed and covered her eyes as the footage was replayed over and over on all the Irish news channels. Again and again, she saw the clip of herself falling on her arse in the muck after being pushed in the chest by Rosaria Kelly, followed by the clip of Doireann and Rosaria's attempted cat-fight. Fauve had had to Luas it home to Kilmacud after the fracas with a big wet muck stain on the arse of her good jeans. That wasn't the worst part of the whole thing, though. The worst part was that it seemed that everyone who'd ever known Fauve in her life had seen those awful news-clips of her and her friends apparently sabotaging a charity launch that was meant to help disabled kiddies buy a few new wheelchairs for themselves. People she hadn't heard from in years saw it and got in touch with her. She'd even got a Skype call from a girl she'd gone to school with who was a doctor now and who lived up a mountain in the Himalayas, providing medical care to poor people, who'd seen the clip on her iPad. Apparently they had really good Internet connections up the mountains. She'd never live it down, the shame of it. Her phone started hopping with texts as soon as the stupid clip had aired for the first, but by no means the last, time.

Her best friend from school, Calista: **Fauve, was that you on the News, you absolute tit? What the Jaysis did you think you were doing? I mean, those poor kiddies!**

Fauve's mother, Elaine: **Fauve, I want you to know that Granny Helene and Grand-dad Joseph are *extremely* upset with you for bringing shame on the family. They're expecting you for dinner on Sunday so they can give out to you in person.**

(Oh, goody, thought Fauve glumly on reading this one. Watch how fast I go.)

Gabby, Doireann's sister: **Well, my shoes are fucked after the muck in the park. What an absolute waste of a day. Do you think Rosaria Kelly would pay the cleaning bill if I sent it to her?**

Oh, fuck off, Gabby, Fauve wanted to text back but decided not to. She was in enough trouble as it was.

Brianne, Fauve's 'perfect' older sister: **Nice one, sis. I always knew you were a total pillock, but now the whole country knows it as well. Congratulations.**

Dr. Cross: **Fauve, I'll see you in my office first thing Monday morning. Don't be late.**

This was the one that worried Fauve the most.

Doireann: **I told you my arse looked big in those trousers! How could you *actually* let me go on live TV wearing them?**

Fauve to Doireann: **Doireann, stop texting me, you plonker, you're sitting right beside me on the couch!**

James, an ex-boyfriend of Fauve's: **I see you're picking on the disabled now, Fauve. Good thing I got out when I did, eh, what with my prosthetic leg?**

Will, Fauve's tactless friend: **Hey, Fauve, I've got an autistic big brother over here you can push around if you like, want to come over here and beat him up? I'll hold his arms for you!**

The fact that this last one was followed by a row of smiley faces did nothing to ameliorate the situation. *Bad taste, Will, very bad taste.*

Will again: **Hey, you and Rosaria Kelly mud-wrestling on the News, good one, Fauve! Shame you didn't get to yank her top down, though. Those tits are delish!**

Brianne: **Is that my pink top you're wearing there? I never said you could borrow that!**

Will again: **Did you actually get to touch her tits? Do they feel real or plasticky?**

Doireann again: **Will we order in pizza or will we cook something or what?**

Fauve to Doireann: **Doireann, will you stop texting me? We're sitting right beside each other, for Christ's sake!**

Brianne: **That *is* my pink top, Fauve, you sneaky thief! I want it back, and I want it cleaned first!**

Will again: **What I wouldn't give to cop a feel of those knockers!**

Doireann again: **We'll call for a pizza, right? I can't be arsed cooking.**

Gabby again: **I should really be sending *you* the bill to get these shoes cleaned, Fauve.**

Brianne again: **Give me back my pink top, Fauve, you light-fingered slag, if you ever want to see Mr. Floppy Willy alive again!**

How did Brianne come to have possession of Mr. Floppy Willy, Fauve's favourite childhood stuffed toy? There was something seriously amiss about that whole situation.

Bernie's, Fauve's local takeaway place: **Buy one snack-box today and get a second junior snack-box absolutely free, free, free! (Offer not valid Monday to Saturday.)**

It was a nightmare. Fauve switched off her phone in desperation, determined to sleep until Monday. Sweet oblivion was what she needed. She fell into it, relieved beyond measure.

"Fauve Delahunty, you stand before this court today accused of heinous cruelty towards the individuals grouped together in the witness seats. How do you plead?"

A camera panned slowly past the witness seats to clearly reveal Bambi, the Disney movie fawn, sobbing uncontrollably into a tissue; Tom and Jerry, the cartoon cat and mouse, clinging tightly to each other and trembling teeth-chatteringly in fear; assorted Teletubbies *(Come ON, thought Fauve, there never was a blue one!)* bouncing about excitedly in their seats, chattering their nonsense talk shrilly to each other; Bosco, the TV puppet, for some reason, shaking his head gravely at the accused while wagging a stern knitted finger; a selection of sweet storybook grannies, complete with spectacles, benign if puzzled what-are-we-doing-here expressions and sewing baskets; the puppy with the bandage round his paw and a patch over his eye from the park, and a long line of new-born baby puppies and baby lambs, each one smaller, cuter and fluffier than the last, seemingly stretching away to infinity.

This isn't fair, thought Fauve wildly. I would never be mean to any one of these sweet helpless creatures, not in a million years! Out loud, she said tremulously: "Not guilty, your Honour."

"*Liar!*" roared the judge, standing up in his seat and pointing an angry finger at the accused. "*Disgusting liar!* You murdered Bambi's mother, didn't you? Didn't you? There's no point denying it; we have Internet footage! And then made her carcass into a rug, on which you then forced Bosco to engage in activity of a carnal nature with this dear little granny from Little Red Riding Hood, while the Teletubbies formed themselves into a shame-circle around them and pleasured themselves *on your explicit orders!*"

All four Teletubbies, including the blue one, burst into howling sobs of remembrance. Bosco looked over at Fauve and smirked slyly, before transforming his expression back to one of abject misery for the judge's benefit.

"I never did!" objected Fauve, two bright spots of indignant colour standing out on her cheeks.

"*Silence!*" bellowed the judge. "You have befouled and sullied the sanctity of this courtroom with your lies and chicanery! I sentence you to a thousand hours of community service, to be spent doing whatever Rosaria Kelly wants you to do! If she wants you to clean her gutters and sweep her chimneys, you will do it. If she requires you to scrub her toilets and do her tax returns, you will do that too, and like it. And if it is her wish that you follow her around every minute of the day, telling her how great she is and polishing her lovely new breasts, then, by God, and the power invested in me, you will do that too!"

From across the court, Bosco sniggered and gave the defendant the two fingers.

***

Fauve woke up screaming, drenched in sweat. Two things weighed heavily on her mind. Was *chicanery* even a real word, and what had she ever done to Bosco to make him hate her so much? She had no beef with him.

Dr. Cross didn't sack her.

"I thought about it, don't think I didn't," she told a tearful Fauve sternly on Monday morning. "I asked you to keep what I told you confidential, and it ended up on the *Six One News*."

Fauve blushed miserably, too ashamed to speak.

"On the other hand," went on the doctor, her expression softening, "I don't doubt that you were acting from a place of genuine kindness."

"*Oh, I was, I was!*" sobbed Fauve.

"I know." The doctor got up and walked round to where Fauve was sitting on the other side of the big desk, and put her hand on the younger woman's shoulder, giving it a brief squeeze. "I'm not saying I'm happy about the whole thing, but I do know that."

"I—I don't suppose it did any good at all?" ventured Fauve timidly. "I mean, they haven't split up or anything?"

"If you mean my husband and Rosaria Kelly," the doctor said drily, "then I'm afraid the opposite has happened. The pair of them are still very much an item, despite your best efforts, and they'll be announcing ..." here, she paused and took a deep breath, "Rosaria's pregnancy in a few weeks, after she's safely passed the three-month mark."

"*Oh, Dr. Cross!*" wailed Fauve. "*That's terrible! Oh, I'm so, so sorry!*"

"Don't be. You had nothing to do with it. That one's very much down to Gregg and his . . . his new girlfriend."

"Will you be okay? I mean, how will you cope with all of this strain and worry?"

"I might take a leave-of-absence around the time the baby's due. My sister has a villa in Spain I might vamoose to for a few weeks. I'm relying on you to show the locum the ropes."

"You can trust me," said Fauve, thrilled to still have her job.

"Oh, and Fauve? No more placards, okay?"

"Cross my heart and hope to die," Fauve said fervently, and the doctor winced.

American Liam came crawling back not long afterwards. He came and stood outside the building on Stephen's Green that housed the medical centre at five-thirty one evening and waited for Fauve to come out. In one hand he held a bunch of rather bedraggled-looking flowers and, in the other, a box of somewhat squishy-looking jam-and-sugar doughnuts, because he knew she had a weakness for them. In a baby-blue sweatshirt she'd never seen on him before and clean jeans, with his blonde hair brushed back from his tanned, handsome face, she had to admit he was looking well, and very American. She herself felt tired and a bit scruffy after the long day, and she wanted nothing so much as a hot bath and a chilled glass of wine. And maybe a jam-and-sugar doughnut, for essential energy.

"Amy gone back to the States then, is she?" Fauve said,

eyeing the wilting blooms and battered cake box with something less than enthusiasm.

He nodded.

"So, what are you now then, bored or something? At a loose end? Thought you'd come and look me up now that sweet little Amy-Pie has gone bye-byes till next time? I'm not here for your convenience, you know." She began walking to her Luas stop home to Beechwood.

"It's not like that, Fauve, I swear it's not. Ames and me, we're all washed up. *Kaput. Finito.* Over. Dead as a dodo."

Fauve paused in her quick walking and looked up at his face. God, but he was gorgeous! Six feet and more of prime American beef and muscle. She tried not to relent towards him (after all, he'd dropped her like a hot spud when he'd found out his precious 'Ames' was coming over, the swine), but the news that he and Amy were finished was getting her hopes up slightly. Who was she kidding? They were already up, up sky-high with a smashing bird's-eye view of the capital from above.

"You broke up with her?" Because of me? were the words she left unspoken. She waited on tenterhooks for his answer. Maybe, if he was properly single now, they could have another bash at things, with everything all out in the open between them this time.

"Well, not exactly. She's met someone else back home in the States, can you believe it? She's thrown me over for some new guy she's met back home. Gave me back the ring and everything."

"I *see* ..." Fauve said slowly. She started walking again, faster this time, so fast she walked past her stop but it didn't matter. She could walk up to the next one on Harcourt Street. The important thing was just to keep walking, walking quite fast, away from Liam.

"Wait up, Fauve honey! Don't you see what this means? We can be together now."

"What, now that Amy's ditched you, you mean?"

He looked at her uncomprehendingly, seemingly puzzled by her bitter tones.

"Well, yeah," he said. "Why not? You and me, Fauve, we're good together. I think we could really have something decent together, if we gave it a go. What d'you think?"

"What I *think,* Liam," she said slowly, standing still to look up sadly into his handsome face, "is that you dropped me for Amy, after keeping her a secret from me the whole time we were together, and now you're only here because Amy's dumped you and you've nothing else on the go. You think I'll have you back in a heartbeat, don't you?"

"It's not like that," he protested, putting his hand on her arm to steady them both as the passengers coming off and climbing aboard the Luas swarmed around them in a fluid sea of humanity. "I really like you, Fauve. You're a top girl. What difference does it make whether I dumped Ames or Ames dumped me? I don't get it. The end result's the same, either way."

"That's precisely why we wouldn't work, Liam. Don't you see, if you'd dropped Amy for me, I might actually believe all that stuff you said about me being a top girl and you wanting to make it work between us. As it is, you're only here because you've nowhere better to be at this precise moment in time. I'm sorry, Liam," she said, shrugging his hand off her arm, "but that's . . . that's just not good enough for me. *You're* not good enough for me."

She turned and walked off quickly, tears in her eyes, before he could see what it was costing her to send him away. Yes, he was gorgeous, yes, they'd had some great laughs and some great sex together, and, yes, a few hours in bed with him was probably just what she needed to help ease the pain of the Dr. Cross-Rosaria Kelly debacle. But — and it was too big a but to get over — she'd only be getting him now because Amy didn't want him any more. He was Amy Cheerleader's reject, her cast-off. It would be the easiest thing in the world to fall back into his arms (and his bed) tonight and turn the clock back to where they'd been before Amy had reared her no doubt pretty little head, but she'd only be getting him because Amy didn't want him, and not because he loved her, Fauve, to distraction. And she'd (mostly) managed, with the help of her three housemates, to get over him leaving her once. Next time he left her, and he probably would, it would be harder to get over him.

"*Fauve, come back!*" he cried out as she walked away, but she kept walking.

She might regret this decision a million times over the next few days and weeks, she might even weaken and want to pick up the phone and text him, but she'd get over it. She'd get over *Liam*. She was doing the right thing. If only doing the right thing didn't suck so bloody much, she thought glumly as she tapped her Leap card against the machine on the Harcourt Street Luas platform. Suddenly he was there behind her again, just as her tram was pulling up slowly to the platform.

"Please, Fauve —" he began.

"*Goodbye,* Liam." The doors of the tram opened and the passengers who were getting off spilled out noisily around them. When they'd gone, Fauve went to board her train home. On impulse, she whirled round suddenly and whipped the cake box from his hands, then hopped on board the Luas just as the doors were gliding shut. She could see Liam's surprised face as she took a giant bite from one of the doughnuts while the train began pulling away from the platform. Men were men and undoubtedly always would be, she thought as she chomped away happily on the sugary, jammy confection, feeling miles better already, but a box of doughnuts was still a box of doughnuts.

She dialled a number on her phone, then, when it picked up, she said: "Heya, Doir, it's me. You at home yet? You are? Grand. Put the kettle on, will you? I'm coming home. And I've got cake."

"*Next stop, Kilmacud; An chéad stad eile, Cill Mhic Oda,*" said the automated female voice after a bit.

Next stop, home, thought Fauve, still chomping away.

Chapter 4

ORLA

Orla Dunlop stood in front of her bedroom mirror and craned her neck round to see the back of the dress. From the front, it looked gorgeous, anyway. Knee-length, sleeveless, form-fitting with a cinched-in waist and a low-cut sort of cowl neck that showed a *lot* of cleavage, way more than Orla generally liked to show. The colour suited her, even though she didn't normally wear this vibrant a red because it would make her stand out too much. Orla didn't really like to stand out. She preferred to blend in, or even to fade into the background if possible. She breathed in and tried to do up the zip at the back of the dress, but it was no good. She couldn't reach it, and she had no intention of asking one of the other girls in to do it up for her.

"*Knock, knock!*" said a voice suddenly, breaking in on Orla's daydream. The door opened and Fauve came in, shutting the door behind her. "Just came up to see if you wanted coffee — Doireann's making some now." She stopped and stared when she saw the dress. "Wow, that's stunning, Orla! Where'd you get it? Are you having trouble with the zip? Here, let me! I'll get you sorted out."

Orla stood there, mortified, her cheeks flaming red with embarrassment. Why did people in this house think they could just barge into her bedroom without properly knocking? They'd done it in the house she'd grown up in as well, just as if she wasn't a proper person with the same rights as anyone else, but a nobody whose feelings didn't matter and could be trampled on willy-nilly! More to the point, why hadn't she remembered to lock the door? The house had been empty when she'd come home but still, she should have known that her housemates wouldn't have been too far behind her. She should have locked the door!

Fauve stepped nimbly behind her and did up the zip. The dress looked even better now.

"Thanks," Orla muttered, hoping desperately that Fauve would wander off back downstairs to Doireann and her coffee, but no such luck.

Fauve sat down on the bed and made herself comfortable. Oh great. Now there'd be no shifting her.

"Seriously, Orla, where'd you get it? It's beautiful. It makes you look like one of those old Hollywood movie stars."

"Come off it, Fauve. It's only a dress, not a miracle-worker." Orla's bark of a laugh was short and self-deprecating.

"I mean it, Orla! Look at you. You're a knockout. I'd love to be able to wear that colour red, but it'd clash with my hair." Fauve's hair, long and thick and healthy-looking, was dyed a bright vivid red. Today, she wore it in two plaits. Orla's was mousy brown, but long too and naturally curly. She normally wore it tied up in a ponytail, but now it was loose and fell well past her shoulders. "What's the occasion, anyway? Is it for Gabby's party?"

Orla nodded self-consciously. "I thought it might do for that, what'd'you think?"

"I think you'll upstage the Birthday Girl, that's what I think," said Fauve with a laugh. "What about your hair? Why don't you put it up? It'd look amazing." She leaped up and began enthusiastically gathering up Orla's cloud of pre-Raphaelite curls and piling them on top of her friend's head.

"I don't know, Fauve." Orla looked doubtful. "With my glasses? I don't think an up-do suits me with these. I can't even wear long dangly earrings in case they look too much with the glasses. You know, too busy, or too fussy, or something."

"Orla, you can do and wear whatever you like — you're beautiful," Fauve said earnestly.

"No, I'm not, but thanks anyway."

"I'm not bullshitting you, Orla. Half the time I don't think you realise how beautiful you are. And, whatever about dangly earrings, which, by the way, look great on you, I think I have just the thing for that cleavage. Wait here and don't move a muscle."

She hurried from the room while Orla stood and fidgeted in front of the mirror, then she returned a few moments later with something small and silver nestling in her palm.

"Close your eyes," she ordered Orla with a grin. She fastened the necklace round her friend's neck then said: "Open them, *ta-da!*"

"It's lovely, Fauve," said Orla, fingering the little silver heart-shaped locket. "But I can't take this, even for one night. It's much too precious."

"Of course you can. No arguments. It finishes the dress off perfectly. What'd'you think, Doireann?" She addressed this to their friend and housemate, who'd wandered up in search of Fauve, who hadn't returned to the kitchen with Orla's coffee order.

Doireann did a very passable attempt at a wolf-whistle. "You look sensational, Orla! Is this for Gabby's party? Because I'm telling you now, my little sister does *not* like to be outshone." She laughed and so did Fauve.

Orla tittered nervously. She couldn't wait for the pair of them to get bored and leave her room in search of other distractions.

"Shoes!" Fauve exclaimed suddenly. "You'll need shoes to go with the dress! High heels, strappy, red if possible, am I right, Doireann?"

Doireann nodded. "May I?" she said, crossing to Orla's wardrobe and opening it without waiting for an answer. She kneeled down and began rummaging through Orla's shoe stash, before coming up triumphantly with a pair of high-heeled strappy sandals in a shade of dusky rose-pink that would do just as well.

Now they'll make me try them on and parade up and down in them, Orla thought in desperation. Why can't they just go downstairs and leave me in peace?

"Try them on, try them on!" clamoured both her friends.

Forcing a smile to her face, Orla slipped on the shoes and aped a catwalk stance for their benefit.

"Come on, walk up and down in them — let's see what they look like in motion!"

Orla's heart sank but she did as she was bid. Why did choosing every outfit have to be such a big production with them? She walked up and down the narrow bedroom in the shoes and dress, feeling ridiculous and even vaguely resentful as they *ooh*ed and *aah*ed over how great she looked. She just wanted to tear the red dress off her body, stuff it in the bin and never look at it again.

"What about a bag?" Doireann said then. "A little red evening bag. A little red clutch purse with a diamanté clasp, or a little spray of diamanté flowers on it would be even nicer. I don't think I've anything suitable. Have you, Fauvey-Wauvey?"

Fauve bit her lip and screwed up her face in concentration. "Not red as such, I don't think. Orla?"

But Doireann was already back in Orla's wardrobe, going through the handbags. "Wow, you've some fantastic stuff here, Orla! And about a million handbags. What did you do, girl, hold up a delivery truck?"

She and Fauve laughed their heads off, and Orla laughed too, but her laughter was strained. Doireann picked out almost the exact right thing, a little satin clutch purse in the same shade of dusky rose-pink as the shoes, with a silver clasp. It was so small it would just about carry a VISA card, a lipstick and a powder compact. What else did a girl out on the town need?

"It's perfect," breathed Fauve, always ready to worship at the altar of great accessories.

"You're completely sorted," beamed Doireann. "I wish I was as well sorted as you, Orla. If I don't get to the shops before Saturday night, I'll be going to my own sister's twenty-first in my friggin' pyjamas."

"Me too," said Fauve. "What about I meet you in the Dundrum Town Centre on Thursday after work? Late-night shopping? I don't think I've anything on. I'll ask Molly from work. She's coming to the party too and I don't think she's bought an outfit yet."

"Grand." Doireann nodded. "Oh, and of course you're invited too, Orla. Even if you're not shopping for yourself, you can help us to choose."

"You star shoppers don't need me." Orla faked a laugh. "I'd just slow you down. Anyway, I think I'm working late this Thursday. I'm on cleaning duty at the crèche."

"Fair enough," Doireann said. "You're sorted for the party, anyway. You'll be the belle of the ball. Hey, is that Sasha coming in the front door now?"

Orla fought down a mounting sense of panic. If Sasha, their fourth housemate, came up here and joined the party, she'd never get rid of any of them. They'd be in here for the night, talking about men and shoes and make-up and Gabby's party. Dredging up the courage from God-knows-where, she opened her mouth and found herself gabbling way too brightly: "Oh God, I'm dying for that coffee you mentioned, Fauve. Will you be a love and run down and make it for me, Doireann? And if one of you would just unzip me — thanks, Fauve — I'll just get out of this dress before I spill coffee on it. I don't want anything stopping me from wearing this on Saturday night. Not after all the trouble you guys have been to, helping me pick out such brilliant stuff to go with it. I'll be down in a minute. God, I'm gasping for that coffee now. Make it good and strong, Doireann!" With a fake laugh, she somehow got them out the door and shut it behind them.

The fake smile slipped from her face and the sigh of

relief she heaved came all the way from the pit of her stomach. She pulled the dress over her head and flung it on the bed as if it were infected. She stuffed it into a carrier bag, careless of creasing it, and shoved it to the very back of her wardrobe, with the rest of the stuff she'd stolen.

She told herself repeatedly that she wasn't a real thief, a common shoplifter like the people who found themselves up in front of a judge for robbing trainers and designer sports gear from shops on Grafton Street or O'Connell Street. She didn't steal for profit, or to sell stuff on, but only because she was unhappy. That's no excuse, she told herself weakly, but the part of her that was presumably stronger continued to do it. She'd only taken the red dress because her mum and stepdad loved her twin stepbrothers more than they ever could Orla, and also because she was still in mourning for David. He shouldn't have left her, he shouldn't be gone, it shouldn't be over between them. *Shouldn't, shouldn't, shouldn't.* A million shouldn'ts, and all she was left with was the stupid red dress that she didn't even want. She'd have to wear it for Doireann's sister Gabby's stupid birthday party at the rugby club on Saturday night, or she'd never hear the bloody end of it from Fauve and Doireann. They'd seen the damn thing now and approved it and exclaimed over it and even picked out accessories to go with it, but the minute the party was over she was putting the dress straight in the bin, as she had no safe means of burning it. She hadn't even wanted it in the first place, but the shop assistant and security guard were both busy with the dotty old lady who couldn't find her purse and was demanding that the shop be searched high and low for it. Orla had just taken the dress off its hanger, pretending to study it a moment before simply stuffing it in her bag and walking out swiftly through the open door of the shop. She hadn't even checked to see if it was in her right size. It was an actual miracle that it had fitted her as well as it did. The whole way home she'd felt her cheeks flame with guilt, and in her mind the dress was ticking away audibly so that other people on the Luas could hear it too, or it was pounding like the heart in that creepy old story by Edgar Allan Poe. She thought she'd never get the blasted thing home. She was only sorry that Doireann and Fauve had seen it, so now she couldn't dispose of it straightaway but had to wait until after the party. Terrific as it undoubtedly looked on her, she'd never hated a dress more.

"Orla, I think we need to talk."

It was a Friday night a few weeks ago. They'd gone out to dinner at their favourite restaurant, a little seafood place along the sea-front in Dun Laoghaire. David had driven them both there in his lovely new BMW, and Orla had noticed that he'd been a little bit quiet on the journey there, but she'd chatted away gaily as usual, with one hand on his thigh as he drove, filling in all the awkward silences with her bright, inconsequential chatter. They'd talked all the time back at the start of their relationship two years ago, about themselves, their jobs (David was a solicitor, Orla worked in a crèche), their aspirations, hopes, dreams, wishes for the future, but now they hardly talked at all. David was always very busy at work though. They hardly even saw each other at times, he was so busy. That was clearly what the problem was. Once David's workload eased up a bit and the other solicitors in his practice started pulling their weight a bit more, things would get back to normal. Their *relationship* would get back to normal. But now David wanted to talk, and Orla's heart sank all the way to her lovely new high-heeled shoes.

"What's up?" she said brightly, trying to keep the fear and trembling from her voice. She took a big long drink of her wine to fortify her for what might lie ahead.

David cleared his throat and gave a little cough. He looked so handsome tonight, in jeans and a blue shirt that both managed to look ridiculously expensive for a smart-casual ensemble. His thatch of dark blond hair was pushed back off his face and his eyes, those eyes that had attracted her so much in the beginning and still did, were as blue as the pale blue sea that she could observe from the restaurant window if she just turned her head to the left a bit. He was so handsome! She sent up a fervent prayer. Please God, let whatever this is not be serious!

"Orla, you know as well as I do that things haven't been good between us for a while now."

Orla stared, shocked. She took another long drink of her wine and looked around for the bottle. The nearby waiter stepped forward immediately and poured her a refill.

"That's only because you've been so busy, and we haven't been able to see each other! Once things ease up for you, things will go back to normal between us." She smiled at him, a dazzling smile that showcased her straight little white teeth and made her huge brown eyes sparkle and shine behind her glasses.

David *ahem*-ed and looked uncomfortable.

"Well, I *have* been busy," he admitted, "but that's not really it, Orla. That's not really the problem."

"Well, what *is* the problem, then?" She said it querulously, like an old lady complaining about the price of fish. She couldn't help it. She hated conversations like this, feared them, even, because they usually only ever went the one way. She was tired of this one already.

David took a deep breath. He looked to Orla like he was biting the bullet that was going to destroy their relationship. "To be brutally honest, Orla, the problem is *you*. You suffocate me. You send me so many texts in a day. You call me morning, noon and night. You leave me a dozen voice messages a day, or you call me when you know I'm in a meeting, just so you can check up on me and see if I'm where I said I was going to be. You call round to my flat on the nights we're not seeing each other to make sure I'm on my own. All my friends have noticed it. I can't live like that, Orla. I feel like I can't breathe in this relationship." He paused for breath.

Orla, her lower lip trembling and her eyes brimming with unshed tears, jumped in with an accusatory "Are you . . . are you seeing someone else?"

David stared at her and sighed heavily. "This isn't *about* me seeing someone else, Orla. Can't you see that? It's about *you*, and the way you can't seem to leave me alone for five minutes, whether it's out of jealousy or a feeling of ownership or just because you're so ridiculously, breathtakingly *needy*, I don't know – and frankly, Orla, I'll tell you now. I'm not happy with *any* of those things. I just can't live like that any more."

"It's Justine, isn't it?" The tears spilled over and streamed down her cheeks unchecked. Justine was a solicitor in the practice where David worked. Orla had met her at one or two of the Law Society dinners and Justine had been all over

David, like the slinky cat she resembled. Her long, poker-straight jet black hair was loose and streamed like a glossy waterfall almost to the waist of her backless, skin-tight green dress, which exactly matched the colour of her exotic-looking, almond-shaped eyes framed by impossibly long black lashes. She kept putting her long, elegant fingers with the blood-red, perfectly manicured nails on David's arm or shirt-front when she spoke to him or — even worse — pulling him down so she could whisper directly in his ear, just as if she was his girlfriend and Orla wasn't standing right beside them with her little glass of champagne in her hand, trembling with jealous rage at David's proximity to such an obvious, *blatant* love rival. She'd wanted to throw the drink in Justine's smug face, and had barely just managed to stop herself.

"Jesus, Orla!" He sounded impatient now. "This has nothing to do with Justine, or any of your paranoid fantasies. It's about you being so clingy. In fact, I wasn't going to say this, but, Orla . . ." He paused and looked uncertain.

"Say what? Say what, David? Just say it, if you have the balls!" She knew she was being a bitch now but she couldn't help it. Things were getting away from her, getting out from under her control, and when that happened, they usually only continued to spiral out of control until they ended in disaster. She was on that course now, like a comet hurtling through space destined for the Earth. She could feel it. Defiantly, she drank some more wine, even though she'd barely eaten a thing and was well on the way to being tipsy.

David picked up his napkin, wiped his mouth and pushed both his napkin and his own plate of barely touched food firmly away from him. "Orla, I think you need help. I know you felt unloved by your mum and stepdad when you were growing up, and I know you felt that your two little stepbrothers took up all your parents' love and attention and whatever else, but Orla . . ." Here he stopped and shook his head, as if he was sorry to have to say this but he was going to say it anyway. "Orla, no one in the world needs to be as clingy and insecure as you are. You have some serious abandonment issues that need to be talked out with . . . I don't know, a counsellor or a psychotherapist or something. I'm not saying this to be rude or patronising or horrible, Orla, I swear I'm not. I'm saying this from a place of genuinely caring about you and wanting you to be all right when I'm not there any more. But I'm not a counsellor. I can't give you the help you need. I can't *be* the help you need. I'm sorry but there it is."

"Have you fucked her yet? That whore, Justine?"

David's face coloured a bright red. Heads were turning towards them in the restaurant now, although most people seemed to correctly sense that they were having an argument and studiously kept their eyes on their food and on each other.

"For the last time, Orla, this isn't about Justine. It's about *you*." He signalled to the waiter for the bill. "Look, get your stuff and I'll drive you home."

"*I'm not going anywhere with you!*" she screeched. She grabbed up her bag and jacket and took her purse out of her bag. "Here!" she added, throwing a few tenners onto the table between them. "I'll pay for my own food, thank you very much. I'm not having someone pay for my food who's been fucking that filthy whore Justine behind my back!"

"Don't be ridiculous, Orla! Of course I'm going to drive you home when you're this upset."

He reached for her arm but she shook it off furiously.

"*Fuck off, you creep!* You're not touching me with the same hands that have touched that whore!" She stumbled from the restaurant in her high-heeled shoes and dived into the first taxi waiting in the rank outside.

She gave the driver her address and then immediately took her phone from her bag and dialled David's number.

"David, I'm sorry, I didn't mean it!" she gabbled when his phone went straight to voicemail. "Please call me when you get this. I promise I won't give you a hard time. Just give me another chance, please! I'll prove to you how much I love you, how much you mean to me!"

She talked till she ran out of time, then she hung up and pressed redial, leaving more or less the same message again when David's phone once more went straight to voicemail. Tears of anger and frustration streamed down her face. Why wouldn't he answer? Her face set in lines of grim determination, she pressed redial again.

He never spoke to her again after that night, despite the many texts she sent him and the calls she made to him. When she was able to get time off at the crèche, she stationed herself across the street from his work and waited for him to appear at the end of the day. When she saw him exit the building with Justine, the two of them seemingly on excellent terms with each other, a murderous rage built up inside her that wasn't quelled even when she saw them both climb into their own cars and drive off in different directions. The next day, not knowing what else to do, she began shoplifting again, for the first time in nearly two years.

***

"I'm just going out for a fag," Orla said. "I won't be a minute."

The party at the rugby club for Gabby's twenty-first birthday was in full swing. The hall was decorated and festooned all over with streamers, balloons and a giant banner which read: *Happy Birthday, Gabby!* The hall was nearly packed to capacity. Gabby was in her second year of art college and it seemed like she'd invited nearly the whole college to her birthday celebration. Her older brother Jason was there with a load of his rugby-playing pals, whose clubhouse they were using for the shindig. Gabby's older sister Doireann was there with a smattering of her own friends, including her three housemates, Fauve, Sasha and Orla. Gabby, Doireann and Jason's parents Maurice and Michelle Rochefort were there also, and they'd invited various friends and relatives along, including an old great-aunt of Michelle's called Bridie who was one hundred and three years old and who enjoyed the party immensely, swilling down glasses of bubbly and beaming benevolently from her wheelchair at anyone who passed by and calling them 'lovey'.

Orla felt overwhelmed. The crowd was just too much and it was sweltering hot in the hall. She'd been told many times tonight by her housemates that she looked fabulous in the red dress, the shoes, the bag and the necklace, but she still felt deeply uncomfortable in the stolen dress and felt like she had the word '*thief*' tattooed across her forehead. '*Shoplifter*' was kind of a euphemistic word for what was really just a plain, ordinary thief, she often thought, the way that 'joy-riders' was just a euphemistic way of saying car thieves. Robbers, people who steal. It just all came down to plain old stealing, when you thought about it. Taking something that didn't belong to you but to someone else. No matter how many fancy synonyms people had for the act.

She felt disgusted with herself. She didn't think she'd ever hated or despised herself as much before as she did right now, standing here lonely and bored, in a stupid stolen dress, at the party of a person she only knew slightly. She'd give anything to be able to just slink away unnoticed in a taxi but there was no chance, as Maurice and Michelle would be dropping Doireann and her three housemates back to Kilmacud at the end of the night and, as they were the parents and sister of the birthday girl, it was safe enough to assume that it would be at the very tail end of the festivities. She honestly didn't think she'd last that long. She was wilting with the heat and the boredom already.

The little group of people she was standing with barely noticed her slipping away. Fauve was deep in conversation with Doireann and one of Doireann's friends from college, a girl called Martina, who apparently went by the nickname of 'Martini' for reasons not too taxing to work out, about the whole Rosaria Kelly fiasco and the aftermath of the 'protest' in the Stephen's Green park. Martini was thoroughly enjoying the story, and nearly choked with laughter at the bit where the little procession of disabled kids entered the park to meet up with Rosaria Kelly, the celebrity face of the charity event taking place, just in time to make Fauve and her little group of fellow feminist protestors look like Hitler crossed with Jack the Ripper for trying to sabotage the happy event. Orla knew the story pretty well by now, as she'd been there in person supporting Fauve, and was glad to be able to make her excuses, which they barely acknowledged, and wander off.

Outside in the carpark, she lit a cigarette and took a long, blissful puff. It was so good to be outside in the cool night air after the heat of the party, although the irony of her choosing to take in polluted air through the cigarette was not lost on her. There were only a handful of people outside smoking. Orla made her way to an empty bench outside the rugby club and sat down just as a taxi drew up beside her and a guy got out of the passenger seat, complaining loudly to the driver. Something about the fare – he was disputing the fare. Angrily, the complaining guy pulled his wallet from his pinstripe trousers, extracted a note from it and handed it grudgingly to the driver, muttering something about "daylight robbery" and how not all thieves wore "effing balaclavas". The taxi drove off, the driver clearly displaying his middle finger with a grin, and the guy put his wallet away and patted himself down, presumably checking for phone and keys. Only then did he turn round and notice Orla, sitting quietly smoking on the bench, trying to make herself as small and inconspicuous as possible. He gave a short bark of a laugh.

"Oh, you saw all that, did you?" he said. "Bastard overcharged me. Eighteen quid to come from fucking Tallaght? Don't make me laugh. Thought he could pull a fast one but I was too sharp for him, the tight-fisted fucker."

Orla, who'd seen him hand over what seemed like the requested amount of money (plus tip) to the driver, said nothing. If this big, blustery guy in the pinstriped suit wanted to show off a little bit in front of a strange woman, well, then, let him. It was nothing to do with her.

"Can I bum one of those?" He inclined his head towards the cigarette. "I could do with one, after the day I've had."

"Oh. Yes, yes, of course." She fumbled about in the little dusky pink clutch purse for her cigarettes and lighter. When he was seated beside her on the bench, all lit up and puffing away, she chanced asking him: "Is your job very stressful, then?" and, when he stared at her, she went on nervously: "You . . . you said you'd had a bad day . . .?"

"Oh, that," he said expansively, puffing out his broad chest and crossing one booted foot over one pinstriped knee. "Well, yes, as the chairman of the whole Mercedes operation here in Ireland, you might say I'm up to my tits in responsibilities. Do you know that not a single transaction to do with the Mercedes brand can take place in the whole of Europe without me signing off on it first? I tell you something, it's a twenty-four-fucking-seven job." He broke off then and looked at her appreciatively.

Orla shivered a little in the night air, feeling a bit like Red Riding Hood under the watchful gaze of the Big Bad Wolf. She even had the right dress on. The burly man watched her as she crossed and uncrossed her legs for something to do, then flushed when she realised she'd only drawn his attention to herself even more.

"I can't believe I'm saying this to a complete stranger," he said, edging closer to her on the bench, "but you are the most beautiful woman I've seen in a long time. I'm Nathan, by the way, Nathan Quilty." He held out a big sweaty paw for her to shake.

"I'm Orla," she said softly, her cheeks scarlet from the compliment. She felt herself warming to this big, solidly built arrogant guy. "Orla Dunlop. Are you here for the party? Well, I mean, of course you're here for the party. What I should say is, are you a friend of Gabby's?" Embarrassed at having been gabbling like a lunatic, she flushed even harder and lowered her eyes, looking down at her hands, folded in her lap.

"Her brother Jason invited me. We played rugby together till I busted the old knee."

"Were you any good? At the rugby, I mean?"

"Well, let's just say that they wanted me for the Ireland team but I had too much on, running the whole Mercedes operation over here. Plus, I had my knee trouble."

Orla had the vaguest feeling that he wasn't telling the exact truth, but she knew that men liked flattery, so she said: "I'm sure it was their loss."

"Yeah, I could have been the next Brian O'Driscoll or Ronan O'Gara, only for my knee. And the job as chairman of Mercedes, of course. What do you do yourself, Orla?"

"I . . . I work in a crèche," she told him shyly.

"Now, that's what I call a proper woman's job," he said with an approving grin and a vigorous nodding of his head. "No real responsibility, just minding a load of snotty kids all day."

"Yes. Yes, I suppose so." Orla knew she should have said something, argued with him, disputed what he'd said, but she had the feeling he wouldn't have liked that, so she said the non-confrontational thing and was pleased when he seemed satisfied with her passive answer.

"Should we go inside? I'll buy you a drink. What're you having? Nice glass of white wine for the pretty lady?"

"Yes, please, that'd be lovely, thanks." Orla, who'd been

swilling Bulmers from a pint glass at the party so far, nodded her acquiescence.

When they were both standing up, he towered over her, even in her dusky pink strappy high-heeled sandals, and his big hand on the small of her back as he ushered her into the hall felt protective. She felt protected by the bulk of him, in a way she hadn't felt since David left.

When they were inside the packed venue, they found a corner together to talk and have their drinks. Orla stood with her back to the wall and Nathan stood in front of her, blocking her view of the room, one arm up against the wall effectively blocking her exit too, but she didn't care. The more she looked up at Nathan and listened to him talk, the more she decided she liked him, was attracted to him, needed to feel like she meant something to him. And the way his eyes were roaming constantly over her legs, hair and breasts was so confidence-boosting after David's painful defection. She felt attractive again for the first time in weeks, enough to begin flirting with him, tentatively at first, and then more overtly. She learned quickly that Nathan liked to talk about himself. All she had to do was listen and look impressed and make the occasional flattering interjection. She was good at that, at making men feel like they were the be-all and end-all. By the end of the night, she had almost convinced herself that Nathan, not David, was the man she'd been waiting for her whole life, and it looked like Nathan was smitten too. She was glad of that. He was dark-haired and handsome in a burly, heavy-set kind of way — not fat, exactly, but comfortingly solid, and his clothes were obviously expensive.

"Are you single, Orla?" he'd asked her earlier in the night.

"Y-yes. I . . . I broke up with someone a few weeks ago. What . . . what about yourself?"

"I'm my own boss," he'd smirked. "Some tart was trying to get her claws into me a while back, but I showed her. No bitch is going to tie me down. Although I might let you have a go sometime ..." He'd leered then, putting his face so close to hers she could smell his beery breath.

By the time the party had started to wind down, they'd had their first kiss.

"Where d'you live, Orla?" he'd asked her afterwards.

"Kilmacud," she breathed. "I live with three other girls. They're around here somewhere. Doireann is Gabby's sister, you know, Gabby, the birthday girl? But I have my own room."

His eyes lit up when he heard this. "Will we order a taxi, so?" he said.

She hesitated. What would the others think of her, bringing a guy home on the first night? *Fuck them*, she thought defiantly. They haven't come anywhere near me all night. I came to their stupid party to please them and then all they do is leave me by myself all night while they gab to their own posh friends. Why should she give a shit what they think, or take their feelings into account? They never cared what *she* thought about anything. She nodded.

Nathan grinned, mopping the sweat off his forehead and neck with a hanky he pulled from his breast pocket, and then they went outside so he could call the taxi. They held hands at first while they waited in the car-park, where a load of people had started to pile into cars and taxis, but when Orla shivered in the cool night air he put his arm around her and squeezed her tightly to him, and she felt so protected she could have cried. When the taxi came, she could hardly wait for it to get them home.

Orla wandered through the shopping centre, humming to herself. She was happy today, ecstatically happy. It was her day off from the crèche, she was shopping for something pretty to wear for her date with Nathan tonight and Nathan himself was texting her nearly every hour on the hour to ask her where she was, if she was with anyone and what she was doing. They were the kinds of lovely, interested texts she would have liked David to send her, but he never did, and, when she sent them to him, he claimed to feel trapped, suffocated, hemmed-in. He obviously didn't know what it was like to feel a real, overwhelming love for someone, an all-consuming, powerful love like the one that existed now between her and Nathan. It was the kind of love that made you want to be with the other person every minute of every day, but if you couldn't, because you both had to work to pay the bills and the rent, then you made do with texts and phone calls during the times when you couldn't be together. Orla thanked her lucky stars every day for sending her Nathan, and just when she'd been so low about David too! Whatever turn of fate that had placed her on that bench outside the rugby club on the night of Gabby's birthday party, at the exact moment that Nathan had been pulling up alongside her in a taxi, had done her nearly the biggest favour of her life. Okay, so Nathan wasn't perfect, but who was? Orla herself certainly wasn't, no one was. So he was a bit of a boaster, so what? That wasn't a crime. So he wasn't the CEO of Mercedes in Europe, but only a humble salesman in one of their Dublin branches, big deal. She loved him for trying to impress her. She loved him! Orla loved Nathan, and Nathan loved Orla. She hugged the words to herself now as she browsed round a little costume-jewellery shop, trying to decide if a new necklace to wear with the dress she was thinking of buying was a must. Nathan loved her in the red dress, the one she'd stolen, so now she could never throw it out. He'd said he'd always remember her in it, the way she'd looked on the night they met. He'd called her his *Lady in Red*. A bit corny, sure, but Orla lapped it up.

Her fingers hovered over a necklace of blue stones on a silver chain that would perfectly suit the dress she'd seen earlier that day in another shop. She took a quick look round the shop while pretending to be perusing the necklaces, which hung on a stand near the open door. The security guard was nearby, yes, but he was yawning his head off and scrolling on his phone. The two shop assistants were looking at something on one of their phones, and two or three female customers, two of them together, were browsing the rings and bracelets. Orla, her heart beating like a jackhammer, made a swift decision. She'd go for it. She hadn't stolen anything since Nathan had suddenly come into her life a month ago. She hadn't felt the urge, and she had a box on top of her wardrobe that was already full to bursting with bits of make-up, jewellery, perfume and toiletries that she'd probably never use because, once she'd got the thing home, she lost interest in it. But old habits obviously died hard. Or maybe she was addicted now, addicted to the risk she was running, to the charge it gave her, the rush she felt. It wouldn't do any harm, surely, to try it once more for luck.

And the necklace was for Nathan's benefit, after all. He'd love the way it looked with her dress, and with her hair down.

She picked the necklace with the blue stones off the rack and slipped it into her handbag. Walking deliberately unhurriedly, she strolled from the shop and had begun to walk quickly away once outside when she felt a hand clamp down heavily on her left shoulder.

"Excuse me, miss, but would you mind stepping back into the shop with me, please?"

Her mother, Yvonne, and her stepdad, Colin, went ballistic. The guards were called to the shop, but because Orla spoke nicely, was of good appearance, hadn't come to their attention before, and expressed lots of tearful remorse while handing back the necklace, they let her off with a caution, even though the store's policy was usually to prosecute shoplifters. Luckily for Orla, the store's boss was on holiday, and the two Chinese girls left in charge in her absence weren't keen to let her know that they'd been inattentive on the job, so they were willing to let the whole thing go, seeing as they'd got their stock back and weren't out of pocket in any way. The guards had insisted that Orla call someone, however, a responsible person, to take her home. She'd dismissed almost immediately the thought of calling Nathan. She couldn't live with the shame of Nathan knowing that she was a thief. That just left Yvonne and Colin. Yvonne telephoned Colin at work and made him come and pick Orla up from the store. He ranted and raved as he drove her 'home', not to her shared house in Kilmacud but to their own family home in Ballsbridge, the house in which Orla had grown up alongside her younger stepbrothers Christopher and Noah.

"After all we've done for you!" sobbed a distraught Yvonne. As usual, she abdicated all responsibility for the affair to Colin, the way she'd pretty much done with everything of any importance from the time she'd married him, but Colin hadn't much more to add, beyond reiterating "After all we've done for you!" a few more times, just to be sure Orla got the message.

What have you done for me, but put me in second place to Noah and Christopher nearly my whole life? Orla wanted to scream back at them, but she knew there was no point. They'd only look at her blankly and uncomprehendingly, as if they hadn't a clue what she was talking about. And, in fairness, they'd fed, clothed, housed and educated her, they'd paid for the childcare course she'd done when she left school, and Colin paid part of the rent for her share of the house in Kilmacud every month. They'd been very good like that, she couldn't say they hadn't. But they didn't *love* her, she knew they didn't. She was the one who made all the moves as regards keeping in touch, and she knew perfectly well that Christopher and Noah were the twin lights of their lives. She sighed and stifled a yawn as Colin banged on.

"The guards suggested that some counselling might be useful," he was saying now. "I'll gladly pay for a course of sessions for you if you find yourself a suitable psychiatrist, or counsellor, or whatever it is they're called."

I bet you would, thought Orla ungratefully, just as long as you don't actually have to *do* anything. A text from Nathan vibrated in her open handbag and she jumped on it excitedly, too pleased to be hearing from him again, for about the twelfth or thirteenth time that day, to be bothered to be surreptitious about it.

The text read: **What time am I calling over later?**
To which she immediately texted back: **Eight okay?**
Grand, c u then. xxxxxxxxxx
She flushed with pleasure to see the row of kisses.

Colin was frowning now at her phone-checking in the very middle of his pompous lecture, but she didn't care. Yvonne had disappeared to go and check on a full roast dinner with all the trimmings for the twins, who'd be home from college in an hour or two, ravenously hungry as they always were, as befitted two full-grown adult males. Yvonne was always terrified that the twins, who were two strong, hefty well-built lads, weren't getting enough to eat, and so she stuffed them full of food whenever she got the chance. Orla wasn't even asked if she'd like to stay for dinner, never mind the night (even though she still had a bedroom here that she never felt welcome enough to use), so she stood up, gathered up her bag and phone and stood on tiptoe to give Colin a peck on the cheek.

"I'd better get back," she told him airily. "I need an early night for work tomorrow. I can't afford to lose my job." She knew that that would have weight with Colin, with his strong work ethic. Everything he had, and he had a lot, he'd acquired by the sweat of his brow. He was a self-made man, as he was fond of telling people at dinner parties, in the import-export line, and he was justifiably proud of having been such a good provider for Yvonne, the twins and Orla.

"What about the counselling? We haven't really finished

talking about the counselling. I told you, I'll pay for a course of sessions or whatever they're called, if you find someone suitable. This shoplifting thing needs to be nipped in the bud. Imagine if any of our friends got to hear about it."

Nip it in the bud? She'd been doing it for years! And as for your precious friends! Is that all you care about, she wanted to ask him, but didn't bother. Instead, she flapped a hand at him as she went out the sitting-room door and said carelessly: "Yeah, yeah, I'll sort it. I'll find one, and I'll text you when I do, okay?"

"You won't forget?"

"Of course I won't forget! Bye, Dad. See you."

Out on the road, she sighed and rolled her eyes. She had no more intention of finding a counsellor than she had in suddenly enrolling in a tap-dancing course. What did she want a counsellor for? She had Nathan. Her phone vibrated with another text.

Where are you, anyway? I've hardly heard from you all day.

Just leaving Mum and Dad's & heading home.

What were you doing there?

Just a routine visit. If I don't show my face occasionally, they worry.

Well, make sure you're ready for me at 8. I'm hungry AND horny!

Don't worry, I'll take good care of you.

See that you do. Laters, okay? x

Laters xxx

I love you, Orla, don't forget that, okay?

I won't. I love you too xxxxxxxxxx Oh, PS, by the way, Fauve and Doireann want to know if we'll come

out with them at the weekend? They've met a couple of guys and they thought we could all go out on a sort of quadruple date thing with Sasha and her new fella?

Orla, what are you bothering with them for? You've got me, haven't you?

Oh, I know, I know. I just thought it might be fun, that's all.

Well, don't think, my little fluffy-head. It doesn't suit you. I'll do the thinking for both of us from now on, okay? For one thing, I'm the man and, anyway, I'm smarter.

Okay, Nathan. I know you are. I really do love you.

I love you too. I'd better get my arse into gear now and do some work, babes. Laters, okay?

Laters xxx.

Well, that decides it, she thought as she eventually boarded the crowded Luas home to Kilmacud. She didn't need a stupid counsellor. She didn't need anyone when she had Nathan, not Yvonne and Colin, not her twin stepbrothers, not even Fauve, Doireann and Sasha. She had Nathan, and he had her. Orla and Nathan. Nathan and Orla, forever. The words had such a nice ring to them. She hugged them to herself all the way home.

Chapter 5

DONNA

Donna took a last look at herself in the mirror and sighed. She was no Kate Moss but she'd have to do. She'd always been a bit on what Mick referred to as the 'cuddly' side. If she hadn't learned to live with that by now, at the age of forty-four, then when would she? And she'd done her best for tonight. The new bronze-coloured dress of silky material was immensely flattering, cinched-in at the waist and alluringly low-cut in the bust. If there was one thing Donna knew she had in spades, it was big, generous boobies. Mick loved them. He never failed to be aroused by the sight of them, even now after more than twenty years of marriage. She'd nursed all three of their kids, James, Adam and Olivia, with these breasts, but she flattered herself that you couldn't really tell to look at them. She'd had the hairdresser put her brown unruly waves of shoulder-length hair into a sexy up-do, and even Donna herself was struck by how chic and sophisticated it made her look. Tendrils curled around her face, making her look younger and more wistful, more like the girl she'd been than the woman she was today, and the style was finished off expertly with the sleek knot at the nape of her neck.

"Going anywhere nice tonight?" the hairdresser had asked her in typical hairdresser fashion.

"No, not really," Donna had replied automatically. Then, embarrassed, she'd quickly amended: "Well, actually, yes, I am, I suppose. A school reunion."

"Oh lovely," the hairdresser had said. "Is it a special year or anything?"

"Well, it's the twenty-fifth anniversary. That's the only reason I'm going, really, because it's a special one. I probably wouldn't otherwise."

"Yeah, I know what you mean," the hairdresser had replied emphatically. "It'd have to be a really special occasion to get *me* anywhere near those bitches I used to go to school with." The two women laughed rather uneasily, and the subject was dropped.

Now Donna finished her mirror inspection with a sigh. She'd used her favourite dark eye make-up, the perfume the kids had given her for last Christmas and the emerald earrings with which Mick had gifted her for their twentieth wedding anniversary to complete her look. Her eyes were a strange shade of cat-like green, and they and the emeralds went well together. Donna gathered up her handbag, a snazzy little bronze-coloured affair that matched her dress, and left the room, locking it carefully after her. Linda's room was just next door. They'd planned it that way.

"*Knock knock!*" called Donna, accompanying her words with some light, actual knocks.

Linda let her in. "Jesus, Donna, you look a million bucks! If I'd known you were going to upstage me, I'd have gone the whole bleedin' hog myself."

Which was ridiculous, of course, as Linda was always particular about her looks. Petite and slim with long blonde hair that hid the greys well, she always looked the business. Tonight, though, the little black dress with the sequins on it looked fantastic on her and the shoes gave her the height she was always complaining that she lacked.

She went straight to the minibar and poured Donna a wee nip of the brandy she'd been imbibing herself. "Dutch courage," she told her friend with a mischievous grin.

"Oh Jesus, Linda, I've already had a couple of glasses of wine in the room. I'll be pissed before we even get downstairs." She'd rather guiltily smuggled a bottle into the hotel in her overnight bag, rather than pay the outrageous minibar prices.

"Good," replied Linda firmly. "No friend of mine is going to one of these yokes sober."

Donna giggled and downed the drink in one go. "Linda, my love, there's absolutely no chance of that."

Oh, Linda was such a tonic, Donna thought as they left the room and descended to the function room in the lift. She and Linda had been best friends in school, and they still were, even though weeks and sometimes months could go by without contact between them. Well, that was life, wasn't it, Donna told herself. Kids, husbands, jobs, pets, bills, illness, holidays, accidents and emergencies and unexpected happenings, they all conspired to keep friends — even Best Friends Forever — from getting in touch with each other. Donna resolved to see more of her friend from now on, to phone and text more often, just as they walked through the imposing double doors of the vast function room in the Victorian Hotel and were slapped in the face with 1989, the year they'd both left school and had gone out into the world.

'*THE VICTORIAN HOTEL WELCOMES THE CLASS OF 1989,*' read the banner that hung above the stage. Donna immediately thought of Carrie's ill-fated prom night in the Stephen King book she and Mick both loved. Huge disco lights, probably got in for the night to make the former students feel at home, Donna thought, were suspended from the ceiling. The bar was doing a roaring trade and, even though Donna and Linda weren't late in arriving, it seemed like a good many of the guests were halfway to intoxication already. Streamers and balloons were everywhere, the three long tables were grouped together to form one long continuous buffet table heaped with delicious-looking food, and, up on the stage, so reminiscent of the one in their old assembly hall in Saint Catherine's, a DJ was playing eighties music that immediately transported both women back to their school-leaving days. There was plenty of room for dancing in front of the stage, and a few couples were already out there, shaking and bopping and strutting their stuff to the songs of their youth. Duran Duran, Spandau Ballet, Culture Club, Bananarama, Nik Kershaw, Howard Jones, Erasure, Adam and the Ants, the Human League, A-ha, Level 42, Men at Work, Jason Donovan and Kylie Minogue, the DJ had them all.

"Will we grab some grub first or have a bit of a bop?" Linda said, casting her eyes around the room for anyone they knew.

"Oh, Linda, love, I'm not nearly pissed enough for a bop, although I *am* pissed. Maybe we should eat something first? I think I need something to soak up the booze."

"Spoilsport," said Linda, but she said it with a grin.

They bought drinks at the bar, grabbed two clean plates

and heaped them with buffet food, then they sat down a little way off from the buffet table and had a good nose at their former classmates while they ate.

"Jesus Christ, Donna. Is that Mary Walshe over there? She's the size of a fucking *house*. She was never that big in school, was she?"

"Jesus, Linda, keep it down, she'll hear you! Anyway, she's probably pregnant or something."

"Oh no." Linda, the expert on everything, was adamant. "That's not a baby bump. That's a chocolate cake and Pringles bump. I should know. I had one myself until I started going back to the gym."

"I don't have time for the gym." Donna said it mournfully, as if it really bothered her, but in truth she hardly gave it a thought. If the good Lord had intended her to lose the weight she'd put on after her three pregnancies, then he'd surely also have given her the motivation to do something about it. As he hadn't, well then, she'd just have to live with it. "Ah, Jaysus, Linda, Mary's coming over here! I told you she'd hear you, you with your big mouth! Hi, Mary! Wow, you're looking really well. That mustardy colour really suits you."

"Donna and Linda!" squealed Mary. "It's so weird seeing you two huddled together like that, whispering away together, just like you used to be at the back of the class. It's like we've never left school. Anyway, listen, I'd like to introduce my husband Derek, we're having our third child in two months' time, that's if the little beggar actually comes out on time. The other two certainly didn't, did they, Derek?" And the ridiculously good-looking man at her side, tall and blond with chiselled cheekbones like a male model, smiled fondly down at her from his superior height and stroked her bump tenderly as if it and its mother were the two most precious things in the world to him.

"Well, that told us, anyway, didn't it?" said Donna, after the loved-up couple had wandered off arm-in-arm in search of food and a place to sit down for the hugely pregnant Mary. "Did you *see* him?"

"*See* him? Did I fuckin' *see* him? That's the kind of hunk I see in my dreams every night. How the hell did lumpy old Mary Walshe bag a divine stud like that?"

"Keep your voice down," giggled Donna. "That's what brought them over here in the bloody first place."

"They're on their third child and he's still looking at her like she's Marilyn Monroe crossed with the latest PlayStation? Jesus Christ. She must be doing something right."

"Maybe she gives fabulous blow-jobs." Donna giggled again, the booze gone straight to her head. She normally didn't drink during the week, and just had a glass or two of wine with Mick at the weekend, although of course Mick wouldn't be drinking wine, he'd be drinking beer. He called wine "the devil's piss" and maintained it had no effect on him whatsoever, which, given his great bulk, was probably true. Donna herself frequently abandoned her wine for one of Mick's beers. Tonight was a Wednesday night (whoever held a school reunion on, ironically, a school night?), supposedly with work in the morning for everyone, and here she was, pissed at barely half-eight.

She and Linda collapsed with hysterical laughter at the silly blow-job remark, clutching each other and shrieking and dropping food off their plates and onto the floor as if they'd never before heard anything quite so funny.

"Donna Ryan and Linda McCabe," said a voice softly from over their heads then, softly, and yet they could still hear it perfectly over the evocative eighties music. "Acting the maggot at the back of the class as usual. Right, well, it's detention for both of you so-called young ladies after school today. I'll put manners on the pair of you yet."

Donna looked up, and suddenly the whole world spun on its axis. She felt woozy and rooted to the spot. "J-Jeremy. Jeremy Larkin. H-h-how are you?"

"I'm good, thanks. And yourselves?" He included Linda politely in his question.

"I'm . . . We're . . . I mean, I'm fine. And . . . and so's Linda."

"That's right, Jeremy, I'm fine," piped up Linda. "Your impersonation of Old Wall-Eye just now was so good, it put the willies up me."

The hysterical laughter had all died away now, to be replaced with puzzlement and open curiosity on Linda's part and shock on Donna's.

"That's good to hear. That you're both fine, I mean. You're both looking very well, I must say. Actually, *um*, Donna?"

She looked up at him questioningly, dumbstruck, from her chair.

"I was, *ah*, I was just wondering if I could have a word with you? In private? I mean, I'm sorry to intrude like this, Linda. I won't keep her long, I promise."

"'S okay, I don't own her. Take as long as you like." Linda shrugged and melted away in search of any familiar faces, wineglass in one hand and a plate of food in the other.

"Could we go somewhere private, d'you think? To talk?" He held out a hand to Donna.

After the slightest hesitation, she nodded and took the proffered hand and allowed him to help her to her feet. Still clutching her wine glass, the plate of food abandoned now on the cluttered table, she found herself standing up in front of him, the top of her head reaching to his shoulder, which was how she'd remembered it. He was nearly as tall as Mick, but nowhere near as broad or as burly. He'd always been lean, but now, after twenty-five years, he looked thin, gaunt even. He still wore glasses, still had all his own hair and teeth, by the look of it, and was dressed deceptively casually in a suit that Donna was sure had cost an arm and a leg. She was close enough to smell the aftershave he wore. She didn't recognise it, but it reminded her of sailors, the sea, the old merchant ships that went round the world in search of strange new lands in centuries past. Something like Old Spice, maybe, but with a modern new twist. She found herself walking with him through the crowded hall, his hand on her elbow guiding her through the throng which, if it wasn't already loaded with drink, was at least decidedly merry by now. She felt like she didn't dare to breathe until they exited the function room and stood together in the relative quiet of the hotel lobby.

"I wasn't expecting to see you here tonight," she said. "I mean, you haven't come to any of the others. Any of the other reunions, I mean."

"Well, this is the big one, isn't it? The twenty-fifth? I got enough letters, emails and texts about it, anyway. I felt myself compelled to come." He gave a lopsided grin that went straight to her heartstrings.

"Linda and me are staying here tonight," she heard herself gabble suddenly. "In the hotel. In case the reunion went on till all hours. I mean, we have separate rooms. She's next door to me. Would you like to c-come upstairs with me? To my room, I mean? We could talk there?"

He nodded, and together they took the lift in total silence, standing apart, not touching, but Donna was painfully aware of his proximity. She unlocked the door of her room with fingers that trembled so much, he had to take the card gently from her hand and swipe it through for them both. Inside the room, he sat down on the edge of the bed, dropped his head into his hands and heaved a huge sigh, one that seemed to come all the way from his stylish, real leather boots.

After a long silence, during which Donna stood awkwardly, fiddling with the bits and pieces she'd put on the dressing-table earlier when she'd unpacked, he said quietly, so quietly she nearly didn't hear him: "How old would he be now?"

"Twenty-eight."

"That's what I thought, but the years go by so fast, you have trouble keeping track."

"Don't they just? Sometimes I can hardly believe it's been so long."

"I know what you mean. Have . . . have you ever been back there? To see the grave?"

"Not . . . not since my Aunty Noreen died."

He nodded, as if he understood. "I see. I don't want to upset you or anything, but I stopped off there the other day on my way back here. I don't suppose you know I've been living near Manchester for a while now?"

Donna shook her head, her eyes wide. "Did you see it?" she whispered, a lump in her throat so big she was surprised she was able to speak at all.

Jeremy nodded. "I took some pictures." He pulled his phone from his pocket, scrolled through it until he found what he was searching for, then held it out to her. "Take a look."

With shaking fingers, she took the phone and began to scroll.

It happened in the mid-eighties, when Donna was fourteen-going-on-fifteen. She went to a mixed secondary school in which the girls, as in nearly every area of life, vastly outnumbered the boys. Donna didn't hate school, but she didn't exactly love it either. She certainly hated Maths, Science and Irish, and just about tolerated most other subjects. She loved Home Economics, and spent her time in school daydreaming about a time when she could be done with books and lessons and meet a nice boy, get married, have a load of babies and keep house for her family, living happily ever after as the fairy tales dictated. She loved music and listened to it constantly, when she was doing her homework, studying for exams (oh God, how she hated those blasted exams!) and doing her jobs around the house. She watched MT USA on Network 2 television every Sunday afternoon while finishing up her homework for the weekend, and listened to the Top Twenty pop music chart on RTÉ Radio 2 on her little Coke-bottle-shaped transistor radio every Sunday lunchtime. She watched *Top of the Pops* every Thursday evening and discussed it with her friends in school the next day, and she fantasised about the members of pop bands Duran Duran and Spandau Ballet on the walk to and from school every day. She had an older sister, Anne-Marie, who was training to be a nurse, and two younger brothers, Aidan and Donall, who were still in primary school. Her mum Joan was a housewife, and her dad Terry worked for the Post Office, in the place where they sorted the mail ready for delivery. They had a dog called Spencer and a cat called Jinx. The cat was very much the boss of the dog.

Jeremy Larkin sat down the back of the class on his own. He was a tall, blond bespectacled kid who kept to himself. He should by rights have been fodder for the school bullies, being lanky and stringy in build and having a 'soft' name like Jeremy, but he was tall enough and just edgy enough that the bullies generally steered clear and only jeered at him from a safe distance instead. He was so quiet that teachers frequently forgot to call on him for answers to questions and, half the time, Donna wasn't even aware of his existence herself.

All that changed when, one dull Wednesday afternoon, she came out of school and found him waiting for her at the gate. He fell casually into step beside her and they walked silently along together for a bit, Donna more puzzled than flattered or excited. When they reached Donna's gate, Jeremy just grinned and said 'See you tomorrow,' and Donna, still rather bemused, said 'See you tomorrow' as well and that was that.

That night, Donna lay in bed and thought about how cute his parting smile had been. They fell into the habit of walking home together from school every day after that. It turned out that Jeremy only lived a few streets away from Donna, but that wasn't why he was walking her home.

Conversations gradually opened up between them. She discovered that Jeremy loved music too, and watched all the same TV shows and listened to the same radio programmes as Donna did. She also discovered that he was named Jeremy after an uncle of his, his father's brother, who'd died tragically young. This gave some meaning to his posh, poncy name, Jeremy thought, and Donna thought so too. Jeremy had a dog as well, a mongrel called Noodles, and a goldfish called JAWS 2. Apparently, he was the unscariest fish who ever drew breath and didn't exactly live up to his famous name. Donna laughed at that.

She laughed a lot when she was with Jeremy. He *made* her laugh. He was funny and witty and kind, and rarely, if ever, said horrible or nasty things about people. The more time she spent with him, the more she realised that she really, really liked him, maybe even *loved* him. She loved being with him, loved it when he kissed her, loved that he didn't have acne like most of the other boys she knew, but just clear, unmarked, slightly stubbly fair skin that prickled lightly against her own skin when he kissed her and held her close. He smelled nice and clean too, unlike some of the boys in her class, and his grin gave her a wobbly feeling low down in her stomach. She kept her friendship and developing relationship with Jeremy a secret from her parents. She only told Linda, her best friend, about it, and, as far as she knew, Jeremy didn't tell his own parents either.

"I hardly ever see them," he told Donna once. "They're always out at work, or playing golf or at their stupid bridge nights. Who cares about stupid bridge, anyway?" Donna got the impression that Jeremy's parents were more well-to-do than her own. His mother, Marilyn, ran a small antiques business and his father, Greg, was a funeral director. Jeremy's older brother, Damian, was in college studying to be an engineer and, a lot of the time, Jeremy was left to his own devices. He had his own key and frequently was obliged to make his own dinner when he got in alone from school. He wasn't alone every day though. Some days, Donna came with him for an hour or two, under the pretence of going to Linda's house to study for the Intermediate Certificate Exam.

"We don't have to do anything if you don't want to," he said, the first time they were alone together in his bedroom.

It was tidier than her two younger brothers' bedrooms, that was for sure, and it smelled a hell of a lot cleaner, too. She would always remember the way the breeze ruffled the spotless white nets that hung at the open window and blew them gently inwards. Such whiteness! She'd never before seen such dazzlingly white bedlinen, like something out of a television commercial for washing powder. She associated such whiteness with rich people only. Poor peoples' bedlinen was grey with all the washing.

"What if I want to?" Donna had replied shyly, before reaching up and kissing him tentatively on the lips. He had lovely lips. They were soft but firm, and never wet or slobbery.

He responded by kissing her hard in return and easing her back down onto his bed. He put his hand up her school jumper and fondled her breasts over her blouse, then, encouraged greatly when she sighed with pleasure and didn't push him away, he took his hand out of her jumper and gently, very slowly, inched it up under the green-and-grey checked skirt of her school uniform.

"I love you, Donna," he told her then, in total earnest, his glasses steaming up with the intensity of his breathing.

"You're the sweetest, kindest girl I've ever known in my whole life."

"I love you too," she said, removing his glasses and placing them carefully on his bedside table. "So, so much." She stroked his face, her two hands on either side of it, and they kissed for so long she felt like she was floating, melting, flying, doing all three at once.

"Is it okay?" he said, and she nodded, without a trace of hesitation or doubt.

She said goodbye to her virginity, and Jeremy to his, without a scrap of regret or anxiety. She knew he was the right person to take it (she didn't know how she knew this, she just knew, that's all), and she gave it gladly, willingly, because Jeremy was The One.

When her parents found out she was pregnant, they hit the roof. Her mother, a sharp-eyed woman, worked it out when she realised that Donna hadn't been taking any sanitary towels out of the 'lady things' cupboard for several months. She confronted her daughter, then slapped her in the face and called her a 'lying slut' for sneaking off to Jeremy's house to have sex when she was supposed to be round at Linda's house, studying for her Inter. Cert, which was now only a few months away. She told Donna's father, who drove the three of them round to Jeremy's house straightaway, to confront the boy and his parents. It mustn't have been one of their bridge nights, because Marilyn and Greg Larkin were both at home, and so was Jeremy, up in his bedroom as usual, playing music and doing his homework. He was shocked into almost complete silence by the sight of all four parents arguing furiously about whose fault it had been that two teenagers of barely fifteen years old had been allowed to have unprotected sex in a completely empty house without either set of parents knowing about it. The Ryans (Terry and Joan) accused the Larkins (Greg and Marilyn) of being lax parents and Jeremy of being a latchkey kid. The Larkins took grave exception to this and Greg Larkin landed a swift box to the jaw of his opposite number, Terry Ryan. Terry Ryan, solid and burly from years of carting around heavy mail sacks on his back and shoulders, retaliated with a punch that broke both Greg Larkin's nose and all chances of good relations between the two families forever. (Greg Larkin was also obliged to take a back seat in the funeral-directing business he worked in for several weeks, lest the bandaging round his broken nose convey to clients an impression of thuggishness which, of course, was all wrong for the company's image.) It *was* mutually agreed, however, that neither teenager would be allowed to associate with the other *ever again*, even though the child growing in Donna's stomach was every bit as much Jeremy's doing as it was Donna's, as much Jeremy's child as it was Donna's.

It was decided by the Ryans that Donna would not return to school until after the summer. She was packed off, as soon as a passage on the ferry could be arranged, to her Aunty Noreen's house in Manchester, with her disgruntled sister Anne-Marie accompanying her on the boat to make sure she got there. "I've better things to do at home than being stuck here, babysitting my stupid slutty sister who couldn't keep her legs closed," she kept grumbling, conveniently forgetting all the times she'd had illicit sex with her own boyfriend. But she hadn't been caught, and Donna had, that was the difference. Aunty Noreen, a widow and Joan Wilson's (her maiden name) older sister, said she'd be happy to keep Donna with her for the few months until the baby was born, so long as the Ryans could contribute a few bob every week towards her keep. The Ryans, being staunch Catholics, naturally couldn't openly approve of the idea of an abortion for their daughter, but privately they thought the whole time that it would have been the best, cleanest and quickest solution all round to their 'problem', if only their religion sanctioned it. Anne-Marie went back home to Dublin, disgusted with her stupid younger sister's foolish and ill-advised actions and the way it was inconveniencing her, Anne-Marie, and Donna was left in Manchester with Noreen, frightened, disorientated, desperately missing Jeremy and their time together, afraid for her future and the future of her child, hers and Jeremy's child. She felt like she had lost her voice, her ability to open her mouth and say what she wanted to happen. It didn't matter anyway. The adults were in control, Jeremy was nowhere to be seen, and Donna was alone.

Noreen arranged for Donna to have her baby in the nearest maternity hospital to them, and for the baby to be given up for adoption straightaway after the birth, or as soon as it could be managed, because that was what the grown-ups wanted. Donna would stay in Manchester for the summer, and return to Dublin, and school, in time for September. She'd miss her Inter. Cert, of course, but maybe she could repeat the year and take it *next* summer instead. Joan and Terry would put it about that she'd been sent to England to stay with her sick Aunty Noreen to help her recover from a hysterectomy and, then, when Noreen was able to look after herself again, Donna would come back home to Dublin and slot back into her life there like nothing had ever happened.

They had it all worked out, the grown-ups, and Donna deeply resented them for it.

She lay in her narrow bed in Aunty Noreen's box-room at night and talked and sang softly to her bump, telling it that, whatever happened, whatever the grown-ups forced her to do, she would always love it, always want it, and would always be there for it, no matter where in the world they ended up. When her contractions started one hot, sticky night in July, she was excited, convinced that she and her baby would somehow end up together, would somehow be all right. It would all work out, she told herself, all through that night and a good part of the next day as the contractions tore her apart and made her cry out, without even knowing she did, for a Jeremy who couldn't even hear her, he was so far away.

No one expected the baby to be stillborn, least of all Donna. When the nurse handed her the little white-faced bundle with closed eyes, she stared at it uncomprehendingly, asking the nurse repeatedly: Why won't his eyes open? Why isn't he crying? What's wrong with him? What's wrong with my baby? What's wrong with Baby Craig? She wasn't even aware she'd named him, let alone why she'd chosen the name she had. When the reality of what had happened began gradually to dawn on her, the doctors swooped in and sedated her.

She went home to Dublin after the funeral, no longer a child, no longer a girl, but a broken woman. She slept through most of the month of August, willing it to be over so that school could start and she could see Jeremy again. Her parents were content enough to leave her alone. They had no idea what to say to her, or what she needed. Everyone agreed that it was for the best if she just slept, got some proper rest.

When school started and there was no sign of Jeremy, she panicked. When one of their classmates told her that Jeremy's family had moved house over the summer (no one seemed to know where they'd moved to) and he wouldn't be returning to Saint Catherine's, she had a breakdown.

Six months later she met Mick for the first time.

The grave looked old and weather-beaten, but you could still read the name on it — *Craig Ryan* — and it looked like some caretaker or other had cut the grass around it recently enough, as it wasn't too overgrown or anything. Also, someone (she guessed Jeremy) had placed a fresh bunch of flowers up against the headstone, the yellows and whites of the gorgeous bouquet standing out hopefully against the weathered grey of the stone. She looked for a long time at the pictures, then she handed the phone back to Jeremy. Seeing her son's grave for the first time in so long had felt like being punched in the gut with the past, and it was a while before she could speak.

In any event, it was Jeremy who spoke first.

"So, how have you been, anyway? I expect you've got married and had a load of kids by now? It was always what you wanted, wasn't it, and you were born for it, anyway. Born to be a wife and mother. That's a compliment, by the way, not an insult. I bet you're a great mother."

"I hope my kids think so."

"So you *do* have kids, then? How many?"

"Three. I married Mick McKenna, from school. You didn't know him. He only joined the school in Fifth Year, after you left. We've been married a long time now."

"I'm glad for you, Donna. You were a lovely girl, and you're a lovely woman. You deserve it. Do they know about . . .?"

Donna shook her head. "Craig? No. No one knows. What about you? Married with kids?" She was surprised to find how interested she was in his answer. She loved Mick and her children, James, Adam and Olivia, with all her heart. But this was Jeremy, her first love, and the father of her first child.

"No kids. I had a long-term partner who died last month."

"Oh, that's awful, Jeremy. I'm so sorry. What was her name?"

"Antoine." He grinned.

Donna's eyebrows shot up. "You're . . . gay? Or . . . bisexual? I . . . didn't know."

"Gay. Well, how would you?" He grinned again. "You were my one and only girlfriend, Donna Ryan. And our baby was . . . was the closest I ever came to being a dad."

"I'm so sorry, Jeremy." And she meant it. At least she'd had Mick and the kids. At least she'd had the chance to be a mother. "What happened to Antoine? Was he sick for a while or was it sudden?"

"He died of pneumonia. AIDS-related, so I guess you'd hardly call it sudden, or a surprise. He'd been HIV-positive for as long as I'd known him. We were together fifteen years."

"Oh God, Jeremy, I'm so sorry. That's . . . that's truly terrible." She couldn't help it. The tears came unbidden and started to fall. A thought occurred to her. "Are you . . . I mean, do you have . . .?"

"AIDS? HIV? No. We were always careful."

"And . . . and what are you going to do now? Go back to Manchester?"

He sighed and shook his head. "From here, from Dublin, I mean, I'm off to Canada to live. For good, I hope. Antoine was

French-Canadian, you see, and he was very close to his family. When his body was flown home to Canada for the funeral, with me watching over it, they were very good to me. There's a lodge in the grounds of Antoine's parents' house that's sitting idle. They've offered it to me to live in, and Antoine's brother has an IT company with openings for a computer science guy, which would suit me. I flew back to Manchester to put our house there up for sale and give notice in my job. This is literally my last stop-off on my way to the Brave New World. Once I get there, I don't plan on ever coming back."

The grin he gave her brought her right back to the mid-eighties and their brief, ill-fated romance.

"Why did you come here?" she said, leaving the armchair she was sitting in and coming to sit beside him on the big bouncy hotel bed. "To the reunion, I mean? Was it really just because it's the twenty-fifth anniversary one?"

"Only partly. I saw that you'd clicked 'going' to the event on the St. Catherine's Facebook page. I wanted to see you one more time before I left this part of the world for good."

"I'm so glad you did. But it's brought it all back."

"I know. I'm sorry for that." He held out a hand to her and she took it, their two joined hands resting on the bedcovers between them. It felt to Donna, not sexual at all, but more like a gesture of genuine friendship between two people who'd once shared something briefly beautiful and very, very sad.

"How did you know where to find the grave?" she asked him then.

He gave a short laugh. "A friend of Antoine's was a private dick."

"I see. Did . . . did you love him very much? Antoine, I mean?"

"He was the light of my life. I've been fumbling around in the dark ever since he left, like a light's suddenly gone off and I can't find the switch to turn it back on again."

Donna couldn't help it. The tears came again. He gently unlaced his fingers from hers and put his arm round her heaving shoulders.

"Can I stay here with you tonight?" he asked. "I've a room booked somewhere else, but they won't care whether I'm there or not as long as I've paid, which I have."

She nodded. "Of course you can. But I can't . . . I mean, I can't . . . *do* anything. I love Mick. I've never been unfaithful to him."

He grinned again. "That's okay, Donna. I doubt if I'm capable yet anyway. I just want to hold you, be near you for the last time."

And that's what they did. They got undressed and got into bed together, eventually falling asleep with their arms around each other, after talking softly for a while about Craig, St. Catherine's, Antoine, Mick, the kids, and Jeremy's hopes for his new life in Canada.

When morning came, Jeremy dressed and left to go to his own hotel.

"I'll never forget you, Donna Ryan," he told her before he went.

Her voice was too thick with tears to manage a reply, but they hugged tightly and she kissed him hard on the mouth, just once, to show him what he meant to her. Then, when he was gone, she got dressed herself and went next door to wake Linda. She had a hell of a lot of explaining to do.

Chapter 6

MAROON-VICKY

"Ed, this is Maroon. She'll look after you. You're in good hands." After delivering the words in her usual brisk and business-like no-nonsense manner, Magda gave Vicky a little push into the room and clicked the door shut firmly behind her.

No one would now disturb them for the hour, but when the hour was up, the light over the door would begin to flash red. This reminded the customer, as well as Vicky, that the hour was up, and it minimised opportunities for the customer to say "Ah, come on, love, just another fifteen minutes, yeah? It's not much to ask, is it?" Vicky could just shake her head regretfully and point at the red light as if to say, "Sorry, bud, if it was up to me, sure, but the Big Boss has me on a timer."

Vicky, who'd only been doing this job for a few weeks now, usually spent the hour waiting for the red light to make its appearance. Never once had the time flown by so quickly or so pleasantly that the red light had taken her by surprise. She was usually counting off the minutes in her mind as the customer laboured away on top of her, forcing herself to think of all the good, useful things she could do for Andrew with the money she was making. Now Vicky went and seated herself on the bed alongside the lanky-looking, middle-aged man whom Magda had introduced as Ed and, with an inward sigh that came all the way from the soles of her high-heeled shoes, held out a hand for him to shake.

"Nice to meet you, Ed," she said, making herself smile.

"You too, Maroon," the man called Ed replied enthusiastically and, in truth, his long lugubrious face had seemed to brighten up when Vicky had appeared on his horizon. Everything about him seemed long and droopy, from his long face, that Vicky guessed was accustomed to wearing a hangdog expression, to his long droopy hands and long, awkward-looking feet, the kind of feet that people in sitcoms tripped over for laughs from the audience.

Apart from being long and droopy everywhere, he wasn't exactly hideous, with shaggy, collar-length dark hair and big dark sad eyes like a puppy dog's. He was probably in his early-to-mid forties, dressed in unfashionable grey slacks, grey slip-on shoes and a dark-green jumper with a brown-and-green checked shirt underneath it. He could have been attractive in a certain light, if it weren't for the depressing air of dejection that emanated from him so strongly that she could almost smell it. Vicky tried not to judge people by appearances, as you could so often be wrong, but she had the strong sense that this Ed fella was not a happy man. He was someone who'd probably long since resigned himself to leading a very ordinary, humdrum, even boring existence, but that didn't necessarily mean he wasn't as resentful as hell about it underneath. Sometimes the dreariest-looking men were the ones who simmered with the most bitterness and rage under the surface, rage against life for passing them by or just for handing them a raw deal.

"What can I do for you, Ed?" She tried to inject a note of friendliness into her voice, as if whatever she could do for him would be a pleasure. Nothing like a big fat lie to get a relationship, even a business one, off to a flying start.

"Could . . . could we just talk for a bit first?"

"It's your hour, Ed. You can do whatever you like." As long as he didn't bore the arse off her for the hour with his petty problems, and then *still* expect to have sex, just as the hour was bloody ending. "Tell me, what d'you do for a living?"

She'd quickly worked out that the ones who wanted to talk only ever wanted to talk about themselves, so, if she quickly got them started on a topic from their own lives, it dispensed with the necessity for any *umm*ing and *aah*ing and any attempt on their part to ask *her* any personal questions. One guy had actually asked her what she did herself for a living. When she'd forced a plastic smile to her face and spread her hands to indicate the small room with the bed, one chair and a bedside table which they were currently occupying, at least he'd had the good grace to go bright red with embarrassment, the dope, and he'd quickly mumbled "Oh yeah, right, sorry."

"I'm a taxi driver," said Ed.

"That must be interesting. Meeting so many different people in a day, I mean."

Ed shrugged. "Not really. I don't know. I suppose so."

"Wasn't there a book out a few years ago by an Irish taxi driver, *Recollections of a Taxi Driver,* or something like that?"

Again, the helpless shrug. "I dunno. Maybe. I don't remember."

Jesus. This one was hard work. "Are you married, Ed?"

she said then, even though she could clearly see the thin gold band on his wedding finger. Maybe talking about his bad marriage (they nearly all had bad marriages; why else would they be coming to her?) would animate him a little bit. They nearly all liked to vent a bit about how shit their home lives were and what total wagons their other halves were.

Ed nodded miserably. Then, to her alarm, two fat tears rolled down his long, stubbly-looking cheeks and landed with a plop on his lap. "She's having an affair."

Oh shit. She hadn't actually meant to make him cry, the big lanky muppet. "Oh, I'm sure she's not. What makes you say that?" she asked him brightly, too brightly.

"I caught them having sex in our bed."

There wasn't much comfort she could offer to that. "Oh. I'm sorry. Is she going to stop seeing him? The other fella, I mean? Now that she knows you know?"

He shook his head. "I wish. They're saving up for a place together. He's married too, you see, to someone else. As soon as they've got enough money together for a flat or something, she'll be off."

"That sounds miserable, Ed. A miserable situation to be in."

"It is." Two more plump tears blazed a trail down his thin cheeks. "She hasn't had sex with me since she started going with this other fella. That's two years now. I haven't had sex with anyone in two years." To Vicky's horror, he burst into tears, proper loud messy snotty sobs.

Oh Jesus. Did she look like a bleedin' marriage guidance counsellor or something? Her heart sinking, she said: "Well, would you like to have sex with me now, Ed? It's what you've paid for, after all, isn't it? Would that cheer you up a bit, do you think?" She tried not to sound like she was babying him (she was an escort, after all, not a bloody babysitter), but, as a mother, it was hard not to slip into using the kind of tone and words that comforted.

Ed sniffled and blew his nose loudly on a wad of tissues she handed him from the box on the little bedside locker. "Dunno," he shrugged. "Maybe. I don't know."

Jesus, Ed, did you have this much trouble making decisions in your marriage? If you did, I don't blame your wife for finding someone else. Aloud, she said: "Well, it's up to you, Ed. Whatever you're most comfortable with. If you just want to keep talking, we can do that too."

"I like you, Maroon," he said suddenly, reaching over and taking one of her hands in his. "You're very beautiful. I expect a load of guys have told you that already."

"Not as many as you might think." She accompanied her words with a light, tinkly little self-deprecating laugh and a dismissive flap of her hand.

"Would you go out with me sometime? I mean, on a date? A proper date?"

"I'm sorry, Ed," she told him firmly. "I have a boyfriend." Not true, this bit, but he didn't know that. "Plus, we're not allowed to mix business with pleasure. I'd lose my job, and I *need* my job." She had this bit off by heart by now and trotted it out any time a would-be Romeo made a similar suggestion, which happened surprisingly frequently. She felt a pang when she saw his hangdog expression deepen into something approaching pure misery, but she crushed it down. It's only a job, she told herself. I am not responsible for the mental well-being of this adult male I've never met before who's old enough to look after himself.

"You must keep yourself always separate from customer," Magda, her Polish boss, had counselled her before she'd started this whole 'escort' thing. "They may have saddest lives you've ever come across, but it is not your problem. You are there to do job, nothing more. You are not responsible for them. Do not permit them to guilt you into feeling bad for them. They are all adults. They can solve own problems."

Vicky remembered Magda's words of wisdom now and held firm.

"Are you absolutely sure you wouldn't like to have sex?" she said. She couldn't believe she was encouraging, even pressuring, a client into having sex with her, but she didn't think she could spend another nearly forty minutes talking to this man who was so downbeat he was actually draining her of her will to live.

After a long silence, he mumbled: "I'm . . . I'm not very good at it. At sex."

Really, Ed? No kidding. You surprise me. "That doesn't matter, Ed. No one's judging you here."

"You promise you won't laugh at me if I'm no good?"

"I wouldn't dream of it, Ed."

"My wife used to laugh at me."

"Well, I'm sorry about that, Ed, but no one's going to laugh at you here, I promise you."

"Can I touch your, erm, your tits?"

"It's all part of the package, Ed," she said, resisting the urge to get up and just walk out.

"And your, *erm*, your down-theres?" He pointed to his

own crotch, just in case she was in any doubt as to his meaning.

"Like I said, Ed, it's all kind of a package deal type of thing," she told him lamely. Vicky, who was never normally a tooth-grinder, found that she was beginning to grind them now, quite badly.

"Can I go to the toilet first?"

What am I, your fucking kindergarten teacher? Jesus. She pasted a brightly artificial smile on her face and indicated with a wave of her arm the door to the tiny ensuite toilet and shower cubicle. She got undressed and into bed while he peed (she could hear it through the door) and had a condom in its plastic packaging ready from the saucer on the bedside table. (She was fairly sure that only one would be necessary.) When Ed emerged from the toilet he sat down on the bed and began to remove his shoes and socks with all the enthusiasm of a man going to the gallows. Off came the unfashionable grey slacks next, followed by the dark-green jumper and the brown-and-green checked shirt. He folded everything neatly and placed them on the chair by the bed. Still wearing his white sleeveless vest and a pair of navy-blue underpants (at least they weren't grubby, baggy, saggy off-white Y-fronts), he dived quickly under the covers and lay on his back as stiff and still as an ironing board. Vicky sighed inwardly. So she was supposed to do all the work here as well then, was she, even though she'd already busted her hump conversationally? Well, it wouldn't be the first time. She put her hand gingerly in the vicinity of the navy-blue underpants and began to manipulate what she found there, her eyes screwed tightly shut the whole time as she forced herself to focus solely on the new pair of trainers she'd be able to buy Andrew with the money she'd be making today, just by being here, now, with Ed. Mister Ed. Stifling a giggle, Vicky realised that the long-faced, lugubrious-looking Ed reminded her of no one so much as Mister Ed, the talking horse from the old seventies sitcom that she'd seen repeats of when she was growing up. The giggle erupted without warning, but she quickly turned it into a moan of passion before Ed could cop it and glare suspiciously at her. When she'd achieved something resembling an erection in the vicinity of the navy-blue underpants, she manoeuvred both of them, not without some difficulty as it must be said that Ed wasn't being much help, into the missionary position and put the condom on him herself. (Ed looked at it helplessly, as if he'd never seen one before and genuinely didn't know what he was supposed to do with it.) Ed huffed and puffed above her for something approximating seven seconds. After approximately seven seconds, he sighed blissfully and said: "Wow, that was fantastic. Thank you, Miss Maroon, so very much."

Bemused, Vicky conveyed the condom and its contents *(don't look at it, just don't look at it, she ordered herself sternly, and do NOT think about it either)* to the waste-paper basket beside the bedside table. She literally hadn't felt a thing, and yet here was Mister Ed, grinning like the Cheshire cat all over his long thin face.

"You enjoyed that then, Ed?"

"*Neighhhh*," he replied.

"What? Sorry, what did you say?"

"I said I loved it, thanks."

"Oh, right. Well, you're welcome."

"Can I come and see you again, Miss Maroon?" he asked

her as he was leaving. The red light over the door was flashing steadily now, and would continue to do so until Ed left.

With the fake smile rigidly in place, she nodded. "You know where I am. And there's no need to call me, *um*, Miss Maroon. Maroon will do just fine."

"I do. Know where you are, I mean. And thanks again, Maroon. That was magical." And then he was gone, swishing his tail behind him, clip-clopping out the door and leaving Vicky to light a cigarette with trembling fingers, even though they weren't supposed to smoke in the rooms. Never mind, she'd open the window in a minute. Jesus. Mister Ed. There was something so mopey and depressing about him that Vicky's mood was now thoroughly downbeat. He was a dozen times worse than the man who made her call him 'Daddy' during intercourse, or the guy who got her to tickle his willy with a feather duster he brought from home. Worse, even, than the man who made her flick his testicles repeatedly with the middle finger of her right hand until his John Thomas eventually stood up of its own accord. She had Repetitive Strain Injury now from doing that.

"I'm handing in my notice," she announced dramatically once she'd finished her smoke and joined Magda in reception.

Magda was leaning over the counter, chatting in Polish to Piotr, the gigantic shaven-headed security guard in a suit who sat in his usual chair with his newspaper and phone and one huge booted foot crossed over the opposing knee. No one ever misbehaved when Piotr was around. Usually he didn't even have to lift a finger. Just the sight and appearance of him was enough.

"I mean it this time. I can't do this any more. I'm done."

"Ed is heavy going, yes?" Magda sympathised.

"Heavy going? Funerals and bereavement are heavy going. Getting a life-threatening illness is heavy going. Haemorrhoids are heavy going. Ed is in a different class altogether."

"Which Ed you mean? Not Ed Half-Dead? You poor thing! I've had him before," said Irina, Piotr's older sister and the person who'd first suggested that Vicky get involved in the 'escort' business, as she breezed through the door of the agency, all ready for her own shift. Vicky normally only worked while Andrew was in school, but Irina was child-free and could work as late as she liked. "Don't worry your head about Ed. He's harmless."

"I'm not *worried* about Ed," Vicky said crossly. "I just don't want to ever see him again, that's all. Or any of them. I'm just not cut out for this. I'm not a fucking machine. I can't just do things like this and not feel them, or not have them affect me in some way."

"Of *course* you are not machine," said Irina soothingly. She seated herself on the couch in the waiting-room and patted the seat beside her.

Vicky sat down reluctantly, not wanting to be talked round, to be persuaded, like she'd allowed herself to be persuaded before. This time, she was really packing it in. She didn't care what Irina or Magda said. She just wasn't cut out for this job, like she'd said. Irina crossed her long elegant legs and lit a cigarette, ignoring Magda's disapprovingly raised eyebrows, then offering one to Vicky. Vicky took it gratefully, even though she'd just had one.

"Just think of Andrew," Irina said. Vicky had told her a lot about her personal circumstances when they'd both been office cleaners together. "I'm not saying that money is everything. But isn't he happier since you've been able to afford a few more things for him?"

Vicky sighed and bit her lip. Fourteen-year-old Andrew's life, with his diagnosis of Autism Spectrum Disorder and Attention Deficit Hyperactivity Disorder ever present in the background, was certainly much happier and more settled now that she was able to afford new clothes and decent food for him and a whole rake of fantastic extra-curricular activities at the special school where he'd been lucky enough to get a place the year before last. Single mothers in council flats in deprived areas of Dublin didn't always have the money to give their kids the comfortable lives they deserved. She supposed she was lucky to have been given the chance to earn a bit of extra cash. Her Aunty June, when Vicky had broken the news to her of her new 'job', had been silent for a while and then she'd sighed and said: "Well, you've got the looks, anyway. I suppose you might as well use them while you've still got them and make a bit of money out of them. Make a bit of money out of men too, the bastards. Just be careful, Vicky love, that's all."

"Autism is a hard cross to bear," Irina said now, puffing away on her cigarette. "You know my mother's cousin Paulina from Poland? She had the gallstones and when they were taking them out I did her cleaning job in her place and that's how you and I meet?"

Vicky nodded, remembering perfectly well the conversation in which the gorgeous Polish Irina had suggested to her that she would make tons more money doing escort work for Magda than she ever would cleaning office toilets. "Well, Paulina has grown-up son with autism. He was hard to mind and so, one day, she had to put him in home. She had no choice. They care for him well there. She clean offices over here and send money back to Poland for son in home. Is best thing for everyone."

Piotr was nodding earnestly in agreement with his sister's interpretation of the situation regarding their mother's cousin's differently-abled son.

Vicky sighed. "Just don't stick me with Droopy Ed again," she appealed to the waiting-room at large. "What did you call him, Ed Half-Dead? I know what you mean."

Magda laughed. "He has already made repeat booking for next week before he leave. He has paid in advance and everything. You must have done very good job."

Vicky groaned out loud and put her head in her hands.

"Cheer up," grinned Irina. "Always let it be like the water off the back of the duck. On Saturday afternoon you will come with me to Smithfield and we will have our fortunes told. You will hear news of many wonderful things that await you in future."

"Our fortunes?" Vicky was sceptical. "You surely don't believe in all stuff that, do you?"

Irina nodded eagerly. "Oh yes. I have my tarot cards read every month without fail by a little woman in Smithfield who is a marvel with the cards and the crystals. Also she do the big one, the ball, you know? The crystal ball? Plus I am also little bit psychic myself. I had a powerful vision once that Piotr's wife in Poland was going to try to kill him. One night she go for him with bread knife. See the scar on his face, just below left eye? Wife did that. If I had not warned him beforehand to be on his guard, he might not be here with us today. Isn't that right, Piotr?"

The enormous giant of a man she referred to as her 'baby brother' nodded gravely.

"Wow," Vicky said. That was quite a story. "*Erm*, if it's not a stupid question, why was Piotr's wife trying to kill him? I mean, he wasn't being abusive to her or anything, was he?"

"Of course not," Irina said indignantly. "Piotr would cut off own hand before he would raise it to a woman. Am I not right, Piotr darling?"

And her baby brother, a quiet man who usually only spoke when he had something to say, nodded ever more vigorously.

"She try to kill him because by accident he flatten her pussy."

"He flattened her *what?*" echoed Vicky.

"He did *what?*" said Magda. It took a lot to surprise Magda. Normally, she was unsurprise-able. But now her perfectly shaped eyebrows were practically through the roof.

"Her pussy, her pussy," Irina repeated impatiently. "You know? *Miaow, miaow*. Her cat."

"He sat on his wife's cat? Was the cat okay?" Vicky, a cat-lover, would have loved a moggy of her own but Andrew didn't much care for cats.

Irina spread her hands philosophically in her brother's direction. "Would you be, if Piotr sit on you?"

Eyeing the man's enormous bulk dubiously, Vicky said: "I guess not."

Magda's phone rang just then. She had a brief conversation with someone, then she rang off and said briskly: "Okay, girls, back to work. Mr. Rogers is on his way in. He wants a proper massage first and then, well, you know how it goes. Who wants him?"

"I'll take him," Irina said with a shrug and a grin at Vicky, who was looking somewhat less downbeat now. "He pay extra if I call him 'Uncle Joe' and ask no questions why he want this. No rest for the wicked, eh, Vicks?"

And Vicky grinned back and rolled her eyes, shaking her head. What else could she do? There were times in life when you just had to stop bitching and get on with it.

On Saturday, they went together as planned to the fortune-teller, Madame Zara, who operated out of a tiny, cluttered barely lit room at the back of a busy little vintage clothing shop in Smithfield. On the little table in front of Madame Zara, a heavily made-up woman in her fifties gorgeously festooned with coloured glass beads and feathers, reposed a set of tarot cards and a purple velvet drawstring bag containing crystals, and there was also an actual crystal ball, big, round and heavy-looking like the ones in the films.

Madame Zara did Irina's tarot card reading for her, seemingly to Irina's approval, and then she turned to Vicky and said in her strangely accented voice (Eastern European like Irina, maybe, thought Vicky): "Do you have a question for me, my dear?"

"What?" Vicky's mind went temporarily blank.

"You must ask her question to which you want answer," put in Irina excitedly. "That is how reading works."

"What kind of question?" Vicky said, her mind only able to conjure up questions like who discovered America and in what year was the battle of Waterloo.

"You know, about life, love, marriage, babies, winning the Lottery, things like that," prompted Irina. "Ask her if you'll find love in the future."

"Will I find love in the future?" parroted Vicky, feeling embarrassed and awkward. She just wanted the whole pointless experience to be over. She was only here because Irina had made her come. She didn't even believe in the stupid tarot cards and stupid crystals and crystal balls. How could an old lady wearing more slap than an RTÉ newsreader be able to see into her, Vicky's future? No one could do that.

"Give me your left hand," said Madame Zara, inspecting it closely when Vicky, nudged by Irina, reluctantly proffered it. "I see that you are not married?"

That's easy enough to work out from the lack of a wedding ring, thought Vicky as she rolled her eyes at Irina, who rewarded her with a sharp dig in the ribs.

"And you have endured much hardship in your life," went on the fortune-teller as she scrutinised Vicky's palm.

Again, no prizes for guessing that I've scrubbed floors and cleaned toilets with these mitts, Vicky told herself, shaking her head in disbelief at the thought that people actually took this mumbo-jumbo seriously. Irina was frowning at her, indicating mammy-like to her to stop fidgeting and sit up and pay attention to Madame Zara.

"I see a young man here," said the fortune-teller now. "A young man with dark hair who means the sun, moon and stars to you."

"Did you tell her about Andrew?" Vicky asked Irina sharply.

Irina shook her head. "Of course not. I tell her nothing. Why would I?"

"Will this . . . this young man with the dark hair have a happy life?" Vicky asked the fortune-teller urgently, realising suddenly that she cared much more about the answer to this question than about anything to do with herself.

Madame Zara deliberated for a minute, then she nodded firmly. "Yes. Thanks to the strong and positive female presence in his life, this young man will choose the right path for himself. He will steer a course through life that will bring him much fulfilment and contentment."

Thank God, thought Vicky, annoyed with herself for having tears in her eyes. Jesus. It wasn't as though she even believed in this . . . this nonsensical quackery, this bullshit. Irritably, she brushed her sleeve across her eyes, hoping the others hadn't noticed. Still, it was just such a relief to hear someone, even this over-made-up charlatan, say that Andrew was going to be all right. That was her biggest fear in life, that Andrew, her baby, her darling, her pride and joy, wouldn't be all right, that he wouldn't have a happy and fulfilling life and that it would all somehow be her fault for being a single mother with none of the advantages that some luckier families had.

"Will he live a normal life?" she blurted out.

The fortune-teller deliberated again, then nodded. "Yes, within the constraints that life has set for him."

That's the autism, thought Vicky excitedly, looking at Irina with shining eyes. The autism was the cause of the constraints the fortune-teller talked about, but he would have a normal, happy and fulfilling life despite these constraints! She wanted to sob with pure relief.

"I see bars now, but not for the boy," Madame Zara intoned. "Someone else you know, perhaps?"

Vicky shot a sidelong glance at Irina, but Irina shrugged as if to say: '*I* didn't tell her.'

Madame Zara was looking at Vicky penetratingly.

Vicky flushed and said quietly: "Yes. I know who that is." Andrew's father, Tommy Keeley, had been in and out of prison since Andrew had been born, mostly for petty crime offences but, this time, he was doing a longer stretch for taking part in a burglary in which a security guard had been shot in the shoulder.

"Tell her if she will find love herself in the future," burst in Irina impatiently. As hard-headed and coolly practical as she seemed to be when it came to making her way in the world (an immigrant working in the sex trade), she apparently had a romantic streak a mile wide in her as well.

"Let me look," Madame Zara said. She then gazed at Vicky's palm so intently and for so long that Vicky began to grow self-conscious and wished she could yank her hand away, if it wouldn't seem rude. "I see a tall, dark handsome stranger," said the fortune-teller, after what seemed like an interminable pause.

Vicky groaned inwardly and rolled her eyes again at Irina, who shrugged and flapped her hands at Vicky as if to say, just hear her out, will you? Give her a chance. Vicky sighed and turned her attention back to Madame Zara, who was getting animated and really into her stride now.

"In one year or perhaps two," she was saying, "but no more than two, a tall, dark handsome man will come into your life and change it for the better. You will find love and happiness with this man. I hear the peeter-patter of tiny feet as well."

"You most certainly do *not*," retorted Vicky, outraged. She already had a baby, her Andrew, and all her energies went into seeing that he was all right. Another baby would take the focus away from Andrew, and she didn't want that. It wouldn't be fair to Andrew. It was bad enough that he had a single mum in a council flat as his care-giver and closest relative, but presenting him with a lowlife jailbird for a father was just taking the piss. She was on the Pill and she always used condoms with the clients as well. She was taking no chances.

"*The peeter-patter of tiny feet,*" insisted Madame Zara in her exotic accent. "This will be a family of much love."

Huh! Don't forget the long sea voyage, Vicky said sarcastically in her mind. Can't have a tall, dark handsome stranger without a long sea voyage in there somewhere.

"Together, you and this man will take a long sea voyage together –"

Vicky's eyebrows shot right up into her hairline.

"Across the ocean to the Land of the Giant Corporate Mouse, and it will bring you all much happiness."

"The Land of the Giant Corporate Mouse? Ah here, I'm done with this."

Vicky stood up and started pulling on her coat. She'd been happy enough to hear nice things about Andrew's future, but this stuff about tall handsome strangers and long sea voyages to the Land of the Giant Rat, or whatever it was, was just utter bullshit.

"It's been, *erm*, interesting to meet you, Madame Zara, but I have to go now. Be seeing you, okay? Cheerio."

She waited outside the vintage clothing shop while Irina paid the woman. It was Irina's treat, even though Vicky, always fiercely independent, had wanted to pay her own share.

"Cross her palm with silver, did you?" she asked Irina with an amused grin when Irina emerged from the shop, blinking in the unaccustomed sunlight after the shadowy murkiness of Madame Zara's cluttered lair.

Irina looked puzzled, then she said: "No, no, she have card machine. She take only VISA and MasterCard."

Vicky said nothing. To some things in life, there was nothing you *could* say.

The weeks went by. Ed continued to come every Monday morning to Stiletto's Kiss-A-Gram Agency & Massage Parlour to see Vicky, and every Monday morning he had virtually nothing new to say about anything. He did, however, continue to act like she'd just handed him the Holy Grail gift-wrapped in hundred euro notes every time he attained a climax (not without a great deal of manful effort on Vicky's part), and every week Vicky brushed off his fulsome thanks and gratitude with embarrassed flaps of her hand.

Then, one Monday morning, as they sat together on the bed prior to Vicky's ritual coaxing of him into intercourse (Ed liked the ritual, and he especially liked the coaxing), he blurted out suddenly: "I'm sorry, but I don't think I'm going to be able to come here any more."

Don't get my hopes up, Eddie baby, please. Out loud, keeping her voice deliberately light and casual, she simply said: "Oh yeah? Why's that, Ed?"

"It's me and Margie," he mumbled, flushing red with the effort of making conversation. "We're getting back together."

Vicky knew she really shouldn't encourage Ed to talk further, but she was curious enough to say: "What? Is she giving up her lover, then?"

"I wish. Nah, he's only gone and dumped her, hasn't he?

His wife found out about them and threatened to put his nuts in a vice and feed them to their pit bull if he didn't drop her straightaway. Drop Margie, my wife, that is. She's a demon. The pit bull, I mean, not Margie."

"That sounds painful all right," agreed Vicky. "I'm not surprised he went along with it. So, how do you feel about you and Margie getting back together, then?"

"It's nothing much to get excited about, Maroon," he told her glumly. "She's made it clear she's only staying with me until something better comes along. And she's told me I can't come here again, not if I expect her to sleep in our bed with me ever again."

"You told her about us?" *Vicky, you idiot, there IS no 'us.'*

Ed nodded. "It just kind of slipped out. She said she was surprised I was man enough to satisfy a prostitute every week like I've been doing." Seeing Vicky wince at the use of the word 'prostitute', he immediately backtracked. "Sorry, sorry, Maroon, that was Margie's word, not mine. I wouldn't expect her to understand the . . . the beauty of what you and I had together."

The beauty of what we had together? Jesus Christ, Ed. I wanked you off once a week because it's my job and my son needed new trainers and a new phone. That's the beginning, middle and end of it. Don't be reading more into this than what there was.

Aloud, she said: "Ed, it's really not my place to say this because I'm not your therapist, but I'm a gobby cow and I can't always keep my trap shut, see?"

He nodded, looking alarmed.

"Are you sure you're willing to . . . to *settle* for what Margie is offering you? I mean, it's not very much, is it? She's using you as a sort of stopgap until, as she says herself, something better comes along. Is that really what you want from your life?"

Ed shrugged. "I dunno. I mean, it's not like I have much else going on, is it? It's not like *you* want to come and live with me, is it? Or do you? I'd treat you like a queen, honest I would. We could go anywhere in the world you wanted for our holidays. As long as we could drive there, I mean. I get really sick when I fly or take the ferry."

"I don't doubt you'd be a good partner, Ed, but like I told you, I have a boyfriend. I'm spoken for. But, goddammit, Ed, I've grown fond of you over the last few months and I don't want you to throw your life away on someone who doesn't give a shit about you."

"I *do* love Margie," he confessed reluctantly then. "If it hadn't been for her boyfriend, I'd have been perfectly happy to spend the rest of my life with her."

"So, you're happy to stay with her then, even though at some point she may leave you again for someone else?"

"I can make her love me again, I'm sure of it," he said stubbornly.

"As long as you're happy staying with her. That's all I really wanted to establish. You're a grown man, Ed. You're free to make your own choices." Vicky sighed a long, tired sigh and put out her hand to indicate the bed on which they were sitting. "Do you want to . . . you know, for old times' sake, before you leave?"

Ed nodded eagerly. "Margie said we can do it once more to say goodbye."

Thank you, Margie, you're a real treasure. Remind me to do YOU a favour sometime. "There was just one thing I wanted to ask you, Ed, though I don't for the life of me know why it matters. What was the dog's name? You know, the pit bull, the one you said was a demon?"

"Tiddles."

Tiddles? Vicky started laughing then. She lay back against the pillows on the newly made-up bed and roared with laughter until she began to cough and splutter madly. After a moment or two of surprise, Ed joined her, and he was laughing too.

Later that day, when she got home from work, she found Andrew slumped on the couch with his feet up on the arm, looking miserable.

"What's up, doc?" she quizzed him, using a form of address she'd used with him when he was younger. "Why the long face?" *Oh, Jesus, not Mister Ed again,* she berated herself.

He shrugged, and turned his face away from her.

"Andrew? What's up?"

"You wouldn't understand."

"I bet I would. Try me."

"Well, it's stupid, but . . ."

"But what . . .?"

"Well, it's just that . . . just that . . ."

"Just that what, sweetheart?" she gently prompted him. To her horror, when he turned his head towards her, she could see the glint of tears in his dark eyes. "What's the matter, honey?" She was thoroughly alarmed now.

"It's just . . . I'm so sick of always being poor!" he blurted out, then immediately looked as guilty as hell for having said anything.

"Has someone said something?" She was instantly on the alert for proof that someone was upsetting her precious baby.

After a moment or two's delay, he nodded reluctantly. "Darren Beirne. He said I couldn't afford those new Nike trainers everyone's wearing in school, and it's because you're a single mother and we're poor."

Vicky sighed. She put a hand to a place just above her eyebrows where a dull headache was forming, the kind that would probably lead to her lying down in a darkened room later with a wet face flannel on her forehead. "Darren Beirne? Is he that little bollix who flushed your swimming towel down the toilet that time? Do you want me to ring the teacher and tell her to give him a bollocking? Because I'll do it, gladly, you know I will. Or I'll ring his ma."

"Mum, don't interfere!" her son groaned. "You'll only be making things worse."

"Andrew," she said earnestly, shoving his long legs off the couch and onto the floor so that she could sit down beside him, "you can't let that little shit bully you. You've got to stand up for yourself."

"I did!" he wailed. "I punched him in the mouth. His lip was bleeding and everything."

"You punched him? How come the teacher wasn't ringing me about it?"

"There's a note in my bag. You've to sign it."

"Right, well," she said then, carefully choosing her words, "although I don't condone violence —" inside, she was as proud as punch that he'd stood up to his bully — that Darren Beirne was a nasty piece of work, "sometimes in life, there's

. . . there's nothing else you can do. Violence is wrong," she reiterated, "but, as I said, well, sometimes in life it's a necessary evil."

"So you're not mad at me?" he said, his eyes glistening with tears.

"Of course I'm not mad at you, you numpty!" She smiled at him and ruffled his hair. When he smiled back, she felt like she always did when he smiled, like the sun was coming out from behind a cloud. She fumbled around in her handbag for a brown envelope stuffed with tenners and handed it to Andrew, who took it with a look of bemusement on his face.

"What's this?" he said.

"It's the money for those new trainers. I was going to get you them for your birthday but you might as well buy them now yourself."

"But . . . but you can't afford this much money for trainers! How can you afford this?"

"Let's just say I cleaned out a few particularly aromatic bogs." Sorry, Ed, for referring to you as a lavvy, she added silently.

"It's not fair that you have to do that kind of thing. All that cleaning and scrubbing, I mean. I know you only do it for me."

"I don't mind, Andy-Pandy. Honestly I don't. It keeps me busy when you're at school. Shure, what else would I be doing?"

"When I'm older, I'm going to get a job and help you, I swear I will! I'd leave school now and get one if I could."

He said it with so much earnestness, it nearly broke her heart. "I know you will, sweetheart, I know! But for now, you just enjoy your schooldays, okay? These are meant to be the best days of your life. God knows, I wasted mine. Anyway, would you like to go in to town and get those trainers now? I could get a bit of dinner going while you're out."

"Mum, you're the greatest."

She was struck anew by the gangling height of him as he unfolded himself from the couch and stood up.

"Andrew?" she called him back as he was heading for the hall. "I just want to get one thing straight between us, okay? I'm not giving you the money for the trainers just because of that little shit Darren Beirne. He's nothing to do with us, and we're nothing to do with him. I'm giving you this money because I want to, and I was going to do it anyway before that little twerp had a go at you. And, for what it's worth, I think you did absolutely the right thing in punching him. He'll leave you alone now. Just don't do it again, okay? We don't want the school on our backs." She smiled at this last bit, to soften the impact of her words.

Andrew grinned back at her.

"I won't," he said. "We still going to Aunty June's for Sunday dinner?"

"You bet we are, Bugalugs."

He grinned again, this time at her revival of another one of her childhood names for him, and then he was gone, off into town to buy the trainers that meant so much to him and his friends these days.

Vicky remained where she was on the couch for a bit, just thinking that she wouldn't be able to give up the escorting any time soon, certainly not while Andrew was still in school, anyway, then she heaved herself up and made her way into the kitchen to make a start on dinner. In an uncertain world, two things she knew for certain. Her son Andrew was her life, and today seemed like a good day for spaghetti.

Chapter 7

CARL

"Right, I'll be off so," Karen said. "I won't be late. You'll be okay?"

"I *have* babysat my own kids before, you know," Carl said. He sounded defensive and annoyed. Defensive that she was acting as if he didn't know one end of a child from the other, despite the fact that they'd had *three* of the blessed things together, and annoyed that she was going out. Yes, goddammit, he *was* annoyed, even though he knew that, logically, he had no real reason to be. After all, he himself was always going out at night. Pints with the lads from work, pints with the lads from the neighbourhood of Lambert Avenue in Terenure where they lived and beyond, pints with the friends he was still in touch with from school and college, pints with the lads from the darts team and pints with the lads from the soccer club and pints with his younger brother Graeme and their dad, and sometimes with their cousins and their dad's brothers, their uncles. Sometimes he even went to the pub alone and just had pints with whoever was at the bar or watching the sports on the big TV. He knew it was unfair that he did all this and Karen did no more than bitch and snipe at him passive-aggressively for doing it. Now the tables were turned, and *she* was going out, and he was sitting here with a puss on him like someone had just taken his precious Netflix away.

"Will *Brad* be there?" he said, the word oozing as much sarcasm as he could muster up.

"Of course he'll be there." Karen was in the hall, flicking a brush through her dark wavy shoulder-length hair in front of the mirror. "Why wouldn't he be there?"

"Oh, no reason. I just wanted to make sure that you all would be having the pleasure of *Brad's* wonderful company on your lovely works night out." He just couldn't seem to mention the man's name without utilising extreme sarcasm. He'd never even met the guy, but, since he'd come to work at the special school where Karen was a part-time substitute teacher, it had been nothing but *'Brad this'* and *'Brad that'* and *'Brad says this and thinks the other and you'll never guess what the slogan on Brad's T-shirt was today and how utterly meaningful it turned out to be!'* and Carl was, frankly, fed-up to his back teeth with hearing about the guy. It was obvious Karen fancied him. Why else would she bring up his name at every possible opportunity? And how come there were suddenly more work nights out than there had ever been before this Brad person came along? Last week had been someone's birthday. Tonight's do was a party for someone called Valerie who was going on maternity leave. God, those teachers had a cushy time of it, Carl often thought. Getting paid to go off and have their sprogs and then, when it suited them, getting paid again to come back to a job that had been safely kept warm for them until they felt like strolling casually back into it. *God Almighty.* He was in the wrong bloody job.

"Don't be jealous, Carl. It doesn't suit you." But she said it with a smile, as if she was pleased he was jealous. How messed-up was that? "Now, let's see. The kids are asleep. Max will need feeding before you put him out. There's a steak in the fridge I've been keeping for him."

"If there's steak in the fridge, then how come I was given mince for my dinner tonight?" Carl was highly indignant. Even the dog was treated better than he was around this place.

"Because it's a bony one I was keeping for him specially. You wouldn't like it, trust me. Don't whinge, Carl. Now, are you sure you'll be all right? You've got the number of the pub and, obviously, I'll have my mobile switched on if you need me."

"Oh, I'll be all right. Don't you worry about me." He crossed his arms and looked the very picture of truculence on the couch, with his legs stuck straight out in front of him and a puss on him. "I'll be perfectly all right here on my own for the night with the kids and Max. I'll just work on my novel for a bit." He was annoyed (but also secretly relieved) when she didn't ask how it (the novel) was going, but instead rushed out the door in a flurry of goodbyes and see you laters and don't-wait-ups.

Don't wait up, indeed, thought Carl, disgruntled, as he headed to the fridge in the kitchen for a can of beer. She'd be getting a lift home later from one of the designated drivers. It just better not be that Brad fella, that's all. *Tsshhhh!* What kind of name was Brad for an Irish substitute primary school teacher in a special school, anyway? Brad was an American name, a name for the captain of the football team, the guy who got to make it with the hottest (and easiest) cheerleaders.

"Brad *is* American, actually," he remembered Karen telling him once. Sure he was. Carl had hated the sound of him immediately. He was probably six foot four and built like a brick shithouse, with healthy ice-blonde American hair and the best American dentistry money could buy. The Americans were so bloody over the top with everything. *Tsshhhh!* He repeated his exasperated noise, liking the sound of it, and opened up the folder on his laptop marked *'MY NOVEL.'* So far, he'd only written a title, *This Gun's for Hire*. He envisaged his novel-to-be as being a sort of Raymond Chandler-James M. Cain-Stephen King crossover with an Irish flavour and cosmopolitan wit, but coming up with original plots was hard. So far, all he'd managed to dredge from the depths of his imagination were *Double Indemnity* knock-offs, where a man pledges to kill his hot girlfriend's older rich businessman husband for the insurance money but then it all goes horribly wrong for some reason. He stared at the blinking cursor, depressed yet again at the failure of his psyche to generate plot ideas. So many of the good ideas had already been taken. Wizarding school for kids was taken. Sparkly teenage vampires, likewise. Hobbits on a quest, you'd better *believe* that was taken. Ditto, the sexy millionaire initiating the shy little college student into the kinky goings-on in his Red Room of Pain. Fucking hell. Why did anyone ever bother their hole writing, or trying to write, anything new, he wondered desperately at times, when anyone with half an ounce of sense could see for themselves that all the plots in the world had already been selfishly snatched up by those greedy bastard writers who'd simply been quicker off the mark? A flicker of an idea came to him then. He sat up straight, his heart starting to race in excitement. No, wait, it was only *Double Indemnity* again, thinly disguised this time as *The Postman Always Rings Twice*. Exactly whom had James M. Cain been trying to kid, anyway, by pretending that *Postman* and *Double Indemnity* were two different books, with two separate plots? Separate plots, his big hairy arse. Carl sighed, mentally batting away the plots of *The Big Sleep* and *Key Largo* like a kitten with a ball of wool. And were detectives, even hard-bitten ones, even *called* gumshoes any more? Maybe that kind of hard-boiled, American man-writing wasn't even in vogue any more. Maybe there'd even been some successful writers since Hemingway and Somerset Maugham and F. Scott Fitzgerald.

Carl sighed again. The world of writing was a load of old bollocks, and the winners in its strange Lottery were those who had simply got to the four or five plots that existed in the world first. It wasn't what you knew, anyway, it was *who* you knew, everyone knew that. Maybe if his dad was a politician and his mum a famous journalist, he might stand half a chance in the incestuous, nepotism-filled world of writing. Or maybe he'd write a shite children's book, carelessly dash one off in five minutes and then sell it for a million quid like all the so-called celebrities did. Celebrities could poop out a bestselling children's book without any effort at all, and everyone would buy it, just because it had been penned by a gay-or-transgender social influencer with a differently abled partner who wrote cookbooks for visually challenged leprechauns in Braille, *as Gaeilge*. Carl sighed again and shut down the programme with his novel on it. Well, his title, anyway. At least he had a killer title. Shure, a good title was half the battle, everyone knew that. Now, if only he could think of an original plot and twist it to fit his marvellous title! He'd be laughing then. Now, however, he threw a pen across the room in frustration. Why was he even doing this? Why was he even pretending to himself that he had any literary talent, that he had what it took to be a successful wordsmith? Oh yeah. Sally Ann Coombes . . .

"You'll never guess who's moving in across the street," Karen had said to him a few weeks ago. She'd been standing at the sink washing up after the dinner and he was still at the table, hidden behind the newspaper.

"No, who?" he'd grunted, not bothering to come out from behind the sports pages.

"Sally Ann Coombes."

He could hear the flourish of triumph in her voice, as if she were unveiling a particularly special birthday cake she'd baked and wanted to show off to him, but he remained where he was, firmly ensconced between the GAA and the Premier League. "Who?"

"Sally Ann Coombes," Karen repeated patiently. "She hosts that afternoon chat-show on the telly, where the celebrities talk about their books and new babies and their weight loss or gain and how much happier they are now that their husbands have left them for younger women. You must know it. I sometimes have it on here in the day."

"That load of old shite?" Carl was scornful. "I can't believe you'd waste your time on shite like that. It's no better than Jeremy Kyle. That's the lowest common denominator in telly terms – chewing gum for the eyes, that is."

"It's company for me sometimes, when it's just me here on my own with the kids after school." She sounded defensive. "Anyway, Sally Ann is moving into the house across the street, with her husband Fabio and their two dogs, Red and Rusty. Two Red Setters."

"What kind of a name is Fabio?"

"He's Brazilian, I think. And, between you and me, I think he's a lot younger than her. I think she left her first husband for him, as a matter of fact. He probably has a huge willy. The new hubby, I mean. A lot of those foreign guys do, apparently."

"Karen!" expostulated Carl, putting down his newspaper. "I'm surprised at you, talking filth like that around the kids!"

"The kids are in the garden," she pointed out reasonably. "I can see them from here. They can't hear me. And I'm just saying, anyway, that's all."

"Well, would you mind not?" he retorted. Just saying, indeed! Talking about other men's tackle made him feel uncomfortable. It was a gay thing to do, and Carl wasn't gay. Besides which, he just had a plain ordinary Irish willy, and he didn't want to possibly hear that it didn't come up to scratch next to an enormous foreign one. Why *did* foreign guys all have such ridiculously impressive willies, anyway? Must be all the sun they got. Irish blokes couldn't help it if they only saw the sun once or twice a year and had knobs like wilted rhododendron as a result. These well-hung foreigners were giving Irish women inflated and unrealistic notions of what size a knob should properly be. And Irish men were expected to just put up with this kind of nonsense! It was unfair, that's what it was. These foreigners were taking unfair advantage.

"Are you jealous, Carl?" Karen was laughing now as she made a start on the more icky pots that she always left till the end.

"Of what? Some Brazilian gigolo who might or might not be hung like a fireman's hose? I don't think so, somehow."

"Sally Ann's much more your type, anyway."

"She's such a bimbo she's practically made of plastic!"

"Oh, so you *do* remember her! I thought that was how you liked them, anyway," she said, with a sharpish edge to her voice. "Big tits and dyed hair."

"I'm not going to dignify that remark with a response," he said, before stalking off huffily to the sitting-room with his newspaper. As if he could ever fancy someone as obviously artificial as an afternoon telly chat-show hostess! He had a life, thanks very much. And he was more of a leg man, anyway, than a titty one. Although, big tits were great, he wouldn't deny that. In the sitting-room, he settled himself on the couch and grumpily read the rest of the sports results.

A few days later, he'd met his new neighbour face-to-face. He was parking his car in the driveway (the garage had too much crap in it; there was no room for his car. It was a bloody disgrace, was what it was – when would Karen ever get around to tidying it out?) in front of the house after work when a female voice he couldn't place yoo-hooed shrilly at him from across the street. He climbed out of the car and stood speechless while two of the biggest, brownest, roundest tits he'd ever seen in his life came bouncing across the road towards him, barely restrained in a hot pink vest-type top with spaghetti straps.

"Hi, I'm Sally Ann Coombes," said the tits, extending a hand towards him in greeting. He took the hand and pumped it up and down a little too vigorously out of nervousness. "I met your wife Karen at the shops the other day. I've been so looking forward to meeting her other half. Carl, I think she said you were called?"

"Well, here I am, *ta-daaaah!*" said Carl in a jokey way, trying his hardest to drag his eyes from the fabulous tits up to their owner's face. It took a few moments. The tits were just that great. Sally Ann Coombes was fifty if she was a day, but goddammit, she was well preserved! Long wavy unnaturally dark-red hair, carefully coiffured, probably dyed, with her heavy studio make-up still obviously in place, and every inch of her body, from the amazing breasts to the long, long legs in the open-toed high-heeled sandals with the wedge heels, was a stunning brown colour so alien to pale, freckly Irish skin that even Carl guessed that it was fake tan. Karen was always slagging him off for not being able to guess when breasts or tan were fake. Both attributes were fake in Sally Ann's case, but Carl would probably at that moment have swapped one of their kids or the dog for a chance to make the beast-with-two-backs with her, just once!

"So, what do you do yourself, Carl?" Her voice, now that she wasn't yoo-hooing from across the street, was all warm and honeyed. It practically invited confidences.

Typical chat-show host, Carl thought admiringly, always on the look-out for a potential studio guest to interest her public. He could well imagine anyone she talked to opening up to her like she was their shrink. "I sell life insurance," he said.

"Oh." He could hear the disappointment in her voice, see her gaze sliding away from him as if she had already lost interest and was planning her getaway. It suddenly seemed very important to Carl to keep her there, to keep her talking, to keep her attention. So . . .

"I'm a writer too, though," he blurted out. "That's my real job."

"Oh, I *see*," she purred, standing so close to him that her pneumatic nipples were nearly boring a hole in *his* shirt, never mind hers. What a tantalising thought that was. "I'm always looking for writers for my show. They make for such interesting conversations. Would I have read anything of yours?"

"*Erm*, not yet, exactly, as such, but . . . but I expect you will soon, very soon!"

"*Mmm*, keep me posted, won't you, Carl darling?" she said, as she began to teeter back across the street in her skyscraper heels.

How the hell did she walk in shoes so unnaturally high? They did go very well with her miniscule micro-denim skirt, though. Not bad for an auld one. Not bad at all.

"Oh, and we must have you over to dinner one night soon! Oh, and Karen too, of course. And *do* please keep me posted about your book."

And that had been that. Now Karen was out living it up in a pub somewhere with this Brad person (yes, yes, he knew that there were other teachers and substitute teachers there too, but it was Brad he had a bee in his bonnet about), and he was stuck at home grappling with his novel, just in case the dinner invite from Sally Ann Coombes actually one day materialised and she'd ask him about how his book was coming along and he'd need to have something to tell her. Why couldn't he think of anything to write about? He'd been good enough at English at school. He'd even won a book token once as first prize in a short story contest in his class. The story he'd written had been about an insurance man (just like him; he was an insurance man too!) who pledges to kill his glamorous girlfriend's husband for the insurance money but it all goes horribly wrong for some reason, and then Karen had come in to announce airily that she was leaving him for Fabio, Sally Ann Coombes' younger husband, the one who was hung like a fireman's hose, and that she was going away to Brazil with him forever and was leaving him the kids and he needn't even *try* to give them back to her because she'd already taken out injunctions against him *and* them, tick-tacks no take-backs!

With a start, Carl jerked awake and realised to his annoyance that he'd nodded off on the couch again in front of *This Stupid Gun's for Stupid Hire*. He was cold, even though it was summer. God, how he needed a beer. Karen still wasn't home. The kids were still asleep and the four little words *This Gun's for Hire* still just sat there on the computer screen, accusingly. Looking at him as if to say: *'Why can't you write me? What's wrong with you? Someone else would be able to do it! Stephen King could it, standing on his head! He would have shat out a dozen books in the time you've taken to come up with that lousy title. You're not a writer, you're just a piece-of-shit insurance salesman and you never wrote a word worth reading in your life!'*

That did it. Carl wasn't putting up with shit like that from his title. He took shit from everyone else in his life; his boss, Karen, the kids, even the dog, that steak-guzzling Hound of the Baskervilles, but he sure as hell didn't need to take it from his title, the title that hadn't even the good manners to morph magically into 80,000 words overnight without his having to break a sweat over it. (He'd even left the programme on and open overnight, just in case the gods of writing felt like performing a miracle in his favour, but nothing. *Zip, zilch, nada. Bah humbug* to it all anyway.) He shut down the Word document, and, then, with a depressed sigh, he googled 'really big tits' and stuck his hand down his pants in readiness. Some things, at any rate, never let you down.

"You're going where, exactly?"

"I told you, Carl. It's a team-building weekend for all the substitute teachers and some of the full-time ones as well. We're staying in the Hilltops Hotel in the Wicklow mountains. They have one of those obstacle courses and an orienteering route through the woods and up the mountains that businesses use for team-building exercises."

"But you're not a business! You're a school. Why would a school need to do team-building exercises, for Christ's sake?" Carl was baffled, not to mention put out big-time. She was planning on going away for the whole weekend? This was much worse than her just going on a night out. How was he supposed to cope with the kids and the house and the cooking for a whole weekend? He could barely boil an egg.

"Why shouldn't teachers do team-building exercises too? We have to work as a team as well, same as anyone else. You don't have to be a business to do them. I'm surprised your lot haven't sent you on one yet, as a matter of fact."

"I'd soon tell them where to go."

"Well, I happen to think it's a good idea, Carl, and I'm looking forward to it. And you'll be fine. Your mum and dad will collect the kids from school and crèche on Friday afternoon and keep them overnight. Graeme's said he'll help. They'll drop them back to you on Saturday, so all you'll have to do is feed them on Saturday and Sunday. You can do that, can't you? They'll be happy with a pizza on Saturday, and I've left a casserole in the fridge for Sunday. All you'll have to do is heat it up." She carried on washing up after the dinner as she talked.

Carl's heart sank. *All he had to do ...?* He loved his kids to bits (Lauren was four, Georgie three and Danny two), of course he did, but he panicked every time Karen left him alone with them. He was no good at all that women's stuff that Karen did so well, juggling nappies and bottles and doctor's appointments while heating things up in the oven, kissing scraped knees better and crooning lullabies at bedtime. Women were so much better at that kind of domestic multi-tasking than men were. And, besides that, there was something about this so-called team-building weekend away in the Wicklow mountains that didn't sit quite right with him.

"How come I'm only hearing about this now, anyway?"

"Carl, it's been pencilled into the calendar for weeks now."

Oh yes, the famous calendar. Karen's Bible. Every time he forgot a birthday, an anniversary, an apocalypse or a visit to the dentist and claimed that no one had reminded him, she'd point him virtuously in the direction of the calendar that hung in the kitchen and say serenely: "It's been in the calendar for weeks, Carl. In all fairness, how can you say you weren't told about it?"

He got up from the kitchen table, where he'd been reading the paper, and stalked to the calendar. To his surprise, and distinct annoyance, the coming Friday, Saturday and Sunday had the word 'HILLTOPS' written across them in green pen and in capital letters. *Well.* Damn and blast that know-it-all, infallible fucking calendar. One of these days he'd take it out into the back garden and burn it, and dance around it whooping wildly like a Native American Indian while he did it, just for spite. He harrumphed loudly and retook his seat, sitting with his hands clasped on the table in front of him like he was the prosecuting attorney and Karen was the witness he was grilling.

"*Humph*, well, that's as may be, but I still don't remember anyone ever actually broaching this subject with me in person, Karen."

"Can I help it if you never listen to me?"

"And furthermore," he went on pompously, really getting into his role as prosecutor now (he'd be getting up and circling the table in a minute, with his fingers at chest-level twanging an imaginary pair of braces, like a barrister in one of those pox-bollocky crime thrillers he was trying to write), "will this Brad person be present at this so-called team-building weekend?"

"So-called? What do you mean, so-called? It *is* a team-building weekend, like I told you. Feel free to ring Marjorie if you don't believe me. I'll give you the number personally."

Marjorie Phillips-Wright was the principal of Treetops special school, where Karen worked.

"And as for *'this Brad person'*, as you call him, being there, well, of course he'll be there. He's a substitute teacher too, like me, isn't he? He works at the school."

"Oh-ho, so he works at the school, does he, eh? So, you'll be alone with this Brad person from Friday after school till some time Sunday evening then, will you?" said the prosecuting attorney, narrowing his gimlet eyes at the suspect-defendant as he got up and approached the stand. He sniffed ostentatiously, for the court's benefit, as if there were something seriously fishy about what he was smelling.

"Carl, there'll be ten or twelve other teachers there besides us, so I'd hardly call that *'alone'*, would you? Anyway, this is ridiculous, the way you keep implying that there's something going on between me and Brad. You're paranoid, Carl, do you know that?"

"My mental acuity and state of mind is not on trial here," barked the prosecutor, quick as a flash.

"Well, I'm not on trial here either," snapped Karen, throwing down her dishcloth with a degree of unnecessary force and preparing to leave the kitchen. "I'll tell you this now, Carl Groves, once and for all, and as far as I'm concerned, then that'll be the end of it. Brad Stimson is just someone I work with, that's all. We get on well, but that's it. I am not now, nor have I ever been, having an affair with Brad, and neither will I ever be in the future having an affair with Brad, okay?"

Methinks the defendant doth protest too much, thought the prosecutor, but he wisely held his own counsel. He didn't want a swipe in the kisser with a wet dishcloth. It would be most humiliating for a man of his immense legal stature. Stimson, though, was seemingly the fellow's last name. Interesting, interesting. Might come in handy sometime.

"Make a note of it, Della," he barked, twanging his braces.

***

"I kissed Brad."

"You did what? What did you say?"

"I said I kissed Brad. I'm so sorry, Carl. I just couldn't keep it from you."

"You kissed . . . you kissed this Brad person . . .?" He could not believe what he was hearing. After a shitty weekend spent trying (but failing miserably yet again) not to give the kids the kind of inept, sub-par care that Karen would give him major shit about when she heard about it (and, make no mistake about it, she would hear about it; the kids told her everything, those disloyal little shits), and trying to think of a plausible plot for his stupid book, he literally couldn't *believe* what he was hearing. He'd had his friends Bill, Joe and Marty over for a game of cards on Friday night when he was alone in the house, and, after confiding in them his suspicions about Karen and this Brad fella, they'd then proceeded to spend most of the night trying to convince him that this Brad fella would be mad *not* to put the moves on Karen if he got the chance.

"She's a very good-looking woman, your Karen," Joe had said with a solemn nod.

"Is she?" Carl had replied, surprised. "My Karen?" When was the last time he'd really looked at Karen, though, he wondered, really properly looked at her? To his shame, he couldn't really remember. He didn't really think of Karen as a person, he'd realised guiltily then, a person with her own hopes and dreams and aspirations, never mind as a woman. She was just chief-cook-and-bottle-washer round here, the one who knew all the secrets to childminding and the domestic arts of which Carl hadn't even the remotest suspicion.

"Oh yes," Joe said, and this time both Bill and Marty nodded solemnly as well. "Lovely dark hair and lovely big . . . *erm* . . ." he'd been about to make the gesture with his hands in front of his chest that universally signified big boobs, but he stopped himself in time with an embarrassed clearing of the throat, "eyes. *Erm*, lovely big dark eyes, that's it."

"You don't really think Karen would cheat on me, do you?" Carl had said miserably then.

"I'm not saying *Karen* would cheat, mate," Bill had said, taking a slice of the pizza they'd ordered hours ago that was cold now, and greasy. "It's more a case of would this guy Brad be nuts not to put the moves on her if he got the chance, and the answer to that would have to be yes. Yes, as in, he'd have to be nuts not to put the moves on her if he got the chance. She's a fine-looking woman, your Karen."

"But would Karen respond to this Brad fella's advances, do you think?" This was Carl.

"Well, only if she's not being looked after at home, if you see what I mean," said Bill, chewing away happily on his slice of cold pizza. "If you catch my drift, mate."

Carl did indeed catch Bill's drift, and he turned ice-cold while looking positively aghast. He and Karen had hardly had sex at all since the birth of baby Danny two years ago. It was about once every month at most, and even then it was more about satisfying Carl's basic needs than any needs or desires Karen might have. To his shame again, he realised that he wasn't even sure what Karen's needs *were* in the bedroom, or if she even had any and if he, her husband, was fulfilling them, which suddenly he very much doubted. If he didn't even see his own wife as a woman, but just as someone, an automaton, say, who put food on the table three times a day and looked after the house and the kids their joint couplings had created, well, then, how the hell could he possibly be satisfying — *ahem* — her bedroom needs? It stood to reason that he couldn't be. And he only had sex with her to tick a box, the sex-box, just to be able to say they still did it and weren't yet decrepit. Oh God, he was a *terrible* husband! No wonder Karen had gone off on this so-called team-building exercise weekend with this Brad fella. To his eternal mortification, he burst noisily into drunken sobs in front of his friends, and cried into his beer for the rest of the night, comforted by his pals who told him that it still mightn't be too late to win her back and that knowing where he'd gone wrong in the past was half the battle, shure.

Now he glared at Karen and said accusingly: "I can't believe you betrayed me like that."

"Don't say that, Carl. It was only a kiss, I swear. I mean, it could have gone further but I stopped it. Brad wanted to go further but I pulled back. I told him I couldn't do it to you, that I loved *you*."

"And I'm supposed to be grateful for this . . . this small mercy, am I?"

"I hate you when you're like this, all sarcastic and judgemental."

"Oh, I'm sorry, am I not reacting the right way? Well, Your Imperial Majesty, won't you please tell me what way I *should* be reacting to the news that my wife of ten years has been having it away with American Brad, Transatlantic Brad, Brad the Yankee Doodle Dandy, Brad the big jock captain of the football team who always gets the hottest (and, let's face it, the easiest) cheerleaders . . .?" He couldn't think of any more racial slurs and so he trailed off.

"You're being ridiculous, Carl. We weren't having it away. No one was having it away. It was one kiss and I pushed him away after it, I swear. It went no further than that."

"Don't do *me* any favours," he snapped, getting up from the bed where he'd been sitting and shoving his feet into his shoes. "I don't need your favours, or your pity."

"Where are you going at this hour of the night? It's Sunday night. Everywhere's closed, including the pubs."

"I'm going for a walk to clear my head," he snarled. "I won't be long. You just get into bed there now and have sweet sexy dreams about Big Handsome American Brad."

"Oh, for Christ's sake, Carl, you're being ridiculous! Come back here, will you? We need to talk about this. . ." But he was gone. The slam of the front door shook the whole house.

Carl walked for what seemed like ages, the image of Karen in the Wicklow mountains kissing the tall, blonde handsome American jock of his imagination fixed firmly in his mind. Whenever he tried to push it away, he could hear his conscience sneering at him with unhelpful little sarky remarks such as, *Well, when was the last time YOU kissed her, Carl?*

When was the last time you bought her flowers or showed her any appreciation or gave her any little token of your esteem? When did you last even give her any indication that you noticed she was alive, next to you in the bed or downstairs in the kitchen or on the couch beside you watching Fair City, or even that she was a woman? Oh, fuck off, you, he'd tell his conscience irritably, but it wouldn't be gagged. It *would* be heard. *You've been neglectful, Carl,* it taunted him. *You've taken her for granted all these years. She has indeed been your chief-cook-and-bottle-washer all this time and you've shown her barely any acknowledgement of what she's done for you and the kids, the whole family. And now Sexy American Brad has happened along . . .*

Carl had no come-back to this. He sighed and kept on walking with his head down and his hands shoved deep in his pockets, until he realised that he'd come full circle on his pointless amble and was coming back up to his own road once more. Ah well. Might as well go in and see what the story was. See if Karen was up to talking things through, although, the way he felt now, all he wanted to do was crash onto the bed with his clothes on and sleep his brains out.

The sound of a car door slamming made him swivel his head to the right a bit. Across the street, Sally Ann Coombes was standing beside her car, waving over to him with a notebook in her hand.

"I left my notes for tomorrow's show in the car," she said with a tinkly laugh. "I'd forget my head if it wasn't screwed on."

"Oh, right," Carl mumbled. She was looking very fit tonight, he noticed, in the same low-cut hot pink top with the spaghetti straps he'd seen her wearing before (the one that emphasised her excellent breasts), this time teamed with high-heeled fluffy blue mules and tight faded-looking jeans. He was mightily impressed that she actually walked around the house going about her domestic business dressed in clothes that most people would consider too uncomfortable for lounging in. Other people did their lounging or TV-watching in sweatpants and slippers. Her carefully sprayed hair fell in dark-red waves down her back and she was fully made-up. She could have just walked off her studio set for all he knew.

"What are you doing, anyway, wandering around like a lost soul at this hour of the night? Been to the shop, have you?" Although her shrewd, TV presenter's gaze clearly took in the absence of emergency fags or milk-and-bread-for-the-morning in his empty hands. She walked over to him.

"*Erm*, I just fancied a bit of a walk, that's all. Clear my head, I suppose."

"Oh dear. Marital problems?" Her tone was ultra-sympathetic, her hand on his forearm applying a comforting pressure.

"Karen kissed someone, on a team-building weekend away with her colleagues in the Wicklow mountains." He hadn't meant to say it. It literally just came out of him.

"Oh dear. That must be awful for you," she purred, the hand on his arm increasing its pressure. "I'll tell you what. Come over to my place and I'll make you a nice strong drink to settle your poor nerves."

"Won't . . . *erm*, won't your husband, *erm*, Fabio, is it? Won't he mind?"

"He's not there," she trilled gaily, leading him across the road. "He's at a club with some clients. He's an interior decorator, you see. Sometimes he has to wine and dine potential clients and take them out on the town."

"I see," said Carl.

Once he was ensconced on her giant leather couch with a

whiskey, staring in bemusement at the framed photos of Sally Ann and her famous talk-show guests that filled every inch of wall space in her sitting-room, Sally Ann herself kicked off her fluffy mules and curled up beside him, smiling at him confidentially.

"*Erm*, you won't . . . *um*, you know that stuff I just told you there, about Karen, I mean? You won't . . . you won't put it on your show, will you? It's really just private, you see."

"Of course not," she purred, practically in his ear. "That's just between us two, a confidence shared between friends."

"Right, well, good. I don't really want to talk about it any more, to be honest with you."

"That's perfectly fine, Carl honey."

Her red-lipsticked mouth was so close to his ear now that her whiskey-flavoured breath (she was having one too) was tickling him. She smelled of a very powerful perfume that she'd obviously applied with a heavy hand. It wasn't unpleasant, but it *was* heady, in that it was going to his head and making him feel woozy, along with the whiskey.

"We don't have to talk about that if you don't want to. What about your book? I've been simply dying to ask you about it. How's that coming along? What's it about, again?"

"An insurance man who kills his girlfriend's husband for the money, but it all goes horribly wrong in some way for some reason," Carl told her glumly.

"That sounds familiar. *Mmmm*, let me think, now. Oh yes, doesn't that sound a lot like the plot of that film, what's this it's called now?"

"*Double Indemnity,*" supplied Carl gloomily.

"That's the one! And wasn't there that other one as well

with a very similar plot? Jack Nicholson was in it? It was a bit raunchy, if I recall."

"*The Postman Always Rings Twice.*"

"Exactly, that's it! And your plot is, what? The same, is it?"

"It's meant to be a sort of modern reworking of the plot, actually."

"That sounds, *erm*, terrific! When will it be ready for publishing? Have you got an agent yet? You're going to need one, you know, to help you negotiate the slings and arrows."

"To be honest, Sally Ann," here he heaved a deep sigh, "I'm thinking of just jacking the whole thing in. Put it with the guitar I never properly learned to play because I hadn't the patience or the staying power and the skateboard I was rubbish at."

He drained his whiskey and put his head in his hands. So many hobbies started and abandoned, and now this whole writing business had gone down the drain as well. Yet another thing that had turned out not to be the one thing in life that Carl Groves was particularly good at. He'd never find his one talent, the one thing that marked him out from the hordes, at this rate. Or maybe he was just a talentless git, a plain old insurance salesman like Walter Neff, but without the glamorous *femme fatale*. Unless he counted Sally Ann. She certainly had the fluffy mules and the cougar-ish disposition, after all.

While he was talking, she had begun to massage him lightly between the shoulder blades with long strong fingers tipped with razor-sharp, blood-red nails. It felt kind of nice, after all the stress of the day, and he didn't resist when she placed her lips against his cheek and then pulled his head round so she could kiss him properly, long and hard, on the mouth.

"We'd better knock this on the head, Sally Ann," he said at last when they pulled apart.

"Why? We're both adults, aren't we?" she breathed sexily, stroking his strong stubbly chin with her red-tipped fingers. "And it's not like your wife's been exactly behaving herself, is it?"

"Don't bring Karen into this, will you?" He shuffled down the couch away from her a bit.

She took his hand and placed it on one firm, round breast, over the hot-pink vest-top with the spaghetti straps. Carl gasped. It felt fantastically firm, not at all hard and plasticky like he'd been led to believe fake boobs felt like.

"Do you like that, Carl?" she purred silkily. "Does that feel nice?"

"You know it does," he said, his breathing ragged. "But . . . but we shouldn't be doing this. I mean, my wife, and your husband, your, *erm*, Fabio, won't he mind?"

"Not at all," she said, sliding one strap of her top down so that the braless breast in Carl's hand was fully bare. "Quite the contrary. He loves it when I have fun with other men. Would you like me to call him and get him over here? He quite likes to watch at times, or he could do you too if you like while I watch? Fabio is great like that. He goes both ways. Have you ever had a caffeine enema? That's one of Fabio's specialties."

Carl leaped up as if he'd been scalded. "*Erm*, no need to interrupt him if he's, *erm*, out with clients and stuff. I'd better be going anyway. It's a bed night, after all, and I need to get to school. I mean, school night, and I need to, *erm*, get to bed." Why wouldn't his stupid thick tongue say the words he wanted to say correctly?

"Isn't bed what I'm suggesting?" She lay back against the cushions and pulled her top down over both breasts. Carl caught his breath at the sight of them. They were magnificent. There was no other word for them. People should come from far and wide to worship them.

"I love my wife," he said desperately. "I'm supposed to be at home, making it up to her for being neglectful, not here with you, having it away!"

"Run away home to the little wifey then, why don't you?" she taunted. "I mean, I thought you were open to having a bit of mature adult fun, but if you're not . . ."

He was in the doorway now, ready to run, when he turned back suddenly. When would he ever get this chance again, he reasoned. He took a deep breath, then made a mad dash at a prone Sally Ann and, muttering a quick apology to both women, Sally Ann and Karen, had a quick squeeze of both breasts. Then, satisfied as to what they felt like, he turned and legged it.

"*You son of a bitch!*" screeched Sally Ann, following him to the door topless with her fake-tanned bosoms bared to the night air. "*I'll see to it that you'll never publish a book in this town again!*"

That suits me fine, thought Carl as he legged it across the street to home, and Karen. If I never see a bloody book again in my life, it'll still be too soon.

Karen was asleep when he reached the bedroom, so, a bit relieved that the serious talk they'd have to have would now need to wait till morning, he undressed and curled up beside her, relishing the familiar feel of her warm body beside his.

He'd missed that on the two nights that she'd been away, he realised now. Promising himself that he'd never take her for granted again, he fell asleep quickly. It didn't even matter to him any longer if this other guy, this Brad fella, was the handsome, tall blond American jock of Carl's imagination. The fact that Karen had turned him down for Carl was all Carl needed to know for going forward. He closed his eyes and fell instantly asleep, a blissful, seemingly dreamless sleep in which firm tanned boobs, husky blond American males and the plots of James M. Cain's novels thankfully didn't feature at all.

Next morning, they both got up as usual with the minimum of chit-chat and got themselves and the kids ready for school, crèche and work. The kids were all in good form for a change (usually, at least one or more of them would be out of sorts and would require extra cajoling), and didn't resist being fed, washed, dressed, kissed, hugged, tickled, reassured and strapped into their various car seats.

On the way out the door, Karen, checking her phone, turned to Carl and said: "Oh, by the way. Here's an interesting thing. I just saw it there this morning when I was scrolling. There's a new film coming out about some kind of maverick assassin or something, and guess what? It's called *This Gun's for Hire*. Wasn't that your title, you know, for your book? The book you were writing? You know, that book?"

Resisting the temptation to grind his teeth and fling his coffee mug at the wall, Carl kept his face neutral as he said: "*This Gun's for Hire?* Nah. Never heard of it." There was nothing else for it. He was closing down both his literary *and* his law enterprises. For good.

"*Make a note of it, Della.*"

Chapter 8

LIZ

Liz took a step back and admired her handiwork. The altar had never looked so beautiful before, she decided, wreathed artistically as it was in blooms from her own garden; freesias, chrysanthemums and roses in three different colours, white, yellow and palest pink, this last Liz's favourite colour of rose because it had been Leah's too. *Sin of pride, Lizzie my girl,* she admonished herself sternly then, *sin of pride.* And in the church too! Although there's nothing wrong in being proud of a job well done, is there? Surely even Our Lord Jesus Christ himself had experienced a soupcon of smugness when he'd pulled off the whole loaves and fishes thing. When she'd tidied away all the stems and leaves and bits of flowery remains into the plastic carrier bag she'd brought with her for the bin, she turned away from the altar and picked up her polishing cloths and tins of polish. Strictly speaking, she was only down to do the flowers today and not the polishing, but polishing the pews till they sparkled and shone was so therapeutic that she usually did a bit before she left. It was so relaxing! It cleared her mind and left her feeling refreshed and happy.

She looked round the church, quiet as usual at this time of the day and empty now save for one man sitting deep in prayer by the confession boxes to the right of the church — to the right as you came in the main door, that was, not to the right as you looked down from the pulpit. Well, Liz would do her polishing quietly like she always did and leave the poor fella to his prayers. In Liz's opinion, you didn't pray that hard with your head practically down on your chest unless you were in real trouble. She selected a pew at random and began her work, enjoying the feel of the smooth wood beneath her cloth and the smell of the pine-scented polish as she moved her arm rhythmically back and forth. When she found herself drawing nearer to the quiet praying man, she realised to her astonishment that it wasn't a member of the public at all but Father Barry, that is to say, Father Barry Galvin, who'd come to take over when old Father Finnegan had died of a heart attack nearly two years ago now. People still referred to him as 'that new young fella, Father Galvin', even though he was fifty-four or five if he was a day, a good six or seven years younger than herself. It was probably just because the parishioners considered him a young fella in comparison with old Father Finnegan, who'd been eighty-seven years old, with only one working kidney and blind in one eye, when the blessed angels had come for him.

"Are you all right, Father?" Liz said quietly now. She sat down on the very edge of the pew where Father Barry was seated, careful not to crowd him, looking at him curiously.

He looked up in surprise, as if he'd been miles away and hadn't had a clue that he wasn't alone in the church.

"Oh, it's yourself, Liz," he said, seeming to give himself a little shake to bring himself back into the present. "I was miles away just then."

"Is everything all right?" Liz queried hesitantly, feeling very bold to be asking the priest about his private business.

Father Barry sighed heavily and put his head in his hands. Liz had never had such a good opportunity to study him this closely before and she made the most of it. He really was a good-looking man, she decided, with the strong, masculine jaw lightly dotted with prickly-looking stubble (just like an ordinary man, she marvelled) and the thick, dark-brown hair liberally sprinkled with grey that he wore brushed back off his face. This close to him, she was even able to observe that he smelled really, really good, as if he were wearing aftershave or something. Fancy a priest wearing aftershave, Liz marvelled again. Were they even allowed to do that? It smelled lovely, anyway, she decided, a fragrance that somehow reminded her of the boats in the harbour at Dun Laoghaire and all things nautical. Gerry never bothered with aftershave. He said it was a load of old rubbish, a money racket, the same way he said all shampoos were only "coloured water" and so what was the point of paying over the odds for a bottle of the stuff?

"Just a bit of family trouble, you know yourself," he said when he'd lifted his head up out of his hands.

Such big, strong-looking, capable hands, Liz thought, lovely hands, then she flushed a fiery red to even be thinking such an immoral thought about a priest's hands. And in the church, of all places! She'd be lucky if she wasn't struck down by godly lightning where she stood.

"I see," she said. "A bit of family trouble?" Liz was no stranger to family trouble, and she sympathised. She didn't at all expect him to extrapolate, and so was surprised when he spoke again.

"My sister's girl over in Tullamore, you know? Stacey, she's called. She's after getting herself into what euphemistically used to be called *'trouble'*."

"I see," Liz said again, more slowly. "Well, things are a lot different today to the way they used to be in my day. Maybe it won't be so bad for her."

"If she were a bit older, Liz, I might be inclined to agree with you. As it is, she's only fourteen."

"Fourteen?" Liz echoed the word in dismay. "That's different. Was she . . . I mean, was it . . .?" She couldn't bring herself to say the word, not to a priest.

Thankfully, Father Barry caught her drift.

"Rape? No, thank God. 'Twas a boy her own age, as clueless and ignorant of the ways of the world as the girl herself. Do you know, they actually think that they can make a go of being parents, the pair of them? The blind leading the blind, that's what it is."

"What do your sister and her husband think about it all?"

Father Barry shrugged. "There's no husband around any more. He buggered off a few years ago. Couldn't handle the responsibility of a wife and four kids. Now the two lads are running wild without a father to curb their excesses, Stacey's expecting and the little one, Tammy, has been to every speech and language therapist in the country because she can't — or won't — speak a word beyond 'Mamma' and 'Dadda' even though she's nearly eight years old."

"That's very sad," said Liz, feeling so much empathy for him and his sister that she forgot to be appalled that he'd said the word *buggered* within the sacred walls of the holy church. "What are they going to do, do they know?"

"Well, there might be an answer to Stacey's problem, at least. Dawn — that's my sister — she thinks Stacey should have an abortion. She's asked me if I can lend her the money for two airfares to Britain and the procedure itself."

"Oh, Father Barry, that's awful for you!" exclaimed Liz. "What will you do about it?"

"What *can* I do, except give her the money? I know, it's ironic, isn't it? Here's me, the chairman of the Pro-Life Board of Directors here in my parish, giving money for my teenage niece's abortion because if she has the baby it'll shame the whole family. It's desperate, isn't it, Liz? Don't ever let anyone tell you that the world isn't rife with hypocrisy." He sighed and put his head in his hands again for a minute.

"I don't think you're being a hypocrite at all," Liz said staunchly, surprised to realise that she really meant it. "All you're being is a good brother and a good uncle, trying to help out your family in a time of great trouble. I mean, if your sister really thinks that the child, your niece, won't be able to cope with the baby . . .?"

"Oh, she definitely *does* think that," Father Barry said grimly, a little vein working in the jawline closest to Liz. "She thinks it would be irresponsible of her, of *me,* to allow Stacey to go ahead and have this baby when she's such a child herself. Even physically, there could be real dangers for someone her age, never mind emotionally. And she has all these plans to go away and study nursing when she eventually leaves school. Stacey, I mean. She's talked about nothing else since she was a kiddie. And you and I know perfectly well, Liz," he went on, turning to his parishioner and fixing her with an earnest stare that made a warm blush suffuse her cheeks, "that, with the best will in the world, babies and studies don't mix. I've lost count of the number of girls I've met over the years who all had the best of intentions when they got pregnant to continue with their studies but, one by one, they nearly all fell by the wayside. Oh, through no fault of their own. Even a mere male like myself can just about imagine how hard it is for someone to bring up a child on their own."

He fell silent and there was no more conversation between them for a minute. Liz thought back to how she'd got married and had Leah after teacher-training college, so her studies had been finished and behind her. But, instead of the career she'd been expecting and looking forward to, she'd been keeping house for Gerry and helping him to further his own accountancy career by cooking elaborate meals and hosting dinner parties for his colleagues and bosses in the firm, and that had been no joke when she had Leah to mind. And just imagine if Leah had been a child with special needs on top of it all! Even *with* a husband, that would have been so hard to cope with, and Gerry hadn't really been a hands-on kind of husband to begin with. All the cooking, cleaning, housework and child-rearing had been left to Liz, and it had also been left to Liz to see to it that Gerry always looked especially good in front of his co-workers, the happy family man with the nice house, the lovely, gracious wife and adorable baby daughter who could read, write and even add and subtract at an early age, just like her clever accountant daddy. Looking back on it all, Liz sometimes thought that she might as *well* have been a single parent, for all the help she'd had from Gerry. Imagine, then, what a monumental task Father Barry's little niece had ahead of her if she really intended to go through with her pregnancy with just an eejit of a boy her own age to help her!

Father Barry straightened himself up now, giving Liz a start because for a moment there she'd forgotten completely where she was and that she wasn't alone.

"Ah well," he said, shaking his head as if to dispel the images there and wipe the slate temporarily clean, "God is good. These things have a habit of sorting themselves out for the best, don't they? What we think of as monumental obstacles today can look like little ant-hills when we look back on them, in a week or a month or a year's time, can't they? How are you, anyway? Has it been two years yet? Since . . . since young Leah, I mean?"

He turned and looked at her properly, and she flushed a fiery red beneath his clear, candid gaze. What honest, gentle brown eyes he had, she thought, noticing for only the first time how piercing they were as well. Of course, she'd never really been this close to him before, or for this long. She nodded.

"Just coming up on it," she said, chewing on her lower lip like she did when she was distressed, or about to become so.

"It doesn't get any easier, does it?" He looked sad suddenly, and a million miles away, and Liz wondered what, or *whom,* he was thinking about to transport him so far away so quickly.

She shook her head mutely, alarmed at the tears that sprang so quickly to her eyes. Dammit! She brushed them away furiously with the back of her hand. To her astonishment, he put his hand in his pocket and pulled out a freshly laundered white linen handkerchief, the kind that often had initials in the corner, although this one didn't, and handed it to her. She took it gratefully and dabbed her eyes on it, wondering as she did so whose job it was to keep him so pristine. The priests' elderly housekeeper, she supposed, an old woman who'd never see seventy again, that was for sure.

"I'll have this washed and returned to you," she said, embarrassed, crumpling the square of no longer pristine white linen to a ball in her hands.

"No rush." He shrugged big, powerful-looking shoulders in the black priest's jacket he wore. "Listen, Liz, I think I've mentioned this to you before, but we still hold the bereavement support group next door in the community centre every month. It's the last Thursday of the month. Our next meeting is tomorrow night, as it happens. Why don't you come along? We don't promise any miraculous solutions or anything like that, but we have tea and bourbon creams on a good night and there's always a good bit of chat to keep your mind off things if that's what you want."

"I'd have to ask Gerry," she said tentatively. *And he normally says no to everything*, she added silently.

As if she'd spoken the words aloud, Father Barry grinned and said: "Tell him you've got an emergency meeting of the Ladies for the Beautification of the Holy Altar."

"Father Barry, are you actually suggesting I tell my husband a little white lie?" she said, the beginnings of a smile playing around the corners of her mouth.

"What the eye doesn't see, the mind doesn't grieve over," he said with a wink.

Liz couldn't help it. She burst out with: "I just have to say this, Father. I can't believe you're so . . . well, so like a normal person! You know, sitting here talking about your niece and your sister and everything. I know that's come out all the wrong way, but do you know what I mean?"

Father Barry laughed as he got to his feet. He towered over Liz, who seemingly hadn't realised before how tall he was. "I know exactly what you mean, Liz, so don't panic. People usually expect priests to act a certain way, like we're not part of the human race or something. They don't expect there to be any more to us than getting lost in Ireland's biggest lingerie department every Christmas Eve and taking part in A Song for Europe."

"Leah loved that show," Liz said softly, the tears starting to her eyes again. "She used to laugh at it till the tears were literally running down her cheeks. We all did. But Gerry won't have it on in the house now since . . . since, you know . . ."

"Time is a great healer. I know it sounds corny, even clichéd, but it's true." He put a hand on Liz's shoulder and squeezed it briefly. "So, might we see you tomorrow night, then, Liz?"

The unexpected physical contact sent a jolt of electricity hurtling through her. "I'll do my very best." Her cheeks burning, she gathered up her polishing cloths, her tins of polish and bag of flower-ends and hurried home to make a start on Gerry's dinner.

"I might have to go out later on," she said nervously the following night as she placed Gerry's dinner, a beef lasagne with half-chips, half-salad the way he liked it, on the table in front of him. "The altar ladies are having a meeting about . . .

about what we'll do for decorations when the missionary priests come in the autumn. You know, for the yearly Mission Masses." She immediately turned back to the sink so he couldn't see her face (lying to him was a lot easier when he couldn't see her face) and, picking up a dishcloth, began to wipe down the already spotless surfaces. It was an action she performed repeatedly when she was anxious. She supposed she might be a little OCD in some ways.

"That's not for weeks yet. Months. What's the hurry?" He was glaring at her suspiciously now, a forkful of lasagne halfway to his mouth.

Liz chanced a light laugh. "Oh, you know what the ladies are like. Audrey Templeton in particular. You can never prepare too much or too soon for a mission Mass." She'd have to keep her fingers crossed that Gerry didn't bump into the gossipy Audrey Templeton around the town. She had a mouth on her like a loud-hailer, that one. She and Liz had one of those passive-aggressive relationships where they'd be faultlessly civil to each other when they met but couldn't really stand each other otherwise.

"Don't be late," he grumped, clearly annoyed that this was an instance in which he couldn't say no, not if it was for the church. But if he could lay down the law about other things, like how late Liz could stay out and other things, he certainly would.

"I won't," trilled Liz, her heart soaring as she scrubbed and scrubbed at the sink with her dishcloth. She could go! It was hard to keep from humming a little tune while she washed up. That would be a sure indicator to Gerry that she was happy and something was afoot. Even if he couldn't work out what the 'something' was, she wouldn't put it past him to put his foot down and spoil everything by issuing a blanket ban on her going out tonight. Playing it as cool as she possibly could, she got through the rest of dinner and the washing-up and made her escape.

The bereavement support group met in the little community centre adjacent to the church on the last Thursday of every month. Tonight was the last Thursday in July. The group would take a summer break after that until September. It being summer, a lot of people had already gone on holiday and were therefore absent.

"You should see it in September," Father Barry joked with her as the session was about to start. "We get so many here then it's like the first day of Back-to-School."

Liz nodded and smiled back. She couldn't believe how excited she was to be attending a meeting of a bereavement support group. She'd washed her short dark curly hair earlier in the day (long before Gerry came home, so he couldn't accuse her of primping and demand to know for whom she was doing it) and spritzed the sprightly curls with something new she'd bought from her hairdresser. She'd had to hide the receipt from Gerry, of course, as he would have had an apoplectic fit to see her buying expensive haircare products from a salon instead of the cheapo own brand stuff from the supermarket, but her hair *did* bounce and shine tonight. She'd tried on every pair of earrings she possessed and experimented with different shades of lipstick, before slamming her jewellery box shut and rubbing her lips clean with a tissue, telling herself in exasperation that she was being ridiculous. Ridiculous to think even for a second that anyone, least of all a parish priest, would be remotely interested in how she looked. She still looked nice, though, in her pale, V-necked lemon sweater over a short-sleeved white blouse, white summer trousers that suited her still-trim figure down to the ground and a snazzy pair of cloggy-looking sandals.

"Not to throw you in at the deep end or anything, Liz," Father Barry said kindly, "but, as we're so few tonight, I thought you might like to go first and introduce yourself and say why you're here. And, because we are so few, you'll have a bit of extra time tonight as well."

Hooray, thought Liz glumly. Extra time to make a fool of myself in front of strangers. "*Erm*, how will I know when I've gone on enough?"

"Don't worry, love, we'll tell ya!" replied a middle-aged man, who looked to Liz the very image of a Dublin taxi-driver. Everyone round the little circle laughed, and, when the laughter had died away, Liz, more comfortable now that the ice had been thoroughly broken, began to speak.

"My name is Liz Grimes and . . . in 2012, my daughter Leah died of stomach cancer in Bulgaria, where she was living at the time . . ."

At the tea break, Father Barry came over to her as she stood rather awkwardly and self-consciously by the table at the side of the room with her cup of tea and a bourbon cream.

"How did you find it?" he asked her.

"It was . . . it was strange, but I suppose cathartic as well," she said slowly. "I've certainly never told a bunch of strangers my private business like that before."

"They're a good group, aren't they?" he said, helping himself to a biscuit, which he then proceeded to dunk with enthusiasm in his tea. "I'm a dunker," he added with a grin, when he saw her looking at him. "And I love a nice biscuit."

"Father," she said suddenly, "could I talk to you privately sometime? I don't mean here, but . . . maybe tomorrow, in the church or somewhere like that?"

"Of course, Liz." He looked down at her gravely. "Is it a personal matter?"

She nodded, her eyes downcast.

"Call into the presbytery then around two? We can chat in my office and, if it's privacy you need, no one need see you going in and out except Old Mags, and she's the soul of discretion." Old Mags was the priests' decrepit old housekeeper, and as far from the soul of discretion as any woman Liz had ever known. Honestly, trust a man not to know that!

She nodded again. "Thank you so much, Father."

"Grand, well, I'll see you tomorrow so. In the meantime, I think we'd better get back to business here. We lock up the hall strictly at half nine. If I don't get everyone out on time, old Jock the caretaker gives me a proper bollocking."

Liz nearly choked on her bourbon cream. She coughed and spluttered so much that the Dublin taxi-driver fella had to pound her on the back a bit.

The meeting resumed.

"It was years and years ago," Liz began tremulously. They were seated in comfortable armchairs across from each other in Father Barry's office in the presbytery. "Leah was only about eight years old. I got pregnant again. It was a shock to me, I can tell you."

"You weren't trying for another baby at the time?"

"Oh God, no! This pregnancy was a surprise. I suppose you think that's a strange thing for a woman to say, when we all know how babies are made, but that side of things had been all but finished between myself and Gerry since Leah was born. As I say, this was a surprise, but . . . but not a happy one." She fell silent for a minute before continuing: "I did a terrible thing, Father. I went to England and I got rid of it. I pretended to Gerry that I was helping Jean — that's my closest friend, Jean Dennehy — to pick out an outfit for a wedding, and, in fact, Jean *did* come with me to London, God bless her, and the two of us stayed with my cousin Maura in Soho, who very kindly drove us back and forth to the clinic I was booked into. I had the procedure done — I can't say the proper word, even now — and I came home afterwards to Gerry, and he was none the wiser that we'd been going to have the . . . the baby boy he'd always wanted." She hung her head and waited for his response.

"Do you know why you did it?" he asked her gently.

She nodded. "I couldn't bring another child into that marriage. I couldn't expose another child to years and years of criticism and petty-mindedness and bigotry and penny-pinching from Gerry, stingy Gerry with his controlling ways and his hatred of anything or anyone even remotely different from the so-called 'norm'. Oh, there wasn't any physical abuse or anything like that. He never hit us. It was just the horrible negative attitude he held towards everything and everyone in the world. Always seeing the worst in everyone, always suspecting people's motives. There was just this poisonous, *toxic* atmosphere around him the whole time, like a cloud of noxious gas or something. It was bad enough that Leah had

had to live through it. I shielded her as best I could, and she was lucky enough to have the kind of personality where Gerry's meanness and nonsense just seemed to roll off her like water off a duck's back — but a boy? He would have taken after Gerry; he might have ended up *being* Gerry! I couldn't take the risk. So I did what I did, and now I have to live with it."

"How would Gerry feel about it, do you think?"

"Oh, he'd be livid. He'd be like a demon. He'd probably kill me. Not so much because of the little baby boy he'd lost, but because I'd done something independently of him, without consulting him or asking his permission. That's the part he wouldn't be able to handle, the part he'd make me pay dearly for, if he ever found out."

"More importantly, Liz, how do *you* feel about it now?"

"Oh, I still feel that I was right to do it. I had a child's life to keep from being contaminated by Gerry. But I'm frightened too, Father, of going to hell for what I've done. I've been worrying about that non-stop since we had that chat about your little niece yesterday. It's kind of brought it all back to me. Do you . . . do you think I can ever be forgiven, Father? I've never said a word about it in Confession, ever. I've always been too afraid that the priest might get angry and throw me out of the church in front of everyone for breaking the most important commandment of all: *Thou Shalt Not Kill.* But . . . but what do *you* think, Father? *Can* I ever be forgiven?"

"Liz, I know I'm supposed to take the party line on this – – you know what that is — you've said it yourself — but I can't help but feel that, sometimes, God knows that people need to do what they have to do, and He cuts them some slack because of it. I'll tell you what, Liz. If it helps, would you like me to hear your formal Confession now? I can give you absolution, then at least you'd have that off your mind."

"Would it be valid, though, if we did it in here? I mean, rather than in the proper confession box?"

"It'd still be valid if we did it on top of a mountain in the desert with a camel and a lizard for witnesses," he said with a laugh.

Liz laughed too then, just a little bit, and then she nodded eagerly, her eyes shining. "We'll do it! I mean, I'll do it. The Confession, I mean." Covered in confusion, she stopped babbling and blushed furiously.

Father Barry rearranged the armchairs so that they had their backs to each other. "That might make it easier for you," he decided, "if you don't have to look directly at me."

"Oh, but I *like* to look at you!" Liz said without thinking, then she clamped her hand to her mouth in mortification. What had she said? Why had she just blurted that out like that? She wanted to die. She could just kick herself for her own stupidity. Father Barry didn't seem to have heard her remark, however; he just went on efficiently rearranging chairs and plumping up cushions.

"There now, we're all set," he said eventually. He sat on one chair with his broad-shouldered, black-clad back to her, while Liz occupied the other.

Nervously, she mumbled the familiar words *'Bless me, Father, for I have sinned,'* then she cleared her throat and uttered them more clearly. It all only took a few minutes, much to Liz's surprise. She'd been carrying around the weight of the shame and guilt for what she'd done for over twenty years, and here was Father Barry absolving her of her enormous sin, in the quiet afternoon sunlight of his presbytery office, in less than five minutes. She could hardly believe it was happening.

"You're a remarkable woman, Liz Grimes," Father Barry told her as she was gathering up her bits and bobs to leave. He bent down to kiss her cheek. Without stopping to think, Liz pulled him down to her and, for one heart-stopping moment, their lips met and locked in a kiss. His lips were firm and soft and infinitely kissable, just like she'd known they would be. It only took her seconds to discern that. Then, with a little agonised cry of distress at what she'd done, Liz pulled away from him. Gathering up her handbag and jacket, she fled from the presbytery.

It was a week or two before she could muster up the courage to go back to the church. Leaving the flowers for someone else on the rota to do, she opted instead to do a bit of clean-up outside, wearing her gardening gloves to pick up discarded crisp packets and plastic drinks bottles from the flower beds and grass verges around the church and the little adjoining cemetery and put them in a black rubbish bag. She gave the presbytery a wide berth. After a while, she relaxed into the work and began to enjoy the feel of the sun on her uncovered head. She'd hardly relaxed for a single second over the last few days, too ashamed and embarrassed at her actions. How dreadful of her, to kiss him like that, as if he were an ordinary free man and not a priest, and she an unattached woman, free to kiss whomsoever she chose! It sent her into a cold sweat just to think about it. She redoubled her efforts to fill her rubbish bag with any bits of flotsam and jetsam she could see floating about the place, just to chase away the memory of what she'd done; then, when her bag was filled to her satisfaction, she set off to take it to the big wheelie bins round the back of the church. Turning the corner, she walked slap-bang into a tall man wearing a long black soutane and dropped her rubbish bag on the ground.

"Liz," said Father Barry, putting his hands on her shoulders to steady her. "I've been wondering how you were. I would have phoned, except we only have a landline number for you and I didn't want to get you into any trouble with Gerry by calling it."

Liz stared up at him in dismay. "Oh God. I was hoping not to see you. I'm so ashamed of what I did. Can you ever forgive me?"

"For what?" His deep rich voice sounded amused. "For paying me the immensely flattering compliment of kissing me? There's nothing to forgive."

Liz looked around them in an agony of mortification lest they be overheard. "But . . . but you're a priest," she whispered, two bright spots of red colour standing out on her cheeks, in stark relief to the rest of her face, which was ashen white, "and I'm . . . I'm a married woman. I feel so ashamed. I've never done anything like that in my whole life, I swear to you I haven't." Confused, she knelt down beside him and began to pick up the bits of rubbish that had fallen out of her untied bag when she'd dropped it.

"Liz, you're to stop beating yourself up about this at once," he ordered, crouching down to help her with the rubbish. "It never happened, all right? You've done nothing to reproach yourself for, okay? Now, give me this rubbish and wait here for me," he went on, straightening back up to his full height and brushing down his soutane with the hand not holding the rubbish bag. "I'll be back in literally two seconds. Don't move." He strode off round the corner to the bins and was back seconds later, minus the rubbish bag. "Come and sit over here with me for a minute, will you? I'd like to talk to you."

He led the way to one of the stone benches that dotted the church grounds. Liz hesitated for a minute. What if someone spotted them together? Then she gave herself a little shake and followed him, albeit nervously. When they were seated at opposite ends of their stone bench, Liz as far away from him as she could manage it so it didn't look dodgy to anyone who might see them sitting there, Father Barry started to talk. He didn't look at Liz as he spoke to her, just chatted away easily to the open air as if she weren't there. Liz was grateful for his not putting all the focus on her, and she gradually began to relax her rigid stance. To any observers, Liz hoped, they would just have been a priest and a parishioner enjoying the beautiful summer sunshine while having a casual chat about parish matters, such as the flowers for the altar, the upcoming missions and the upkeep of the church and its grounds.

"I was in love once," he was saying. "I was only about twenty-eight. I'd left the seminary, I had my Master of Divinity under my belt, and I'd been assigned to my first parish. I wasn't the parish priest, of course, just an underling. But I was so proud of myself, you'd think I'd been made Pope."

He paused, and Liz smiled in spite of her nerves. She could just imagine him, young, eager, all set to change the world with the fire of his fervour and enthusiasm.

"Part of my work — and it's the same now as it was then, as you'll know yourself — was to visit any invalids in the parish and try and give them some comfort if I could. One such man was called Pat — and he'd been more or less bed-ridden ever since a bad dose of tuberculosis in the eighties. Anyway, this man Pat had a wife, a patient, long-suffering woman who put up with all his grumbling and complaining and bitterness about his lot in life and never uttered a word of complaint herself. She was beautiful, in a faded, tired kind of way, and I began to look forward more than I can tell you to my visits there. Before long, I was head-over-heels. Lost, to her beauty and her generous, compassionate loving nature."

He paused for a minute, and Liz felt a painful dart of envy shoot through her at the thought of this beautiful patient woman she'd never met who had captured Father Barry's heart so completely back in his younger days. How handsome he must have been then, she thought, looking at his chiselled profile as he gazed off into the distance, the strong jaw that was never quite stubble-free and the thick brown hair liberally flecked with grey at the temples and swept back off his face. You could almost imagine him as a film star of some kind, or a handsome priest in a mini-series about forbidden love or something, like Father Ralph de Bricassart in *The Thorn Birds*. Liz shook her head slightly to dispel the images that were coming into her mind and directed her attention back to what Father Barry was saying.

"For the first time in my life, I was really, truly in love, Liz. I knew it was real love, because it hurt me to think about it, it was so intense. And I know that she felt the same. We talked about running away together, that's how serious it was. But we couldn't work out how to do it without devastating the husband, who depended on her for everything."

How Liz hated her at that moment! She felt almost sick

with jealousy. If the woman had been sitting beside her on the bench right now, she might have clawed her lovely eyes out.

"Then the inevitable happened. She fell pregnant. By me, I mean, as the husband was no longer able to . . . was no longer capable of the act. There was no question of an abortion, as she was a staunch Catholic.

Not that bloody staunch, thought Liz bitterly, if she was fooling around with a priest when she was supposed to be married!

"We had no clue, not a clue, what to do for the best. So I went to my parish priest and told him everything."

"What happened?" breathed Liz.

"Things happened pretty quickly after that. After only a few days, I was moved to another parish, about as far away from her as you could get. Money was to be taken from my pay every week and paid into a bank account towards the upkeep of my, well, of the baby that was now well and truly on the way. I wasn't allowed to see her, not even to say goodbye. My parish priest thought that, in this case, least said, soonest mended, and that a clean break was best for all concerned. I wrote her a letter when I was in my new parish, but I never sent it. Too cowardly, I suppose. Too afraid of stirring things up again."

"What happened to her? And the baby?"

"The husband found out eventually, of course, that she'd been unfaithful. How else could she have conceived a child? Bedridden or not, he beat the living daylights out of her, and she miscarried."

"Oh God, no!" Liz's hand flew to her mouth. How could she have wished all kinds of harm on this poor woman? She'd be needing another emergency confession at this rate.

"The last I heard, although this was years ago now, they were still together, still miserable, no doubt, but stuck with each other, nonetheless. I blamed myself for everything, for ruining her life because of my own selfish, lustful desires."

"Well, she was an adult too, wasn't she? She had a mind of her own as well. It was her decision as much as yours to enter into the . . . well, the affair."

"She came off much worse, though. The penalties were nearly all hers to bear. She paid dearly for her association with me."

Liz bit down hard on the unkind remark she'd been all set to make about the love of Father Barry's life.

"You know, Liz," he said earnestly, turning to her now to look her full in the face, "I sometimes wonder if the reason I went to my parish priest in the first place was because I knew that, if I did that, all the responsibility for whatever happened next would be taken away from me, that Mother Church would solve my dilemma for me without me having to lift a finger. Yes, I loved her with all of my heart but, when she fell pregnant, I think I got scared. Maybe I even wanted out but I didn't want the messy trouble of having to extricate myself, and that's why I went to my priest. I was a cowardly shit, that's what I was."

"Don't say things like that!" cried Liz fiercely. "You're a brave, kind, generous, noble honourable man, and any woman would be lucky to have you!"

"Don't canonise me, Liz," he said grimly. "I'm no saint. But I can now spot a potential disaster when it's speeding down the motorway towards me at a hundred miles an hour, and that's what I wanted to talk to you about. I've . . . I've put in for a transfer to another parish, Liz. I think it's best that we don't let this . . . this thing that's between us get off the ground. Best that we nip it in the bud. That much I learned, at least, from all that . . . all that business . . ."

She stared at him in dismay. "But you can't leave! You just can't! Not when we're only getting to know each other!"

"Liz," he said, his tone deadly serious, "I won't lie to you. Yes, you remind me in many ways of *her*. Yes, you're a woman I could so easily love. But I'd be no good for you. I'd ruin your life the way I ruined hers. I won't take that chance."

"Is it really me you're protecting," she said, "or just your precious self?" She put her hand to her mouth, aghast that she'd just talked to him like that.

He shrugged and got to his feet. "Probably a bit of both. I told you I was a coward, didn't I? Probably more so in my old age than I was back then. I've become used to my comforts now and a nice quiet uncomplicated existence. I guess I just want to keep it that way. Maintain the status quo, if you like. I know it's a cop-out but I can't, or won't, change it. Goodbye, Liz." He held out a hand to her and she took it automatically and let him squeeze it, hard. "You're a good woman. I hope you find some kind of happiness in life. God knows you deserve it."

And then he was gone, round the side of the little church and into the presbytery. Stunned, Liz gathered up her gardening gloves and made her way slowly out of the church grounds and down the road to her Luas stop like someone in a trance. The sun was shining brightly enough for sunglasses and the birds were singing but Liz noticed none of it. She sat stock-still in her seat on the Luas and let it carry her homewards without taking in anything of her surroundings. What did anything matter now? Her heart was broken.

For once, Gerry was home before her. He was seated at the kitchen table, the newspaper open in front of him, sniffing disapprovingly and making her pointedly aware that *he* was aware of the lack of dinner preparations under way anywhere in the vicinity. Liz nervously began to potter about, looking in the fridge to see what they had in. It was a Tuesday, and Gerry normally enjoyed a nice big fat juicy steak on a Tuesday while she herself nibbled on a pork or lamb chop.

"Guess who I met in the post office today, buying a TV licence while I was renewing the car insurance?" he greeted her with.

She shrugged, tying on her apron and getting ready to peel potatoes and chop vegetables, like she did every boring, meaningless day of her life. "How should I know?" she said dully. What did she care who he'd met in the post office, and what did it matter, anyway? What did anything matter, now . . .?

"Audrey Templeton."

Liz paled. She stood at the sink with her back to him, hardly daring to breathe.

"And guess what she told me?"

"What did she tell you?" Liz's voice cracked on the words.

"Well, it's a funny thing," Gerry said, obviously milking his moment for all he was worth. He came and loomed behind her as she stood at the sink, fiddling with this and that with trembling fingers. "She told me that the altar ladies haven't had any meetings yet about the Mission Masses, and certainly no emergency night-time ones. Wasn't that a strange thing for her to say?"

There was a crash as the plate Liz was holding slipped from her fingers and fell to the floor.

Chapter 9

JAMIE

What a fabulous day it was! Much more of this, Jamie Sweetman reckoned, and the Irish people, more typically accustomed to rainy summers in the past, would start to expect sunshine as their God-given right. Last year's summer, the summer of 2013, had been an absolute scorcher. The sun, that golden orb in the sky not instantly recognisable to most Irish folks, had blazed in the sky for nearly three consecutive weeks and, by the end of its reign (no rain at all), everyone you met was burnt red-raw on the forehead, the nose and the V of chest skin visible just beneath the neck. Global warming, Jamie decided as he headed homewards from the Swan shopping centre in Rathmines carrying his two shopping 'bags for life'. If it was this hot in 2014, God alone knew what kind of summers the years ahead had in store. Irish people just weren't made for this kind of heat. Even Jamie, a young strong male of twenty-four-going-on-twenty-five at the very peak of his fitness and health, was beginning to wilt, and it wasn't that long of a walk between the Swan centre and his flat in Ranelagh. He looked longingly at the park across the road from him now, before deciding that a quick sit-down on one of the benches and a swill from his water bottle would be just the ticket. He had nothing in his bags for life that would suffer greatly for not getting them home and into the freezer for an extra ten minutes. He crossed the road, nipped in at one of the park's open side-gates and selected a bench. There was space at one of the benches between an elderly man and a harassed-looking young mother with an empty pram who seemed to be keeping an eye on her offspring in the playground. Jamie sat down and settled himself and his shopping between its other two occupants, had a long cooling swig of his water bottle and closed his eyes behind his sunglasses for a minute. Just for a minute, mind. It was beautiful here in the park, and a light breeze was beginning to blow, which really took the kick out of the heat. He couldn't, wouldn't, stay here all day. He had to get his shopping home at some stage . . .

He was startled awake, some ten or fifteen minutes later, by a ball lightly striking the side of his head and knocking his sunglasses askew. What the feck . . .?

"I'm so sorry," said the harassed-looking young mother on the bench beside him. The elderly man had wandered away while Jamie had been snoozing and there were just the two of them left on the bench now. "Joseph, that's very naughty! You've hurt this poor man and knocked off his sunglasses, and while he was having a nap, too!" The blonde chubby toddler she'd been berating stood in front of Jamie, giggling unabashedly.

"Oh, I was just resting my eyes," Jamie said, shocked to find how deeply he'd slept for those few minutes in the sun. He could have been robbed of his shopping, his phone, his wallet, anything. A quick check reassured him that he was still in full possession of his belongings, if not his faculties. Fancy his nodding off in public like that! The sun must be more powerful than he'd taken it for. "I'm not hurt, anyway, it's fine."

"Well, even so," said the woman. "Joseph, say you're sorry to the man!"

"Thowwy, man," lisped the child, still giggling.

"Butter wouldn't melt, I see," Jamie said with a grin. "He looks like a proper little angel, this fella, doesn't he?" The little boy had blonde hair and blue eyes and did, indeed, look positively cherubic.

"I bet you wouldn't say that if you heard him yelling for a drink of water or the toilet at two in the morning."

"I can imagine." To his gratification, the child came and stood beside him, looking up at him without a trace of shyness. "What's your name, young fella?" he asked him, even though he'd already heard his mother call him Joseph.

"Jo-fish," said the child. He pulled the opened water bottle out of Jamie's bag for life and began to shake it. "Jo-fish thirsty. Jo-fish want a dwink of this."

"Joseph, you can't have that! It's the man's drink. You've got your ba-ba, anyway."

"It's okay, I don't mind. But don't drink this one," he told the child. "This one's yucky, because I've already drunk out of it, see? Yucky, right? You can have this new clean one that's not opened, see?" He opened the fresh one and held it out to the child, who took it.

"Yucky," giggled the boy, pointing to the first drink before drinking from the second.

"Yes, that's right, yucky!" Jamie, enchanted by the openness and friendliness of the little fella, was happy to play along.

"That's very kind of you," the woman said, before adding: "Joseph, say thank you to the man!"

"Fank you, man," said Joseph.

Jamie felt his heart melt a little bit. What a pet the child was! The mother looked so stressed, though, so worried. She wasn't wearing a ring on her wedding finger and he wondered if she was bringing up the child on her own.

"It's no trouble at all," he said. And he meant it. Jamie was a people person. He was easy to talk to and he never minded listening to people or trying to help them out if he could. "You're too trusting, Jamie love," his older sister Marie had said to him in the past. "That's your problem. You leave yourself too open to getting hurt and dumped on." But he always tried to give people the benefit of the doubt, and what was wrong with that? He'd almost rather get hurt himself than wrongly turn away someone in trouble.

"Jo-fish need a wee-wee," announced the child.

"Oh, God," said the mother, before turning to Jamie and adding: "I'd better try to get him home, I suppose. We're potty-training at the moment but I carry nappies around with me, just in case. It's just there's nowhere around here to put one on him, and he won't get in the pram when he needs the loo. It's uncomfortable for him, I suppose."

"Jo-fish need a poo-poo," said the child now.

"Where do you live?" Jamie asked her.

"We have a flat in Camden Street."

Not by any means a million miles away, but Jamie

reckoned it might be a bit of a trek for a mum with a buggy and a child who'd refuse to get in it because his bladder was full. He hesitated a moment, then he said: "You could come back to mine to get him sorted. It's just around the corner there, up Liston Drive."

"Oh, we couldn't put you to such trouble," the woman said.

Jamie shrugged. "It's no trouble. It's literally just round the corner there."

"Well, if you're sure?"

"Sure I'm sure. You two don't look like serial killers to me." He grinned, and she smiled back. She had quite a pretty smile when she showed it.

"Okay, then, thank you, you're a lifesaver."

He towered over her when they stood up. He was tall and, with his gym physique, quite burly. She was small and slight and slim, with long dark wavy hair held back by two flowered combs. Her sleeveless sundress, cinched in at the waist, was flowered too and reached nearly to her ankles. Her legs were bare, her feet in flat white canvas summer shoes. Her eyes were dark like her hair and looked huge in her thin, almost haunted-looking face. She would be quite attractive, Jamie thought, if she didn't look so worried all the time. Mind you, he reminded himself, maybe he'd look worried too if he was a young vulnerable woman with the sole responsibility for a small child.

Her name was Aileen, she told him as they walked back to his flat, he carrying the sleepy Joseph in his arms and the woman he now knew as Aileen pushing the buggy with Jamie's two bags for life sat squarely in its seat. She was twenty-eight years old, a little older than Jamie, Jo-fish was three-and-a-half and she was separated from the father of her child, to whom she had never been married. The father, Russell, sounded like a real winner, Jamie thought. Unemployed, heavy drinker, didn't always pay the maintenance for his son, unreliable, often disappeared for weeks on end without so much as an hour's notice. Russell and Aileen were going through one such period of enforced separation now, and Aileen was stressed, worried, permanently exhausted and fed-up. Not that Russell was much help, apparently, when he *was* around, according to Aileen.

"He prefers to just sit and watch Sky Sports with a can of lager to doing anything with Joseph and me," she was saying as they came to a halt outside the rundown-looking, old three-storey house on Liston Drive where Jamie lived alone in one of the apartments, a grandiose word for what was basically a grotty flat more properly intended for students.

The long front garden was in serious need of a good grass-trimming and weeding, and the bins just inside the gate smelled none too fragrant in the heat. The house was divided up into six flats, two on each floor, all equally grotty and badly in need of decoration and repair. The front door, with the paint peeling off it in strips you could pull if you were so minded, was open now, and two Jamaican men, colourfully clad in Hawaiian-style short-sleeved shirts, shorts and flip-flops, were sprawled on the steps that led up to the house, smoking and listening to very loud reggae music on the boom-box they'd brought outside with them. Jamie and the Jamaican men, who lived on the ground floor with their wives and children, nodded their hellos at each other as Jamie handed over a drowsy Joseph to his mother and himself manoeuvred the buggy and the two shopping bags up the front steps.

"Smoke, man?" one of them said, holding out a joint to Jamie.

"Another time, mate, ta." Jamie drank and took occasional recreational drugs (indeed, he'd bought some good stuff from his Jamaican neighbours in the past), but in general he was careful what he put into his gym-honed body, which was his temple, after all. "Is it okay if we leave the buggy down here?" he added to Aileen.

She looked doubtfully round the hall, which was crammed with bicycles and prams already.

"It'll be perfectly safe, I promise you. Or, lookit, if you prefer, I'll just bring it upstairs with us. It's no trouble."

"No, no, it's okay, we'll leave it here – shure I've got the baby-bag and my handbag."

There was no mail for Jamie on the hall table, he saw as they passed it. Good. He got nothing but bills, anyway. Together they climbed the two flights of stairs to his flat.

"Toilet's in there," he told her.

He took the shopping into the kitchen and began to quickly unpack and refrigerate it. Good thing they were back home, he thought wryly, as some of the items were starting to look distinctly soggy. When Aileen returned from the tiny bathroom — shower, toilet and sink and nothing else, not even a cupboard for toiletries, just a rickety shelf — with Joseph, the child waddled straight to the battered old couch in the sitting-room area that was half kitchenette and curled up on it like a cat.

"Ba-ba," he said, holding out his hand with his big blue eyes scrunched tightly closed. Aileen extracted a baby's bottle filled with milk from the capacious baby-bag that now sat, opened, on the floor beside Jamie's couch, and handed it to the child, who took it and began to suck on it greedily with eyes closed. Then, she arranged the cushions on the couch so that the bottle in his hands could lean against them and not fall from his mouth. When she'd finished her little motherly jobs, which Jamie had been covertly watching with fascination and which she'd performed with the efficiency born of years of practice, she turned to her host and said: "He'll sleep for hours now, I'm afraid. Two or three at least. Is that okay? He has a nappy on, so he won't wet the couch or anything."

"That's fine. Will you have a beer? I'm going to have one myself. We've earned it, after walking here in this heat, I reckon."

"That'd be lovely, thank you. Although it feels, a bit, you know, sort of decadent, drinking in the afternoon? I normally don't break out the wine until after Joseph goes to bed for the night."

"I've no wine in – are you sure beer's okay?"

"It's more than okay," she said with a laugh, taking the ice-cold can he proffered and opening it before taking a long cool drink from it.

She came and sat at the table by the window, and, after a moment's hesitation in which he felt like a big awkward yoke in his own home, he sat down across from her.

"This is lovely," she said, looking round the flat. "I really like what you've done with the place. Did you do the flowers yourself? And choose the pictures and cushion-covers and little ornaments, or did they come with the flat?"

Jamie felt a flush suffuse his face suddenly. "No, I picked them out myself." A vision of his father, Jim Sweetman (sweet by name but not by nature, Jamie would have said), knocking seven bells out of him after he'd caught him in the hall one day, arranging flowers from the garden in a little pottery bowl, came unbidden to him but he batted it away. Jim Sweetman had come down on any behaviour he called 'faggotty' like a ton of bricks. That had included the poetry Jamie had scribbled in the little notebook with the Irish birds on it and the little pale-pink-and-white statuette of the graceful, pirouetting ballerina that Jim had hurled into the bin one day and smashed irrevocably in one of his rages. Jamie had looked everywhere for a replacement, but he'd never found one exactly like it again, which made him sad.

"You've got a real knack," she said admiringly.

"Ta," he said self-consciously. How his father would laugh scornfully, and then rage, at the cushion-covers and little matching throws he'd dotted around the couch and armchairs, at the way he'd tied the heavy velvet curtains back with bits of patterned material he'd admired in a haberdashery shop once and wound a spray of dried flowers in with the ties, just because of the way they looked. It made him feel good to make things look nice. It had been a crime in his father's house, but now Jamie had his own flat, grotty and all as it was, and he could do what he wanted with it. His father would never see this flat, so it was safe to arrange it how he liked. He moved Aileen gently away from the topic of décor and asked her a bit about herself.

It turned out that she'd worked on the deli counter in a convenience store before she'd become pregnant, and that her landlord had kicked her out of her flat when he'd found out that she had a baby in tow. Now she lived in a 'dump' of a bedsit on Camden Street in Dublin 2, and there were four flights of narrow stairs up which to drag the baby and the bags and the shopping every time she went in or out. She no longer worked, and lived on rent allowance and something she called the One Parent Family Allowance. It was a bit grim, she admitted to him as they broke open their second, and then their third beers, cold and dripping with condensation from the tiny fridge.

The sun was streaming in at Jamie's open sitting-room window and the sunshine and the beer were combining to make him feel very mellow indeed, even without the weed his Jamaican neighbours had been offering him earlier.

"What about your parents?" he asked his guest. "Don't they help at all?"

Aileen shook her head and made a sort of derisive snorting sound. "You must be joking. They've never liked Russell, you see, and when I got pregnant, they said I was mad not to get rid of it and wash my hands of Russell. Instead, I had the baby and they washed their hands of *me*. They've actually said that I've made my bed, would you believe, and that now I have to lie in it. Like this is the Victorian times or something. I can't go back until I've ditched Russell, but I wouldn't go back even if I *did* ditch Russell. I mean, how dare they dictate to me whom I can and can't see? I'm not their . . . their *possession*."

Jamie nodded understandingly. "Parents," he said with a half-grin.

"What are yours like?" She looked at him curiously.

He shrugged. He never liked getting onto this subject, whether with friends, co-workers or potential lovers. "My dad was laid off work with an injury when I was a kid. Since then, he's just sat at home drinking and lashing out at whoever gets in his way."

"And your mum?"

Jamie stiffened. Mums were supposed to love their children, to shield and protect them, no matter *what,* from the slings and arrows of life and from rampaging fathers hell-bent on causing damage, but not Nora Sweetman. Jamie, as the youngest of their four kids (Niall, Gerry and Marie were all older and married, with their own kids and homes), had probably got the worst of his father's aggressive behaviour, and his mother had never intervened, not even once that Jamie remembered, to protect him from Jim Sweetman's particularly destructive brand of wrath.

"Not up to much," was all he said now. What was there to say?

"Poor Jamie," Aileen said softly, putting her little hand over his bigger one on the table and stroking it with her thumb.

"Hey, don't feel sorry for me," Jamie said with an embarrassed laugh, extricating his hand from hers, pretending he needed it urgently to run over his short spiky ginger hair. "I'm fine. You're the one bringing up a child on your own. That's the hardest job there is, surely?"

"You don't get any thanks or appreciation for it, though. No one ever treats you like you're doing an important job, even though you're raising the next generation of human beings."

"Yeah, it's gas when you think of it like that, isn't it?"

She nodded, then she took his hand again and resumed stroking his skin, clammy from the heat and, now, nervousness. He tried to pull away, but she held fast.

"Aileen," he said, taking a deep breath, "we can't."

"Why not?" She was smiling over at him. She really did look very pretty when she smiled. Her lips looked soft and red (and kissable, he had to admit) and her teeth were small and white.

"Well, I'm gay, for one thing," he said desperately, wondering why, if he really *was* as gay as he knew himself to be, he suddenly felt so damned languid and horny. It was the heat, he thought, looking round him like an animal caught in a trap. It had to be the heat.

Aileen expressed no surprise at his words. "But there's no law against it, just the same, is there?" she said softly. He felt her little bare foot rub suddenly against his leg, bare too in the Bermuda shorts he wore. He felt the hairs on both his legs prickle and stand up. The same thing happened to the hairs on his arms and head and on the back of his neck. Her little foot reached his groin and slipped inside the material of his shorts to rub, gently at first and then more insistently, against his underwear, and the sensation it produced there was electric.

"Can we go to your bedroom?" she whispered.

Swallowing hard, not knowing what else to do, Jamie nodded.

They went out together all that summer and into the autumn. Jamie worked five days a week in the men's clothes shop on Parnell Street that had employed him since he was nineteen, and he spent every weekend and most evenings with Aileen and Baby Joseph, who very quickly grew to adore his Unka Jamie. Jamie took his two weeks' holiday in July and, rather than going off to Ibiza or somewhere on a lads' sunshine holiday with his mates, he spent every minute of it with Aileen and Joseph. They stayed over almost every night of his holiday, with Joseph tucked up on the couch with his baba and his beloved stuffed rabbit, Big Ears, and Aileen and Jamie's sweat-soaked bare limbs entwined together in Jamie's rather lumpy double bed.

The three of them fell into a routine remarkably quickly in the beginning. Aileen would wheel Joseph over to Liston Drive from Camden Street most afternoons, arranging to be there around the same time that Jamie would get home from work. Jamie would come jogging up (that was how he travelled home from work every day while he was living in Ranelagh; it was great exercise and he enjoyed it) and Aileen and Joseph would greet him happily. Jamie would shower quickly in the cramped, mould-infested bathroom and then cook the three of them dinner. He loved cooking and was pretty good at it. Aileen was full of praise for his culinary efforts, but she never offered to cook anything herself.

"Oh, I'm not nearly as good at it as you are," she'd laugh, before pulling him down to her for a kiss.

Jamie came to their upstairs flat in the old four-storey building on Camden Street a couple of times, and slept with Aileen on her pull-out couch while Joseph slumbered in the tiny bedroom in his single bed, but it was so squashed that they only did it once or twice.

"Your flat is so much bigger and nicer than ours," Aileen

would say, hugging him, and Jamie could see that it was and, besides, he never minded them coming to his place. They were good company for him (let's face it, he was lonely, goddammit), the sex was good and frequent between him and Aileen, and Jamie quickly found himself growing to love the blonde cuddly Baby Jo-fish (that was what they both called him, Jo-fish), something he never thought he'd get the chance to do.

"I mean, I'm gay. I know I'm gay. I've been gay my whole life, or at least since I was old enough to know what the word meant. Maybe even before that. I thought I'd accepted that I'd never be a father because I'm gay. I thought I'd come to terms with it, but how could I have, when after about five minutes in little Jo-fish's company all the feelings about being a dad that I thought I'd repressed come bubbling up to the surface? When I look at Jo-fish, I know I'd give anything in the world to be a dad. To be *his* dad. How messed up is that?"

Aileen would laugh and say: "That's not messed up at all. It just goes to show what a lovely person you are, and what a great dad you'll be some day. Look at how good you are with Joseph. You're practically like a dad to him already. I wish you *were* his dad. As far as I'm concerned, you are his dad. A dad is someone who's there for a kid. Not someone who's off doing their own thing, who doesn't give a shit about the kid they've made with someone. Like Russell." She'd grimace then and shudder, as if she were shaking the very thought of Russell off of her.

"Would Russell be okay with me . . . I mean, with me hanging around you guys all the time? Hanging around you and Jo-fish, acting like a sort of dad to the lad?" Jamie worried about that all the time, worried that he might be stepping on someone else's toes, even those of the absent Russell.

"If he's not around to see it, then it's none of his business," Aileen would insist, then she'd put her hand between his legs and manipulate him to a state of arousal so that he could make love to her. Jamie noticed that she'd never allow conversations about her ex-boyfriend, Russell, to go on for too long. She was probably right, he decided. What was the point of dwelling on the fella if he'd pissed off on his little family, left them in the lurch the way he had? As time passed, Jamie persuaded himself to worry less and less about the absentee father, Russell, and he concentrated more and more on becoming attached to Aileen, wanting her, needing her, but loving the child most of all.

Jamie and Jo-fish got on "like a house on fire", according to the child's mother. Jamie played with him endlessly when they were together. He never tired of pushing the child on the swings in the park or of kicking a ball to him in the little back garden of the house on Liston Drive. He loved it too when other people in the park looked fondly at the two of them together, smiled at them indulgently for being, as they saw it, a loving father and son happily at play together. It made him feel 'normal', and, at times like that, he'd feel like his heart was going to burst, it was so full of love for the child. In the flat, Jamie built complicated Lego houses and model aeroplanes and other constructions, thoroughly enjoying the challenge of following awkward-looking instructions and finishing up with a recognisable structure, much to the child's delight.

"You're so good at following the instructions," Aileen would say with a laugh, looking up from Jamie's big television (he'd recently treated himself to the biggest set he could afford) and the film or series she was watching. "I'm rubbish at that kind of thing."

"Oh, it's easy when you've got the knack," Jamie would reply with a grin, before going back to glueing or screwing little bits of plastic to other little bits of plastic while Jo-fish watched him wide-eyed, gurgling with delight. Jamie would look over at the boy every so often and he'd feel an explosion of love inside him so intense it almost felt like an actual physical pain.

"What are you playing at, Jamie, love?" his sister Marie said, when he called over to see her one day he had off from work. "It sounds to me like this Aileen one's just using you. She's got her feet well under the table at your place, with you doing all the cooking and cleaning and entertaining her son while she puts her feet up or goes gallivanting round the place, shopping or meeting her pals and whatever else she gets up to on her little jaunts."

"She's only gone *gallivanting*, as you put it, a couple of times," he said defensively. "And it was only to the Swan Centre to pick up milk and a few other bits for the lad." He flushed as he said this, knowing full well that he'd babysat for Joseph a good few times during the evening while Aileen went out for a coffee or a drink or a meal with her friends. Once or twice, he'd even kept the child at his place overnight while Aileen got a proper break by going to a club in town with her girlfriends.

"I just feel so trapped, Jamie," she sobbed to him more

than once, "all cooped up in that tiny flat with just the baby for company. I'd go mad if I didn't get out every now and then. I'd kill myself, I would."

"I don't mind taking care of Jo-fish," he'd told her eagerly. "He's no trouble at all, shure he's not. He's very easy to mind."

"I know, he's a little dote, isn't he? Everyone says that about him," she'd said, beaming all over her face at the prospect of a night out and a proper break, the poor girl. Jamie would babysit the lad and, the whole time Joseph was in his flat, he'd feel so happy, like he was a proper dad for the first and only time in his life. He didn't even mind the extra washing-up or bed-making or cleaning he had to do when the child was there. It was all worth it. For Jo-fish, for *his son,* as Aileen actively encouraged him to think of the little boy, it was an absolute pleasure.

"And what about when the child's father turns up again, like a bad penny?" Marie was chain-smoking now at her kitchen table in her house in Crumlin, with her mouth all pursed up like a cat's backside with her obvious disapproval. "That's you out on your ear then, isn't it?"

"That's not going to happen," Jamie said, almost confidently. "Even if he does turn up again, which Aileen doesn't think he will because it's been months now, she swears she's not going to take him back again. All that's over and done with as far as she's concerned." He was *almost* confident because, even though he believed Aileen ninety-nine per cent about how she would never get back with Russell, there was still a tiny part of him that feared the man's reappearance. Fate wouldn't be so cruel, though, would it, as to give him Aileen and, more importantly, his little baby Jo-fish, and then snatch them away again after such a short time? No, Jamie reasoned. *Nothing* could be that cruel. And, as the weeks progressed, he *was* finding it a little easier to think of Russell as being completely out of the picture, and of himself, Jamie, as taking over the parental role himself. Stepping into the breach, as it were, bridging the gap, being the father figure, even the *father,* that the child needed.

"*Huh,*" Marie said, leaving Jamie in no doubt as to her opinion regarding Aileen's reliability, her *ability* to really mean it when she said she'd never have Russell back, *'even if he begged on his hands and knees in the dirt,'* to use her exact words. "And what about all the money you've been spending on them?" Marie went on indignantly. "The last time I was out at your place, it looked like a bleedin' toy shop."

That was because Jamie stopped into Smyths' toy store in town most lunch times now to pick up a toy or 'something nice' for Jo-fish. He'd bought him everything from traditional toys like teddy bears and action figures to the latest 'technology' gadgets, like the iPad the child could use to watch cartoons on. Jamie loved the way the checkout girls would admire his choice of purchase and say things like: "Ah, that's lovely, that is. You've just got the one kiddy, is it?" and, grinning like a big eejit all over his face, he'd say: "Yeah, a little fella of three-and-a-half, he's called Joseph." And the girls would smile indulgently at him and say: "Ah, he's very lucky to have a dad like yourself, always buying him such lovely stuff," and Jamie would leave the shop and go back to work feeling like he was ten feet tall and walking on air.

"You're spoiling him," Aileen would say when she'd be

admiring the latest toy or gadget, but she'd be smiling as she said it and she never told him to stop buying stuff, for which Jamie was grateful. He loved buying stuff for his little Jo-fish. It made him feel good and it brought the child such happiness. Where was the harm in it? He'd bought stuff for Aileen too, of course, so that she wouldn't feel left out. The usual things like chocolates and flowers, perfume, candles and bath stuff, but he'd bought her some more expensive stuff too. The perfume she'd wanted, endorsed by some female celebrity or other, that had cost nearly seventy euros, and the gold bracelet she'd admired in the window of a jeweller's shop and which he'd bought her for her birthday. She'd been so delighted with both the perfume and the bracelet that he'd felt brilliant about himself and life in general, and their relationship in particular, after he'd given them to her.

"I earn more than she does," he told his sister defensively now. "That One Parent Family Allowance she's on doesn't exactly allow for many luxuries or treats." Aileen got something called Rent Allowance to help her to pay her landlord but, other than this, the One Parent Family Allowance was all that she and Joseph had to live on. Jamie didn't know how much it was exactly but he knew it wasn't much, certainly not enough for the kind of comfortable, secure life he thought that Joseph, yes, and his mum too, deserved to have.

"Why doesn't she go out and work for her money like the rest of us?" Marie had worked nearly her whole life in the same launderette, and now she managed the place.

"You know perfectly well why. She's got no one to mind Joseph. And he won't be going to school for another eighteen months. She might do something part-time then."

"There's childcare and child-minders." Marie was sticking to her guns.

"Which all cost money. More money than most single parents can afford."

"Oh, you're an expert on single mothers now, are you? Have you given her any money? I'm only asking because I'm worried you're being taken advantage of, Jamie, love."

"That's none of your business, Marie. You've no right to ask me questions like that." He stiffened and went red in the face while she stared at him steadfastly.

Marie sniffed triumphantly. "That means you have. Jamie, love, you earn barely over the minimum wage yourself. You can't afford to be keeping her and her child as well as yourself. You're being taken for a ride, Jamie, love."

"You've no right to talk about them like that!" Jamie flushed even hotter when he thought of all the fifties he'd slipped Aileen for groceries, for stuff for Jo-fish, even for a night out with the girls.

"Oh, Jamie, are you sure?" Aileen would always say with her eyes wide and, then, when he'd grin and tell her he was perfectly sure, she'd fling her arms around him and call him a darling and a treasure, and his heart would soar with gladness. Anything he could do to make her and Joseph's life easier, he wanted to do it.

"Look, you haven't liked Aileen from the start," he accused his sister now, referring to the one time the two women had met, the time Marie had called over recently to his flat and found it looking *"like a bleedin' toy store"*. Marie had been cold and sniffy and snippy towards Aileen, and the younger woman had reacted by prickling up like a porcupine. Jamie didn't blame her. Marie had been positively awful to her that day, practically accusing her to her face of being a conniving little gold-digger just out for what she could get. It had taken ages for Aileen to get back to behaving normally around him again after Marie's visit.

"I think I'll take Jo-fish home," she'd said after Marie had left the flat in a huff.

"At this hour? Do you have to? He's grand here, isn't he?" Jamie had been dismayed.

"I just think I need a little bit of space tonight, Jamie," she'd said quietly.

He'd felt bereft to see them go, and had started bombarding Aileen with texts and calls (not his usual easy-going, laid-back style at all) almost as soon as she'd left, asking her if they were okay and when they were coming back. They hadn't returned for a couple of days, during which time Jamie had felt absolutely desolate. He hadn't felt normal again, happy again, until the pair of them were back in his flat and he was holding Jo-fish's sturdy little body against his in a bear-hug once more, breathing in the baby-smell of him, while Aileen looked on with a fond smile at the pair of them.

"I thought you were meant to be gay, anyway, Jamie, love? What are you playing at, messing around with this girl and her child? You're only setting yourself up to be hurt. As soon as her fella comes back from wherever he's gone off to, she'll be back with him in a flash, or she'll go off with some other fella that catches her eye. You can tell she's a flighty young one, that Aileen." Marie was sitting across from him with her arms folded, a fag drooping at the side of her mouth. She was an expert at holding conversations with a ciggy perfectly in place.

"And I thought *you* didn't want me to be gay?" Jamie retorted bitterly. "You certainly seemed dead against it when I came out. You, Dad, Niall, Gerry, all up in arms about it. I just can't win with you people, can I? When I'm gay and going out with guys, you don't want to know me. When I'm going out with a woman, you still think I'm doing the wrong thing."

"It's not like that, Jamie, love. I'm not proud of how I reacted when you first told me, but it's been a few years now and I've had time to get used to it. I've learned to accept that this is what you are and I'm okay with it. I was only upset about it at first because I knew you'd be in for a hard life, being gay and always being a target for the gay-bashers out there. I'd be lying, even now, if I said that that's the kind of life I'd have wanted for you. But it is what it is, isn't it, and you are what you are. I can't speak for Dad and Niall and Gerry, though. They'll never change. It's just the way they're made."

Jamie preferred if possible not to think about the way his homophobic father Jim and two older brothers had reacted to his coming out. It hadn't even been a proper 'coming out,' involving or implying a heartfelt chat between two parties about something deep and meaningful. His father had found out accidentally, probably the worst possible way for him to have done so. While rooting about in Jamie's bedroom for cash to spend on booze, he'd uncovered a stash of gay porn under the bed. When Jamie had come in from work, his father had blind-sided him with an attack that took the shocked young man completely by surprise. The physical altercation had ended in Jamie's being thrown out of the house in the rain, amidst much hostility and vituperation on his old man's part. He'd managed to persuade a friend to put him up for a bit, and he'd never gone home again, except to pick up his stuff one day when his dad was at the doctor's. His relationship with his father, never a good one or a strong one to begin with, was irreparably in shreds.

As Marie got up to refill the kettle, Jamie sat at the kitchen table with his head in his hands and thought about what she'd said, the remark she'd made: *'I thought you were meant to be gay, anyway?'* That one. That stung. He *was* gay, he was still gay. There was no change there. He still fantasised about men when he daydreamed, he was still aware of the presence of attractive men around him when he went out and about or into work, and he fantasised about men in order to be able to have sex with Aileen. She didn't know that; he wouldn't dream of telling her, but if he didn't do it, the fantasising about men thing, he doubted if he would be able to get hard for her and stay that way long enough to make love to her. He missed going to gay bars, like the George on George's Street or, his favourite, the Glam Bar on Capel Street, a bit of a way up from Panti Bar. He missed his gay mates, whom he had no time for now he was seeing Aileen, and he missed the excitement, the rush he used to get when he saw someone he liked in a bar and it turned out that that person liked him too. The eyeing each other up, the unspoken words that passed between them in a loaded look, the electrifying first touch and the satisfaction of good hard sex, hard bodies crushed together slick with intermingling sweat. He knew that people thought that gay guys were promiscuous because they supposedly had sex at the drop of a hat without being in a meaningful relationship first, but straight people did that all the time too. Just look at the action in Copper Face Jack's or in Flannery's on a Thursday or Friday night. Straight people didn't get castigated for it though, even though sometimes straight people's sex resulted in unwanted pregnancies that caused the mother much pain and anxiety and left the fathers as free as air to walk away from their responsibilities. At least gay guys were only hurting themselves, and not bringing an innocent little third party into their complicated emotional or sexual machinations.

But, if he was still gay, Jamie wondered as his sister handed him his tea with a tired sigh, and if he missed the life, the life*style,* then what *was* he doing with Aileen? He was certainly very fond of her, but he knew that he only loved her as a friend and not really as a girlfriend or potential life partner. Mostly, aside from the obvious fact that he adored little Jo-fish and regarded him as a son, the son he might never have if he remained gay, as it were, mostly he was with her, with them, because they made him feel *normal.* When he went out with them, with Aileen beside him pushing the buggy or with Jo-fish up on his shoulders squealing with delight at every new sight and sound, he knew that people saw them as just a normal family: a mummy, a daddy and an adorable little boy. Sometimes people complimented them on 'their' gorgeous little son, and, when that happened, Jamie's heart filled with gladness. He never corrected their mistake, and neither did Aileen. No one looked askance at him any more for being a single gay male; groups of guys who might have previously given him grief over his sexuality, even though he never felt that he looked particularly 'gay', paid him no attention now, for which he was grateful. Not that he couldn't look after himself — he could — years of punishing gym sessions and self-defence classes had seen to that — but it was a relief not to have to be on his guard against homophobic attacks all the time. Now, the type of guys who formerly might have slagged him off or even attempted to beat him up if they found him coming home on his own late just glanced at him uninterestedly, their eyes sliding away immediately again, bored. Nothing to see here, move along. Not that he wanted Aileen, or her presence, to protect him against homophobia. That was just a pleasant side-effect of their being together. No, the real benefit was simply how normal being with her and Jo-fish made him feel and, despite his strong sexual need to find a man he fancied and fuck him good and hard, he was in no rush to go back to being a member of the gay community.

"She'll only hurt you, Jamie, love," Marie said, taking a sip of her tea and fumbling in her bag for her cigarettes.

"She won't," insisted Jamie.

But she did.

One evening in mid-September, he jogged up to the house after work to find that they weren't waiting for him in the garden as usual, Jo-fish charging round like the Road Runner from the cartoons exploring everything and getting into everything. Jamie didn't panic at first. Sometimes they arrived at the house on Liston Drive after him, or they went to the shop on the corner while they were waiting for him, to get Jo-fish an ice cream, maybe, or buy a bottle of wine or a few beers for dinner. He let himself in, had a quick shower and then made a start on dinner. To his surprise, they still hadn't arrived by eight o'clock, by which time his lovely vegetable stir-fry was nearly ready to be served. Jamie phoned Aileen on her mobile, but it was switched off. Now, that *was* odd, because Aileen was like Jamie in that respect: she never, ever switched her phone off. He left a message, trying to keep it bright and breezy when, in reality, his stomach was in knots. "Hey, you two, what's up? The stir-fry's ready to eat and no one's here to eat it! Give me a call when you get this message, okay? I love you both, 'bye." But, when he still hadn't heard from her by eleven o'clock, at which point he was no longer expecting them to turn up at the flat, he gave up waiting and went to bed, after first tidying away the toys he'd left out for Jo-fish. He had a new rocking-horse for the child hidden in his wardrobe under a pile of towels and shirts. He was saving it for Joseph's birthday on September the twenty-third. He couldn't wait to see the look on the little boy's face when he saw Old Dobbin. Jamie had longed for a rocking-horse his whole childhood, but he'd never received one. Instead, he'd been given footballs and football boots and miniature toolkits and guitars and Meccano sets, even though he'd never expressed an interest in such things before. It was just that his parents, or maybe just his homophobic father in particular, had obviously been desperate to bring out the boy in him, even when he'd been as young as four and five years old. Jamie sighed and went to bed. This evening was obviously a dead loss. He'd see what the morning brought.

Jamie heard nothing from Aileen for five days. On the third and fourth days, he'd stopped off at the house on Camden Street and pushed the bell for Flat 4, but no one had answered. Aileen's flat was at the back of the house as well, so he wasn't able to look up and see if he could spot any activity going on behind the net curtains. He continued on with his journey home both evenings, puzzled, worried and hurt.

On the sixth day of no communication at all from Aileen, just as he was on the verge of calling the Guards and reporting the pair of them, mother and son, missing, he received a text from Aileen which read: **Jamie, please don't hate me, okay? Russell's back and he wants to give it another go. I owe it to Joseph to try again. He needs a father, after all. Please don't try to contact us any more. It's for the best. And I'm truly sorry for any hurt I've caused you. Best wishes, Aileen. PS. Jo-fish sends a kiss.**

Jamie stared at the text, dumbfounded. Just like that? Just like *that?* Three or four months of his life, and the relationship was over, just like that? Gutted, he sat on the couch in his flat for ages with his head in his hands, trying to figure out what to do. There was no one really he could talk to about all this. Marie would only say I told you so, albeit in a motherly kind of way. None of his gay mates would have much sympathy either. The ones he'd told had looked very doubtful about his entering into a relationship with a woman, given that he was supposed to be a gay man. Well, there was no *supposed to be* about it; he *was* a gay man, through and through. He always would be. But the child, the child! His heart hurt, it ached so much for little Jo-fish, for the clean baby-lotion smell of him and the good hefty weight of the boy in his arms. Above all, he missed feeling like a *father*, that marvellous feeling of being normal and not a freak that he'd revelled in the whole time he'd been dating Aileen. What was he meant to do now, just go back to being a gay man in a climate where gay men were not always welcomed? There was talk of a referendum for gay marriage next year some time, but who knew if it would ever even happen or how it would turn out? Jamie turned now to his phone and rattled off dozens of texts to Aileen, begging her to take him back, to consider giving their relationship another chance. After all, he was a better, more viable option as a father for the child than Russell, surely? He was responsible, kind-hearted, a good cook, good with his money, had a steady job. Admittedly, the flat was a kip but he could find better. Aileen replied to none of his texts but one, the one where he'd asked her if he could call over to their flat to drop off all the toys he'd bought for Joseph that still lay around his own space. Not that Jamie wanted rid of them; on the contrary, he'd be gutted when they were no longer there to remind him of the child, but he'd bought the stuff, the teddies, the action figures, the board games and the fire trucks for Joseph, and he wanted him to have them, to get some use, some joy, some fun out of them.

Can I drop them round tonight? he'd texted her.

After a while, her response: **Not tonight. Tomorrow night, okay? 8 o'clock.**

Grand, see you then, he replied, deliberately leaving out the words *'looking forward to it,'* in case she thought he was reading too much into the simple invitation to come round and drop the child's toys off.

He went to bed literally trembling with anticipation. He hardly slept for excitement at the thought of seeing the two of them again and, at promptly seven forty-five the following night, he piled the boxed-and-bagged-up toys, including the cumbersome brand-new rocking-horse which he'd painstakingly wrapped, into the back of a taxi and gave the driver the Camden Street address.

"You got the whole of bleedin' Smyth's in the back there, buddy?" the driver commented.

"Something like that," grinned Jamie, thrilled to be asked. "They're . . . they're all for my son. It's his birthday soon, you see, on the twenty-third."

"Ah, separated, are ya, buddy?" the driver asked, his voice warm with sympathy.

"Yeah," Jamie replied mournfully. "But I'm trying to get her to take me back, see?"

"Is that what all the toys are in aid of?"

"Well, for starters, anyway. I've . . . I've got a little something else up my sleeve too." He blushed bright-red as he thought of all the effort he'd put into making tonight a night to remember.

"Well, the best of luck, mate. That's fifteen quid there, mate. Yeah, I'm separated meself, what is it, about eight years now. Mind you, the kids are all grown-up now but it's never the same again with them once you've moved out of the family home and into some shitty auld bedsit. It's just never the same."

Jamie nodded his head enthusiastically to show he understood the grimness, the bleakness of the lot of the separated man. Together, they wrestled the rocking-horse and the rest of the stuff out of the boot of the taxi and onto the street outside the building that housed Aileen's flat. The stairs up to her flat at the back of the house were narrow and dimly lit but he should be able to manage it. It might be a bit tricky, manoeuvring Old Dobbin round the two bends in the staircase, but he'd be grand. He tipped the driver a couple of extra quid for his trouble, which resulted in a bout of handshakes and shoulder-clapping and back-slapping and "good man yourselfs" and other expressions of goodwill.

"Best of luck now, buddy," the driver said kindly as he climbed back into the driver's seat. "I'll be thinking of ya when I light a candle to St. Jude at the weekend. Once a week I do it, and he's never failed me yet."

"Patron saint of lost causes and hopeless cases, isn't he? That's me for sure, anyway."

"Ah, go on out of that," said the driver good-naturedly. "You'll be grand, buddy. Nice young fella like yourself." He beeped the horn a time or two as he drove off down the road in search of fares.

Jamie, feeling all warm and fuzzy inside after this lovely sympathetic manly exchange, pushed the buzzer for Flat 4, filled with more confidence than he'd come out with, thanks to the kindly fatherly taxi-driver. Nothing happened for several minutes and, cautiously, he pushed the buzzer again. Surely Aileen wouldn't invite him round, only for her not to be in when he called? No, he comforted himself. Aileen would never do that. No matter what had transpired between them, she'd never do that. She wasn't a thoughtless, inconsiderate cow. He'd just pushed the bell for a third time and had turned away from the door, chewing his lip as he wondered was he going to have to call another cab to take himself and Old Dobbin and the other toys back home again, when the front door opened a crack. It wasn't Aileen anyway; he established that straight away.

"*Erm*, I was buzzing Aileen's flat," he said nervously. "Flat Four. She's expecting me."

"Yes, I know," said the tired-looking, dark-haired young woman who'd answered the door, speaking in a foreign accent that might have been Polish — certainly it was Eastern European, anyway. "I am Nina. I live on ground floor. You are Jamie?"

Jamie nodded, a sinking feeling in his stomach suddenly. What was going on here? How did this total stranger know who he was?

"Aileen tell me you come. You bring toys for baby. Aileen say you leave them with me."

"Where is she? Why isn't she here? She knew I was coming."

Nina gave the kind of exhausted shrug that indicated that she neither knew nor cared. "You bring in toys?" she said, turning away to go through the open door of her flat. It was as cramped and musty-smelling as Aileen's own flat, but it was much untidier. There was baby stuff and nappies and toys everywhere. A baby or toddler could be heard crying from another room with a closed door. Nina's reaction to the crying was to turn up the volume on the portable telly. Jamie hesitated, then he started to bring the toys in from outside, if only to stop them from getting robbed by a casual passer-by, but he wasn't happy about this whole situation, which seemed dodgy to him.

"Are you sure Aileen's not in?" he asked Nina, who'd sat back down on the battered settee and resumed watching her programme and finishing her half-smoked cigarette.

Nina shrugged. "She go out with baby and baby's father to see movie, then go for foods. Go upstairs and look for yourself if you don't believe me."

Jamie flushed deeply at the mention of the baby's father. That selfish, lazy excuse for a man, Russell, was out now with Aileen and Jamie, enjoying a film and a meal, while he, Jamie, was stuck leaving bags and boxes for the child he'd loved with this foreign woman who was staring at him now with almost a pitying look in her hard, glittery eyes.

"What is it?" he demanded after he'd deposited Old Dobbin on a space on the stained old carpet (not that there was much space available in the cramped apartment), not caring a hoot if he sounded unfriendly. "What are you looking at me like that for? What are you smirking at?" She wasn't exactly smirking, so he was being a little bit unfair there, but she was certainly gazing at him strangely, and he felt he had a right to know why. It seemed he had fuck-all rights in this general situation as it was, but maybe he had a right to know the meaning behind her pitying look.

"You are Sugar Daddy," she said impassively, muting the telly and giving him her full attention suddenly.

"What? What did you say? What do you mean by that?"

"You are Sugar Daddy," she said again, but there was no malice in her tone. "That is what Aileen call you – Sugar Daddy. She show me all the time the things you buy for her and baby, the bills you pay, the things you do for her."

Jamie coloured bright red, feeling more embarrassed than he ever had before in his life. Suddenly he felt overwhelmed by a desire to get away from this place. He turned to flee the tiny cluttered flat with its overpowering smell of cooking and the glittery-eyed, fag-smoking oracle who dwelled there and told him harsh, horrible *painful* truths.

"You take Nina's advice," she said. "She is what you Irish call gold-digger. We babysit for each other because we need each other for that, but always I know what she is. You are good man. I can tell. You will find woman who will love you for you."

"Sugar Daddy?" he whispered. "You're sure that's what she said about me? That that's what she called me?"

Nina shrugged. "Why would I lie? If she loved you, she would be here now, but she go out with baby and baby's father so she does not have to see you. She is coward too. She wants the easy way out of the mess she has made of your kind heart. I tell you this, which Aileen has asked for me to keep secret. Sometimes when you babysit, she is with baby's father. They have the sex, or go for foods, while Sugar Daddy mind the child."

With that Jamie was gone, out the front door of the rundown-looking building and off at a trot. He suddenly had a terrible dread of Aileen and Russell returning to their flat with Jo-fish in tow, the little fella wearing a golden crown from Burger King or waving a plastic toy from MacDonald's or wherever they'd gone to eat. He couldn't face them, couldn't face the sight of them playing Happy Families together while he was going back to a darkened, empty flat. He couldn't bear it. It was too much. He had to get away. He jogged up as far as the canal. It was dark and not that many people were around as he took the small velvet ring box out of his jacket pocket at Portobello and dropped it in the murky waters. So much for that, anyway. Never again, he promised himself fervently as he watched the black water ripple outwards and outwards and outwards. Never again would he lose his heart so easily to someone who only wanted to hurt him. Never, *ever* again.

He went back to his flat, back to his life and back to his job, and tried to act as if nothing untoward had happened. A few weeks later on a Friday lunchtime, a good-looking, slim young man in his mid-twenties walked through the door of the men's clothes shop where Jamie worked. He looked familiar to Jamie, who thought he might have recognised him from Glam Bar, a popular gay place on Capel Street where he'd recently resumed spending his own Friday and Saturday nights. He hadn't felt much like partying or living it up after Aileen and Jo-fish's traumatic departure, but it had turned out to be good for him. It brought him out of himself and took his mind off things. It was a million times better for him than moping alone in the flat, missing his little ready-made 'family'. Now the good-looking young man was browsing through the shirts and belts, and grinned engagingly at Jamie when the latter came over with an offer of assistance, his heart fluttering like mad all the while in his chest with the excitement of knowing already that he found this particular customer desperately attractive.

"Do I know you?" the young man said suddenly, after they'd spent a while looking at shirts and debating colours (and the dark-haired young man's slightly sallow colouring) together. "I mean, I think I've seen you before somewhere. D'you ever go to Glam Bar?"

Jamie nodded, blushing to the roots of his short, spiky

ginger hair. He was elated. He *knew* he'd seen this gorgeous guy before, and in a gay setting too! "It's practically my second home."

"Mine too. It's a wonder we haven't met properly before now."

Jamie marvelled at this fact too. They chatted about the bars and mates they had in common for a bit (it turned out, not that surprisingly, that they knew a lot of the same people) and, then, when the young man was paying for the four shirts, the belt and the pair of jeans Jamie had persuaded him looked really good on him (well, they did! He had a super-lean figure verging on downright skinny that brought out Jamie's protective side), he said unexpectedly: "Are you doing anything tonight? Only I'm going to Glam Bar with a few friends. It's my birthday," he went on shyly, "and after the bar we're all going back to mine for a house party. Should be an all-nighter, if you're up for it. You'd be more than welcome to come along as my guest. Well, it's my party, anyway. I'll invite whoever I want."

He grinned, and the sight of it set Jamie's heart fluttering so much he nearly thought he might be having actual palpitations.

"I'd love to come," he said, willing his voice not to croak. "I'm Jamie, by the way," he added, holding out his hand for the other man to shake. "I'm pleased to know you."

"I'm pleased to know you, too, Jamie." The touch of his hand on Jamie's was electric. Jamie felt a desire he hadn't experienced in weeks. "My name's Callum."

Chapter 10

PHILIPPA

"Right," said Kate Sheehy-Bulger, donning the tortoiseshell spectacles on a chain around her neck that made her look like an editor from the nineteen-fifties and peering over the tops of them at the list in her hand, "you can choose from the following: One: Father of five cross-dresses to help him relax."

Both of the women in front of her remained silent. Philippa studied her nails and yawned delicately.

"Two: Looking fab at fifty!"

This time, both women groaned loudly and Denyse said: "We've done that one to death, surely?"

"Three: Irish nun leaves the convent to marry prisoner on America's Death Row. You don't get to travel to America, but you *do* get to Skype both the nun *and* her intended."

There were interested murmurs from both women. "I might take that one," Denyse Wheeler said, and Philippa, not overly pushed, shrugged her acquiescence.

"Four: Being vegan in the fast-food era."

Both women groaned even louder and Philippa put two fingers down her throat and made vomiting noises, which made her editor roll her eyes and *tsk-tsk* in disdain.

"Five: And, finally, we have a mystery bag!"

Kate said this last bit with a flourish and Philippa immediately sat up straight, stuck up her hand like a schoolgirl seeking permission to *dul go dtí an leithreas más é do thoil é* and squealed: *"Teacher, teacher! Over here, teacher! I'll do that one, Miss! Miss, Miiiiiiiiss, over here, please! Look at me, teacher, look at me!"*

"It's like running a bloody kindergarten, working in this place," Kate tutted as she opened the envelope containing the details of the so-called *'mystery bag'*.

While she was doing this, Philippa turned to Denyse and said: "You're definitely happy to do the nun and the murderer, are you? You won't change your mind when you find out what's in that envelope?"

"*Nah*," Denyse said. "There's probably just another fashion show or cocktail party for daytime telly presenters in there, anyway. I feel like doing something a bit meatier this month. But, hey, what makes you think that my Death Row guy is a murderer?"

"Well, he didn't get on Death Row by robbing the pension book off a little old granny, did he?" Philippa retorted. "Oh no. He got on Death Row by clubbing the little old granny to death with her own walking stick, then taxidermy-ing her corpse and sticking it on his couch as company for him for when he comes home in the early hours of the morning all exhausted from his killing sprees. That's your average American serial killer for you." She folded her arms and smiled smugly at her superior knowledge of the subject, even though it had been acquired only through watching Alfred Hitchcock's *Psycho* just the once, years ago.

"God Almighty, Philippa, you've got an awfully gory

imagination on you for an Irish person," said Kate, to her head features writer. "You're wasted on the magazine. You should be writing your own horror novels. Be a kind of Stephanie King or something. Now, here we are," she held up the A4-sized sheet of paper she had taken out of the envelope. "An interview with Jem Trueblood in the Clifton Hotel. You'll be talking to him about his latest film and any projects he might have in the pipeline. You'll be taking a photographer with you, and I'm telling you now I want *loads* of photos, topless if possible. He's very open to showing off his body so it shouldn't be a problem. Okay, Philippa? *Philippa?*"

Philippa sat dumbfounded, her mouth open, apparently lost for words, while Denyse put her head in her hands and groaned theatrically. "Why didn't I hold out for the mystery bag? Jem Trueblood is going to blow my nun right out of the water!"

"The details of the interview are all in here," Kate said now as she handed the envelope and sheet of paper over to Philippa, who took them wordlessly. "I suggest you do a load of research on him first, which shouldn't be too hard as he's been in every newspaper and magazine in the civilised world since that bloody film came out."

Philippa nodded, still all picture and no sound.

"Are you all right?" asked Denyse, speaking extra-loudly as to an invalid, leaning forward and putting a hand on her friend's arm. "Do you need anything? Can I get you anything? Water?"

"Wine," gasped Philippa. Her face was pale.

Denyse looked at her watch. "Can you wait till lunch-time?"

"If I must," croaked Philippa.

***

Philippa spent the rest of the morning at her desk in the office of *Ladies' Secret Things,* the magazine for which she'd written for nearly ten years and which was named for a brilliant quote from the Christmas episode of clerical sitcom, *Father Ted.* She'd gone to the Ladies' room straight after her meeting with Kate and Denyse, the other main features writer for the magazine (they usually divided up the features between themselves, though Philippa was technically and on paper the magazine's lead features writer), and splashed a ton of water on her face to revive herself. It had done the job, after a fashion. She had more or less recovered from the shock of hearing that, in a very few days from now, she would be going to the swanky-as-feck Clifton Hotel in Ballsbridge to interview the hottest male actor in the world right now since doing the Hollywood movie *Garbage King,* in which he'd played a young homeless man who'd come from nowhere to become the biggest rock star on the planet because of his intensely personal and relatable song lyrics. The fact that the actor who played the rock star was Irish was a big talking point for the Irish media and the tabloids. Philippa's hands were shaking as she clicked into the various news stories about him and made notes on her pad with her pen. (She prided herself on still using the basic tools of her trade.)

"That's not his real name, is it, Jem Trueblood?" Denyse, whose desk was next to Philippa's in the open-plan office, was all agog for the juicy details and had so far barely touched her nun, despite the fact that the nun's intended was destined to walk the infamous Green Mile in less than a week's time, barring another miraculous intervention from the Governor of the state in which they were currently residing and, although he'd intervened a few times already, it was now said to be unlikely that there would be any more such stays of execution.

"*Nah*, of course it's bloody not," Philippa scoffed, looking up the guy's Wikipedia page on the Internet. "His real name's Ken Jones, he's twenty-nine years old and he lived in Rialto before going to Hollywood and hitting the big time. His parents still live there, and apparently they're very good about giving interviews and showing people round his old bedroom for a modest price. More, if you want to take some of his old teddies or footy posters away with you as a souvenir. We might do a follow-up interview with them after I do the big one with Jem."

Denyse grinned. "Quite the little cottage industry they've got going for themselves there. What else, what else, go on!"

"Well," said Philippa, scanning several online articles at once, or trying to, "it says here that his long black hair is all his own." Denyse made a *'phwoar'*-ing sound at this. His long glossy tresses, as dark as a raven's wing, had been made a huge big thing of in the film — they'd had him running around topless with his hair down like Anthony Kiedis from the Red Hot Chilli Peppers in their video for the song, *Under the Bridge*. "But the tattoos he was sporting on his chest in the film were drawn on for the movie."

"*Awww*," Denyse said, disappointed.

Jem Trueblood had been bare-chested for most of the film; the producers had obviously decided that his magnificent six-pack of rippling abdominals were to be a major selling point, and they'd been right. Women all over the world had swooned at the sight of him. It was like Valentino brought back to life for the movie moguls, and they'd run with it. They'd exploited the young man's obvious physical attributes to the max, and their actions were still paying off in spades. *Garbage King* had nearly broken the box office, never mind the Internet.

"What else, what else?" said Denys. "Is he single or what?"

"*Mmmm*, maybe just for the moment. It says here that he had a hugely passionate love affair with his female lead, Carrie Ashton, the American actress, during the making of the film, but when the film was over she went back to her ex."

"What a dozy cow! Something wrong with her eyesight, obviously. I'd give my left diddy to go out with him, and so would most women in their right mind. These Hollywood chicks are spoiled for choice, that's their problem. When you can choose between Pierce Brosnan and Colin Farrell, you start getting picky. What did he do before he was a big famous Hollywood movie star, anyway?"

"This is the funny thing. Apparently, he's a failed musician in real life. He got turned down by two Dublin music colleges for being tone-deaf, and he's been told off by the Guards a load of times too for busking without a licence. But not just that. Crimes against music, was how one Grafton Street shop-owner put it. Seemingly, he drove customers *away* from the shop with the racket he was making."

Denyse burst out laughing. "So, he's a failed musician in real life, but he's hit the big-time playing a rock star? You couldn't make this shit up, could you? Is that not his own voice he's using in the movie, then?"

"It feckin' well is not. The voice belongs to a forty-three-year-old country singing wannabe from Nashville who was desperate for his big break. Only in Ireland, Denyse, my love, only in Ireland. Or, in this case, Nashville."

Philippa, while still scrolling down through the Jem Trueblood news stories, dashed off emails to everyone she could think of, telling them all her big news about interviewing the movie star.

She started with her two older sisters: Nicola, who was married to Shane and had two children, Little Kimmie-short-for-Kimberley and Little Nicky-short-for-Nicholas, and Geraldine, who was still single but actively seeking a partner on Internet dating sites, and then their younger sister, the baby of the family and of the four sisters, Coco-born-Christine-but-nicknamed-Coco-because-of-her-love-of-fashion-and-her-idol-Coco-Chanel. They all responded pretty much immediately, and they all asked Philippa the same question: "*When's he coming?*"

"*When's he coming?*" Denyse parroted, quoting the line from *Father Ted*.

"Saturday," Philippa told/emailed/texted everyone simultaneously. She was practically jiggling with excitement. "I've to meet him and his publicist at five o'clock on Saturday in the Clifton. I've to announce myself at the front desk and then I'll be given a special pass to go up to the room."

"Up to his *hotel room?* Oh, fucking hell, can I come?" Denyse's eyes were out on stalks.

"You can in your arse. You've got your nun and your murderer."

"I don't want them any more! Can we do a swap?"

"*Tick tacks, no take-backs*, Denyse, you know that's our motto!"

"Fine," sulked her co-worker. "But I would have given you anything you'd asked for."

"You don't have anything I want," smirked Philippa, turning smugly back to her computer.

Three years earlier . . .

Nicola O'Brien (Denby, as was) picked up the phone and pressed the 'answer' button, but she could hear nothing but muffled sobbing for several minutes. After saying "Hello? Who is this? Pip, is that you?" a number of times, the voice she knew better than she knew her own managed to spit out the words: "N-N-N-Nicky, it's me, Pip. C-c-c-can I c-c-c-come and stay with you for a bit? It's all over between me and B-B-B-Brian!"

The relationship Philippa had thought would last forever came to a horrible end on a beautiful Greek island, on a holiday that she'd thought would cement herself and Brian's relationship back together for good. He'd been distracted and sort of distant for months before the holiday, citing problems at work whenever she tried to talk to him about it. He was always too tired for sex, too wrung-out after long, pressure-filled days at work to do more than grunt out a "*Not tonight, Josephine*" and fall asleep when she tentatively made romantic overtures. They'd been living together in Brian's Phibsborough flat for nearly three years, and Philippa was hurt and confused by the gradual change in his behaviour. He hadn't even wanted to go on the holiday, the one she'd been so sure would save their relationship and put things back on an even keel between the two of them.

"What the hell is this supposed to be?" he'd said when she'd presented him with the brochures.

"Well, *erm*. They're what they look like, Brian. Travel brochures."

"I can see that. But where do you think I'm going to get the time to go swanning around some Greek fucking island? I'm up to my tits in work, Philippa. I've told you this time out of fucking number, and you still think you can just book a *holiday* for the two of us without checking with me first? Have you not listened to a word I've been fucking saying to you the last few months?" He said the word *'holiday'* the way you might hear someone else say *'paedophile'*, his voice was so contemptuous.

He'd sounded so angry, she'd actually been scared. Brian had never talked to her like that before, in the whole three years they'd been together. She'd backed away nervously and bumped into the table behind her.

"I . . . I thought you'd be pleased," she said, flushing a dull, dark-red colour. "I thought you could do with the break. I . . . I thought you were working too hard."

"That's an awful lot of *thinking*, Philippa. Maybe you should stop *thinking* for the both of us, because, I can tell you now for nothing, you're shite at it."

It was too much for Philippa. She burst into tears. Brian immediately became contrite. He crossed the room in two strides and took her in his arms.

"I'm sorry, Philly. I'm being an ungrateful bastard, aren't I? I'm sorry, I'm so sorry for making you cry. Can you forgive me?"

"I just wanted to do something nice for you," she wailed, dampening his shirt-front with her tears.

"I know, I know," he soothed, stroking her long chestnutty hair away from her wet face. "I know. And I've spoiled it by being a bastard, as usual."

"You're not a b-b-b-bastard, you're not!" Her voice rose even higher and he shushed her gently. *"I'll k-k-k-kill anyone who says you are!"*

"There's no need for that," he'd grinned, and then suddenly he was her beloved Brian again. He'd been gone there for a minute, but now he was back. "Look," he went on earnestly, releasing her from his bear-hug but taking her two hands in his own, "we'll go on the holiday, okay? The Greek islands at this time of year sound brilliant." It was autumn. "It's off-season so there won't be very many people there. That was clever of you, Pip. We'll have the place to ourselves. We'll have a ball."

"Do you really think so?" she gulped, still tearful.

"Course I do," he said, ultra-cheerfully. He bent his head and kissed her then.

She kissed him back fervently, glad that they were no longer fighting. The kiss became heated and, then, suddenly, he was picking her up and carrying her to the bedroom and dropping her onto the bed, where they clawed and tugged at each other's clothes until they were naked and he was deep, deep inside her, thrusting in and out while he kissed her face and hair wildly and she raked her fingernails up and down his broad bare back.

Afterwards, Philippa began excitedly to pack their bags and prepare for the holiday of a lifetime.

***

The two weeks in off-season Greece were a disaster. They squabbled constantly, about stupid fiddly things like where to go for the day or what time to have dinner, and Brian, who worked in IT like half the men of Ireland today, spent an inordinate amount of time on his phone. Day and night he was checking it.

"I told you, Philippa," he'd explain irritably when she complained, "there's a lot going on in work at the moment. In fact, I shouldn't really have come on this bloody holiday at all. I've left all the lads in the lurch, with this massive project we have on. I only came because you pressured me into it. Guilted me, more like." At the sight of her face crumpling at his harsh words, he'd sigh even more irritably and snap at her: "There you go again, guilting me with the big, sad fucking Bambi-eyes."

"I'm not guilting you," she'd say, frantically brushing away with her sleeve the tears that threatened to fall, but she was heart-broken at his words and behaviour. Or did she only have herself to blame, she wondered sometimes, was this situation entirely of her own making? She'd tried to paper over the cracks in their relationship with a sunshine holiday, like so many had done before her, but if a relationship wasn't working in Dublin, Ireland, why should it work on a Greek island, however remote and idyllic the location? That was a mistake so many women made, Philippa knew. She'd written a bloody article about it herself once for the magazine, shure. She'd even used that exact expression, *"papering over the cracks*". How could she have been so blind, so stupid, as to walk into exactly the same situation herself with her eyes wide open? But hindsight was a great thing, and, besides, it was easy to give good sound advice to a person you didn't know. It was a whole different ball-game when this shit was happening to *you*.

She tried to put a brave face on it all, but by the time the last day of the Most Disappointing Holiday Ever rolled around, she was almost ready to give up the ghost. Almost, but not quite. And then a sort of miracle happened, but not the kind that brought a lifetime of happiness, fulfilment and wonder.

As Philippa was packing to leave for the airport to catch the plane home, Brian went into the shower without taking his phone with him. That was the miracle. He normally brought it with him everywhere, like Philippa did too, but, unlike Philippa, he even took it with him when he went to the toilet, the way other blokes might take a newspaper. He either had an advanced case of phone and social media FOMO *(Fear of Missing Out)*, or he just didn't want to risk leaving his phone down anywhere Philippa might see it.

When she found it on the bed under a pile of his shirts that he'd laid out for her to pack, she picked it up curiously. Should she look at it? She felt torn between ethics and a raging, wholly feminine, desire to see if he'd been up to anything he shouldn't. She clicked into it, keeping an ear out for the shower the whole time. She should be able to hear it when he switched it off. When he came out of the bathroom a few minutes later, a towel round his waist and another one in his hands while he briskly dried his short brown hair, he saw her sitting on the edge of the bed with his phone in her hand, her face impassive, unreadable. It didn't take a genius to work out what she'd seen.

"So, you know then?" he said coolly.

She nodded. Then: "How could you? Iona was my friend. My fucking *friend*! I introduced you."

Brian shrugged. "We never meant for it to happen. We never meant to hurt you."

"You had her round to *our* flat, you fucked her in *our* bed, and you say you never meant to *hurt* me? Wow, I'd hate to see what you'd come up with if you were really trying."

He seemed to bite back an answering retort. Instead, he just held out his hand for his phone. He seemed nervous and fidgety without it.

"Can I have it back, please?"

Philippa stared at him, and then at the phone, as if she hadn't a clue what he was on about. Suddenly she got up and darted through the open French windows out onto the balcony. She raised her arm to throw the phone.

"*Don't do it, you silly little bitch!*" he roared, barrelling at her at top speed.

But he was too late. She'd thrown it as far as she could manage it, which, as she couldn't throw for toffee, wasn't very far. But the phone made a satisfying cracking sound, nonetheless, when it hit the patio floor three storeys down and shattered into a hundred pieces, much to the surprise of the two Greek waiters who'd been smoking in a doorway out of sight of the balconies above them. Looking up, they instantly let loose a barrage of swears and insults. Even Philippa, who spoke barely any Greek, had no trouble working out what they were saying.

"*You spiteful little bitch!*" Brian bellowed, grabbing her arm and yanking her roughly in off the balcony. "*That phone cost me a couple of hundred quid!*"

"*Let go of me, you bastard!*" Angrily, she shrugged off his touch. How dared he have a go at her about the stupid phone, when he'd been having sex with Iona Beirne, one of her oldest and closest friends, for what looked like months now? How actually dared he?

He grabbed hold of her shoulders in the flimsy sun-dress and started shaking her hard. "*You crazy bitch!*" he kept repeating, over and over. "*You crazy fucking bitch. That phone cost me two hundred quid!*"

Her head waggled back and forth as if her neck was broken. It was a horrible, scary feeling.

Without his hand there to hold it in place, the towel round his waist fell suddenly to the ground, exposing his recently showered, shrivelled-up nether regions. He stopped shaking her and stooped, cursing, to retrieve it. Philippa, glad he wasn't shaking her any more, began to laugh out loud out of sheer nervousness and relief.

"What are you laughing at, you mad cow?" he snapped.

"*It's just so . . . so f-f-f-funny,*" she managed, before a hysterical shriek of laughter came out of her, purely involuntary. "*Your t-t-t-towel fell off!*"

He shoved her then, killing the laughter stone-dead straightaway. She fell backwards onto the carpet, banging her head off a chair, and burst into shocked tears. Brian ignored her and strode naked across the room to grab his clothes. Philippa stayed on the floor, crying, for what seemed like ages. After a while, she got up and went and stood in front of the bathroom mirror, staring miserably at her red eyes and blotchy cheeks. She washed her face and went back in the bedroom to finish packing.

And, just like that, the relationship she'd put her heart and soul into for nearly four years was over. They'd travelled together in the taxi to the airport in stony silence, and they'd sat together on the plane back to Dublin the same way. It had been agony for Philippa, who longed the whole time to put her hand on his thigh in a gesture of conciliation or affection, but she couldn't bring herself to do it. Every time she felt her fingers beginning to stray, an image of Brian and Iona, naked together, sweat-soaked, making love, or of Brian shaking and shoving her, would intrude rudely on her consciousness, and that would quell the desire for contact. But only temporarily. Before too long, the fingers would feel like straying again. She was a nervous wreck by the time the plane touched down in Dublin Airport.

The rest had been horrible, truly horrible. They'd been living together in Brian's flat in Phibsborough, so Philippa was the one who had to move out, which she did on the day of their return to Ireland.

"You don't have to move out straightaway," he said awkwardly, once he'd realised she was *packing* packing, as in moving out. "You can stay for a few more days, if you need to."

"Don't do me any favours, will you?" she said tightly as she continued to stuff bras and knickers into a plastic bag. That bastard! Nearly four years together, and he could give her *a few more days* to sort somewhere to live? He could go and fuck himself from a great height, and so could her ex-friend, Iona Beirne. In any case, she couldn't stay in his flat, sleep in his bed — or even on the couch — if they weren't a couple, if they weren't staying together, as she'd thought they would, forever. It was too sad.

So she'd phoned Nicola, the sister to whom she was closest, and Nicola had said (bless her!) that of *course* Phillipa could come and stay with her and Shane and the kids in their house in Harold's Cross, for as long as she needed.

Even though she knew she wouldn't like the answer, she asked him then, her stomach knotted in jealousy: "Is Iona going to move in here?"

"*Erm*, I dunno. We . . . we haven't really talked about it yet."

I'll take that as a yes, Brian Delaney, you two-timing bastard, she decided sadly as she went on packing.

"I'm sorry things didn't work out between us," he had the cheek to say as she was leaving. Nicola had driven over to collect her with the kids in the back of the car, and they were now waiting for her outside the house. "I . . . I *do* wish you well, you know, and all that."

"Fuck you, Brian," she said tiredly, dropping her keys on the hall table with a clatter.

That was then, and now was now. She'd been (mostly) single for three years — the odd one-night-stand when she was tipsy and horny didn't count — and licking her wounds in private while, all around her, life went on, her friends all got engaged, married and pregnant (and not always in that order, either) and . . . horror of horrors, Brian and Iona had got married too and promptly had a baby girl called Isobel. Of course, Iona was the first woman ever in the world to get married and have a baby and, boy, didn't she boast about it non-stop to their mutual friends!

"I hope the baby has her father's hairy back and shoulders," Philippa had said to Nicola on the day of the christening. She'd heard about the event through these self-same mutual friends on Facebook. Then, feeling like the bad witch from the fairy tales who came to the christening to put a curse on the baby, she'd dived face-first into a bottle of wine and stayed there for the rest of that weekend.

Now, in 2014, she thought she could say with some degree of confidence that she was Officially Over Brian. Yes, Over with a capital O! She was still relatively young at thirty-two, she'd taken good care of her skin and her figure and her long wavy toffee-brown hair with the chestnutty glints in it (those, she put there herself), she still craved good sex with every fibre of her being and, for the first time since Brian, she thought she might actually be (drum roll, please) Ready to Move On. She was interviewing the hottest guy on the planet in a few days' time and she was damn well going to look her best for it and, if something were to accidentally happen between the two of them, well, then, what of it? There was no law against it, was there, for two single people to have a little bit of fun in their own time, and behind closed doors?

Philippa scrolled down through her phone for the numbers of her hairdresser, her nail technician and the lady who waxed her, well, legs and . . . things. She made an appointment at Legs 'n' Things for the Thursday before the interview, to give any post-waxing redness or soreness time to calm down. She was going all out for Saturday. You might even say that she was going for the Full Monty . . .

***

It had taken her several days, but she was finally ready. She'd been waxed, oiled, primped, preened, polished, straightened, sprayed, massaged, made-up and lightly tanned to within an inch of her life. Her long chestnutty hair was loose and fell nearly to her waist. The colour went well with those in her short-sleeved, flirty little summer dress, a floaty confection of psychedelic pale-browns and yellows and oranges, sixties-style, that made her legs look extra-long and her boobs nicely round and full in the low square neckline. Her high-heeled sandals were made of the softest pale-brown suede and she had a wide-brimmed hat in the same colour and fabric to finish off the ensemble. She looked spectacular, and she knew it. She thought fleetingly of Brian, wishing sadly that there was some way to let him know what he was missing out on. Ah well. That was then, she told herself firmly as she added the finishing touches to her make-up, and this was very definitely now.

Her phone rang just as she was ready to grab up her handbag and head down to the front door to wait outside for Dónal, the photographer, who'd be accompanying her to the interview and photo shoot. Damn it, she thought, frowning, as she rooted around in her bag for the phone, this had better not be Dónal saying he'd be late. She'd timed this whole thing so that they'd arrive at the Clifton together in plenty of time to meet Jem and his agent. There was a tiny margin of error to allow for minor slip-ups like traffic jams, etc., but positively not for Mucking About or Acting the Maggot. This was Philippa's biggest and most important gig since coming to work for *Ladies' Secret Things,* and no one was going to balls it up on her. She needed it. She really did. You might even say that she had a lot riding on it. To her relief, it wasn't Dónal, phoning to say he'd be late or couldn't come because he had a gangrenous leg. Even a gangrenous leg wouldn't be a decent enough excuse to bail out on the photo shoot. He didn't take the pictures with his damned leg, did he?

"Hi, Coco lovey, I can't talk now! I'm literally on my way out the door this minute to do the interview. Look, I've told you all already, I'll email or phone everyone tomorrow with all the juicy details, okay? Okay, Coco lovey? Okay?"

There was no answer, just a strange sniffling noise. Puzzled, Philippa looked at the phone. Yes, it was definitely Coco's number that had come up on the screen. "Coco? Coco, are you there?" she chanced.

There was more sniffling, then her sister's voice said weakly: "P-p-p-pip, c-c-c-can you c-c-c-c-come over?"

"Over? Over to where, Sutton? Coco, what's the matter?"

More sniffling, then: "M-M-M-Matt."

"Matt, honey? What's he done? Is he all right? Are you all right? Has he hurt himself? Has he hurt *you?*"

No answer, just sobbing.

Right. That was it. "Coco lovey, I'm coming over, okay? You're in the flat, right? Stay put. I'll be there as soon as I can. Okay, honey? I'm hanging up now, but I'm coming straight over, okay? Okay?"

"K-k-k-kay," whispered Coco.

Damn it, Philippa thought grimly as she grabbed up her bag and ran downstairs. That Matt fella had better not have laid a hand on her sister. To her intense relief, Dónal was pulling up outside the house in Rathmines (it was divided up into flats, of which Philippa had one) in his old jalopy just as she stepped outside and locked the front door. Thank Christ for that. She couldn't be doing with having to battle her way out to Sutton on the DART today. It was a gorgeous summer's day and half of Dublin was probably heading to the beach. The other half, as usual, would be in town, causing traffic jams and long delays. She climbed into the passenger seat beside her photographer, careful not to squash the hat.

"*Swit-swoo*, Philippa, looking good, girl!"

Philippa smiled her thanks at Dónal for his appreciative acknowledgement of her appearance. Well, she'd gone to a lot of trouble to look her best, hadn't she? Then she said: "Change of plan, I'm afraid, Dónal. We're going to Sutton, not Ballsbridge."

"Oh?" Dónal began pulling away from the house. "This Jem Trueblood fella in Sutton now, is he?"

"I wish," Philippa said glumly. "No, he's still in Ballsbridge, worse luck. No, the thing is, see, my little sister Coco's in some sort of trouble, and I've got to go to her."

Traffic was heavy now, but at least it was moving. She thanked her lucky stars that she wasn't having to try and commandeer a taxi in the blazing heat to take her to the DART. Thank God for Dónal. They were practically halfway to Sutton already.

"Trouble? What kind of trouble?"

"I don't know exactly. Something to do with her boyfriend, Matt, I think. They may have had a row or something."

"I see. And what about the job? What about this Jem Trueblood fella? Are we not going to interview him, then?"

"Dónal, I honestly don't know! I'm going to try to ring his agent now to tell him we'll be late. Maybe we can meet them later this evening, or tomorrow or something. If there's time after Coco, we might still swing it, but it's twenty to five already, shure." She clicked her tongue in frustration when the agent's phone went straight to voicemail.

"Hi, you've reached Alan Freebourne of Freebourne Publicity. Leave a short message after the tone and I'll call you back when I get a minute." The voice sounded suave and American and sort of *rich*, somehow.

Beeeeeeeeep.

"*Erm*, hi, Alan, it's Philippa Denby here from, um, *Ladies' Secret Things*. I'm, *erm*, supposed to be interviewing Jem Trueblood in the Clifton at five?" Philippa groaned inwardly. She'd planned to be swanning in to the Clifton Hotel in Ballsbridge round about now, looking cool, calm and collected and definitely not sweating like a labourer in a heatwave, the way she was now. She sighed and continued leaving her message. "Anyway, *um* . . ." she searched her memory frantically for his name, "Adam, I mean, *Alan,* the thing is that something's, *erm*, something's come up and, *erm*, I'm afraid I'm not going to be able to make it at that time. But, *um* . . ." here, her voice went up hopefully, "I was just wondering if you and . . . and Jem will be around for the evening? Because, if so, I could pop round later when I'm done doing the . . . the thing that's, *erm*, come up, if you see what I mean, and we could see if we could try the interview then? Anyway," she gabbled frantically, anxious to finish before the time ran out, "if you could just call me back, that'd be great. My number is 085-835 . . ."

Beeeeeeeeep.

"Shit," she said to Dónal. "Didn't get to finish that, there. But never mind. He'd have my number already anyway, shure." She put the phone back in her bag, before whipping it out again immediately to see if he'd called back.

"Are we going to get in trouble with Kate then?" Dónal asked her now, a little frown of puzzlement and concern drawing his eyebrows together. "I mean, I don't mind helping you out, Philippa, you know that, but I don't fancy losing my job either. I've got a mortgage now, and two wives and two sets of kids to feed."

Philippa remembered then that he did indeed have two sets of financial responsibilities, one to his first wife and the kids thereof, and the second to the new wife. It was funny, she thought. I mean, here's me with no husbands whatsoever to my name, and here's Dónal with two wives and two sets of kids. She wondered for the umpteenth time why the Universe didn't parcel things out a little more equitably.

"It won't come to that," she assured him, with more confidence than she was feeling. "I've known Kate Sheehy-Bulger for donkey's years. She won't fire us. She'll be okay about it, when I explain to her what happened."

"You'll take full responsibility for the whole thing, then?"

"Yes, yes," she said crossly. "If that's all you're worried about."

"I only worry about two things, Philippa me darling," he said with a grin. "Hunger, and being put out on the street."

"I told you that's not going to happen! Kate will be fine about it once I explain to her. Now, can you just turn left here? It's Number Six, Orchard Drive, Sutton. That's the road there, see? Can you just pull in here, please? Thanks, that's perfect."

"Want me to come in with you?"

Philippa hesitated. On the one hand, she didn't necessarily want people from work knowing her private family business, even though Dónal was dead sound and a good colleague to have. On the other hand, she didn't know what she was walking into and she might conceivably need a bit of muscle with her for back-up. Not that Dónal was muscly. He was dark-haired, slight and slim of build and only about five-foot-six in height, but, what the hell, Philippa decided. He was here, and he was at least a man. He might be able to help. "Come on, so," she said, getting out of the car, grabbing her bag but leaving the hat to remain seated alone, crush-free, on the back seat. Philippa had an inkling that summer chic and glamour weren't going to be called for in this situation.

Dónal did likewise (got out, that is; he had no hats to supervise), then he locked the car and the two of them went in at the gate and up the garden path to Number 6. The front door was open, which was good, as Philippa didn't have a key. They pushed it gently and went through it into the house. The little rented two-up, two-down was in silence. In silence, except for a moaning, keening sound coming from what was presumably the sitting-room, on the right-hand-side of the front door as you went in. Coco and Matt had been living here for about a year, and Philippa would have been ashamed to admit, to Dónal or to anyone else, that she hadn't been out to visit them in months and months and months, even though the DART went there every single day and it wasn't exactly inaccessible. The guilt was prickling at her like mad now as she called her sister's name gently and pushed open the sitting-room door.

Coco-born-Christine-but-nicknamed-Coco-because-of-her-love-of-fashion-and-her-idol-Coco-Chanel was curled up in a ball on the floor beside the couch, with her mobile phone on the carpet beside her. She was clutching her knees and rocking back and forth making those awful keening noises they'd heard from the hall. Dónal looked at Philippa, his eyes grim. The sitting-room had been trashed. The coffee-table had been overturned, and the magazines (including some back numbers of *Ladies' Secret Things,* Philippa noticed with a pang of remorse and regret for not having paid more attention to her baby sister recently) and a jug of flowers had obviously gone with it. The ornaments and knick-knacks had all been swept off the mantelpiece and the sideboard, and it looked like someone had put their size twelve boot through the television, which sat on a table in the corner of the room. Philippa stared at the wreckage, appalled. What the *hell* had happened here? She flew to Coco and took her trembling sister in her arms.

"Coco! Coco, are you all right? Are you hurt? Did Matt do this?"

Coco just sobbed in her big sister's arms. Philippa checked her over as best as she could for injuries. She had a black eye and a cut, bleeding lip for starters, but Philippa worried that she might be hurt elsewhere. "Coco!" she said urgently, lifting her sister's little pixie-ish face carefully by the chin so that Coco could look into her face. "Are you hurt anywhere else? I've got to know, Coco, please tell me, will you?"

Coco looked at her sister with eyes that were huge and brimming with tears. "I think I've lost the baby," she whispered.

"The *what?*" echoed Philippa, aghast.

"The baby," repeated her sister dully.

Cautiously, Philippa lifted the hem of Coco's long black floaty dress, the kind of hippy-ish garment she normally wore with her beloved Doc Marten boots, and peeped underneath it. There was blood all over Coco's legs, and a small puddle of blood on the floor. None of it had been visible under the dark-coloured dress, which was why they'd missed it at first. Philippa gasped.

"*Call an ambulance*," she barked at Dónal, who didn't need to be told twice. "Who did this to you, Coco-Pops?" Here, she reverted to one of her favourite nicknames for her younger sister. "Was it Matt?"

Even as she asked the question, Philippa knew it was Matt. It was always the boyfriend, or the husband. Who else would beat a woman to a bloody pulp in this horrific way? Philippa had written tons of articles for the magazine on this exact subject. But, she realised now with dismay, as she held her sobbing sister tight and waited with her for the ambulance, she'd written every single one of them from the cosy standpoint of someone who'd neither experienced domestic violence herself – well, except for that brief episode with Brian – nor witnessed it happening to anyone she knew. Now it was happening to her beloved baby sister, and it was suddenly a whole different ball-game. A ball-game that was colder, harsher and starker than it had ever appeared to her before. She cringed now when she thought of the blasé, flippant way in which she'd dashed off those articles to fill a few pages in the magazine. **'It's so important to tell the people around you what's going on, so that they'll be aware and can help if necessary,"** she'd written gushingly. And here she was now, only finding out by accident that her baby sister was a victim of this horrible crime herself, and was pregnant to boot! What kind of a terrible person was she, she wondered desperately, that her baby sister, to whom she'd always supposedly been close, hadn't felt able to tell her that she was pregnant, and that her live-in boyfriend was abusive to her? Philippa felt about two inches tall. **"And always remember that it's not your fault. Nothing you've done has caused this violence and aggression in your partner. It's his choice to be violent. It's nothing to do with you."** And here she was now, dying to ask her own sister what she'd done to make Matt so angry that he'd trashed their home and beaten her up! She felt deeply ashamed of her glibly written articles and her blinkered outlook on a topic that had only really come home to her today. And with a massive bang, too.

"Are you okay, lovey?" she asked Coco now. But Coco wasn't answering. Her eyes had closed and her head drooped to one side. "*Coco, Coco, wake up! For fuck's sake, Coco, wake up! Stay with me, Coco, lovey, for Christ's sake, stay with me! Oh, Dónal, I think she's lost consciousness!*"

"The ambulance is here," he said grimly.

"Are you sure she's going to be all right?" Nicola asked, her eyes wide with worry.

Philippa nodded. "She's lost her baby and she's sustained a concussion, but the doctor says she'll be fine." She took a long sip of her hospital-coffee-machine coffee and grimaced when she realised she'd left it to go cold. They were seated on hard plastic chairs outside Coco's hospital bedroom, talking together in hospital-hushed voices. Nicola, the second oldest of the four Denby sisters, had left her two kids, Little Kimmie-short-for-Kimberley and Little Nicky-short-for-Nicholas, with her husband Shane to come to the hospital. Their eldest sister, Gerry-short-for-Geraldine, was currently on holiday in Spain and Philippa and Nicola had decided together that there was no point upsetting her about Coco while she was in another country and not able to do anything to help. Let her have her holiday, they decided jointly, and we'll fill her in when she gets back.

They hadn't told their parents about what had happened to Coco either. Their father, Colm Denby, had left their mother years ago to go and live with a much older woman, something his daughters had found hard to understand and even harder to forgive. If she'd even been some brainless bimbo, some dollybird, with long legs and big boobs and bleached-blonde hair, maybe they'd have been able to follow his reasoning, but Margaret Leach had already been old when Colm had gone to live with her, years ago. The girls' mother, Jacqueline Denby, was an artist who'd made a name for herself a few years back. She'd spend hours in her studio every day, even when her daughters had been growing up, standing in front of the canvas on the easel, with her long tangled salt-and-pepper hair loose down her back, her feet bare and a sleeveless long dress about her person, winter and summer alike, for ease of movement. She spent her days completely wrapped up in herself and her painting, and only emerged periodically from her studio to have sex with one of her much younger men, the 'toy-boys', as her disgusted daughters called them. As much as the four girls might have craved the love and attention of a mother, they realised early on that they were better off relying on each other. As a result, the bond between the girls was very strong; the bonds that tied them to their parents much weaker. Some people shouldn't be allowed to be parents. Each daughter still felt short-changed in the area of parental love, and, if they could change the situation, they undoubtedly would have. But, for now, Coco was the important one.

"I didn't even know she was pregnant, did you?" Nicola stage-whispered to her sister as a couple of male orderlies went by, wheeling an old man wearing an oxygen mask on a trolley.

Philippa shook her head. "No. None of us did, unless she told Gerry, which I doubt." Philippa was usually the sister in whom Coco confided things. She was gutted that Coco hadn't this time. Why hadn't she, she wondered? How come she was only finding out today, through sheer accidental misfortune, about Coco's unborn baby and Coco's abusive partner? With a pang of guilt, she realised that she'd been so wrapped up in herself and her own problems since she'd broken up with Brian that maybe Coco hadn't felt able to talk to her. Coco, as the youngest of the four girls, was probably the one who'd suffered the most through the lack of parental love and guidance. She, Philippa, should have been there for her more. She hadn't even visited them — Coco and Matt — in months, since not long after they'd moved to the house in Orchard Drive. She was a terrible sister. She deserved this awful situation being thrust upon her. But did Coco? Of course not. Coco was the sweetest, most optimistic, sunniest-tempered person you could ever hope to meet, and she was a talented fashion designer who'd started working at a small (but prestigious) independent design house straight out of art college. She'd always wanted nothing more than to design her own clothes and be a proper fashion designer one day. How dared this asshole, Matt Courtney or whoever he was, try to prevent her from reaching her goals? When she saw him again, and the Guards were out looking for him now, she'd be hard put to keep from throttling him personally, the evil fecker.

The doctor came out of Coco's room now and both women jumped on him.

"Don't panic," he said, holding up his hands in a calming gesture. "Your sister's going to be fine. But the Guards are going to want to speak to her later. I'll leave a note on her chart saying that I don't think she's up to that today. The staff can have me paged if the Guards want to hear it from me personally."

"*Can we see her?*" both women chorused together.

The doctor nodded. "She's awake at the moment, but she won't be for long. I've given her something to help her to sleep. You can pop in and say hello, but keep it short, okay?"

Both women scampered past him into Coco's room. They stopped short when they saw her, lying back against the pillows so white and still, with the bandage round her head and another round her left hand, a place Philippa hadn't even known had been injured.

The tears spilled down Coco's chalk-white face when she saw her sisters.

"My baby's gone," she whispered.

"Oh, Coco-Pops, why didn't you tell us you were

pregnant?" Philippa said, seating herself in one of the hard plastic visitors' chairs while Nicola took the other one.

"I was waiting till I'd told Matt," Coco said miserably. "He'd always said he never wanted kids, so I was afraid to tell him."

"How far along were you, lovey?" This from Nicola, while she stroked the fingers of Coco's unbandaged right hand.

"Five months. I'd had my scan from Holles Street. My b-b-b-baby was a b-b-b-boy."

"Oh, God, Coco," Philippa said. "Was that what you and Matt were fighting about, today?"

Coco nodded, then winced as if the action had hurt her head. "He found my contraceptive pills. He could see I hadn't been taking them. He thought I did it on purpose, to trick him."

"And had you?" Philippa asked her sister softly, very softly, so as not to distress her.

There was a long silence, then Coco nodded. "I think so," she said miserably. "I just wanted a baby so much. Someone to love me, who'd never leave me. I did trick him. I did." The tears began to fall in earnest now. Nicola shot a warning glance at Philippa.

"That's probably enough talking for now," she said firmly, and Philippa nodded. Coco's eyes were already growing heavy and starting to flutter closed.

"Poor Coco," Nicola said when they were back in the corridor outside Coco's room on the hard plastic chairs. "Imagine wanting someone to love her so much that she was prepared to trick Matt into getting her pregnant."

"Can you blame her, with parents like ours?" her sister said bleakly. "Still and all, though, I'd like to get my hands on that bastard, Matt. I'd teach him a few things about hitting women. He wouldn't be hitting any women again in a long time, I can tell you that much."

"Violence never solves anything. Let's just be grateful that it'll be all over between them after this. Be grateful for small mercies, Pip."

"I suppose." Philippa seemed genuinely reluctant to relinquish the idea of teaching Matt 'a few things'. "Even Coco isn't daft enough to get back with him after this. How are Shane and the kids, anyway?"

"Oh, they're grand, thank God. And what about you? How's work? How's Denyse, and Kate, and all the gang?"

Philippa, after experiencing a momentary pang of sorrow that she hadn't a husband or kids herself to ask after, said with a wry grimace: "Can I get back to you on that one tomorrow? I'm not sure I'm even going to *have* a job, after Kate finds out I had to ditch Jem Trueblood for a battered sister." She nearly giggled when she realised how like something out of a chipper that sounded. Christ. She'd hardly slept a wink since finding out about the Jem Trueblood gig. Maybe she was growing hysterical. That was all she needed.

"Kate will be fine about it, I'm sure," soothed Nicola. "She's got a family of her own, hasn't she? Daughters and all that? I'm sure she knows that sometimes you just have to drop everything else for family."

"That's easy for you to say, sis. Still, we'll see how things go. My personal guess is that she'll be livid and handing out redundancies. Still, we'll see."

***

Kate Sheehy-Bulger *was,* in fact, livid about the Jem Trueblood thing, but she didn't sack anyone, and she was actually quite sympathetic in the matter of the 'battered sister'. Philippa was relieved she wasn't going to lose her job, quite a cushy number overall, over the incident, or cause Dónal to lose his. She'd been envisioning all kinds of militant scenarios in which she took Kate Sheehy-Bulger to court for wrongful dismissal, and had the whole might of Ireland's community of battered wives and girlfriends behind her to support her in her fight, but she was kind of relieved that Kate was such a decent stick and that she wasn't going to have to take her unfair dismissal case all the way to the Supreme Court after all.

"Have you seen this?" Denyse demanded when Philippa reached the *Ladies' Secret Things* office on Monday morning. She was brandishing an early edition of one of the tabloid newspapers.

"No, giz a look." Philippa plonked herself at her desk and took the paper from Denyse's hands. After receiving her message to say that she wasn't coming, Jem Trueblood's agent, Alan Freebourne, had clearly decided to take his client out on the town for a night's drinking and night-clubbing. The delicious Jem Trueblood was plastered all over the papers, pictured drinking champagne out of an up-and-coming young supermodel's belly-button. Philippa groaned loudly and put her head in her hands. Damn and blast it, anyway! That could have been *her* belly-button, she mourned, if she'd only made it to the bloody interview instead of haring round the countryside helping endangered sisters. Not that she begrudged helping Coco, of course she didn't. But if only Coco hadn't chosen that exact time to be needing her sister's assistance! But she *didn't* choose it, Philippa reminded herself sternly. Matt was the one to blame here, not Coco. Philippa wanted to be absolutely crystal-clear about that. With a sigh heavy enough to blow the papers off her desk, and an even heavier heart, she got down to work, before suddenly remembering something else and turning to Denyse.

"By the way, what happened with your one, the nun? How did the interview go?"

"Oh, brilliant," Denyse said nonchalantly, in a way Philippa took to mean that she'd been dying to talk about it. "I did the interview with her while she and her convict were waiting for the execution, then she and the convict committed suicide together with some little vials of poison she'd smuggled into the prison in her prayer book. It had one of those false insides, you know? Like you see in the fillums? Only, in the fillums, people normally hide guns in them. Or bottles of hooch in the Prohibition times. Anyway, there was murder about it, if you'll excuse the pun. It's all over the media in America, how this fella cheated the electric chair with the help of his Irish nun-slash-lover. Some of it's filtered over here as well, though, which is good news for me, because I did the last ever interview with her."

"Surely it's lethal injection now, and not the electric chair any more?"

"Yeah, well, yes, I suppose so. Shure, when I said yes to doing the interview, I thought they still hanged people over there or shot 'em by firing squad. I was gobsmacked to hear they'd outlawed all that type of thing ages ago."

Philippa cringed, put her head down and got stuck into her work (a feature on whether or not texting and Facebook messaging were jointly ruining the art of conversation, a piece she could have rattled off in her sleep), only stopping at two in the afternoon to read a text from Nicola, whose turn it was to visit Coco in hospital today. She read the text, then dropped the phone on to her desk and clapped her hand over her mouth.

"What's the matter?" asked Denyse in alarm. "Is something wrong?"

"Coco's out of the hospital," Philippa said, her hands visibly trembling as they reached for the bottle of water she habitually kept on her desk. She took a long thirsty swig of it.

When she was finished, Denyse said: "But, that's a good thing, isn't it?"

Philippa shook her head. "Not necessarily. Not in this case. Matt came to collect her, and apparently she checked herself out and went off with him. She's gone back to him, Denyse. She's back with Matt."

Denyse chewed on her lower lip, as Philippa dropped her head into her hands once more and groaned loud enough for everyone in their open-plan office to hear. But this time, it was for more than just a supermodel's belly-button. It was for Coco.

Chapter 11

MICHAEL

Michael Redmond got off the 46A bus when it reached Donnybrook Village. He would walk the rest of the way, as he did every evening from Monday to Friday after work. He'd been having a lovely chat with an auld fella on the bus about how it was the man's fiftieth wedding anniversary today, except that his wife had died last year from emphysema and so she'd be missing it. But the old man was an optimistic sort. He was on his way out to his daughter's house in Stillorgan now to have a big celebratory roast dinner with all the trimmings, after which he'd go out for an anniversary pint (or ten) with his son-in-law and three grown-up grandsons. He didn't even need to worry about getting himself home to his council flat in town tonight, as he'd be staying the night in his daughter's house. They had a little boxroom that was perfectly adequate for his needs and he always slept like a top there. He looked forward to his great sleeps there. In fact, if it wasn't for the absence of his dear wife of fifty years, it seemed like this jaunty auld fella, full of smiles and hope, had the tough business of life well and truly sussed. He'd worked hard all his life as a bus driver, and now he was retired and reaping all the benefits that that cosy time supposedly had to offer. Michael sincerely hoped that he'd be even half as content as this auld fella when he reached that age himself.

"Well, this is me," Michael said when the bus rolled to a stop in Donnybrook Village. He put out a hand to the old man, who was seated across from him. "It was nice talking to you. I'm Michael, by the way."

"I'm George," replied his travelling companion. The two men clasped hands warmly and then George said: "The best of luck to you, lad, in the future."

"You too. And enjoy your anniversary dinner."

"I always do, lad," replied the old man with a cheeky wink.

As Michael walked away from the bus stop, he was surprised to find he had a lump in his throat. He was not a recluse by any means and he always enjoyed chatting to people, even complete strangers, but there was something about this auld lad that had really touched him. The old man's contentment, his optimism, his joy in simple pleasures like a roast dinner he didn't have to cook himself and a night spent in the pub with members of his family; it all made Michael want to cry somehow, and Michael was not usually the crying type.

You're jealous, he told himself as he walked briskly to the shops. *You're jealous of the auld lad because he's as happy as Larry and you're not.* Then: *Bullshit,* he cautioned himself sternly as he gave himself a mental shake and dismissed the old man from his mind. He picked up a bouquet of rain-washed white roses from outside the supermarket. Polly adored white roses, and the fact that they'd been bathed in rainwater before they reached her would only make her love them all the more. Polly, as a poet, was a hopeless romantic. Raindrops on roses and whiskers on kittens were all grist to her poetic mill. Michael took the roses to the check-out inside the supermarket, along with a bottle of red wine, Polly's favourite. It must have been Be Nice to Michael Day, because even the usually surly check-out girl was beaming all over her face this evening.

"You're in a good mood today," he chanced as he handed over the money.

"You bet I am," she said, waggling the fingers of her left hand at him. On the ring finger reposed a massive, showy engagement ring.

"Congratulations! Have the two of you been together long?" He was surprised as he spoke to feel a pang of what could only have been envy. What was *he* envious of, he wondered, what reason did he, Michael Redmond, have to be jealous of a check-out girl whose boyfriend had popped the question? He'd had numerous chances to propose to Melissa, the one woman he would ever have even considered marrying, but he'd blown it, like the big gobshite he was, and now Melissa was gone, fled to England, and their beautiful little daughter Eugenia was buried under the earth, out in Glasnevin Cemetery, and it was all his, Michael's, fault. At least, that was how he'd always seen it.

"*Are you joking?*" squawked the check-out girl raucously. "It took me ten years of waiting to finally get this baby on my finger." She waggled the beringed hand again and smiled broadly. "What about yourself?" she added coyly. "You're not buying the wine and roses for yourself, I'm guessing."

"How do you know?" he said, mock-indignantly, as he bagged up his wine in the brown paper bag she'd given him. "I *could* be buying all this stuff for myself, I'll have you know."

"Enjoy your evening," she said with a grin and a wink. Everyone was winking at Michael today. Clearly it was Let's all Wink at Michael Day as well. "You know," she went on, with a speculative look at her customer, "you'd be quite a decent catch for someone some day."

"Thanks very much," he said dryly. "Oh, and congratulations again on your good news."

"See ya tomorrow."

"Yeah, see you tomorrow."

He walked up Rainbow Drive, thinking about the Happy Check-out Girl *(now there was a book opportunity that Hans Christian Andersen or the Brothers Grimm had missed, surely?)*. Normally, she was as prickly as a porcupine with a toothache, but today, love and excitement for the future had transformed her into a thing of beauty and a joy forever.

He let himself in the front door of the house where he lived. Old Mrs. Turner, as deaf as a post, who lived in the ground floor flat, was pottering about in the hall with a cloth and a tin of polish. She was a big fan of Michael's. She thought he was *'a lovely young man'*, as Polly was always teasing him. She was forever grateful to him for sometimes picking up her groceries for her from the supermarket and doing any heavy lifting for her that needed doing.

"Oh, Michael, lovey," she twittered when she saw him now. "Look, I've had an official letter!" She fished it out of her apron pocket and handed it to him. "Does it mean what I think it means, lovey?"

"Wait now and I'll tell you." He scanned the letter swiftly and handed it back to her with a grin. "Well now, Missus, if you think it means that you've had a bit of a win with your Prize Bonds, well, then, you'd be right. Congratulations, it's five hundred euros!" He spoke loudly because of her poor hearing.

"Oh, Michael, lovey! Whatever will I do with it?"

"Go on a sunshine holiday and get an all-over tan for yourself? Splash out on a Ferrari and a toy-boy and drive all the auld fellas crazy when you whizz past them on the street?"

"Oh, Michael, lovey, you're an awful messer!" But she looked as pleased as Punch with herself as Michael wished her a good evening and headed on up to the stairs to the flat he shared with Polly. Everyone he'd met this evening had been so pleased to see him. It was a nice feeling.

When he unlocked the door of his flat, he immediately detected a distinct drop in temperature. Polly was in the kitchen, standing at the sink with her back to him.

"Where the hell have you been till this hour?" she said tightly, in a tone he recognised, without turning round to face him. The set of her back was rigid with disapproval.

He was only a few minutes later than usual, but he knew better than to bring that to her attention. Instead, he said: "I was getting you these, actually." He held out his offerings.

"Oh, Michael, they're beautiful, thank you!" she gushed, as she flew to him and buried her tiny little pixie-face in the blooms. "Oh, and they have teensy-weensy little raindrops on them, too! I must write a poem about them while you put them in water."

He did as she asked while she hurried to the bedroom to

fetch the red velvet hard-backed notebook in which she wrote her poetry. (She always objected vociferously when he called her 'his little poetess'. "You don't hear of anyone's going to the doctor*ess*, do you? Or buying their cabbages from a greengrocer*ess*?" He had to concede that she was right.) His stomach rumbled when he smelled the dinner cooking in the oven, a lasagne and garlic bread, judging from the delicious aroma, and the bits and pieces of what was clearly a side-salad scattered around the counter-tops. Polly was a good (if untidy) cook when she bothered, but she didn't always bother. Today she *had* bothered, and Michael, who'd worked through his lunch at the advertising agency today in order to catch up on a project on which he was a little behind, was absolutely starving. It was important, however, not to appear too impatient.

"Can I help with dinner at all?" he asked, as nonchalantly as he could manage it.

"No, it's all under control," she muttered, her head bent over her red velvet-backed poetry notebook, the tip of her little pink tongue protruding from the side of her mouth like a child's. Her extraordinary long red hair fell over her face and shoulders and down her back. The dark-red colour of it was wholly natural, and so were the corkscrew curls which she sometimes revelled in and sometimes hated and threatened to cut off, although Michael was sure she never would. Small and slim and shorter even than the average Irishwoman, with her hair long and loose she looked like a fairy from a child's storybook, or the kind of woman who might dance naked round an open fire at Stonehenge while the sun rose on the morning of the summer solstice. Little girls they passed on the street often clapped their hands in delight when they saw her and exclaimed: "Mummy, Mummy, it's Merida from the movie *Brave*!" She was the most strikingly unusual-looking woman Michael had ever known. It was a clear case of opposites attracting, the advertising executive in his thirties with his feet firmly rooted in the material world, and the ethereal sprite of a girl of twenty-five with huge green eyes and a spirituality and psychic quality about her that appealed to a Michael who'd long grown bored of his choice of advertising (and medical advertising in particular; it was all cold and flu remedies and cures for baldness, impotence and flatulence) as a career. She reminded Michael of a tiny Kate Bush, who'd been Melissa's favourite singer, but Polly's singing voice, sadly, put one in mind of a cheese-grater caught in a collision with a blender. She even reminded him of Melissa, who'd been both an artist *and* a poetess. Sorry, sorry, poet!

"So, how did you spend your day?" he asked her when dinner was finally on the table at about twenty-five-past seven. He wolfed down the lasagne, garlic bread and salad she'd put in front of him, delighted that today had been one of Polly's 'Earth Mother' days, in which she deemed cooking for herself and Michael an occupation fit for a poet of her stature.

She sighed. "I've spent most of the day on the phone, trying to co-ordinate everything for the Anniversary Dinner."

Michael's heart sank. He'd been hearing about this fortieth anniversary do for Polly's parents for months now. Polly, who, as a poet with few other skills, was unemployed, was considered to be the one member of her family with enough time on her hands to organise the do. The way she talked about it, however, you'd think she was trying to co-ordinate a get-together of the United bloody Nations. Michael was sick and tired of hearing about it.

"Then I started work on the seating plan," she was saying. "I'm exhausted now from racking my brain all afternoon trying to work out where to put Uncle Horace and Uncle Geoffrey."

"What's the big deal about these two uncles?" He spoke with his mouth full.

"They hate each other's guts. They haven't spoken in about twenty years. Surely I've told you this before?"

"Probably." He forked up his last mouthful of lasagne and ate it with relish. "Just stick 'em as far away from each other as possible. It'll be grand."

"You don't take this seriously at all, do you, Michael?" She was pouting now, a bad sign.

"Of course I do." He washed his food down with a big drink of the wine he'd brought home. "But there's no need to stress about it as much as you do. It's just a party."

Immediately he knew he'd said totally the wrong thing. Her tiny little pixie-face, with the huge eyes and trembling mouth, framed by the glorious hair, was turning bright pink, the way it always did when she was agitated or becoming enraged.

"Look, I didn't mean it's not a big deal, okay?" he backtracked hastily. "I just think you shouldn't stress about it as much as you do, that's all. For your own sake, I mean. For the good of your own health and well-being. That's all I meant."

But it was no use. She was in one of her moods now, huffily carrying plates to the sink and passive-aggressively scraping the leftovers loudly into the bin, letting him know that he was in his usual place again: the wrong. He was there so often these days that he was strongly considering making it his permanent address and having cards made. Michael sighed. This sulk could literally go on all night. Polly wasn't usually amenable to any efforts on his part to nip things in the bud. Still, he had to try.

"The food was delicious tonight, Polly. I really enjoyed it. Thank you."

"That's all I am to you, isn't it?" she grumbled as she continued to clear away plates and bowls. "A bloody slave. And I know you think I'm lazy, idling around the place here all day writing my silly poems and organising the silly little party for my parents' anniversary. I know you think I'm some kind of waster, an idler, just because you have a so-called 'proper job' in a big fancy office that requires you to wear a suit and tie and kiss your boss's arse religiously every half-hour."

"Polly, you're wrong. I don't think that about you at all, honestly I don't."

But it was too late. She snatched his empty plate from him, turned away as if to bring it to the sink for washing, then turned back and brought the plate smashing squarely down on his head. Then she fled to their bedroom, sobbing loudly. His heart sank all the way to his boots. He couldn't believe she'd done this to him. Again.

They had met in a graveyard, of all places. Glasnevin Cemetery, where Michael's only child, his daughter Eugenia with his ex, Melissa, was buried. He'd been there to put flowers on her grave (Melissa was living in the UK now and so he was the only one left to do it), and Polly had been out there to visit the grave of one of her grandfathers. She'd brought the family dog, Skippy, with her, and the little fellow had slipped his lead amongst the paths that weaved their way around the massive necropolis. Michael had been kneeling at the grave, tidying it up a little and absent-mindedly pulling out a stray weed or two, mostly just enjoying the warmth of the sun and the feeling of peace that came over him whenever he came here, when the exuberant overgrown puppy came hurtling along at top speed before skidding to a halt in front of Michael, his tail wagging a mile a minute.

"*Grab him, will you? Oh please, don't let him go!*" came a girlish voice then.

Michael had looked up then, and saw a woman running towards him. Her small pert breasts bounced up and down in the khaki-green vest top she wore with trousers, and an inordinate amount of red, corkscrew-curled hair streamed out behind her as she ran. Michael was entranced. What vision of loveliness was this? He'd never seen anything quite so enchanting. He obligingly took hold of the dog, who in any case didn't seem like he was trying to escape or go anywhere, and who licked his face ecstatically on being held.

"Oh, thank you so much! Oh, Skippy, you naughty dog, what are you trying to do to poor Mummy? You're such a bad, bad little doggie, aren't you? Putting Mummy and the nice man to all this trouble. I wuv you, you bad dog, you! Do you wuv Mummy, too?"

Michael watched in bemusement as the tiny little woman knelt down beside Eugenia's grave and covered the excited dog in kisses and cuddles and endearments. Close-up, she was even more striking. Her skin was creamy-white with the lightest smattering of freckles. Her green eyes were as brilliant as emeralds and set wide-apart in her tiny little heart-shaped face. Her lips were naturally red and full and her teeth tiny and white. The khaki-green vest top (beneath it, she'd been braless) and combat trousers were teamed with clumpy Doc Marten boots, but the whole ensemble just served to emphasise her fragility and delicate frame. Michael, a big, well-built man of six feet in height, was surprised to find that he wanted to protect her, to shield her from the slings and arrows of outrageous fortune. Small, petite women affected him like that sometimes (Melissa had been on the slight side herself), but this little sprite, who'd come lightly tripping out of the clear blue sky to fling herself down next to Eugenia's grave and the excitable puppy, was blowing his mind.

"I'm Polly," she said now, extending a hand towards him in greeting. "I'm so sorry about Skippy. He's such a naughty doggie, aren't you, Skip?" The dog was in his element, being petted and patted by both his diminutive owner and by Michael, who loved dogs and usually got on well with them. Michael took the proffered hand and shook it, liking the way her smaller hand seemed to be immediately swallowed up by his larger mitt.

"I'm Michael. That's okay, he's fine. He's a grand little fellow. What breed is he? Mongrel, is it?"

"Pretty much," laughed Polly. "He's a year old but he's still as excitable as a puppy. He keeps charging off to chase birds or butterflies he hasn't a hope in hell of catching, the silly little noodle-head. Don't you, Skip?" She enfolded the mutt in a bear-hug, sitting there cross-legged on the narrow grass verge between Eugenia's grave and the main gravel path.

Michael was utterly enchanted. He hadn't lost his heart to any woman in a good long while, but this woman? He could feel himself surrendering his paltry defences already to *this* woman.

"*Erm,* what brings you out here today?" he ventured. "If you don't mind me asking, that is."

"I don't mind *you* asking," she responded coyly. "My grandfather — my mother's father – died about three months ago. He's buried over there, by the gate." She pointed with her small elegant fingers, the nails painted the same hard, brilliant green of her eyes.

"I'm sorry to hear that," he said out of politeness.

"That's okay." She shrugged. "I'm getting used to it. Who's Eugenia?" she added, pointing to the little headstone. "I mean, is she someone belonging to you?"

"She's my daughter, actually. *Was* my daughter. She died in 2004. Meningitis."

"Oh my God, that's awful. And your . . . your wife? Is she okay? I mean, is she still alive and all that?"

"Oh yes. She's alive all right, only we split up the year Eugenia died. And . . . and she wasn't my wife. We were never married."

"Oh, how awful for you, being all alone at a time like that!"

Was it his imagination, or did she look faintly pleased at the knowledge that he hadn't been married to Eugenia's mum? "I got used to it. Listen, I'm on a day off from work today. D'you fancy driving back in to town with me and going for a cup of coffee or something? That's if you're free, of course. D'you live round here?"

"Drumcondra. I know a great little restaurant there where

we can sit outside with Skippy, if you'd like to give that a try?" The dog's ears pricked up at the mention of his name and he began to yap joyfully.

"Sounds good to me. Will he go in the car, d'you think?"

"Yes, of course, he loves cars. You'll be lucky if he doesn't try to drive the thing. Won't he, Skippy darling?"

The three of them strolled through the sprawling cemetery to the gate, and then up the road a bit to where Michael had parked his car. The sun was shining. It was a glorious day. Michael felt incredibly relaxed as they all trooped along. He felt so good that it wouldn't have surprised him at all if the girl called Polly had slipped her hand into his as they walked. It would have felt totally natural and right.

He drove them into Drumcondra, and they sat outside the restaurant Polly had recommended, a friendly little family-run place whose staff had no objection whatsoever to bringing out a bowl of water and a little plate of tasty sausages for Skippy. They ordered cup after cup of coffee, talking non-stop about themselves as they drank up the sunshine as well as the hot beverage. At least, Polly talked. Michael learned that she wasn't really a girl at all but a woman of twenty-five, who'd been to college but hadn't finished it, and who'd been more or less permanently unemployed since then.

"There aren't many jobs out there for poets," she said ruefully, spreading her hands in a gesture of *'what can you do?'* and Michael said he supposed that was true enough. "I'm working on a collection of poetry, though, and when I have a whole load of them that I'm happy with, I'll start submitting them to publishers. *Then* we'll see the money rolling in!" she finished exuberantly.

Michael hadn't the heart to tell her that he didn't think there was much money in poetry, unless you were Seamus Heaney, or someone like that. He knew all that through Melissa.

He found out that Polly still lived with her parents in Drumcondra, having nowhere else to go at the moment. She had older married sisters and brothers whom she saw fairly frequently, but so far she was the only one in her family who hadn't gone down the traditional route of university followed by a career or steady job followed by marriage and kids.

"Well, I'm only twenty-five, for God's sake," she said, in a tone that suggested to Michael that it was utterly ridiculous to expect someone to have found the life path they wanted to pursue by the tender age of only a quarter of a century. Michael, who'd wanted to be a hotshot advertising executive for as long as he could remember, and who'd gone after it and pursued it ruthlessly until he'd achieved it (the fact that he was now bored to death with it was neither here nor there), couldn't really relate, but he'd nodded as if he did nonetheless.

"I have plenty of time to decide what I want to do with the rest of my life, don't I, Skip darling?" She appealed directly to Skippy, who slobbered on her face obligingly before woofing half-heartedly at a passing dog, then settling down comfortably to lick his balls.

Michael found her utterly charming. She reminded him a lot of Melissa, not so much looks-wise, but in her chosen *métier*. Melissa had worked as an illustrator of children's books (she presumably still did, though she lived in England now), and damned talented she'd been at it too. She'd also been a talented poet — she'd possessed countless notebooks filled with poems for which she'd done the most exquisite little illustrations, and all in her spare time as well — but she'd been as driven as Michael in her own way, not floaty and dreamy like Polly. Polly kind of reminded him, in the nicest possible way, of a child's red balloon, that bobbed here and bobbed there and bobbed everywhere, but never really *did* anything or achieved anything very much, or went anywhere of any significance. That didn't annoy him when he first met her, though. When he first met her, he thought she was the most refreshing, free-spirited little wood nymph he'd ever come across in his life. And she was beautiful, oh Lord, she was beautiful! Her beauty was like something otherworldly, almost like Melissa's had been. He was smitten, and smitten hard. Loving two lady poets in one lifetime, what were the chances of that, he often wondered, and him a dull-as-dishwater advertising executive?

He drove her and Skippy home to Drumcondra later that day. Then, the next evening, he called again to her house by arrangement and took her out to dinner. She clearly knew that green was the colour that suited her best, as she was garbed in a floaty green confection that nonetheless wrapped around her small curves in all the right places. Her jewellery was green too, a striking-looking necklace that drew the eye to her modest but perfect cleavage, and a pair of earrings that flashed like her eyes and swung flatteringly when she moved her head, which she did frequently. She became animated when she talked, and waved her hands about and shook or nodded her head a lot. Michael enjoyed watching her talk, even if the words that came out of her mouth often took the form of her misinformed opinions on things and didn't always make a whole lot of sense. Polly liked to talk, and, in the beginning, Michael was perfectly content to let her.

"You're a proper little chatterbox, you know that, don't you?" he'd say, looking at her fondly with an indulgent grin when he'd tried unsuccessfully, yet again, to get a word in edgeways.

She'd just smile minxingly, accepting his words as the compliment they were meant as, before continuing to talk at top speed about whatever subject was holding her attention for the moment, the words just tumbling over each other in her eagerness to get them out.

He'd asked her to move in with him, into his flat in Donnybrook, after they'd been dating for three months. She brought Skippy with her, a budgerigar in a vintage Victorian-style cage, called Homer Simpson because of his bright yellow colour, a mountain of vintage clothes and hats and, to Michael's surprise, a gramophone, an actual gramophone, and a selection of gramophone records. Her things lent to his bachelor flat a touch of class, as long as they managed to keep an over-exuberant Skippy from chewing everything from the couch cushions to Michael's slippers to the notes from his latest work project.

The sex, once Polly moved in, was phenomenal. She writhed and wriggled beneath him and screamed as if he were doing things to her that no one had ever thought to do to her before. She adored posing for him when he bought her naughty lingerie, and she knew how to do things with her lips, teeth and tongue that left him feeling like he'd been run over by the Luas, but in a good way. If there *is* a good way to do that. She was wild and uninhibited and careless in her love-making, and this imparted a danger to it that turned Michael on and kept him coming back for more. It felt like there was nothing she wouldn't do to please him in bed and, for Michael, this was an enormously satisfying feeling.

The first time she was violent towards him happened two months after she moved in. He'd had a long pain-in-the-arse day at work, and had come home at seven in the evening, cranky, hungry and tired, to find Polly still in bed, with the devoted Skippy curled up in a ball at her feet. Michael, to his shame, had not reacted too well to the sight. He'd pulled the covers off her, dislodging a sleepy Skippy, demanding loudly to know what normal person slept till seven in the evening, and what did a guy have to do around here to get a bit of dinner? Michael wasn't a bad cook by any means, but, since Polly had moved in, the cooking had fallen mostly to her because she was the jobless one, the one at home all day.

"*I'm not your slave!*" she'd screamed at him, alarming him. "*And this isn't the fucking nineteen-fifties, either!*"

"I never said it was. I'm just starving, that's all. It's been a long day." Shocked by her vehement response to his grumbling, he tried pouring oil on the troubled waters, but Polly was having none of it. When he sat down on the bed with his back to her to take off his shoes and socks for the shower he had every evening after work, she picked up the alarm clock on the bedside table and hurled it at the back of his head.

It made contact sharply with his cranium, his short hair not affording him much protection in the skull department, and he leaped to his feet as a reflex, swearing loudly. *"What the fuck, Polly?"*

"Now see what you made me do!" She burst into messy tears and threw herself onto the pillows in a storm of weeping. "Oh, I'm so depressed!"

Thoroughly freaked out, rubbing the back of his head where he was sure he could feel blood, warm and wet, he crossed to the bed and took her in his arms, soothing her as one might soothe a child or a panicked animal. "Come on, Polly, love, don't cry! I'm sorry, I'm sorry! I never meant to upset you, I swear. I'm just a big grumpy bastard and I don't deserve you. Come on, sweetheart, dry those tears and let me see your lovely smile!"

"Does Michael still love his Polly-Wolly-Doodle?" she sniffled in a baby-voice, wiping her nose on the bedcovers.

"Of course he does!" He bent his head to kiss her then, and she pulled him down immediately and locked her arms around his neck so he couldn't move. (Thin they might be, but there was surprising strength in those wiry little arms.) They made love then, wild, passionate love that counted, Michael reckoned, amongst their very best times.

Afterwards, Polly was in a rare good humour as they chopped vegetables and prepared meat and potatoes together, side-by-side in the kitchen. Chatting away lightly about everything and anything, positively beaming with a radiant good humour, she made no reference whatsoever to their argument, or to the fact that Michael had a bandage from the medicine cabinet taped over the bloody gash on the back of his head.

Michael, taking his cue from her, said nothing either, and

the incident was glossed over. Just like all the others that followed . . .

Now, Michael swept up the pieces of broken dinner plate with a heavy heart and a throbbing skull. It was always left to him to clean up the damage after one of Polly's 'outbursts', as he called them to himself (and he always did it, too, in case his not doing it provoked more violence). Clearly he found it too painful to call them what they really were, an attack or an assault. If he'd done to her what she'd done to him over the course of the last two years, he'd probably be in jail right now, and rightly so. But, because he was a big, strong heavy-set man and she was only a little slip of a thing, he hadn't even dared to call the Guards, for fear they'd laugh at him.

"A mighty fella like yourself?" they'd say incredulously. "And you're seriously telling us that this tiny little woman here is after assaulting you? Would you ever feck off out of that and let us get back to dealing with real crimes and real assaults? Or maybe you're the real abuser here, Michael Redmond? Maybe you're the one doing the assaulting and you're trying to spoof us? Pull the other one, Michael Redmond. It's got bells on . . ."

And then they'd leave, laughing at him amongst themselves, and there'd be a black mark against him forever for having called them out on false pretences, as they'd see it. He'd had terrible dreams, nightmares really, in which both men he knew and was friends with *and* strange men alike all stood around laughing and pointing at him, saying things like: "Defend yourself, man! You're six-foot-odd and built like a brick shit-house and she's five-foot-nothing — defend yourself, for eff's sake!"

But he couldn't really, not without hurting her. He could try to take away whichever implement she was using to batter him (lamp, kettle, china or brass ornament) and pin her arms to her sides until she calmed down, but he was so afraid of hurting her that, often, she'd have battered him bloody before he could get her weapon of choice away from her. She'd come at him with a kitchen knife once, screaming like a banshee, and even then he'd resisted the reflexive impulse he'd had to just punch her in the kisser and lay her out flat, and had merely wrestled the knife away from her, cutting his hands in the process, before she could do any real damage.

So many times, he'd almost confided in a good friend at work, an ad-man like himself, or in a guy he'd been to school with and had been friends with most of his life, but every time he felt the urge, the same thing stopped him, an overwhelming feeling of shame that he couldn't shake, no matter how many times he spoke sternly to himself and told himself that he wasn't to blame. That wasn't what other people would think, was it? They'd think he must be to blame for it somehow. Why else would that tiny, beautiful little woman feel the need to lash out at him like that? He must be at fault in some way, mustn't he? He must be to blame. Sometimes he wondered if the whole thing was some kind of horrible penance for the way he'd been so unfair to Melissa and Eugenia, refusing to marry Melissa and give them both the security and protection of his name, purely because he was a commitment-phobic coward. Maybe it was karma, coming back to bite him big-time on the ass.

Or maybe it was *Polly* who was really at fault here, but Michael either didn't like or couldn't stomach this unpalatable theory. How could Polly, his beautiful, delicate little Polly, be at fault in this or any other way? She was the foxiest little enchantress he'd ever met in his life before, the sex between them was phenomenal, and when she was in a good, stable mood, she was the best company he could ever remember having. It was only when she was in one of her dark moods that the violent stuff was in danger of happening. Even then, he reasoned, how could he even blame her for her dark moods when he knew full well why they happened? She had told him about her grandfather, her Granddad Rory, the one whose grave she'd been visiting with Skippy when they'd first met. She'd told him how this grandfather, whom she'd adored and hero-worshipped, had sexually abused her from when she'd been about five to when she'd been twelve or thirteen and her periods had started. She'd told him about the numbing fear she'd felt when this Granddad Rory had come into her room at night when he'd been staying with them, and done things to her that made Michael want to dig the old man up and punch him repeatedly in the mouth. How could anyone be normal after such experiences? No wonder poor Polly was the way she was, and no wonder Michael felt like he couldn't betray her by 'telling' on her. If it helped her to occasionally take her troubled feelings out on Michael, then he'd put up with it for her sake. He had to. What choice did he have? He was up to his eyes in it now.

The day of the long-awaited fortieth anniversary party for Polly's parents, Martha and Brendan Yates, dawned bright and clear.

"You'll have good weather for it anyway," he remarked to

Polly over breakfast, but Polly, absorbed in one of her interminable lists for tonight's shindig, merely grunted in response. Poor Polly, he thought as he dipped a bit of toast in the runny part of his egg. This had all been way too much for her, organising this entire celebration all by herself for nearly the whole of this last year. He felt a huge resentment towards her siblings, who'd allowed her to take this whole thing upon her own frail shoulders just because she was the only one amongst them who hadn't got a job or a family of her own. The sooner this whole thing was over, the better. Polly could get some rest and not be all uptight and touchy all the time, biting his head off every time he spoke to her, so that he was afraid now when he spoke of saying the wrong thing and rubbing her up the wrong way. She could go back to being her loving, carefree joyful self. Although, Michael pondered as he left for work, under strict instructions from Polly not to be late for The Party, how long had it been since she'd been like that? He was disturbed to find he couldn't remember.

"Isn't it lovely to see Polly enjoying herself, so happy and bubbly?" Polly's mum, Martha Yates, stood at a quiet corner of the buffet table alongside Michael and smiled benevolently at him.

"Yes, it's good to see her that way, after all the stress of the last few months."

He watched Polly as she bustled importantly round the hotel ballroom, greeting everyone and ticking their names off on her clipboard and issuing instructions to someone, he didn't know who, on her headset. The long-awaited anniversary party seemed to be going well, thank Christ. For his part, he'd turned up on time after work, wearing the new suit that Polly had picked out for him herself, and carrying his and Polly's present for her parents, a crystal punch-bowl that had left quite a dent in Michael's bank balance. Still, it had been what Polly wanted, and, after all, it was only a small thing to do for her, but it had made her so happy. He was glad the party was going well. He certainly didn't want to be at fault himself if it wasn't. Polly would go ballistic, and that was something Michael wanted to avoid at all costs.

"It's such a shame her Granddad Rory can't be here tonight," Mrs. Yates was saying now.

"Yes, it's a shame. How long has he been dead now?" Michael absentmindedly nibbled at an olive, watching Polly stand on tiptoe to murmur something into the ear of the disc-jockey she'd hired for tonight, a game auld lad who was sixty-five if he was a day, but he had all the old records that Martha and Brenda had danced to in their youth, so that made him suitable in Polly's book.

"Dead? He's not dead. My father's not dead. He's in a nursing home, in County Meath." Martha Yates was staring at him in surprise.

Michael accidentally swallowed the olive he'd only intended to nibble on. Once he'd stopped coughing and spluttering, he said: "Sorry, Martha. I must have misunderstood Polly — I thought she said he'd died. How long has he been in the, *erm*, nursing home?"

"Oh, about twenty years now. Since Polly was about four or five. He has MS, and now he has Alzheimer's as well." She was looking at him curiously now. "Michael, did Polly tell you that her Granddad Rory was dead?"

That's not all she's told me about him, he thought grimly, remembering what Polly had told him her Granddad Rory was supposed to have done to her, when the whole time he was in a nursing home in another county, unable to get around under his own steam. Aloud, he said: "Well, yes, but, as I said, I probably misunderstood her."

There was a silence. Martha Yates bit down hard on her lower lip. To Michael's eyes, she seemed to be deciding whether or not to say something. Then she took a deep breath. "Michael, dear, Polly is a marvellous girl but . . . but, you know, sometimes, she tells lies. Did she ever tell you why she left university?"

"*Erm*, well, yes, as a matter of fact, she did. It was too stifling, she said, it had too many rules and restrictions for someone of her free spirit." He could imagine exactly how that had happened. Someone like Polly didn't thrive or flourish where there were too many constraints or regulations, although he'd been mildly surprised when she'd told him that it was a Bachelor of Arts she'd been doing. He'd always imagined the Arts in university to be a fairly flexible affair, and not the draconian drag she'd claimed it was.

"It was a little different to the way Polly said it was, I'm afraid. There was a man there, a lecturer. Polly . . . well, she accused him of trying to rape her, in his own room after a tutorial one day. It was terrible. The Guards were involved and everything. The case collapsed when the lecturer turned out to be gay and living with another man. Why would a gay man try to rape a female student? Anyway, Polly eventually admitted she'd lied about the attempted rape. She'd made a pass at him, he turned her down and Polly, well, Polly got angry and told the lie that caused all the trouble. The Guards should have charged her for making wrongful accusations, by rights, but the professor, he just wanted the whole horrible mess to be over and done with and he didn't press charges. The Guards let her off with a caution for telling them lies. But her father and me . . ." here she inclined her head towards her husband, who was deep in an animated conversation about the Champions League with a group of other like-minded auld lads across the crowded ballroom, "we . . . well, this is going to sound awful . . ."

"Go on, please," said Michael tightly. His jaw was already sore from holding it so rigidly and trying not to react the way he really wanted to, at what Polly's mother was saying.

"Well, we . . . we booked her into a clinic for a while. Six months, as it turned out to be. She had some therapy there and they said she was cured of the need to tell lies, but sometimes . . . well, sometimes, I just don't know."

"What are you two having such a deep confab about?" Polly had materialised out of nowhere to come and stand at Michael's elbow, clipboard and head-set still in place, and her glittering green eyes hard and cold with suspicion as she stared up accusingly at her mother and boyfriend.

"Just what a fantastic job you've done with this whole night," Michael said, pulling her to him with a hand round her waist and bending his head to kiss her on top of her flame-red hair, which looked spectacular tonight despite the fact that Polly had to eschew the tiara of real green, red-and-orangey brown end-of-summer leaves she'd chosen for herself to wear, in favour of the headset that allowed her to keep in constant touch with the waiters, the DJ and the one rather elderly bouncer, which, after all, was more important.

She smiled up at him, happy once more. "It's a wonderful party, Polly. Well done, love."

"Yes, it *is* a huge success, isn't it?" she giggled. "Are you enjoying it, Mummy?"

"It's the best party I've ever been to in my life, darling," her mother said with a smile.

Polly flew at her instantly for a hug, but, while the two women embraced enthusiastically, Martha Yates exchanged a look with Michael over the top of her petite daughter's head that seemed to warn him to be careful, somehow.

He didn't tackle her until the next day, Saturday. He was off work and they'd both slept late, recovering from the party, which had gone on till the early hours of Saturday morning. He'd been racking his brains to try and come up with a way to tackle her about it without seeming to be confrontational, but in the end he'd just blurted it out while they were in the bedroom, getting dressed to go for coffee and the newspapers, like they did every weekend.

"Polly, whose grave were you visiting the day we met?"

She whirled round from what she was doing at their dressing-table, startled. "What?" she said.

"I said, whose grave were you visiting the day we met?"

"My Granddad Rory's grave, of course. I told you that." A tell-tale wave of colour began to rise up from her neck to flood her cheeks. She turned back to the dressing-table and resumed fluffing up her hair, humming lightly but never once taking her eyes off his face, reflected in the dressing-table mirror.

"Are you quite sure about that, Polly?"

"Of course I'm sure about it!" she snapped, whirling round once more to face him, properly this time. "Of course I'm sure that it's my own grandfather's grave I was visiting when we met! Why wouldn't I be sure?"

He felt the familiar fear take hold of him and squeeze him round the heart. She was getting angry. Any minute now, she'd let fly at him and hit him with something, or she'd throw something. He looked round the room wildly to see what weapons were to hand for her. Her hair-dryer, the alarm clock which had already been used as a missile against him, a couple of lamps, a few knick-knacks. Whatever she did, however she chose to try to hurt him, he'd have to stand his ground this time. He couldn't live like this indefinitely.

"Because I know for a fact that your Granddad Rory isn't buried in Glasnevin. He isn't even dead, is he, Polly? He's alive and living in a nursing home in County Meath. He was in there, incapacitated, the whole time you claimed he was abusing you."

"So that's what you and that evil *bitch* who calls herself my mother were talking about behind my back last night!" she snarled, getting up from the dressing-table chair, and causing Michael to take an involuntary step back, though he was ashamed to do so. "You *do* know that she's evil, don't you, my mother? She's never liked me. That's why she tells lies about me, see? She's jealous of me, that's why! She's always been jealous of me, because my father prefers me to her, because I'm young and beautiful and she's a dried-up old hag! He prefers to fuck me over her, that's why she's jealous! She's never loved me! Can't you see that, Michael?"

"No more lies, Polly," said Michael wearily. "Has anything

you've ever told me been the truth?" He turned his back on her to dig a shirt out of the wardrobe. Almost immediately, he felt a sharp, stunning pain in his back, directly between his two shoulder blades, and heard a dull thud as a fairly sizeable object hit the floor. He turned round and looked down. She'd thrown her heavy wooden jewellery box with the sharp steel-tipped corners at him. He'd bought it for her himself, on their holiday to Italy earlier in the year. Now it lay on their bedroom carpet, open, her trinkets and bits-and-bobs of jewellery spewing out of its gaping maw. She sat on the bed, staring at him, watching for his reaction.

"Get out, Polly," he said evenly. His hands were trembling with the shock but his voice was steady. "Pack your bags and get out of my flat. I don't want anything more to do with you." However much of a let-down he'd been to Melissa in their relationship, he was sure now that he wasn't meant to pay for it for the rest of his life by being Polly's punching-bag. Even Melissa herself, as angry and disappointed as she'd been with him, would surely never have wished that on him.

"You don't mean that, Michael!" She stared at him in disbelief.

"Don't I?" He got her suitcase down from the top of the wardrobe, careful not to turn his back on her fully again, and dumped it on the bed. He began opening drawers and cupboards and throwing her things into the suitcase willy-nilly. She flew at him, her fingernails clawing at his eyes, scratching at the skin of his face and drawing blood, her bare feet kicking out at him. He held her at arm's length while she spat bile at him and called him every name under the sun, repressing as best as he could the urge to hit back. No matter what she did to him, he wouldn't hit her. But, after she'd kneed him painfully in the balls, he pushed her backwards onto the bed away from himself, where she lay for a minute, shocked that he'd taken some action against her at last.

"Get *out*, Polly," he said again, all traces of his former weariness gone. "I'm going out for a walk now and, when I come back, I want you gone from here. And don't bother telling people that I'm some kind of wife-beater, either. I'm not like your other victims, terrified of publicity. I don't have anyone to protect except myself. If you try to defame me or drag my character through the mud like you did with that poor lecturer, I'll prosecute you into the middle of the next century and I won't give a solitary shit who knows about it. Understood?"

She burst into wild, passionate sobs. *"Don't make me go, Michael! Don't send me away, please! I'll change. I'll be different, I swear!"*

"If I thought for even a minute that that was true . . ." he started, but then he stopped. Leopards, especially poisonous, insidious ones like Polly, didn't change their spots. They either couldn't, or they simply didn't want to. However much you might have wanted them to.

He quickly got dressed, then he took a fifty-euro note out of his wallet and dropped it on the bed beside her. "For the taxi home to Drumcondra. Never let it be said that I left you stuck."

"I don't *want* to go home to Drumcondra!" she wailed, manoeuvring herself face-down on the bed, kicking her legs and pummelling the pillows like a child having a tantrum. "I hate it there! It's so boring. And they watch me like a hawk there since I came out of the clinic! It's like being in prison."

"That's not my problem any more, Polly." He grabbed up his jacket from the back of a chair and left the apartment. As soon as he shut the bedroom door behind him, he heard the crash as something small and made of china was hurled against it, with an accompanying scream of thwarted rage and frustration from the room's remaining occupant. Another ornament bites the dust, he thought wryly as he ran lightly down the stairs and out the front door into the rainy street. Oh well. Ornaments could be replaced. The human skull, and a person's sanity, not so easily. He strode briskly down the road, enjoying the feel of the late summer rain on his upturned face.

Chapter 12

BECKS

Becks was going out the door to work in the morning when her dad stopped her. He cleared his throat awkwardly a time or two before saying gruffly: "*Erm*, Becks love, I was just wondering if you'd, *erm*, be coming straight home from work tonight or if you, *erm*, if you were seeing Ian tonight?" He was red in the face after this unusually long speech. Stephen Jamieson was a man of few words. He always had been, even before . . . even *before*.

Becks took a deep breath before replying, fiddling with her hair in the hall mirror to help her to appear nonchalant. "Ian and me are all washed up, Dad. We're not together any more."

Her dad looked surprised and, if anything, even more awkward. "Oh. I'm sorry to hear that. When did this happen?"

"Weekend," Becks said gloomily. "I don't really want to talk about it, to be honest."

"Okay, so, love. Whatever you say." He sounded relieved, as all Irish dads would at the thought that they didn't have to talk to their adult daughters about feelings and relationship stuff a moment longer than necessary.

Becks felt a twinge of sympathy for him suddenly. He couldn't even pass the buck by saying: "I'll put you on to your mother," like most other Irish dads could.

"Why were you asking about tonight, anyway? D'you need me for something?"

"No, well, yes, sort of. I just wondered if you'd come home for dinner. I was going to, *erm*, do something nice for us."

"What's the occasion?" Becks narrowed her eyes suspiciously. Stephen never went in the kitchen more often than he had to. Mind you, having said that, he had a couple of speciality dishes he trotted out every once in a blue moon that would make your mouth water. Becks hoped that, tonight, whatever his motivation for going back in the kitchen, it would be his deliciously creamy chicken korma. It was literally to die for. It'd give her something to look forward to after a long day of trying her damnedest to Avoid Thinking About Ian.

"No occasion," he mumbled, ushering her towards the door as he spoke. "There's just someone I want you to meet, that's all."

"Meet?" echoed Becks incredulously, just as she was shoved gently out the front door and onto the garden path. "Who? Is it a woman?"

"Yes, meet. It's not a big deal. It's just a friend. See you tonight, then. Have a good day at work."

And then the front door was shut, quietly but firmly, in Becks' face. *Humph!* She stared at it for a moment, then turned and hurried down the garden path and out the gate to her bus-stop, too curious to be miffed. Her dad wanted her to meet someone! Well, it had to be a special someone then, surely? Stephen Jamieson only brought a woman home to meet his daughter once in that same blue moon under which he ventured into the kitchen. Over the years since Becks' mother, Joanna, had left him — left *them* — he'd only brought home a handful of girlfriends, and none of them had even come close to replacing Joanna as his wife or (God forbid!) as Becks' mother. Becks certainly didn't want a stepmother, wicked or otherwise, but over the years she'd grown to accept that it was unfair of her to expect Stephen to live the life of a monk for the rest of his life just because his selfish, flighty young wife had left him for her lover, and dumped Becks on him as well into the bargain. If Becks was allowed to date people and to at least attempt to find romantic happiness, then it would have been unreasonable of her to expect her dad to live only for his daughter and his work as a self-employed carpenter with his own small but generally thriving business.

Not that her attempts to find romantic happiness had been yielding much fruit lately. All that stuff with Ian Holloway had been the last straw. If ever there was definitive proof that you shouldn't mix business with pleasure! Becks was furiously angry with herself for having broken her own rule, but Ian, the new resident graphic designer at Linklater's Publishers, Portobello, had been just a little too good-looking, just a little too smooth with his patter and flattering words, just a little too ready to swear undying love and fidelity forever. People who swore undying love on five minutes' acquaintance invariably didn't mean it. They might *think* they meant it, but all they were really feeling was just the first flush of passion, and, when that wore off, which it always did, they were left looking about them awkwardly, trying to get out of the mess they'd created for themselves. Ian wouldn't love and adore Becks for all eternity any more than he'd love and adore Man United Football Club for all eternity (no, wait, bad example, *terrible* example!), but then neither would Becks love Ian till the end of time. As a matter of fact, she'd kind of gone off him after about three dates. No, this little blip wouldn't mar her whole happiness for the rest of her days, but she wished with all her heart that she hadn't blotted her work copybook by sleeping with one of the staff. Still, she'd worry about Ian when she got to work. Sufficient unto the day is the evil thereof, wasn't that what they said?

She pushed Ian out of her mind resolutely, looking out the bus window idly as they sat in traffic, then she found that her mind wandered immediately to her dad and how, like most Irish men, he was utterly hopeless when it came to talking about Feelings, Relationships or Sex. A conversation that required all three to be discussed simultaneously was almost beyond him entirely. Suppressing a giggle, she remembered the day years ago when he'd given her the Talk on the Facts of Life.

She'd been about twelve or thirteen. He'd actually brought the subject up himself, in fairness to him, without any prompting from her.

"*Erm*, Becky love," he'd mumbled one day when they'd both been seated on the couch after dinner, watching a programme about the Eurovision, "I've noticed that you've been . . . growing, erm, *things* . . ." here, he pointed, without actually looking himself, in the general direction of her newly blossoming front bits, "and whatnot, and Mrs. Beech tells me that you've asked her to buy, erm, other *things* from the supermarket for your, erm, time. Erm, time of the month, I mean, d'you know what I mean?"

Mrs. Beech was the staid, heavy-set housekeeper Stephen Jamieson had hired to look after his household after his wife had left him. She'd stayed on till Becks had turned eighteen and was able to do the household cooking and cleaning by herself.

Now, an innocent, wide-eyed Becks gazed across at him with a query in those eyes.

"She wondered if maybe it was time I gave you the chat about, erm, well, what I mean to say is, the old Birds and the Bees chat, Becky love."

"Birds? Bees?" She stared at him, bemused.

"Maybe I'm not explaining myself very well."

He pulled a clean hanky, painstakingly ironed by Mrs. Beech, out of his trouser pocket and wiped the sweat off his forehead and neck with it. His eyes looked watery behind his glasses and he tugged frequently at his short brown beard, sprinkled liberally now with salt-and-pepper, a thing he did when he was agitated. He'd had a beard and glasses since Becks had known him. Becks couldn't imagine him without them. She often wondered if he'd come out of his mother's womb sporting them.

"What I mean to say is that, well, now that you're growing up and becoming, erm, a young lady and such-like . . ." here, a dull brick-red flush, beginning at his neck, began to crawl up his face and suffuse it with colour, "there are certain things that you're going to need to know. To equip you, for, you know, life. And . . . and things." He looked at her imploringly, begging her to understand.

"What things, Dad?" Her eyes were as big as saucers.

"Well, you're going to, erm, grow up and start to have relationships with men. I mean, boys, boys, of course, not men! Not men yet, anyway, not until you're eighteen at least. And, when you do, you know, start to have relationships and such, you're going to have to be prepared for . . . for certain things that they're going to want to do. These boys and . . . and men, I mean."

"Like what, Dad? What things?" She couldn't have sounded more innocent.

"Like, well, for instance, they might want to . . . to touch you on certain places, like . . . like your, *erm*, front things . . ." he flapped, again without looking, in the direction of her chest, "and, and, *erm*, down below as well . . ."

"Down below?" Becks' voice rose to a squeak and her dad's face turned an interesting shade of purple.

"You know, down below. You . . . you've probably started to grow hair down there by now . . . No, don't tell me!" he added in alarm, when Becks opened her mouth to speak. "I don't need to know. All you need to know for now is that it's perfectly normal to, erm, have hair down there. And, when you're much, *much* older than you are now, say, when you're in your thirties or forties . . ."

Becks' eyebrows shot up into her hairline at this; she mightn't be ready now but she had no intention of waiting till she was an old maid to have sex.

"You might meet a man you love and who loves you and that's when . . ." here, he looked round him desperately as if seeking an escape route and tugged so hard on his beard that he made himself wince and his eyes water even more, "that's when you might want to have what we adults call *sex* with him, see?" Again, he looked at her imploringly, as if to say, please don't make me go into any more detail, please, I'm begging you!

"Sex?" she echoed, all innocence. "How does it work exactly?"

"It's . . . let me see now, how best to describe it . . . it's when a man and a woman take off all their clothes and lie down together . . . and, and certain things get hard and then the man puts them somewhere dark and warm and safe and . . . Except, it's not really safe, not unless you . . . Oh, Christ Almighty, I wish your mother was here!"

Sweating profusely, he dropped his head in his hands in the attitude of a broken man.

"Don't upset yourself, Dad," she consoled him, patting him on the shoulder. "You did a great job of explaining everything. I think I've got the basics down now, anyway."

"Really, Becky love?" He looked up hopefully, his eyes glittering with tears of frustration and misery behind his glasses.

"Really, Dad," she echoed, barely able to keep a straight face.

She fled to the bathroom where she laughed so much she had to stuff a hand-towel in her mouth so he wouldn't hear her. Poor Dad! She already knew all about the so-called Facts of Life. Mrs. Hoey, the Home Economics teacher, had explained them fully to Becks' class about a year ago, and Noreen Sheehy-Bulger, her best friend at school, had obligingly filled in any gaps, as she had older sisters and they all had boyfriends and it was surprising the amount of surreptitious knowledge Noreen could accrue when she hung around her sisters and they didn't know she was paying close attention to their private conversations. Becks was, therefore, probably at least as well up on the subject as any thirteen-year-old in her peer group. It had just been so funny to watch her mortified dad try to explain it all to her. She could not *wait* to tell Noreen all about it at school on Monday.

Now, the bus rolled to a stop at Portobello and Becks got off, revelling in the glorious summer day and the short walk to Linklater's Publishers, where she'd been working as a reader and occasional receptionist for several years now. Of course Ian was there, crouched over his computer in the back office with his back to everyone, working on his designs for book covers. Old Mr. Edmund, her boss, was there too, of course, signing for a delivery in the front office.

"Good morning, my dear," he said, once the courier had left, with the same olde-worlde courtesy which made everyone around him feel comfortable and welcome. "How was your weekend?"

"It was okay." She bit her lip, then while she had the courage, blurted out: "Look, Mr. Edmund, there's something I need to tell you. Me and Ian are all washed up. We've had a fight and we're finished. *Kaput*. Broken up. *Finito*. And, the thing is, I don't really want to talk about it. In fact, I definitely don't want to talk about it, so I hope that's clear. And I don't particularly want anyone saying *'I told you so'* either."

"My lips are sealed," he replied, making the zipping-his-lip-and-throwing-away-the-key gesture.

"I know," she said, relenting and wanting to hug him suddenly. "And I know you didn't think it was a good idea for me and Ian to mix business with pleasure but we did, and now it's finished and it's all a total mess and you were right. But . . . but thank you for stepping back and letting me make my own mistakes and for not saying *'I told you so'*."

"No one here will give you any grief, I promise," Old Mr. Edmund said kindly. "The subject's closed as far as I'm concerned, and I'll see to it that everyone here respects it."

Becks smiled at him. She knew he would. He was an old darling, a proper teddy bear, and he'd been so good to Becks, a favourite of his, that she was coming to see him as a sort of surrogate grandfather figure. She'd never had grandparents, another thing that had set her apart from the other girls in school when she was growing up.

"Thank you," she said. "I know you will. By the way, you'll never guess which confirmed bachelor might have found himself a new girlfriend, after donkey's years of just sitting on the couch in front of the telly with the remote control and a six-pack of beer?"

The working day had begun.

The first thing Becks noticed when she put her key in the front door of the house in Sycamore Drive later that day was the smell of chicken korma that wafted out of the kitchen and into the hall. *Mmmm*, Dad had made his speciality, goody. She was bloody starving, having skipped lunch that day, both in anticipation of a top-class feed from her dad tonight and also because she'd had some work to catch up on. And why was she behind in her work, she reminded herself sternly as she took off her jacket and smoothed back her long, light-brown hair in the hall mirror, why had she been a bit less conscientious than usual lately? Because of Bloody Ian. Because she'd broken her own rule about never dating someone she worked with and it had all gone tits-up, that was why. Old Mr. Edmund, as the small staff at Linklater's affectionately called their boss, would have been well within his rights (morally, anyway, if not legally) to bawl her out for it, but, probably because she was his favourite employee and normally his best worker, with a real feel for the books they published and the authors they met and mentored, he hadn't, for which she was immensely grateful, and instead was letting her make up the time *and* the work. God bless his patience and tolerance, anyway.

The second thing Becks noticed was the very expensive-looking fitted leather jacket, petrol-blue and as soft as butter, ladies' wear, that was hanging on the hook next to Stephen Jamieson's scruffy work jacket, the hook where Becks normally hung her own coat. *Humph*. Well. So that was the way of it, was it? She hung her light summer jacket on a different hook and took a long appraising look at the petrol-blue one and even briefly fingered the material. Well, this chick certainly had good taste for an auld one, whoever she was. Becks, who'd inherited her mother's love of fashion and accessories and flair for throwing an outfit together, could always tell. The sound of laughter and social chit-chat emanated from the kitchen. Becks plastered a huge fake grin of welcome to her face and opened the kitchen door, fully prepared to be kind to whomever it was who was making Stephen laugh out loud in the kitchen right now. Whoever she was, she must be a bloody miracle worker, because Stephen Jamieson had never really laughed much since his wife had left him, and that was a long time ago. Maybe she was one of those women who tried to be constantly funny to keep a man's interest. Stephen had certainly attracted a few of those try-hard types over the years, but the relationships had never lasted. Stephen's relationships never lasted. Stephen was a very poor communicator and that drove women nuts, just like it had driven Joanna, his wife, nuts. Had probably driven her *away,* if the truth were known.

Becks entered the kitchen just in time to see a smiling Stephen hold a loaded cooking spoon to the red-lipsticked mouth of a very glamorous woman and the woman take a nibble of whatever was on the spoon and declare it delicious before smacking her lips together in a gesture of satisfaction.

"Hi, all. Am I, *erm*, am I interrupting something?"

"Oh, Becks, hi, love," her father said, looking all flustered and red in the face. She'd never walked in on him play-acting with a woman before. "We didn't hear you come in."

"Obviously." For a minute, Becks had trouble keeping the smile on her face. "I'm Becks, by the way." She stuck out a hand to the other woman, who had recovered her composure after being caught out getting spoon-fed by her lover, who also just so happened to be Becks' father.

"I'm Veronica," the strange woman replied. "Veronica Lacey. I've looked forward very much to meeting you. Steve's told me so much about you."

Oh, has he now, thought Becks, annoyed. Good for *Steve.*

Hurray for *Steve*. Good old *Steve*. Aloud, she mumbled: "I wish I could say the same."

"What was that, Becks dear?" flashed back Veronica.

"Oh, nothing, nothing at all," trilled Becks, turning to her father and adding: "Is there anything I can do to help here, *Steve*, erm, I mean, Dad?"

"Well," he said, looking bemused as always when he had one or more females to deal with, "nothing much out here. Dinner's more or less under control. Tell you what, though, could you take Veronica through to the dining-room? You two can get acquainted and I'll bring the grub through in a bit?"

He looked happy for once, excited even, like a little boy on Christmas morning who discovers that that bastard Santa has actually brought him the game he wanted, for once. Becks wasn't used to seeing him look so, well, *jolly*. And, speaking of looks, he'd gone to a lot of trouble to jazz himself up for today. He'd had his brown greying hair neatly cut, he'd trimmed his brown greying beard and he was wearing what looked like a new blue shirt with his good jeans and brown boots, which Becks had ironed herself last weekend. (The jeans, not the boots.) She had to admit that he scrubbed up all right and was totally looking like an eligible bachelor in his early fifties today. And as for Veronica, well . . .!

Well, for starters, she was way younger than Stephen, who was fifty-two. She was only about forty, maybe even younger. Becks had been expecting someone older, probably because most of her father's previous girlfriends had been closer to his own age. This spring chicken had a full head of glossy, jet-black hair cut into a sharp, swinging bob. Her make-up was flawless, if dramatic (red lips and smoky eyes) and a tad over-done for a summer's evening, her short-sleeved, pale-blue-and-white-patterned summer dress had definitely not come off a rail in Penneys and every inch of the flesh on display (bare legs, arms, neck, a bit of cleavage) had all been fake-tanned to within an inch of its life. Her high-heeled strappy sandals matched her dress and so did her handbag. Becks was no slouch in the style stakes herself, but this woman was making her feel frumpy. She was so well put together, it seemed as if the whole effect had been organised down to the last detail by a team of Swedish engineering experts with slide-rules and protractors who measured things. Becks, more than a little miffed, led the way to the dining-room, where her dad had set the table for a meal.

"So, what is it that you do again, Becks?" Veronica asked her when they were seated. "I know Steve's told me, but I just can't seem to call it to mind at the minute."

"I work in a publisher's."

"Oh. *Books.*" She said it in the same way that you might mention something else from the Stone Age that was now obsolete. *Oh. Woolly mammoths. Oh. Cavemen. Right. I see.* Then she compounded Becks' fury by adding: "I didn't think anyone really bought books any more. I thought they read everything now on those Kindle-y things, after the success of *Fifty Shades?*"

"No!" expostulated Becks. One of her pet hates was people saying things like that about the book trade. "Yes, I'll admit that Kindles are very popular at the moment, but I think you'll find that most people still like the feel of a real book in their hands and will never go one hundred-per-cent-digital as long as there's still a physical book industry alive and kicking."

"No need to be so touchy, dear," Veronica said with the most patronising smile that set Becks' teeth on edge immediately. "I meant no offence. I haven't picked up a book since I left school and that's the way I prefer it."

Becks felt herself break out in a cold sweat. How could her father, not much of a reader himself, in fairness, even consider dating a woman who admitted freely that she hadn't picked up a book in years, when Joanna, his former wife, had passed on to Becks her passion for reading, her love for the printed word in physical book form? Her lower lip began to tremble with indignation, but, before she could formulate a haughty answer, her father swiftly interjected as he entered with the food.

"Tell Becks what *you* do, Veronica sweetheart, why don't you?"

Veronica flashed him an angelic smile before telling Becks tightly: "I work in PR."

"Oh now, don't be modest, love," went on Stephen, dishing out the plates of steaming hot, deliciously creamy chicken korma with the accompanying naan bread and poppadums. "She's got her own company, haven't you, love? That's how we met, isn't it? I was doing some carpentry work for Veronica's company, wasn't I, love, putting up some shelves and filing cabinets and what-have-you, and we got chatting and . . . and that's pretty much the way of it, isn't it, love?"

Becks didn't care for the way her father kept deferring in every sentence to the haughty-faced Veronica, who seemed to expect such deference as her right and proper due.

"Oh, right," said Becks. "For a minute there, I thought you meant that you'd gone to her looking for PR or something mad like that. I mean, what would you be wanting with PR?"

"Well, actually . . ." Stephen looked uncomfortable, as if he didn't have a clue how to finish his sentence and was hoping someone else might step in and do the honours.

"As a matter of fact," Veronica put in smoothly, "Stephen and I have arranged for my company to take over all of *STEPHEN JAMIESON'S CARPENTRY* PR needs from now on."

"But that's always been my job!" wailed Becks, stunned. Well, she had a look in her dad's appointments book every Sunday night, *if* she had time, and reminded him of where he was meant to be in the morning. Oh, and she occasionally put a funny meme about tradesmen or just life in general up on the Facebook page she'd created for her father's business last year in a moment of boredom, but she was ashamed to admit that she hardly ever looked at it when she was (compulsively) checking her own social media pages. Maybe that wasn't quite the same as doing his PR. *Shit.* Now this woman was going to muscle in on what should have been Becks' patch by rights, but Becks hadn't a leg to stand on because she'd grievously neglected her patch and left it to die of thirst without so much as a droplet of water to ease its agony, so it served her right. *Fuck.* Fuck it anyway.

"Veronica has a lot of good ideas for expanding the business," her dad said enthusiastically. "Don't you, love?" This last was directed at Veronica, who smiled back indulgently.

"Word of mouth's always been good enough for you before," muttered Becks sulkily. Her dad's business had always just been a van and a tool-bag, a mobile phone and the odd advertisement in the *Buy and Sell* (when he'd first started out, shure, it had been cards in the window of the local hardware shop), but that had been pretty much it. In what ways Veronica was hoping to *'expand the business'*, Becks was sure she didn't know.

"Word of mouth!" echoed Veronica with a brittle little laugh. "Word of mouth!" She said it the same way she'd said *'books'* earlier. "In this day and age!"

Stephen Jamieson obviously caught his daughter's expression as he said anxiously: "All Veronica is saying, Becks, love, is that things have moved on a bit in recent years and that maybe the business should, *erm*, move with the times a bit too. That's, *erm*, that's all she's saying, love."

You never gave a shit about the business 'moving with the times' when it was just you and me, Becks thought. Out loud she said, but not without an Herculean effort: "Well, that's, erm, great, Dad. I hope it all works out well for you. I mean, for the business."

Stephen looked relieved and went to go and see about the dessert, a fancy tiramisu he'd bought in the supermarket because his culinary efforts didn't stretch to desserts.

Becks and Veronica sat in stony silence in his absence, Becks fuming with repressed anger, toying with her glass of wine, and Veronica checking her phone. How bloody rude, thought Becks angrily, bringing her phone to the dinner table like that, when she'd been invited specially and everything! She conveniently forgot that she herself spent most meals on her phone normally, or with a book propped up against a sauce bottle in front of her, while her dad read the newspaper or watched the News. Now, her righteous indignation flared up inside her, making her want to slap the phone out of Veronica's perfectly manicured hands.

"Aren't you a little old to be still living at home at your age?" Veronica said later on, when they were all poised awkwardly on sofas and armchairs in the sitting-room, the two women with glasses of wine and Stephen with a can of beer. "Twenty-six, I think Steve said you were? Me? I couldn't wait to leave home. I left at eighteen and never looked back. The thought of still being stuck in that dump with my parents at the age of nearly thirty . . . well!" She gave an exaggerated shudder to illustrate her point.

Becks choked on her wine, coughing so hard that her dad had to come round and bang her on the back. "Sorry," she spluttered through tight lips. "Went down the wrong way there."

How dared this Veronica woman, how very bloody *dared* she come round here and cast aspersions on the fact that Becks still lived at home with her father at the age of . . . that bitch, to even *mention* her age! . . . nearly . . . nearly *thirty*! Where the hell else was she meant to live? Becks and her dad were pretty much alone in the world. Stephen Jamieson had no family living. Becks had no brothers or sisters or cousins. Joanna, Becks' mother, the one who'd left them both when Becks had been five, might have had relatives still living, but she'd been estranged from them since before Becks had even born. Becks wouldn't have had the slightest clue how to go about tracing them, and she doubted if her dad would have, either. It made *sense* for the two of them, Becks and her dad, to live together. It *did.* The four-storey old house in Terenure was plenty big enough for the two of them. And Becks, being the only child, would obviously be the one who'd end up caring for Stephen when he was in his dotage, so didn't it make more sense for her to be already *in situ?* She'd always assumed that, when she got married and had kids, that she and they (husband, kids, pets, bicycles, barbecues, camping equipment, swing sets, she wanted the full works) would all come and live with Stephen in this house and be one big huge happy family. She'd missed out on the rough-and-tumble of a big family in her childhood. Without Joanna, the house had been very quiet. Becks had flitted through it silently from empty room to empty room like a little ghost, with her books and her dolls (in particular Baby Audrey) always in tow, while Mrs. Beech the housekeeper watched afternoon telly in the kitchen as that evening's dinner cooked. Even when her father came home in the evenings, he'd either go to the pub or drink in front of the box for the night and Becks would still be alone. When she got married, she would have loads of kids and change all that, but that was still in the future, worse luck. Ian certainly wasn't going to be the one to make all her dreams come true. In the meantime, however, it was none of this Veronica woman's business where she lived or how old she was. The bloody cheek of the woman!

"Dad, are you sure it's a good idea to have another can?" she managed brightly through gritted teeth. "You want to be able to drive Veronica home safely after dinner, I'm sure?" She hadn't seen a car in the driveway besides her dad's van, so she felt it was safe to assume that Miss High-and-Mighty

Veronica Lacey hadn't arrived at the house under her own steam.

"Oh, don't worry about me, Becks dear," Veronica said sweetly. "Steve's invited me to stay the night." She smiled over at her embarrassed boyfriend, who grinned foolishly back. There was a wealth of implied intimacy in her words.

Becks felt her chicken korma and rich tiramisu dessert churn in her stomach, prior, she feared, to making its way back up her throat.

"Oh, lovely," she faked. "Can you please excuse me for a minute? I've just remembered an urgent work call I promised to make this evening." She fled to the coolness and peace and quiet of the landing, where she waited until her stomach had settled sufficiently before dialling Bloody Ian's number. He answered on the third ring. Becks abruptly cut short his attempt at the pleasantries.

"Ian, look, this is an emergency or I wouldn't be calling you. In fact, you're the last person in the world I'd be calling. Yes, yes, all right, I know I shouldn't be saying things like that if I want a favour from you. Look, I wouldn't be asking this if I wasn't completely desperate, but can I crash at yours tonight? My dad is planning on having . . . *barf,* having *sex* with his girlfriend in this house tonight, and I have absolutely, positively *got* to get away from here before it happens."

"Bummer," Ian said sympathetically. Then, salaciously: "Your old man has a girlfriend? At his age. Fuck me. Is she hot, this girlfriend? How old is she? Good tits? Legs? What?"

"Ian, you're a total pig, but I don't have time to go into any of that now. Can I crash there or not? I can sleep on the couch. I'll sleep anywhere, as long as it's not here."

There was a silence. "The thing about that, Becks, *um* . . ." Ian began.

Then a woman's voice, as sugary as nectar, came on the phone.

"Becks, sweetie, is that you? Is everything all right, sweetie?"

Becks froze. That was Corinne, the new receptionist from Linklater's. That fucker Ian had replaced her already? They'd only broken up at the weekend! She pressed the 'End Call' button and sat on the top step of the stairs clutching her phone, shivering despite the warmth of the summer's evening, until it was time to go back downstairs and be falsely polite once more.

Later that night, when her father's double bed started creaking and rocking, Becks, curled up in the foetal position on her bed, resolutely stuck her headphones on and turned the volume on her music up as loud as she could bear it for the rest of the night.

When she woke up, it was with a headache and a distinct feeling of disgruntlement. The same awful dream had been running through her head all night. In it, she'd come home from work to find her father assiduously hoovering the sitting-room, clad only in a backless apron and nothing else, while Veronica sat with her feet up reading a magazine and stuffing her face with chocolates. The sight of her father's hairy backside in the backless apron as he went about his household chores was quite bad enough, but when Veronica snapped her fingers and rapped out sharply: "*Footstool, activate!*" and Stephen Jamieson began to get down on his hands and knees by the couch so that his strict mistress could rest her stiletto-clad feet on his back, Becks, desperate to avoid the sight of the full moon rising, clawed her way out of the dream like a woman being buried alive with shovelfuls of earth, waking up struggling to breathe. *Jesus Christ on a bicycle!* What a nightmare that had been! One of her worst ever, and she still regularly had the one about her mother, tapping on her bedroom window in the middle of the night like Cathy in *Wuthering Heights*, begging to be let in. It took a long hot shower and many cups of coffee before the horror of the hoovering dream began to recede even slightly.

Life went on. Becks still went to work every day, trying to have as little to do with Ian the Womaniser and Corinne the Slut as was humanly possible, but, with a premises as small and cramped as Linklater's was, it wasn't easy to keep her distance all the time. "We do all have to work together," Old Mister Edmund had reminded her gently when she'd complained. Ian kept trying to talk to her and let her know that his relationship with the gorgeous Corinne, a perfectly groomed Dublin 4 girl with an annoying super-posh accent, was only on the most temporary of footings and that he would throw her over in a heartbeat if Becks would only take him back. But Becks wasn't at all sure that she even *wanted* Ian back. He was a two-timing sleazebag who'd slept with a woman called Lorraine who worked in a nearby pub while they'd been going out together, and he'd got with Corinne practically the day they'd broken up. Only a complete and utter louse would do that. Even though Becks disliked the prissy, perfect Corinne intensely, she felt kind of sorry for her as well, knowing that Ian was prepared to give her the old heave-ho just as soon as ever Becks said the word. Well, Becks wasn't saying the word. She deserved better than Ian Bloody What's-his-name.

So, Becks mourned the loss of yet another romantic relationship while simultaneously striving to make Linklater's the best publishing company for poetry, memoir and children's books in the whole of Ireland *(The Irish being such terrific storytellers, the raw material was all already there)*.

In the meantime, the relationship between her father and the haughty and obnoxious Veronica Lacey, PR Queen Extraordinaire, seemed to be gaining ground. Stephen Jamieson went round the house and about his work whistling, with a permanent grin on his face. Veronica stayed over at the house in Terenure two or three times a week, so he clearly had plenty to whistle and grin about. On the nights when his girlfriend stayed over with him, his bed creaked and groaned all night and horrible sex-moans could be heard all over the house, but not by Becks, who staunchly stuck her headphones in her ears the moment she shut her bedroom door behind her of an evening.

Every time she came home from work on an evening when she knew that Veronica was going to be there, she banged and clattered and sang at the top of her voice out in the hall while she was hanging up her jacket, so they'd know she was home and she wouldn't be confronted with the nightmarish sight of her father's bare arse in the backless apron doing the hoovering while Strict Mistress Veronica sat with her feet up in the sitting-room, stuffing her face with effing Quality Streets. God Almighty, she wondered crossly sometimes, why did so many Irish men want to be dominated by women? She could only presume that it was what came of having bossy Irish mammies telling them what to do throughout their childhoods. They couldn't live without being told what to bloody do by strong women. It was becoming a real problem for modern women. Every second bloke nowadays wanted his arse slapped and to be tied up and verbally abused during sex. Becks had no proof (apart from her nightmare) that Stephen Jamieson was that way inclined, but she wouldn't be one bit surprised if he was, given the way that he was so deferential to Veronica in everything he said and did. And that Veronica one was a bossy bleedin' cow, a real wagon.

Then the lovers had a row, their first one that Becks knew of, but it was a big one. For a while now, Veronica had been skulking round the house with a tape-measure, gazing speculatively at the windows and doors as if wondering what best to replace them with, once she was safely installed as the mistress of the house. Becks was filled with horror at the thought of a new broom sweeping clean the house's tatty old *décor* and replacing it with modern monstrosities. Yes, the house was old (actually, it was very old) and a bit rundown-looking, and the fixtures and fittings hadn't been changed since the Jamiesons had moved in in the late eighties, when Joanna had been pregnant with Becks, but . . . but that was the *point*. *Joanna* had chosen the décor, the furnishings and wall-coverings and floor-coverings and curtains. This battered old faded dusky-pink velvet couch in the sitting-room was the same one Joanna used to lounge on, chain-smoking and with her long bendy legs dangling over the arm, bemoaning the fact that she'd been born in the sixties and not in the twenties, for which her tall, thin flexible frame and short blonde bob would have been ideally suited. She'd loved the costumes, the jewellery and the make-up of the twenties as well, and the music, the dancing and the old films too. She was never happy in these modern times. She always knew she'd been born in the wrong era. A tarot card reader had told her that, but it had only confirmed what she'd already known, deep down in her heart. The long coffee-table was where she'd put her feet while she was reading, or just sitting and smoking. The heavy glass ashtray, which she might have taken with her when she left because it had gone missing at around the same time, had been replaced with a cheap plastic one because Stephen smoked too. Even Becks had the odd puff, when she was stressed.

The big floor-length window in the sitting-room was where Joanna had sat on the window-seat, smoking and looking out at the rain on wet days, bored, restless and depressed because the sun she loved wasn't shining and she couldn't go and lie naked in the privacy of the back garden like she loved doing, lapping up the sun's rays while her little Becka-Boo, as she'd called her, chased the squirrels back up their trees and read her favourite comics, the *Beano,* the *Dandy* and the *Twinkle, especially for little girls.* Becks had been so happy when her mother had been there with them. The thought of Veronica or Stephen's getting rid of anything Joanna had chosen or enthused about when they'd first moved in filled her with dread. She couldn't handle the thought of it. She just couldn't.

The row between Stephen and Veronica was not exactly

about couches or curtains, however. Becks had come downstairs for a snack one evening to find a wholly unexpected shouting match going on in the kitchen. Veronica and Stephen were standing at opposite ends of the table, glaring at each other.

"What's going on?" said Becks, looking curiously from one angry face to the other. These two never argued, never mind fought like cat and dog. What the bloody hell was going on?

"She wants to tear down the summerhouse!" yelled Stephen.

Becks had never seen him so angry. His face was bright red and there was a vein throbbing in his neck.

"What?" Becks rounded on Veronica, who quailed a little. "What the hell? The summerhouse? I'll have you know that my dad made that with his own hands in honour of my mother when she left us. It's a place to remember her by. What the hell do you think you're doing, talking about tearing it down like that?"

Now, Veronica seemed almost close to tears. "I never said just tear it down. That's not what I meant. I just meant that it's perhaps just a shade too big and . . . and *overpowering* for the back garden, and that if we had it taken down and put in a little water feature instead, an ornamental pond, get a few koi fish in maybe . . . And, besides, I didn't know it was anything special or something to do with your mother, with Joanna, how could I?"

"Don't say her name! How dare you say her name! You're not fit to wipe her boots!" bellowed Stephen, banging his fist down on the table and making the crockery on it jump.

"Okay, Dad, take it easy now, she didn't mean any harm by it!" Becks instinctively came round to Veronica's side of the table, and placed a hand protectively on the older woman's arm. "I'm sure Veronica didn't mean to upset you. Okay? No one's tearing down the summerhouse, all right? Why don't we all just calm down and I'll make us all a nice hot cup of tea, okay?"

"Fuck the tea," Stephen said, opening the fridge and extracting a fresh six-pack of beer. He stomped out of the kitchen and into the sitting-room with it.

"I think I'd better go," Veronica said.

Becks looked at her in surprise. She was shaking like a leaf. Of her usual confidence and arrogant air, there was no sign.

"Is your car outside?" Becks couldn't remember if it was or not. "Or would you like me to call you a taxi?"

"I've got my car."

"Yes, but look, are you okay to drive? You don't look very . . . I mean, you look a bit pale. Will you at least stay for a cup of tea? Put some colour back in those cheeks."

"I'd rather go, if you don't mind. Besides, I don't think Steve . . . I don't think he wants me here at the moment."

She looked so despondent that Becks felt sorry for her. "Of course he wants you here," she said kindly. "But . . . but maybe you're right. Maybe it's for the best if we just give him some space for now. I'm sure he'll be his usual easy-going self again when you talk to him tomorrow. He's probably just tired. You know how hard he works."

Veronica looked doubtful. Becks stayed with her while she gathered up her handbag and jacket, both of them casting wary glances at the closed sitting-room door as they passed it. Becks gave the older woman a brief hug at the front door, then she stayed at the door, arms folded, watching worriedly, like a mother hen, as Veronica tap-tap-tapped down the garden path in her high-heeled shoes, out the open garden gate and into her car.

Veronica turned and gave Becks a subdued little wave before she drove off down Sycamore Drive. Becks waved back, then closed the front door quietly before standing uncertainly in the hall for a few moments staring at the sitting-room door. It was closed, but not just closed. It was *closed* closed, and she was nervous about opening it and seeing what kind of mood her father was in now. In the end, she took a deep breath, counted to three, turned the doorknob and walked right in. Stephen was seated in 'his' armchair in front of the television, which was showing a football match. His head was lowered, a can of lager in his hand, which rested on the arm of his chair. As she came closer, she realised that he was either asleep, or pretending to be. Either way, he clearly wasn't open for business.

"Goodnight, Dad," she whispered, dropping a kiss on the top of his head. Then she went to bed but, after all the disturbance of the evening, it was a long time before she slept.

Life, and the relationship between Stephen and Veronica, eventually returned to normal. Becks was secretly disappointed that the row hadn't split the pair up, while knowing she was being ungenerous to think so. After all, she was free to choose a life-partner for herself (not that she was having much luck with that at the moment), so why shouldn't her dad be, too? Because he's my *dad,* was her answer to that, even though she knew that that was selfish and childish. And she was disappointed too, because the brief rapport that had developed between herself and Veronica on the night of the Big Row seemed to have dissipated like a morning mist. Veronica had seemed to soften a bit towards her that night, and now she was back acting like the two of them were enemies, each vying for the love of the same man.

"I know I couldn't stand her when I first met her," she complained to Old Mr. Edmund, who was as gossipy as an old woman when it came to matters of this nature, "but, I don't know, after she had that fight with Dad over the summerhouse, I thought she and I could be, well, not mates exactly, but, well, not deadly enemies either, you know?"

"Be patient with her," Old Mr. Edmund advised. "She'll come round eventually, when she realises that the two of you are not actually in competition with each other for your father's love and attention. There's plenty of room for you both in his life."

"Try telling her that," Becks had mumbled before turning her mind reluctantly back to her work. Veronica was as prickly as a bagful of premenstrual porcupines. She, Becks, wouldn't hold her breath while waiting for the other woman to 'come round', as Old Mr. Edmund had optimistically put it.

Then, one afternoon Becks came home earlier than usual, fully prepared to make the usual unholy racket in the hall so that Stephen and Veronica, if they were at home and having sex anywhere in the house outside of Stephen's bedroom (she still wasn't convinced that her dream about Stephen in the ass-less apron doing the hoovering was only a horrible nightmare and not a ghastly premonition), would have time to cease and desist before she caught them in *flagrante delicto,* a prospect which made her truly gag.

She got off her bus at the top of Sycamore Drive and strolled down the road to her house, not even really thinking about Stephen and Veronica but about Ian, and whether it would last between him and Corinne, the new receptionist at Linklater's. She felt like a bit of a dog-in-the-manger on the subject. She was fairly certain (about ninety per cent) that she didn't want Ian back, but neither was she particularly thrilled about Corinne's having him. She was even half-thinking of telling him she wanted him back, just so she'd have the satisfaction of seeing Corinne get dumped like a hot spud. Did that make her evil, she wondered, or just human, with human frailties and weaknesses like everyone else? Should she try to rise above the whole thing, keep her dignity while leaving the Terrible Twosome to get on with it? She was deep in thought, still pondering this weighty moral question when she reached the house.

Stephen's van was in the driveway, so he was at home after all, and, parked outside on the street by the kerb, was Veronica's snazzy little red car, with the words *VERONICA LACEY, PR CONSULTANTS* emblazoned across either side of it. Great. *Sigh.* They were at home then, and that meant that they were most likely making the beast with two backs somewhere on the premises. The government should really outlaw parents, and anyone of parental age, from having sex with anyone other than their lawfully wedded spouses, and even then they should keep it strictly behind closed — no, locked! — doors and do it only on one day a month at the very most. It was just too stressful and vomit-inducing for the adult children of such ageing swingers. Mentally preparing the words of the song she was planning to sing aloud when she entered the hall so as to alert them to her presence, Becks came round the side of her dad's van to find a distraught and tearful Veronica sitting on the front doorstep.

"What's up? Where's Dad? Is he okay?" Becks was alarmed. God Almighty. What the hell was up with the pair of them now?

"He's fine," sobbed Veronica, not without a tinge of bitterness. "He's perfectly fine and dandy. Happy as Larry. He's thrown me out, the bastard. He wouldn't even give me time to collect my handbag and phone and stuff. And my car-keys are in my handbag, so I can't even go home until he lets me have them. Thank God you're here. I was afraid you wouldn't be home till after six as usual and I'd have to sit out here all day."

Becks was appalled. A sobbing woman on the doorstep? This wasn't at all good for relations with the neighbours. Did Stephen want the reputation of a man who bullies women, because that was what was going to happen if incidents like these were going to become commonplace occurrences? And poor Veronica looked a mess. She had cried all of her expensive make-up off, and, in the absence of a tissue to wipe her eyes or blow her nose, it looked like she'd been using the hem of her black-and-white summer dress for that purpose.

"What happened? Why'd he throw you out?" Becks knew that asking that question was a bit like asking a domestic-violence victim what they'd done to anger their attacker, but she was genuinely curious as to what would make her normally mild-mannered father do such a thing. Mind you, he hadn't been all that mild-mannered on the night of the Big Row about the summerhouse, had he? He'd turned into a different person that night, a frightening person who shouted and roared and banged his fists on the kitchen table, making everyone around him jump in fear. The only other time that she'd seen him like that was on that dreadful day over twenty years ago when he'd come home from work unexpectedly at lunchtime to find his beautiful, vivacious wife Joanna, with his pretty little daughter Becka in tow, preparing to leave him for the man Becks had only ever known as Uncle Vic.

1993 . . .

Rebecca dutifully climbed up on to the window-seat with Baby Audrey in tow and looked out at the rain-washed street. No way was she packing her favourite doll in the dark cramped luggage, to get scared and squished in the boot of the taxi. Baby Audrey would be sitting right there on her lap with her when she was in the taxi, being driven away from Sycamore Drive in Terenure for ever. Rebecca's eyes widened when she saw the big white van with the words 'STEVEN JAMIESON CARPENTRY' printed in big letters on the side of it suddenly pull up to the garden gate where the taxi was soon going to be. She knew that somehow this meant danger for Mummy's lovely plans, the plans that included her daughter Rebecca, whom she loved so dearly. Rebecca scrambled down off the window-seat, leaving Baby Audrey behind her in her haste. She bolted into the hall and up the stairs, shouting: "It's Daddy! Mummy, it's Daddy! Daddy's here!"

Mummy stuck her head out of the bathroom door, a loaded mascara wand in her hand and an expression of annoyance on her face.

"What on earth are you yelling about, Rebecca?" she said irritably. "Haven't I told you a thousand times that young ladies simply don't shout?"

"Daddy's home." Rebecca was red-faced at being told off by Mummy.

"What!" Mummy, by contrast, went chalk-white.

"He's outside the house," said Rebecca. "I saw his van from the window just now."

"Fuck!" breathed Mummy, before tearing down the stairs to see for herself. "What the fuck is he doing here in the middle of the day? How does he know? Who told him? He'll spoil everything! He'll spoil everything!"

She reached the hall at the same time as Daddy, who'd just put his key in the door. They said nothing as they stood and stared at each other. Daddy took in the little pile of suitcases in the hall, topped by one of Mummy's antique candy-striped hat-boxes, bursting at the seams with her precious treasures.

"Rebecca, go up to your room," Daddy said in a quiet voice that was somehow scarier than if he'd been shouting.

"But, but, Daddy, Baby Audwey!" Rebecca reverted without realising it to the lisp she'd had when she was younger.

"Now, Rebecca." Still in those dangerously quiet tones.

"But, but Daddy . . ." she began.

"Now!" he roared, and, with one last pleading glance at Mummy, whose face was pale under her make-up, Rebecca fled.

"It was because I suggested throwing out all those big old photo albums with all the photos of Joanna in them," Veronica said, between harsh, gulping sobs that seemed wrenched out of her. "You know the ones in his bedroom? In the wardrobe?"

How could Becks not know? How many times had she gone into her father's bedroom, into his wardrobe, while he was out working, and pulled out the giant pile of albums, then sat on his bedroom floor with them for hours and hours, poring over the photographs of Joanna? Joanna Jamieson, or Joanna Tate as was, had been exceptionally photogenic, with her shiny blonde bob, her long bendy flapper legs, as she'd called them, and her mobile, expressive, red-lipsticked mouth painted in the style of her idol from the twenties, Clara Bow. Steven had taken hundreds of photos of his wife, some of which included his daughter Becka, but they were mostly just of Joanna. Becks didn't blame her father for mostly wanting photos of his bright, intelligent, sparky wife with the radiant smile and mercurial personality and not ones of his quiet, mousy daughter. Who'd want a picture of plain, dumpy Becks when they could have one of the brilliantly dazzling Joanna Tate?

Becks was absolutely aghast to hear that Veronica had suggested throwing such precious albums away. There were years and years of Joanna's married life documented in those albums. They were irreplaceable. *Irreplaceable.* But, somehow, she knew that there was no point in telling Veronica this. She'd obviously felt justified, as Steven's girlfriend, in asking him to do an *'out with the old, in with the new'*, and some people might even say that she had a point. Either way, Becks knew there wasn't much point in arguing the toss with the woman over it. It would only be a waste of their joint breath. Becks had her opinion, Veronica had hers, and never the twain would meet. So she wisely kept her own counsel on the matter.

Out loud, Becks said: "And that's when he threw you out?"

Veronica nodded, still sniffling. "He grabbed my arm and practically frog-marched me down the stairs and out the front door. I kept begging him to at least let me get my things, but he wouldn't listen. It was like he wasn't even there inside his own head, somehow, if you know what I mean. He just wasn't there." She blew her nose loudly into the tissues from the little packet Becks had fished out of her bag for her.

"Right, well, that's no good. And he's in there now, is he? In the house, I mean?"

Veronica nodded vigorously. "Look in the front window, shure. He's watching the telly and having a beer. I knocked and shouted and rang the doorbell and banged on the knocker but he didn't even turn a hair. Nothing, not a flicker. He could be stone-dead in that chair for all I know. He hasn't moved for hours."

A cold shiver ran through Becks, despite the warmth of the day. A quick glance through the front window on the right-hand side of the door as you were facing it confirmed that Steven Jamieson (she could only see the back of his head, and his left arm as it dangled loosely over the left arm of his chair) was indeed unmoving in his favourite armchair, facing the television. Beer cans, some clearly empty and some still unopened, littered the carpet around his chair.

"Right," she said grimly, more firmly than she felt. "Let's sort this. You come in with me now, Veronica. You go straight up to Dad's room, or wherever it is that you've left your stuff, get them and bring them downstairs, okay? I'll check on Dad myself."

Veronica seemed relieved not to have to join Becks in that particular task. When Becks unlocked the front door with her own key, glad beyond measure that her father hadn't bolted it or deadlocked it from the inside, which he so easily could have done, Veronica fled upstairs while Becks went to the right, through the open sitting-room door and over to where her father sat, eyes closed while, on the television, some kind of dreary afternoon talk show was switched to mute. It was that Sally Ann Coombes woman again, with the dyed dark-red hair and the big fake tits. Her guest, a middle-aged man in a suit, seemed to be reading aloud from a book. Becks recognised her, Sally Ann, because she was the talk show hostess du jour at the moment, but she hadn't a clue who the man was, except for the fact that he was clearly a writer. Sally Ann was a great supporter of the arts, as she was always saying on her show, and she often had celebrity writers on to plug their latest cookbook or sporting biography. Never any normal unknown people, though, just always celebrities with something to plug. Funny, that.

"Dad, Dad, are you okay? Dad, wake up!" Frantically she shook him by the left shoulder. To her immeasurable relief, he opened a pair of bleary, hungover eyes and looked at her in bemusement. The smell of beer emanating from him made her feel nauseous.

Thank Christ, he was alive! She sent up a silent prayer of gratitude, then she pulled herself together and said, more sharply than she meant to: "Right, Dad. You stay exactly where you are for the moment. I'll make you some coffee and a bite to eat in a bit, okay? I just have to check that Veronica's all right. Don't move now, okay? Do you hear me?" But he was already drifting comfortably back to sleep. Becks left him and hurried back to the hall. Veronica was coming down the stairs with her handbag. She grabbed her jacket from the hook next to Stephen's in the hall and began to put it on.

"Are you . . . I mean, will you be okay?" Becks asked her tentatively.

"What do you care?" snapped back the older woman. "You never liked me. You never wanted me seeing your dad in the first place. No point in being hypocritical now, is there?"

"I never disliked you. I just . . . I just didn't want you demeaning him by making him wear the ass-less apron to do the hoovering in," Becks said sadly.

"What?" Veronica looked at her as if she'd suddenly become deranged. "What are you on about?"

"Sorry, never mind I said that. It's just something stupid that's nothing to do with anything. Look, I'm sorry that things haven't worked out between you and my dad. If it's any consolation, I don't think he should have lost his temper with you, either today or that other time, the time about the summerhouse and . . . and all that. I'm ashamed of him for shouting at you, and for throwing you out of the house today as well. I think he should apologise, but, if he doesn't, and he's pretty stubborn when he wants to be, then I hope you'll accept my apology as a sort of proxy?"

Veronica's hard face softened a little. "Thanks. That's something, I suppose. Look, Becks, can I give you a piece of advice? I've had a bit more life experience than you, and it's something I've been wanting to say to you, or your dad, for a while now, so I need to kind of get it off my chest, okay?"

"Okay." Becks' heart sank to the soles of her summer

sandals with the small cork heels. When people asked if they could give you a piece of advice like that, it was rarely anything you wanted to hear. Quite the bloody opposite, usually. Now she stood in the hall, in front of her father's departing girlfriend, and waited to hear this marvellous piece of free *'advice'*.

"It's Joanna," Veronica said earnestly. "She's everywhere in this house. She's all over it. It . . . it *pulsates* with her, somehow. She's in the walls and in the furniture and even in the air inside the house. I know there are no photos of her lying around the place . . ." They're all in his bloody wardrobe, like a bloody shrine, was the unspoken implication, "but she's still in every fibre, every dust mote, every corner of this house. The house *is* her. She's still here. I don't know how, but she is."

Becks stared at the older woman in surprise. She was spot-on, of course, but how could she know so much about them, and about Joanna in particular, on so relatively short an acquaintanceship? Veronica must be a psychic, a *sensitive,* or something.

Before she could open her mouth to reply, Veronica rushed on: "It's not healthy, Becks dear. Not for you, and not for your father. You've both made Joanna's leaving here into the biggest, most important, most meaningful and significant thing that ever happened in the history of the world. If you're ever to forget her, get over her, you both need to get away from this house for good. Otherwise, you'll just continue to live in the past every single day for the rest of your lives. You'll never move on. You'll never get over her. You'll never forget her."

Becks stared. "Why on earth would we ever want to forget her?" she asked in genuine puzzlement. "My mother was the most important person in the world to me, and in Dad's world too. We want to *remember* her, Veronica, not forget her. You're wrong about that, quite wrong."

"Becks, I know this is going to sound a bit odd, but my grandmother was the seventh child of a seventh child and she *knew* things. I mean, she *knew* things that no one else did or ever could have. My mother was always saying that I'd inherited something of her second sight and I'm telling you, Becks love, that Joanna is still *here* somehow, here in this house. Unless you and your dad get right away from this place, you'll never be free of her."

While Veronica spoke, Becks had been unconsciously edging the woman more and more towards the front door. Veronica stumbled backwards over the hairy, scratchy brown doormat, in situ since Joanna's day and fairly shabby-looking now, grabbing on to the front door to right herself. She looked at Becks curiously, seeming not to know what to make of the serene smile on the younger woman's face.

"Goodbye, Veronica. I do genuinely hope that you'll be all right. If you've left anything behind you, just let me know and I'll forward it on to you, okay? It's no trouble at all."

Becks opened the front door and ushered Veronica through it. While Veronica stood there, on the step, looking as if she might be about to speak further, Becks closed it gently, bolted it and then deadlocked it carefully. On her way to the kitchen to make her slumbering, boozy father a cup of coffee to aid him with his hangover, she ran her fingers along the walls of the house, along the shell-pink flocked wallpaper with the seagulls in flight on it that Joanna herself had chosen over twenty years ago. The seagulls flying made her feel *free,* she said, free to flit or fly wherever she wished, instead of just being forever chained to this dreary old mausoleum of a house with a husband and child. Veronica was right. Joanna *was* in the walls of the house. Of *course* she was. Where else would she be? It was *her* house, after all. If you stood still and quiet for long enough, you could almost hear the walls breathing, in, out, in, out, in, out, and the breath they breathed was Joanna's. Becks was positively mystified as to why Veronica had thought that that was a *bad* thing. The woman must be mad. Well, she was gone now, and maybe it wasn't the worst thing that could happen. Whistling the tune of a song she remembered her mother crooning to her when she was a baby, Becks put the kettle on and rooted about in the bread bin for something nice to make her dad's sandwich with. It was just the two of them again now. Well, the *three* of them really, she amended with a smile. Just the way it *should* be.

Chapter 13

LAURA AGAIN

2015

"Why did your last relationship end, babes?"

They were in bed together in Laura's flat, a few days after Christmas, and they'd just had the most incredible sex of Laura's life. Paul was such a wonderful lover, the way he liked to vary things up a bit by having Laura climb on top of him, for example, instead of just doing it in the missionary position all the time, and even getting her to slap his face a bit while she was up there and call him dirty names. How wonderfully kinky and inventive and uninhibited he was! In a million years, she could never get tired or bored of having sex with Paul. It was just so refreshing to meet someone who didn't just want to do the same thing over and over again like they were on a bloody loop or something. Now, though, she hesitated, wondering how best to answer his question. It wasn't that she was having trouble remembering what had happened. She'd never forget it as long as she lived.

She'd been in work as usual, sitting at her monitor, daydreaming, if the truth were told. She was daydreaming about her and Harry's wedding day, if they ever got that far. Of course, he'd have to leave his wife first and ask her for a divorce, which that cow Helen would refuse to give, and, anyway, Harry was dragging his heels about telling his wife about himself and Laura (nothing new there, alas; all guys were the same when it came to telling their wives about their mistresses). Laura knew that the chances were that she and Harry Grattan could spend long frustrating years stuck in this waiting phase, waiting for Harry to tell his wife about them, so, in the meantime, she treated herself to such self-indulgent luxuries as the odd bit of daydreaming. About their wedding day, her wedding dress, their honeymoon and the new house they'd move in to when they were back from honeymoon. What if, instead of the traditional church wedding, they disappeared off to a tropical island somewhere and were married on the beach, both barefoot and dressed in simple holiday clothes, with just the celebrant in attendance? Lovely as that sounded, however, Laura knew that she couldn't live without the full church wedding and all the trimmings. Her whole life, things had been done arseways because she had no dad and there was no man around, just Eleanor, who was almost as flighty and as hopeless sober as she was drunk. There'd been an array of (usually much younger) suitors, of course, but none of Eleanor's relationships ever lasted long and there wasn't a single one of them that Laura would have considered fit to be a Daddy-substitute. In any case, she was planning to ask her Auntie Vera's husband, whom Laura called Uncle Derek, even though they weren't technically related, to walk her down the aisle and give her away, when the time came. She was happily composing a guest list for the Wedding of the Future (would there be any way, she often wondered, that she could avoid inviting Eleanor at all, so that her drunken tearfulness and outrageous flirtations with much younger men wouldn't ruin yet another family occasion?) when the office door opened with a bang that reverberated round the fair-sized room. An attractive, stylishly-dressed black-haired woman in her midforties stormed up to the front of the room, in which Laura and four others — three women and a youngish lad — all sat working away and demanded loudly: "Which one of you is *Laura Brennan?*"

Everyone in the room turned to look at Laura, who squirmed in her seat and blushed. Goddammit, this was Helen Grattan, Harry's wife! Laura recognised her from a photo she'd seen once on Harry's phone. He hadn't shown it to her himself; she'd sneaked a peek at it when he'd left it behind him to go to the toilet while they'd been in a pub together once.

"Oh, it's you, is it, you over-made-up bitch? You're Laura? What the fuck do you think you're playing at?"

"I don't understand you," squeaked Laura. "I mean, of course I can *understand* you, but what I mean is that, erm, I don't know what you're talking about?" She squirmed and fidgeted in her seat some more, feeling far from her usual (reasonably) confident self as the older woman continued to tower over her.

"I'll tell you what I'm talking about, Laura Brennan, shall I? Recognise this, do you, you slut?" Helen Grattan pulled a lanyard out of her jacket pocket and dangled it in front of Laura's face. It was Laura's identity card for work, with her name and photo on it. It was a terrific photo. She'd had her hair done specially for this photo, and a professional make-up job as well. No way was she going to have a shit photo taken and have to spend the rest of her working life looking like Myra Hindley on her work I.D. Card as had happened one time, yonks ago, thanks to a bad hair day. But how did Helen Grattan, of all people, come to have it? Unless . . . Laura wanted to put her head in her hands and groan out loud. She'd only gone and left it in Harry's car, hadn't she? It had obviously fallen off while they'd been making love, and she'd never even missed it till now. Still, a lanyard that had fallen off didn't necessarily signify anything sinister, did it, she told herself hopefully. Harry might just have been giving her a lift home.

Her hopes were dashed when she saw what Helen Grattan was holding out to her in her other hand, her expensive-looking nose wrinkled in distaste. A pair of pink-and-white checked panties that Laura knew were hers. They'd been part of a Marks & Spencer's six-pack job, and she'd only been wearing them because she hadn't been anticipating having sex with Harry on that particular day. Still, they hadn't been on her for long, as Harry drove them both to a favourite secluded spot and pulled them off her in his haste to make love to her. They'd had fast, furious sex and, afterwards, he'd dropped her home, neither of them thinking to check that she had all her bits-and-bobs with her. Well, clearly she hadn't. That had been a couple of days ago, and now the other three girls in the office were all goggling at her disgustedly as if she was the lowest of the low or something, and Helen Grattan looked as if she'd like to kill her.

Her face suffused with a scarlet blush, Laura grabbed the panties and the lanyard from the other woman and stuffed them in her handbag, which sat on the floor at her feet.

"Well, slut! Have you nothing to say for yourself?" Helen Grattan's voice rose shrilly till it could probably be heard on the street outside. She was leaning over Laura's desk now, with her hands, the nails manicured and painted blood-red, flat on the polished wood surface. As she screamed into Laura's face, Laura could smell the wine on her breath. Maybe she'd had a glass or two of Dutch courage before she'd come here.

Laura was saved the trouble of answering by the sudden appearance on the scene of Harry Grattan himself. He'd been in the toilet when his wife had arrived. Now, alerted by the sound of raised voices, he arrived into the melée with a puzzled expression on his handsome, dark bearded face, drying his hands on his trousers.

"What's all the shouting about? Helen, what are you doing here?"

"I'm returning some of your slut's property, Harry, that's what I'm doing. Property she left in your car."

Harry's face fell as he looked from one woman to the other. From the looks on both their faces, the game was obviously up. "Can we discuss this at home, please, Helen?" he said, with an attempt at a conciliatory smile.

She flew at him. She beat on his chest with her fists and scratched at his face with her long, blood-red nails. *"You bastard! You filthy, unspeakable bastard!"* she kept screaming. *"I can't believe you've done this to me again! And with a slutty little office scrubber, as well. I hate you, Harry Grattan, I fucking hate you and I wish you were dead!"* Her voice rose until it reached almost deafening levels and tears of anger and hurt spilled freely down her heavily powdered cheeks.

"Right, that's it, Helen, I'm driving you home, okay? Is the car outside? Right, let's go. Come on. Let's go. Come on." His attempt at manhandling his wife out of his office didn't go well.

She launched herself at him again, screeching: *"Don't you dare touch me, you bastard, don't you dare touch me! And I want this slag gone, do you hear me, Harry? I'm not moving an inch from here until you tell her to go! Do you understand me, Harry? I want her gone!"*

Harry Grattan heaved a huge sigh. Rubbing his chin hard in a delaying gesture, he said nothing for a minute while he presumably absorbed the situation. Then, in front of the six pairs of eyes that were now watching him intently, he shrugged fatalistically and said to Laura off-handedly: "It might be best if you *do* go."

Laura stared at him. "For now, do you mean, or for . . . for good?"

Harry sighed again, while Helen Grattan stood by and watched Laura triumphantly. "Well, for good, I suppose. I'm sorry, Laura, but it's for the best. It couldn't work now, not now that everyone knows about it. I'll see you get what you're owed. But, for now, just go, will you, for Christ's sake?"

Laura paled. She was losing her job, and her lover, in one fell swoop, and not one person in this lousy fucking office was going to stand up for her, speak on her behalf? She looked around wildly for even one ally, but the three women and one youngish male studiously avoided her eyes. Oh yes, right. She'd forgotten what a snooty bitch they all thought she was. She hadn't bothered with a single one of them since she'd come here, only Harry, and now they were seizing with both hands the opportunity to pay her back for it. They'd be glad to see her go, this lot. On legs that weren't quite steady, she stood up and crossed to the storeroom to fetch a cardboard box for her work stuff. By the time she returned, box in hand, Harry had managed to manoeuvre his tipsy, still angry wife to the front door.

"Stay away from my husband, you dirty little slut! Get your own man, that's if you even *can*." Satisfied with her parting shot to her husband's bit-on-the-side, Helen allowed herself to be manhandled by a severely irritated Harry out the door and into the car, belonging to her husband, that she'd driven here today on her slut-shaming mission.

Laura, meanwhile, willed herself not to cry as she emptied the contents of her desk into the cardboard box in front of the four members of staff who remained in the outer office. She'd only been here about a year, but there was plenty of clutter. Old bits of make-up, tissues used as make-up wipes on which she'd blotted her lipstick, an empty water bottle, sweet wrappers, bits of paper with phone numbers on them, used pens, Luas tickets, bus tickets, a couple of old celebrity magazines. Most of it was utter rubbish, but anything that could be salvaged, she took, including the plant she'd bought for her desk that she had thought would brighten up her work-space a bit, and the framed photo of a cat. It wasn't her cat; it was the photographer's model cat, just one of those pictures that was already in the picture-frame when you bought them, but Laura liked cats, though she hadn't owned one since the cat she'd had in her childhood had been run over by a car. She put the plant, the cat photo and anything else that wasn't rubbish into the box and grabbed her handbag and jacket, and then, with her cheeks flaming red with embarrassment, she'd done the walk of shame through the office and out the front door. The dead silence as she did her little walk was broken only by a solitary snigger, otherwise you could have heard a pin drop. Laura didn't think she'd ever felt so ashamed. She hurried to the nearby Luas stop, praying fervently that she wouldn't meet anyone she knew on it or have to talk to anyone while she was in this state. Only when she'd closed and locked the door of her Stephen's Green flat behind her did she give vent to the tears she'd been holding back. Imagine, Harry Grattan, that actual bastard, choosing his wife over her in front of her very eyes! The hurt she felt was like an actual physical pain. Like her mother did, she chose to numb it (or try to numb it) with alcohol, but that only worked to an extent. The pain was still there when she sobered up, something Eleanor never seemed to cop on to.

Naturally, she didn't tell Paul any of the details of this sordid little tale. She didn't want to put him off her completely. So, when he said, "So, why did your last relationship break up then?", she answered breezily: "Oh, Harry and I were just too different from each other, that's all. We each just wanted different things."

This answer seemed to perfectly satisfy Paul, who said: "And what *do* you want, my lovely Laura?"

Not for anything would she have told him what she really wanted; a husband of her very own, a home, a family, a whole bunch of cats, a garden, a normal, happy life where no one was a single parent struggling on their own and no one's Daddy abandoned or ever left their children. Paul, a married man who presumably already had all that good stuff with his wife Barbara (she wasn't sure about their cat situation), wouldn't want to hear that kind of thing from his sexy young mistress. Instead, she told him what she thought he wanted to hear. "Oh, just the usual things. Great sex, a few drinks, a good night out, good fun, the odd holiday, just a nice good time while I'm still young enough to be able to enjoy it. You know?"

"Oh, I know, my lovely Laura, I know. And you know how I know?"

She cuddled into him, loving that he was here with her in her bed, instead of enjoying Christmas at home with his wife and family. "How?"

"Because you and me are kindred spirits, my lovely Laura, that's how. We want the same things, and we're young enough and good-looking enough to be able to go out and get it." He took her hand and placed it on his flaccid penis. "Do you know what I'd love you to do?"

"What? Tell me! Anything you want to do, we can do." Sex was the key, Laura knew, to keeping a relationship with a man going. Men cared more about sex than anything else, so, as long as Paul was in her bed, she'd shoot oranges out of her fanny while singing the Marseillaise backwards if he wanted her to, if it would keep him by her side.

"I love a really dominant woman," he said, moving his hand over hers on his willy. "How would you feel about dressing up for me a bit, say, in stockings and suspenders, and bossing me around a bit? A bit of spanking, a bit of face-slapping, a bit of the old verbal abuse, stuff like that? Would that grab you at all, do you think?"

Mildly surprised, but relieved that it wasn't anything more

outlandish, Laura nodded in excitement. "Of course I could do that! I'd love to, if it makes you happy."

"Just being here with you makes me happy, my sweet Laura, my love. But, since you're offering, maybe you could just get on top of me there for a minute and have a bash at it now. At being a kind of a Miss Whiplash character, if you get me?"

"Do you like being, erm, being whipped and all that stuff?" She wasn't really sure how she felt about that kind of thing. It was a bit more 'out there' than she was used to.

"I don't mind a good whipping, sure. But we'll just start with a nice easy bit of light spanking for now. I don't really need Barbara catching me with whiplash scars all over me, much and all as I might enjoy it. Not that we have sex together any more," he added hurriedly. "Not since Lucy was born. So, erm, are you going to start any time soon?"

"I'm not sure what to do," Laura confessed, feeling a bit silly as she sat, naked, atop his willy, her mind completely blank, unsure as to what he wanted her to do.

"Just do what you feel like," he said lazily, clasping his hands behind his head and very obviously waiting for her to get the ball rolling.

"*Erm, okaaaaay*. Right." If she was to do what she *really* felt like, she'd climb down off his thingy, get back into bed with him and cuddle him till they both fell asleep. But, clearly, that wasn't what he meant. Hesitantly, she began to move on top of him. He groaned as if he appreciated the sensation. Encouraged, she moved a bit more and moved her hands onto his neck. He groaned even louder and begin to thrust up into her, harder and faster.

"Hit me, Laura, my sweet, lovely Laura! Hit me!"

Tentatively, she slapped his face as lightly as she could manage it. "Was that . . . was that okay?"

"*Mmmm*, oh, yes, but try it a little harder now, okay? Don't be shy. I won't break. Do it good and hard now."

She walloped him with all her strength across his cheek. He yelped in pain.

"Jesus, Laura! Are you trying to mark me or what?"

"I'm so sorry!" she apologised. "I didn't know how hard you wanted it."

"Somewhere between the two extremes will do. Not too soft, but not too hard, either. Let's try it again, shall we? Practice makes perfect, after all. We'll get there. Ah, shit, my cock's after going soft now with all the waiting and hanging about. You'll have to get off and suck it first for a bit, okay?"

Confused and not a little irritated, Laura did as he asked.

The Great Affair had really and truly begun.

She went back to her mother's house in Phibsborough for New Year's, even though she would have preferred to stay on in her own flat, where she would have bought a crate of wine and hermited it for the couple of days until the celebrations were over. Laura hated New Year's. Whatever about Christmas, New Year's Eve was a cold, lonely time to be without a man and without a real family, and Paul had already told her that he wouldn't be able to see her again until the festivities were well over.

"It's a time for family, worse luck," he'd said ruefully, before giving her a kiss so deep and passionate, she'd felt like he was sucking her heart out through her mouth. Paul was such an amazing kisser. No one had ever kissed her like that before, not even Harry. She hardly missed Harry at all any more, not now that she had Paul. The kiss almost — *almost* — took her mind off the fact that she'd be in her mother's house for New Year's Eve and New Year's Day.

"I'll be on my own if you don't come!" Eleanor had wailed.

"You know you've got an open invitation to go to Auntie Vee's on New Year's," Laura had reminded her. "We both do."

"I'm not going. It'll be all about Marge and the new bloody baby. Why she had to go having it on Christmas Day of all days, I'm sure I don't know. Looking for notice, probably."

Like you're not the biggest attention seeker for miles around, Laura could have said but didn't. Eleanor would only have a fit. So, she locked up her flat off Stephen's Green on New Year's Eve around lunchtime and took the bus to Phibsborough, only to find that her mother had gone out somewhere for the afternoon, shopping, probably. That was typical of Eleanor, not to let Laura know that she'd be out when her daughter called round. So Laura put the wine she'd brought with her to see in the New Year in the fridge, and took her overnight bag up to the little room that had been hers since she was a child. The room overlooked the scrubby little back garden that still contained her childhood swing set. The sight of that one solitary swing (not even a double set; there would have been no need) always made her sad. It reminded her of her lonely childhood, as the only child of a single parent who'd frequently abdicated her responsibilities as a mother and foisted Laura on to one of her sisters, mostly Laura's Auntie Vee. No siblings of her own, very few friends, and no father. Not even a dead father, or a separated or divorced father, but simply no father at all, as if she'd come solely from Eleanor and no one else. Laura sighed heavily and turned away from the window. This whole house reminded her of her fatherless bloody childhood. No wonder she always dreaded coming here. And now her mother wasn't even in. The house was deathly quiet. The whole street was quiet. Everyone was busy doing last-minute New Year's shopping or off seeing friends, or they'd already started drinking in the pubs or in each other's houses to celebrate the coming of another year. Laura was more conscious at this time of year that she had no close friends. At school, she'd been the quiet Little Miss Prissy Pants, as the other kids had called her, with her perfect golden plaits and pristine uniform, her nervous, timid personality and No Father. When school ended forever, she'd been too busy looking for the Perfect Man, the one who would make her lonely childhood and the unfortunate circumstances of her birth up to her, to bother with friends. Still, never mind, she told herself now as she sat down on the edge of her bed and lit a cigarette. She had Paul now, and that was all that mattered. After she'd stubbed out the cigarette in the cheap plastic ashtray on her bedside table, the rickety one that had caused more night-time glasses of water to spill during her childhood than she could ever possibly remember, she lay down on the bed, intending just to close her eyes for a minute.

She drifted off into an uneasy sleep, and a dream in which she was pursuing a laughing Paul through a fairground Hall of Mirrors.

"Which one is real, which one is the real Paul?" she asked herself over and over, but Paul just kept on laughing and disappearing around yet more corners. When she eventually woke up, she had a splitting headache, and she wasn't even hungover.

It was the sound of banging and clattering from downstairs that had woken her. She sat up on the bed bleary-eyed and immediately checked the time on her phone. It was quarter to seven in the evening on New Year's Eve, and pitch-black outside. Holy shit. She'd lain down, with the intention of just resting her eyes for a minute, at about twenty past three. Crikey, she must have been tired. Still fully dressed in her jeans and sweater, she shoved her feet into her shoes and went out on the landing to see what the racket was. The landing light was already on and Eleanor was coming up the stairs, laughing and chatting away non-stop to her companion who, as he mounted the stairs behind her, turned out to be the Awful Thomas. They were wearing their coats and hats and the two of them were carrying big department store carrier bags of stuff they must have bought in the sales, which were already in the shops.

"Look who I found in town!" Eleanor trilled gaily when she saw Laura, seeming not to notice the look of dismay on her daughter's face.

"Howyeh, Head," Thomas said cheerfully.

Laura ignored him.

"Mum, can I have a word with you, please?" It was said through gritted teeth as Laura tried very hard not to lose her cool in front of the Awful Thomas. "In private, if you don't mind," she added pointedly, as Thomas stood there on the landing with Eleanor and didn't look as if he were planning on shifting himself any time soon. They both smelled strongly of fags and booze.

"Tommy, love, go on in the bedroom and make yourself at home," Eleanor told the younger man brightly. "I'll be in in a minute."

"Don't be long," said the Awful Thomas as he shuffled off down the landing to Eleanor's bedroom. To Laura, he looked even scruffier than she remembered him being over Christmas.

Eleanor giggled like a schoolgirl at his inane remark, then, when Thomas was out of earshot, she turned to her daughter and hissed: "Laura, it's New Year's Eve, for Christ's sake! I really hope you don't intend to start getting on your soapbox and preaching at me."

"Where did you find him?" Laura hissed back. "Was it really accidental, you bumping into him?"

"Of course it was," huffed Eleanor indignantly. Then she lowered her voice to a conspiratorial whisper as she went on: "What was I supposed to do? I found the poor lamb begging on Henry Street. I couldn't just leave him there to starve, could I?"

"Begging? On Henry Street? With . . . with a little plastic cup and everything? Doesn't he have any pride, and a girlfriend and a child, as well? Whom he lives with?"

"They've had another fight and she's thrown him out of the house. The poor thing hadn't eaten a scrap of food since yesterday morning, so I took him for a bite to eat and a few drinks, that's all. There's no harm in that, is there? It's New Year's Eve. You wouldn't leave a dog outside in the cold without a morsel of food on New Year's Eve, surely."

"I don't care that you fed him. But why did you have to bring him back here with you? Some guy who's actually been out begging with a plastic cup on Henry Street? Will we just hand over our purses to him now so, to save time?"

"He's not a thief," huffed Eleanor.

"He stole our bath-sets on Christmas Day, remember? Our Christmas presents to each other. Or don't you care?"

"You don't surely begrudge him a few little rubbishy scented soaps? He needed them, as Christmas presents for his . . . for his own family."

"For his girlfriend and child, you mean. The girlfriend and child he'll run straight back to the minute he's got what he wants here. Well, don't come crying to me when he does another runner, okay? You've been told he's not free, so it's your own fault if you get hurt." She conveniently forgot about Paul and her own situation while she was loftily castigating her mother from her perch on the moral high ground.

"Little judgemental Laura," said her mother, close to tears. "You've always been the same. What gives you the right to judge other people and look down on them from the dizzying heights of your pedestal? What makes you so bloody perfect that you can afford to look down your perfect little nose at me and Thomas? Are you really that snowy-white and squeaky-clean yourself?"

"I never claimed to be perfect!" Laura was deeply aggrieved now. "But . . . but, well, I actually had plans for tonight, believe it or not, but I cancelled them to come here to you because you were crying about how you were going to be all on your own for the evening. Now I'm here, and I find that you've brought that Thomas fella back with you like he's some kind of stray dog that's followed you home. And it's obvious to anyone with eyes that you're planning to spend the evening with him, so what the hell am I supposed to do now?"

"There's plenty of food and drink downstairs," said her mother in a conciliatory tone, her eyes sliding sidewards towards the door of her own bedroom, behind which they could both clearly hear a drunken Tommy fumbling about taking off his clothes and whistling loudly and out-of-tune. "And there's loads of good telly on. You'll have a lovely evening."

"I don't *believe* you," said Laura. "I can't actually believe that you'd do this, on New Year's Eve, of all nights. All right, I'll stay the night, but only because I can't be arsed faffing about with public transport on New Year's bloody Eve. And . . ." here, with her nose wrinkled up in distaste, she gestured towards Eleanor's closed bedroom door, "and I'd better not hear or see anything I don't want to hear or see, or there'll be trouble, okay?"

Eleanor, all smiles now that she'd got her own way (her boyfriend was back and her only child was dancing attendance on her once more), kissed Laura on the cheek and disappeared into her bedroom at the speed of light, with a backwards wave and the words "Happy New Year, love!" trailing off on her lips.

Utterly disgusted, Laura went downstairs and mooched about in the kitchen for something to eat that wouldn't require any preparation. She slapped a few slices of cooked ham and a couple of slices of cheese between two bits of bread and took the lot into the sitting-room with a bottle of wine (it was Eleanor's wine, but tough titty; Eleanor owed her, big-time, for tonight) and her cigarettes and phone.

Paul had said when she'd seen him last that he'd do his very best to call or text on New Year's Eve but he couldn't guarantee it. "I'll be up to my tits in kids and wives and parents-in-law," he'd said matter-of-factly as he laced up his shoes while seated on the edge of her bed after they'd made love, "so don't hold me to it, okay?"

"Okay," she'd said obligingly, as if she really didn't mind one way or the other, but she *did* mind; oh Lord, how she minded!

Now she flopped on the couch dejectedly and picked up the remote. Of course Eleanor wouldn't have thought of buying anything resembling a Christmas TV guide, so that at least Laura would be able to see what shite they were laying on for the stuck-at-homes tonight. Eleanor had been buying clothes for the Awful Thomas as well, expensive-looking clothes too, judging by the carrier bags they'd been hauling upstairs earlier, but anything as mundane as a Christmas TV guide, you could *fuhgeddaboutit*. Dispirited and increasingly agitated-slash-disturbed by the sounds of vigorous sex coming from upstairs (Eleanor was most definitely a howler and a screamer), she turned on the television and began to flick.

She didn't see Paul again until they went back to work in the New Year. But, much to her relief, their affair hadn't been just a festive fling or office Christmas party sex. It began to really take off in the New Year. It seemed that the separation at Christmas had made Paul more, not less, interested, in her, for which she was devoutly thankful. She'd spent the whole of Christmas worrying herself sick that the gloss of their sexual union might wear off for Paul once the decorations were down and the tree lights back in their box in the attic for another year, free to mysteriously tangle themselves up again in plenty of time for next year. They settled into a cosy little routine as the weeks went by, much to Laura's relief. By the time she'd gone back to work at Phelan's in the New Year, she'd convinced herself that she was head-over-heels in love with the tall, dark and handsome junior manager and that she couldn't live without him. Paul wasn't able to stay over very often at Laura's flat, but two or even three nights a week he was able to stay very late, telling his wife that he was working late on a difficult project and then unwinding by watching a footy match at a mate's house. Laura was thrilled at all the time he seemed to want to spend with her. He'd sometimes leave his car in the Phelan's car-park and get the Luas back to the Stephen's Green with her after work, but the chances of their being seen together by someone from work were quite high this way. More often than not, therefore, he'd drive himself to the Stephen's Green car-park while Laura made it back ahead of him on the Luas, then he'd spend the whole evening grumbling about the shocking price of car-parking fees, in between having wild, uninhibited sex and eating the tempting little food dishes she'd prepared for them both.

Laura lived for the days when Paul would be coming to her flat after work. She loved shopping for nice things for the flat — a gorgeous lamp, some Egyptian cotton bedsheets, cushions and throws for the bed and couches — that would make it as comfortable a bolt-hole for Paul as possible, a little love-nest for them both. She enjoyed shopping for their nights in as well, buying pricey little cocktail party nibbles to whet Paul's appetite post-sex. His appetite for the sex itself seemed to know no bounds. He had a fantastic body, he was well-hung and, even though he was in his mid-thirties, he had the sexual energy and stamina of a much younger man. The only thing was . . . Well, he only ever seemed to want to have sex in the exact same way these days. Laura on top of him, dressed in sexy lingerie, riding him hard, slapping his face and giving out to him for being a naughty boy, a dirty boy for touching his filthy thing without permission and fantasising about women while he was doing it. The sex was out of this world; it was just that, well, sometimes Laura just wanted to be held, and Paul didn't seem interested in that type of thing, except after the sex when he sometimes needed a little kip. But that was just Laura holding *him* while he snoozed. It wasn't the same as Paul lying on top of her, making love to her tenderly while gazing soulfully into her eyes and whispering sweet nothings into her ears, if both activities weren't mutually exclusive, simultaneously.

One time, early enough into their relationship, maybe about March or April of 2015, Laura had taken her courage in both hands and tried asking him for what she wanted, instead of just leaving it all up to him as usual. He'd reached her flat at around a quarter to six, which was good and early and would give them plenty of quality time together before he headed home at around ten or even eleven. He was in high good humour, as excitable as a puppy on account of the sex they'd have.

"Aren't you going to, erm, well, put on something sexy?" he asked her, when she'd climbed into bed beside him, naked.

"I just want to feel your skin against mine," she said shyly, lying down beside him and cuddling into him, with her arm resting across his chest.

"Erm, is everything okay, Laura? Are you on a go-slow or something?" He seemed puzzled, and she knew exactly why that was. By this stage, she'd normally be sitting astride him, riding him hard and fast (like a cowboy bank-robber en route to Mexico, just ahead of the posse that wanted to see him dangling at the end of a rope), her tits spilling over the top of some tight, basque-y confection that left her pussy and ass uncovered, barking orders and abuse at him while slapping him hard across the face and even sliding her hands around his neck and choking him a little tiny bit. This was what he liked. This was what he expected to get, what he expected Laura to give him, every time he called over. He liked her to wear stockings and suspenders with high-heeled shoes as well, and these made for very uncomfortable bed-wear. Tonight, her shoes were all in the wardrobe, and the stupid stockings and suspenders in a ball in the drawer.

"I just thought we could do it the normal way for once," she said lightly, trying to disguise how worried she felt about asking him to deviate from his preferred routine. "You know, erm, missionary-style? If that's okay with you . . .?"

There was a silence, then: "Oh. Okay. If you want." His tone was cold enough to freeze the milk. "Well, I suppose you'd better get me hard, so, then, if you want me to be able to do anything for you."

For me? I thought it was meant to be for both of us? she wanted to say but didn't. She bit the words back, fearing an argument, and began to use her hands and mouth to 'get him hard', like he'd said. *He's sulking, he's actually sulking,* she thought as she wriggled into position after she'd helped him achieve an erection and waited for him to make a move. With a huffy sigh, he climbed on top of her, his stony facial expression leaving her in no doubt as to what he thought of this madness. She lay beneath him expectantly, smiling up at him with her blue eyes shining at their closeness. The smile died on her lips when he deliberately closed his own eyes, entered her and began thrusting in and out mechanically, an expression of sullen concentration on his face. *What's he concentrating so hard on,* she wondered, *or is he having to fantasise that we're doing it the other way, in order to stay hard?* Whatever was going on with him, he pulled out of her straight after he ejaculated and said he had to get home. He was knackered and needed an early night if he was to be able to keep up all this 'living a double life' stuff.

Terrified that he was never coming back, Laura watched him go with her heart in her mouth.

When he came back again the following week, she made damned sure she gave him everything he wanted: the sexy lingerie, the hooker shoes with such high heels they made her dizzy to wear them; plenty of choice words to describe naughty men who wanked without their mistress's permission whenever they got the chance, men who needed to be slapped and disciplined before their mistress could feel in any way satisfied with them again. She gave him the full works, and he lapped it up like a cat with a saucer of cream.

Laura breathed a huge sigh of relief when they parted on excellent terms later that night. Paul was in the best mood she'd ever seen him in, and seemingly all she had to do to keep him that way was to be his own private and personal dominatrix for as long as he wanted her to be. It was going to be exhausting work, though, doing this for him several times a week every week, watching him lying there with his hands clasped behind his head pretty much *waiting* for her to start into her *'act'*, as Laura now called it. She was bloody exhausted after being so *'on'* for him all night. She'd be dead of tiredness in a year if she had to do this for him every time they met. As she sat on the edge of her bed to take off the uncomfortable hooker shoes (sparkly, purpley, glittery, she wouldn't be seen dead in them in public, but Paul had licked them with such great abandon earlier on, even the undersides), her phone rang. Thinking it was Paul, she answered it without thinking.

"Laura? I'm so cold," said her mother.

"Mum, seriously, what d'you want at this hour? I'm knackered and I'm literally about to go to bed. I have work in the morning, even if you don't."

"I just miss Thomas so much," whispered Eleanor.

The man Laura called "the Awful Thomas" had done another runner on New Year's Day and gone back to his girlfriend and child, although this time he'd stayed to have dinner first, a turkey casserole cooked by Laura and comprising a load of festive leftovers, mainly turkey. (It had turned out that he wasn't a vegetarian at all.) Eleanor had been devastated once more, especially when he didn't reappear a few days later like he had at Christmas. This time, he'd taken forty euros of

Eleanor's Disability money from her purse with him and was presumably scared to show his face again for a while.

"Now will you see him for what he is, Mum?" Laura had said, exasperated.

"I don't care about the money!" Eleanor wailed. "I just want my Tommy back!"

"Well, you can't have him because he's gone, and let's hope it's for good this time." Laura should have remembered that being cruel to be kind never worked on her mother. Eleanor had dissolved into floods of tears and New Year's Day, like Christmas Day, had been ruined, courtesy of "the Awful Thomas".

Now, listening to her mother sob on the other end of the phone, her heart sank as she realised she wouldn't be getting to bed any time soon. Worn out from performing like a circus monkey for Paul, now she had to act as counsellor and comforter to her mother.

"What did you say, Mum? You're mumbling. I didn't catch that."

"I said I took some pills. My sleeping pills. Tired now. Cold. Want to sleep."

"*Pills?*" Laura screeched in dismay. "*Are you fucking kidding me? How many?*"

"Don't know. A few."

"How many is a few? Mum, tell me!"

"I said I don't know. Want to sleep now."

"*Mum, don't you dare go to sleep, do you hear me? I'm coming over, okay, Mum?* And I'm calling an ambulance, too, okay? Mum, stay on the line, will you? I just need to get dressed!"

She hurled herself around the flat, throwing on clothes and

grabbing up shoes, bag, wallet, phone, keys and all the rest.

She arrived at her mother's house, in a taxi she'd picked up at the rank by the Green, to find Eleanor drinking tea and flirting madly with the three good-looking young male paramedics. She had only taken a couple of pills, and had already vomited them back up naturally through her system. Laura was late for work the next day as a result, and was docked an hour's pay by Young Mr. Phelan, who ran the company now for his ageing father, whom everyone at work called Old Mr. Phelan. The thrill of power and being in charge had clearly gone to Young Mr. Phelan's head, and he'd smirked delightedly when he was telling her about how he was docking her pay for *'tardiness'*. Who the fuck but the Americans said *'tardiness'*? The man was an odious creep. Laura had practically to prop her eyes open with matchsticks during that day's work. Paul kept sending her sexy texts and emails from his little junior manager's glass cubicle, visible to Laura from her desk in the 'typing pool', as they called it, and it was all she could do to show willing and respond in kind, pretending she was up for horny fun right now and was so turned on that she was actually going to sneak away to the Ladies' Room and play with herself while thinking about him *'fucking her'* the whole time. As if she wasn't ready to drop from exhaustion from having to constantly mind her mother and please Paul all at the same time. As if she could muster up even an ounce of enthusiasm for sex, after the night she'd had! It was comfort and support she needed from Paul, not more bloody sexy texts and emails.

Why aren't you going to the jacks? he texted her eventually. **You said you were going.**

I'm going now, she texted back with a winky face.

That's a good girl, he texted back with a whole row of winky faces.

When she was in the Ladies' Room, he phoned her from his desk. His office was clearly empty of other staff, and anyway, as it was made entirely of glass, he was able to see when anyone was approaching. "Tell me what you're doing to yourself," he demanded. "Put the phone down between your legs. I want to hear it."

Laura bit back an hysterical laugh. Why didn't he just say *'Put your pussy on the phone to me'* and be done with it? Sitting on the closed toilet with her knickers and tights very definitely still in place, she uttered some fake moans and made some rustling noises with toilet paper that she hoped would satisfy him. He seemed more than satisfied, and before long she began to hear noises from his end that she didn't doubt for a second were real. When she was back at her desk, he texted her another row of winky faces, along with the words: **Can't wait to ride you sideways on Thursday night!** Except, it won't be sideways, will it, Paul, she wanted to reply, because you don't do sideways, do you? You don't do any way at all except your own way, and I'm starting to think that you'll never change, and you'll never want to do it any differently, no matter what *I* want. With a rapidly sinking heart, she made a start on her work.

The weeks passed and turned into months. The affair gathered pace. The sex was fantastic, though the method was always of Paul's choosing. Laura was locked into it now — it was partially her own fault — and there seemed to be no way to change things. They talked a lot, too, though; it wasn't just sex. Paul wasn't one of those strong silent types who suffered a bad or indifferent marriage in silence. He didn't seem to mind talking to her about Barbara and their two small daughters, Jessie and Lucy, and the most intimate details of his and Barbara's sex-life. Back when they'd *had* one, that was. Apparently, she didn't like giving blow-jobs, as Paul put it, and she thought the whole S&M thing was only for perverts and deviants and she didn't even want to *know* about it. *(She was more into M&S than S&M, he'd joked once.)* Paul had to keep all his kinky desires to himself when he was at home, and he resented it like crazy.

"Thank God I've got you," he told Laura frequently.

It always sounded so heartfelt, the way he said it. She never knew whether to be flattered by this or not. Was he just using her to live out his dirty fantasies?

"Do you still love her?" Laura asked him once as they were lying together on her bed after a particularly passionate bout of S&M love-making, if you could really call something 'love-making' that didn't seem to involve any love-making at all, only slapping and shouting.

"Well, of course I still *love* her as such," he'd replied, after taking a moment or two to think about it. "I mean, she's the mother of my two children and we've been together since we were kids, so I'll always *love* her, if you get me. But I'm not *in love* with her, d'you know what I mean? That spark was extinguished a long time ago. Love flies out the window when the kids start coming and the bills are rolling in and you're arguing and knocking lumps out of each other more often than you're talking normally. And as for the sex, well, you can forget it. It's all, *I've got a headache, we'll wake the kids and*

I've just got them settled, I'm not in the mood, I'm a bit full after that curry, what do you think I am, some kind of fucking machine that can have sex to order or something? You never do anything romantic for me; how'd you expect me to be in the mood for sex twenty-four-bloody-seven?

"And that's just you, is it, Paul?" Laura attempted a feeble joke here.

"I'll have you know, my good woman, that I've never turned down sex in my whole life," he said, mock-indignantly, tickling her under her armpits until she begged for mercy.

"But . . . but you *do* love me, don't you, Paul?" She held her breath until he answered her.

"Of course I bloody do," he said, putting his arm around her and pulling her head down to his chest while they chatted. "If only I'd met you first, my lovely Laura, my Laura, my love. We'd have been so happy together. We'd never have argued, like me and Barb do, and the sex would have been just out of this world. And you'd never refuse me, either, would you, love?"

She shook her head vehemently, her eyes filling with tears as they always did when he talked like this. Sometimes her heart felt like it would break when he talked about what might have been. It was always what might have been, too, and never what *might be,* in their future. When she asked him about their joint future, hers and his, he fobbed her off with things like, *I guess we'll just have to wait and see how things turn out, won't we,* or *we can talk about it again when the kids are older, I couldn't leave Barb on her own with two small kiddies to bring up, but maybe when they're older...?* He'd trail off then and act as if the subject was closed, after having been satisfactorily dealt with by him. But Laura was never satisfied with it. She ached to know how he really felt about her, where she stood with him and what their joint future held, if anything at all. He was so hard to pin down, no pun intended. Not when there was bondage or S&M to be dished out; then he practically pinned *himself* down. But, on the subject of Their Relationship, well, it was a bit like pulling teeth to get anything out of him. As long as they were having fun, as he put it (he placed a huge amount of store on 'fun', like most men), covertly sending each other sexy texts or emails in the workplace under the very noses of their co-workers and bosses, or back at Laura's flat playing Mistress & Slave (no prizes for guessing who played whom), he was in a grand mood. Laughing, joking, full of quips and energy, enjoying the thrill of their stolen hours. The minute she brought up the subject of Their Relationship, however, or feelings, or his and Barbara's marriage, it was a different story. Then, he'd be sulky, moody, rushing to get away, remembering a promise he'd made to Barbara to get something from the shops before they closed or to his kids to do something with them before they went to bed. This happened as regularly as clockwork. If he was trying to impart a message to Laura by so doing, she wasn't slow on the uptake. *Be cool and maintain the status quo and everything will be hunky-dory,* was the message she was getting loud and clear. *But push me about the future or Our Relationship, and I'll go running back to my wife and kids faster than you can say commitment-phobe, okay?* Laura got the message all right, and for nearly two whole years she tried to live by it. She mostly succeeded. The only times Paul got tetchy was when she pushed him, however gently, to leave his wife and come and live with her.

"The timing's got to be right, Laura," he would whine. "I can't just march up to her and say, *Oh, by the way, my wife of over ten years, I'm leaving you for a younger woman, oh, and did you iron me a shirt for today, I can't seem to find any clean ones?* That'd go down well, wouldn't it?" He looked at her as if to say, '*Well, aren't I right?*'

"Other men seem to manage it," she'd say stubbornly. That would really get his goat. He'd get on his high horse then and say: "Well, bully for them! Congratulations to these other men who've managed to successfully leave their wives without hurting anyone – these dudes should really get a medal for their marvellous achievement! But maybe I'm just a little more grateful for all my wife has done for me over the years, and a little more reluctant than *those* bozos to hurt her and my kids and tear my family apart at the drop of a hat. These things take time, Laura. You can't just make these things happen overnight, you know. The timing's got to be spot-on. It's got to be right."

"But when will the time be right?" she'd wail, worn out from it all.

"I'll know when it's right." Now it was *his* turn to be stubborn, and Laura would have to leave it.

Then, one day, something seemed to snap in her.

It was the autumn of 2016. This coming Christmas, it would be her and Paul's second anniversary. Two years of the most fiercely intense sex she'd ever had, and also two years of never really knowing where she stood with Paul or how much she meant to him, but being afraid to rock the boat in case she inadvertently scared him away. She was tired from always having to be '*on*' for him. She couldn't have an 'off' day or a bad hair day or a day when her period was making her feel grotty and under the weather, in case he was repulsed and ran back to Barbara. She could never be just herself for him, in case just herself wasn't enough for him, or good enough. She always had to be smiling and brightly welcoming, welcoming him into her flat, which always had to be perfect and pristine, and into her body, which she had to practically starve so she could continue to fit into the stupid sexy basques and corsets he liked her to wear for her dominatrix act. She was so tired from it all, even tired from endlessly cleaning the flat in case it wasn't up to Barbara's standards. (Barbara was apparently a clean freak.) She couldn't afford to let it get even the tiniest bit messy in case Paul decided that he could never live with her because of it. She still loved Paul, loved him with all her heart. He was *'the one'*, after all. She knew that. That wasn't in doubt at all. She just longed for a *'normal'* life, where she could be herself with him, relax with him instead of always having to be *'on'* in his presence, and maybe occasionally do something together like watching a DVD, anything that didn't involve sex, or Laura screaming at Paul the way he liked it to get in his 'shame-corner' and reflect on his filthy actions, the dirty little maggot.

Then, one day in the autumn of 2016, she arrived at the Stephen's Green on the Luas after work and, instead of having to head straight for her flat to get it and herself ready for Paul, or to the supermarket to buy nibbles to tempt his fancy and a decent bottle or two of wine (Paul wasn't coming over tonight; they had some boring bloody relatives coming over for dinner, or so he'd said), she broke with tradition, bought a choc-ice at the newsagents' outside the Green and took it into the park to relax while she ate it. It was still warm and sunny and old ladies everywhere were marvelling at the fact that they hadn't had to turn on their heating at home yet. There was an empty bench beside the duck pond and she sat down on it, enjoying the illicit thrill of eating a choc-ice, because normally she had to avoid both chocolate *and* ice cream, in order to be able to fit into the lingerie Paul favoured on her. The last thing she needed was a roll of stomach flab showing under her stupid basque thingies. While she sat and ate her choc-ice and daydreamed idly while watching the ducks, a man approached the bench with a very pregnant woman and settled her onto the bench beside Laura. She was blonde, like Laura, and the warm breeze lifted the edges of her hair, just like it did Laura's. She was beautiful, maybe the same age as Laura (who was now twenty-eight), and she looked so radiantly happy, sitting there cradling her enormous bump in the pink maternity summer dress, being fussed over by her husband (they were both wearing wedding rings; Laura always looked at people's ring fingers first), that Laura felt an immeasurable sadness flow through her by comparison.

"Are you sure you'll be all right?" the man was saying. God, but he was gorgeous! The original Mr. Tall, Dark and Handsome, he was even taller than Paul and — dare she even think it, it was such a blasphemous thought — better-looking, and there was no mistaking the adoration in his eyes as he looked down at his pregnant wife. "I'll only be a minute, and I've got my phone if you need me for anything, anything at all."

"Will you just go?" laughed the woman. "You're flapping

over me like a mother hen. Go on, will you? I'm sure I can survive for five minutes on this bench without you."

"If you're sure?" he said solicitously, and this time she flapped at him to go.

"He's so protective," she said to Laura laughingly after the man had gone. "He's only gone to the Gents' at the top of the Green. You'd swear he was going to Siberia, the fuss he's making."

"How far along are you?" Laura asked the woman enviously.

"Seven months," said the woman. "We've just come from Holles Street Hospital, actually. We had our first scan today." She fished around in her handbag for a grainy photograph which she handed over to Laura. Laura couldn't really make out what it was supposed to be, but she nodded and smiled and made all the right noises and the other woman seemed perfectly satisfied.

"Is it your first?" Laura asked then.

The woman nodded, laughing. "Can't you tell by the way he's treating me like I'm breakable, or a precious piece of porcelain or something? By the time we've had four or five of the little buggers, he'll probably be juggling them — and me — like bloody oranges!"

Laura laughed politely, then excused herself and fled. Her heart felt like it was breaking in two, and the last thing she wanted right now was to wait until Mr. Perfect Husband 2016 returned from his trip to the Gents' and started fawning over his beautiful wife again, as if she was the first and only woman in the whole world ever to be having a baby.

As she walked quickly out of the park and started heading

towards her flat, she blinked back the tears that threatened to fall and tried very hard to control her breathing. That was what *she,* Laura, wanted, a loving, devoted husband all of her very own who loved her and worshipped the ground she walked on! Oh, Paul worshipped her all right, but only when he was on his hands and knees with his bare hairy arse in the air licking her stiletto-heeled shoes during one of their sex sessions. They didn't make love; they had sex sessions. Maybe she should actually start charging him by the bloody session. The floodgates opened properly when she got home. She lay down on her bed, still fully dressed, and sobbed her heart out for the best part of an hour.

When the tears had all dried up, she sat up and wiped her eyes on a tissue from the box on the dressing-table. She'd cried all her lovely pricey work make-up off.

She wanted what that woman in the park had, she told herself repeatedly as she went to the fridge for the bottle of wine that would probably now replace dinner. She wasn't even hungry, anyway, after the choc-ice and with the unseasonal heat and everything. She wanted a home, a husband and a baby of her own, but she wanted them with Paul, and she didn't want to have to share him with Barbara or Jessie or Lucy or *anyone*. She didn't care if that sounded unreasonable; it was just the way it was. Why should they have everything, anyway, while she had nothing? It was about time the tables were turned. It would serve Barbara right to be the one on the outside for a change, looking longingly in at all the things she couldn't have. Laura hardened her heart against Paul's family, who hadn't done anything at all to warrant the way Paul treated them. The very next time she saw him alone —

he'd be coming to her flat for sex as usual after work tomorrow, just as if she were a hooker he paid to do a job for him — she was going to pin him down (but not the way he liked!) and demand to know when he was going to tell Barbara that he was leaving her for Laura, like he'd promised to do all those times in the past nearly two years. Vaguely, admittedly, but a vague promise was still a promise. She would give it to him straight. She might even give him an ultimatum. Crudely speaking, it was time for Paul to shit or get off the relationship pot. When was he leaving Barbara for her? It was high time she knew where she stood. She could hardly wait for tomorrow to come.

Most Definitely Not The End . . .!

Printed in Great Britain
by Amazon